The Evolution of Ethan Poe

Books by Robin Reardon

A SECRET EDGE

THINKING STRAIGHT

A QUESTION OF MANHOOD

THE EVOLUTION OF ETHAN POE

Published by Kensington Publishing Corp.

The Evolution of Ethan Poe

Robin Reardon

KENSINGTON BOOKS
www.kensingtonbooks.com

KENSINGTON BOOKS are published by

Kensington Publishing Corp.
119 West 40th Street
New York, NY 10018

ISBN-13: 978-0-7582-4680-6
ISBN-10: 0-7582-4680-3

First Kensington Trade Paperback Printing: August 2011
10 9 8 7 6 5 4 3 2 1

Printed in the United States of America

For Sarah, who helped me discover
the best way to tell my stories

" 'Tis some visitor," I muttered, "tapping at my chamber door—
Only this, and nothing more."

—Edgar Allan Poe, "The Raven"

The Evolution of Ethan Poe

Chapter 1

I wish my mom's divorce lawyer wasn't so freakin' *hot*. The man is gorgeous. On the other hand, maybe it helps keep my mind off of what's really going on. In any case, it's distracting.

So is my stupid brother Kyle's recent little outburst, the one where he came up with a totally unique way to gear up for the start of school. I don't have a clue where he got this idea, but just last week, he buys one of those giant bags of ice cubes from the Store 24 next to Nick's Pizza in that string of about five stores out on Route 154. He clears some space in the middle of the toolshed that Dad built in the backyard four years ago, plunks the bag of ice in some old tin bucket he got from God knows where, cuts the bag open, shoves his right hand in, and sits there. And sits there, until Mom panics because she doesn't know where he is, makes me call all his friends looking for him—no luck with that—and finally gets in her car to scour the area. I wander into the yard, the phone from the kitchen in my pocket in case Kyle calls or Mom does. And I hear a noise from inside the shed, like broken pottery sliding across a surface.

I pull open the door, and there he is, back against the shaky support for a shelf attached to the side of the shed. Kyle's hand is deep into melting ice cubes, his teeth gritted with determination.

"What the fuck!"

"Ethan! Get out!" His voice is shrill, panicky, and too much white shows around the brown of his eyes.

"What are you doing? Get your hand out of there!" Whatever he thinks he's doing, it can't be good. I step over old green plastic pots, terra-cotta shards, a bent trowel, swirls of stiff green hose worn in places with the crisscrossed fibers exposed. Kyle is seventeen, a year older than me and just as skinny, but more than one year taller. Or maybe I'm more than one year shorter. Anyway, I'm trying to yank his arm to get his hand out of the ice, and he's fighting me. Finally I give up and instead attack the bucket so I can spill the contents. He fights this, too, but he has only the one hand to work with, so I win.

Feet sliding on tumbled lumps of ice, he runs from the shed toward the house, his right hand curled against his navy blue God Is Now Here T-shirt. From what I can see, the hand looks like the claw of some dead creature. I follow, dialing Mom's cell number as I go, and let her know I've found Kyle. The universe must have been conspiring to bring everything together, because she's pulling into the driveway when I call.

Mom's no lightweight; she's tall like Kyle and solid, and between the two of us we manage to drag him out of his room, down the stairs, and into the kitchen. Mom threatens to tie him to the chair if he doesn't stay put, and she takes the plastic bucket she uses when she mops the kitchen floor and starts to fill it with lukewarm water. You don't spend your whole life in central Maine without knowing how to treat minor frostbite, and she hasn't moved more than a few miles from where she was born.

I can tell by the look on Kyle's face that he's in pain now that his hand is warming up. It couldn't have been too badly frozen, or it would have been longer before the pain set in. Mom doesn't care about the pain, evidently. She rants at him as water fills the pail in the sink, one hand on her broad hip and the other now flying into the air, now landing on the faucet, now pushing strands of dark brown, unmanageable hair away from her face, ineffectively trying to tuck them into the frayed red elastic that's holding some of it in check.

"Of all the damn fool things! You boys are supposed to be helping me! Have you forgotten that? Now that that low-life father of yours isn't here. Kyle Poe, what the hell did you think you were doing?" Mom was probably cute when she was young, with a round face and dark eyes that sparkle when she's in a good mood, but right now she looks like one of the Furies we studied in Greek mythology.

Through gritted teeth, Kyle's only response is, "Don't say damn. Or hell."

Of course this sends Mom into a new fit. "I'll say whatever the hell I want to! Ethan, put a chair beside your damn fool brother."

I comply, nervous because Mom doesn't usually swear *this* much; she must be more than mad. She sounds almost afraid. She lifts the pail, now heavy with water, and half waddles to the chair I've set beside Kyle. It hits the wooden seat with a liquid thunk. Mom grabs Kyle's right arm above the wrist, the curled hand now less white than pink with the blood returning, and lowers the claw slowly, half inch by half inch, into the water as Kyle gasps and grinds his jaw.

Water level halfway up the forearm, Mom stands straight, both hands on hips now, and glares at him. "Talk to me, Kyle. What did you think you were doing?"

His words halting with an effort not to reveal his pain level, Kyle says, "Matthew five, verse thirty: 'If your right hand causes you to stumble, cut it off, and throw it away from you. For it is more profitable for you that one of your members should perish, than for your whole body to be cast into Gehenna.' "

Mom looks confused. "And how on earth did you trip over your right hand, I'd like to know?"

If she doesn't know what he means by "stumble," I sure do. My right hand has brought me to my back on the bed or pressed against the tiled shower stall many times in the last few years. And the "member" in question isn't at the end of my right arm. But unlike Kyle, I don't have a problem with either member. I *look* for opportunities to stumble, every day. Every night. But Mom doesn't know what Kyle means. She prods, "Well?"

Kyle just shakes his head, and seeing how much pain he's in, Mom finally gives up and practically falls into the fourth chair at our ancient Formica-top table, red with gray and black rounded arrowheads scattered across the entire surface. Most of the stuff in our house comes from other people's yard sales. Only recently has it struck me how out of place the straight-backed wooden chairs look around this relic. The chairs themselves aren't new—far from it. But at least they match each other. And they look more at home on the battered, wide pine boards of the floor than the aluminum legs of the red Formica table. Honestly, you'd think we didn't have any money. We aren't rich, I don't mean to say that. But we could afford some decent kitchen furniture. And I know there's enough money put away someplace to give both Kyle and me a good start at college, though we're both expected to contribute to that. As for the secondhand stuff, Mom's just really big on "living light on the land."

Mom stares at Kyle. I watch her uneasily and glance occasionally at my brother's strained face, eyes shut. Everyone seems to avoid pointing out that Kyle hasn't explained himself further. Maybe Mom has figured out what he means. Finally she says, "Honestly, Kyle, going to church is one thing. Punishing your hand..." Her voice trails off, and Kyle doesn't do anything to fill in the blanks.

We sit there like that, with Mom getting up a few times to add more warm water to Kyle's pail, before I start getting restless. "I'm gonna clean up the mess in the shed," I throw over my shoulder on my way out of the kitchen.

With an ancient stubby broom I sweep the melt-softened cubes and water out through the shed doorway, my mind barely focused on what I'm doing. *Low-life father.* If your father is low-life, what does that make you? Middle-life? And that's only if your mother is high-life. Whatever that means.

I collect the broken pot pieces in the bucket, my irritation with Kyle growing deeper and closer to real anger with the clang of each shard that lands. He'd started to get all holier-than-thou sometime in June, as far as I can remember, not long after Dad left. Dad hasn't gone very far, what with his public works job with the town. He rents the room over the Barstows' garage where Mr. Barstow's mother had stayed until she died, the kitchen nothing more than a tiny sink, a small stove, and a half refrigerator on a couple of square yards of linoleum in the corner.

Dad gave Kyle and me this big lecture just before he got in his pickup truck to drive away, about being men now and shouldering some of the responsibility around here. I remember thinking, *Do men ever want to cry as bad as I do right now?* But Kyle looked really serious, and he must have taken things quite to heart. Because the first thing he did was start going to church every Sunday. Not long after that, he took it upon himself to commit to paper the chores we'd each always done without the formality lent to them by virtue of being written down and attached to the side of the refrigerator, where they're now held on display by a magnet shaped like the Christian ichthus—that primitive fish symbol the early disciples supposedly used. Then he started ordering me around, reminding me pointedly when my chores weren't done, adding to the list as he felt necessary to make sure everything was cared for. Protected. Right.

It doesn't help that Mom seems to alternate between approving of Kyle's responsible approach to life and being amused by it. I just want him to knock it off. I mean, who does he think he is, my father or something? Maybe she'll think again after today's little exhibition.

I was never into church that much, but in the past year or so it's actually begun to make me nervous. That is, once I realized what the Bible says about me. About people like me.

In a skirmish with the old hose—stiff and unwilling to let me curl it into a mass I can tie and drag to the pile going to the dump—anger wins out over irritation. I curse under my breath, partly at the hose, partly at Kyle. He's ruined things for me, just when I'd got up enough guts to talk to Mom. I've been waiting for the right time, you know? Because, I mean, you can't just dump this onto your parents. Parent. It's hard enough finding the courage to tell your mother you're gay. I don't know if I'll *ever* be able to tell my dad. And I sure as hell don't plan to tell Kyle, so this afternoon looked like a good time. Mom went out last night to meet Jimmy Korbel, just for a few beers, not a real date; the divorce isn't final yet. But she came home in a great mood. And then when it looked like Kyle was away someplace for the afternoon, it seemed like this would be the day. So I spent a little time in my room, white earbuds jammed into the sides of my head, collecting energy and attitude from my favorite music, but before I could quite bring myself to turn off the iPod and go look for Mom, she found me. That's when she told me that Kyle was missing and I had to help find him. End of my plan. And now I don't know now *when* I'm going to say anything.

Getting ready for school is part fun, part chore for me. If I hadn't just bought a lot of Goth-inspired stuff, we'd have gone shopping for back-to-school clothes. But Mom's attitude is, "You made that bed, Ethan. Now you lie in it." I don't get it; does she think I regret the choices? Hardly.

But I do need a new winter coat. So the day after Kyle's weirdness she says she and I need to go on a shopping trip. She stares at me a minute when I tell her I want to get a used coat, from a store in Bangor I heard about called This Time For Sure. When it sinks in that a used coat will be cheaper, she nods, no doubt picturing a maroon parka or some such hideous, practical item. And of course, it appeals to her habit of reusing other people's cast-offs. She says, "We'll go there after my next appointment with Mr. LeBlanc."

This is the hot lawyer I mentioned. Guy. That's what he told me to call him, not Mr. LeBlanc, even though that's how my Mom refers to him rather pointedly when she talks to me. Guy, pronounced in the French manner. Rhymes with Gee, as in Gee Whiz. Rhymes with Jeeeeesus-God, but that man makes my pants too tight every time I think of him.

He's not that old, either. I mean, I've never done it with anyone, but the idea of doing it with him is not so far-fetched. He's just tall enough to be a couple of inches above me, and I love the way his dark hair falls in waves around his head, with that one curl that looks like it's accidentally placed just off-center of his forehead, like he doesn't know it's separated itself from the rest of his hair, like he doesn't know it helps make him gorgeous. Plus, I half suspect that he's gay. That's my fantasy, anyway.

So when Mom and I show up for her appointment the last weekday before school starts, I've got my tightest black jeans on, the ones where the big teeth on the silver zipper show because there's no fabric flap over them, and my black T-shirt with the holes I put in it and then carefully frayed to look like they aren't deliberate—kind of like that curl. And when I tuck the shirt into the jeans, one of the holes is almost but not quite right over my right nipple, so it peeks out depending on how I position myself. I want Guy to notice this.

Mom tries to make me change before we leave the house, of course. "Ethan, for God's sake, put on something decent!" So I top the look with a white shirt, a couple of sizes too big, not tucked in so I can take it off or just let the fabric fall aside as I want. We're already a little late, or I think Mom would demand more of a change.

Guy is as gorgeous as ever in a light-colored suit and a blue and white striped shirt with white collar and cuffs. He's the Light to my Dark. Even with such beautiful clothes I wish he'd take them off. I want to know how much hair is on his chest. For starters. I take off my white shirt as if to open the bidding, and Mom glares at me. Too bad. And it pays off. I swear, at least three times my little peek-a-boo trick catches Guy's eye, in just the right spot. Just the right way.

He's *got* to be gay. I step out of his office with a smile I hide from Mom.

A bell over the door at This Time For Sure tinkles when we walk in. Mom is quickly buried in a section of fiber-fill parkas, which is what I expected. She calls me over a few times to try something on, and each time I go over without protest, saving my energy for when I've found something worth fighting for. And I find it.

There's this long blue-black (of course) coat, kind of like a navy pea coat on steroids. The collar can flip up high to cover my ears, the sleeves are ideal at just a tad too long, the pocket linings are actually intact, and on the back—seemingly out of character with the rest of the coat—in light gray, between shoulders and hips, is this huge bar code design.

Wacko. Perfect. I bury my hands in the pockets and wander over to where Mom is still digging into stuff I wouldn't wear on a bet, and I wait for her to look up. Finally she does.

Her eyes roll up and then close for a nanosecond, she makes a clucking noise with her tongue, and she says, "Ethan, you can't be serious."

I've been through enough of these scenes to know that when she says, "Take that thing off this minute" or "Yes, dear. Very funny. Now try this on," she isn't going to go along with it. But when she says, "You can't be serious," if I play my cards right— which means patiently trying on anything she wants me to—I might get my way. She hands me another couple of parkas, and I try each one on, quietly but deliberately putting my long pea coat back on each time, until she finally takes a good look at me and says, "How much is that thing, anyway?" She fingers the dense wool while I tell her it's only seventy-five dollars. She pulls the pockets inside out. She opens the coat and examines the lining and looks for how well it's attached to the coat. She takes it off me and goes over it for moth holes. She smells it in several places. There's just nothing wrong with this coat. And the parka prices are only a teeny bit less.

I know it's over when she folds it over her arm and says, "If I buy you this thing, Ethan, you're going to wear it. Do you hear me?" I nod, barely breathing. "What are you going to wear shoveling snow?" I look at her, surprised; Dad always plows the driveway, and all Kyle and I ever have to do is the walkway and the steps. "Don't look so shocked. Did you think your father was going to keep doing everything for you even though he doesn't live with us now?"

Given that I have something I want to talk her into, it seems counterproductive right now to point out that she's the one who made him leave, not me. "We still have that old parka Dad doesn't wear anymore, the one with the stains."

Her look at me is half glare, half warning. "Find yourself something to wear on your hands."

I want to hug her. Maybe the grin I throw her is enough.

The gloves are another great find. There are thin black leather ones with no ends in the fingers, and a thicker pair of black suede ones with full fingers, and I can wear them together. The whole lot costs only fifteen dollars.

Mom says, "Are you happy?" I grin and nod. "Happy enough to let me look around a little for myself?"

By the time we leave, I've picked up another pair of black jeans and a black leather jacket that's nearly free, and Mom's found a shearling coat that she doesn't take off until she's paid for it. I'm thinking we might come back here again and wondering how much cred I've got with her now.

On the way back to the car I notice something I hadn't seen on the way here, probably because I was looking just for This Time. Right next door there's a body art place. Photos of tattoos and piercings pretty much cover the front windows so you can't see in very well. I'll bet they don't always want you to see what they're doing to people in there. One close-up of a nipple with a barbell through it makes me gasp. It had been one thing when I let my best friend, Jorja Loomis, push a needle through my frozen left earlobe last July, but this? I mean, wow. Then I look hard at one tat, a yin-yang circle. I have a T-shirt Mom bought me last June, white with a red and white yin-yang symbol on it. I can't remember ever wearing it; if it had been black, maybe. But I do know yin stands for inward, or female, and yang is outward, male. The two together are balance. And, in a way, they're also androgynous. A balance of male and female, not all one or the other. And it hits me all of a sudden: This is me.

Mom pulls at my arm. "Forget that, Ethan." This is one of the times she means it. But the seed has been planted. Before another day has gone by, I've started my tattoo fund.

Jorja gets on the bus for the first day of school decked out for real. Kyle's on the bus, too, but we never sit together. Jorja and I had pretty much decided to go Goth together early last spring, getting black stuff cheap at Walmart. Goth came and went around here a few years ago, and now that it's kind of out of fashion it's that much more appealing; no one else will be copying us—been there, done that, bought the safety pins, using them on diapers—and we can let it be known that we *like* being outliers. She makes her way toward me, hugging her book bag to her chest, head down so that the look her eyes give you from under her eyebrows is kind of scary. As usual, there's more black makeup than skin around her eyes, but the reddish-blond hair falling in strings around her face kind of dampens the effect. She plunks down beside me in the seat that everyone knows is saved for her, trying to pretend she doesn't care whether I notice the black fishnet gloves that hook over her thumb and not the fingers. Makes me wish it were cold enough already to wear my own new gloves, and that new coat.

"Gloves in summer?" I ask, pretending it's a genuine question.

She looks at them, shrugs. "I have a pair that pull all the way over my elbow for when it snows." She half glances at me to be sure I've caught the irony, but then something outside the bus catches her eye. It's the flimsy marquee outside her church. In slightly crumpled black capital letters it says, A PRAYER A DAY KEEPS THE DEVIL AWAY. From the corner of my eye I see her send two thumbs-up toward the sign. And I know she's serious. She already prays in school, even when someone might be looking. Before last winter, when we hooked up as best friends, I thought she was doing it to be sarcastic. Now I know better. Even so, I still think she does it at least partly to be noticed. After all, it's proof that she's an outlier by choice.

If I'm an outlier—and I guess I have to admit that I am—it's not because I want to be. It's just safer. And hanging with Jorja is protection for both of us. I mean, she's so heavy-duty Christian that she doesn't want boys approaching her for sex, and when the other kids see us together so much, they won't guess about me. So I go along with putting on this show—like the Goth thing—to pretend I'm an outlier by choice.

It was my idea, actually. Goth, that is. You can tell, just by looking at photos of Edgar Allan, that we're related. Kyle, with his light brown hair and chipmunk cheeks, takes after Mom's side of the family. But with my wide forehead, black hair and eyebrows, and a long nose, I look like the famous Poe except for the moustache and the dark eyes; my eyes, for some unknown reason, are blue. I even have a widow's peak, and even though Edgar Allan didn't, it seems appropriate somehow. He was Goth inside. Maybe I'll get there someday, but for now I'll do my best to look the part.

Jorja and I don't sit together in every class; that would be lame. So we arrive separately to Biology today just before lunch and sit a few rows apart.

The teacher this year is new. Or, not new exactly. She grew up here, went to college in Orono, and came back to teach. Not that Orono is that far, but it's just far enough that Sylvia Modine could insist on not living at home, I guess. I don't really know her that well. I don't really know her at all.

I know her brother, though. Not as well as I'd like. Imagine Kevin Bacon at sixteen, in one of his blonder phases, and you've got a pretty good idea of what Max looks like: dark blond hair just mussed enough to make you wonder if he just got out of bed, a prominent chin, and a look in his blue eyes that's either *I* might *be pulling your leg* or *I'm imagining you naked.* Max Modine has had my attention for about a year now. I can't say whether I've had any of his, but I'd sure like it. There have been a few times when I thought that maybe, just maybe . . .

Of course, he may not know he's got my attention. This is just so wrong. It's not fair! It's okay for people to think I'm with Jorja even when I'm not, but if Max and I were together—I mean, if he's even gay—it'd be a freak show around here.

So now Ms. Modine is our Biology teacher. I suppose if I were straight, I'd think she was pretty. Long hair, light brown with blondish streaks, and one of those enthusiastic voices that makes me want to pull something over my head and hide. And she makes me want to hide right away.

"Good morning, class! I'm Ms. Modine, and before anyone has a wisecrack about it, yes—my brother Max is in the class. Anyone got anything to say about that?" She waits, her face smiling but her eyes challenging, and no one says a word. A few kids turn in Max's direction for a second, and I realize I've blown a chance to look at him when it would be safe—when others were looking at him, too. Crap. Guess I'm working too hard to avoid being seen looking at him.

Ms. Modine has big plans for us, it seems. Dissecting frogs, field trip to a fish farm, twig identification after the leaves are off the trees, all kinds of fun. She assigns us some reading for tomorrow's class. I don't pay much attention until I hear a couple of girls make squealing noises; we're to be prepared to discuss the circulatory system of a Japanese beetle.

"I'll bet you never thought of a beetle having a circulatory system, did you?" is Ms. Modine's snarky comment. That's probably not how she meant it, but that's how I heard it.

After school, on the bus ride home, Jorja tells me I'm coming to her church for Teen Meet with her. She likes to order me around. Sometimes I let her. I'm not sure why I don't today, except that I've never agreed to go to this meeting before, and I don't feel like it today, either. I'm pretty focused on the back of Max's head two rows ahead of us.

Jorja sees this. Her voice hissing into my ear is almost painful. "You can't do that! You know that! It's your cross to bear." She punches my arm hard as she gets up for the stop in front of her church, Society of Nazareth. I know what she means. She knows I'm gay. That's why she feels comfortable with me. But she also believes it's this huge sin to give in to the temptation to actually *be* gay, so she needs to believe that I would never act on it. She prays for me all the time, sometimes to be strong and resist temptation and other times to be straight, and every once in a while she checks in: "Are you still gay?" One time she'd had some kind of vision that told her the prayers had worked, and when I insisted I was still gay, she said, "You're not just telling me that to get into my pants or anything, are you?" This made no sense to me, so all I could do was assure her that I was still gay. Still me.

Following Max's ass with my eyes as he gets up for his stop, I'm thinking maybe, just maybe I'll say something to Mom today. About me. But as we approach our stop, Kyle pokes my shoulder on his way forward in the bus. "Grass-cutting day," he says, like I'd forgotten. I had, but I still don't want him reminding me. And mowing the yard is not a small task. We have two full acres. Guess "true confessions" will have to wait.

Mom is standing on the front stoop, arms crossed on her chest, her head cocked at Mr. Phinney, who has his campaign persona in full swing. He's running for the open seat on the school board for our district, which includes us and two other towns. No one was running against him until a few days ago. But now Etta Greenleaf has joined the race.

Ordinarily I wouldn't pay much attention to this kind of thing. What do I care? School is school, whoever's on the board. But Etta is famous. No one calls her by her last name. She's lived here, like, forever, though she did move away for a little while. And mostly she's kept to herself, in a small house that used to belong to her father, who'd been caretaker for the old Coffin estate, when the Coffin family owned this big tannery. It's closed now, and the Coffin house burned down way before my time.

There's a lot of rumors about why Etta came back and why she's still here, but I think the most likely one is that her father didn't leave when the Coffins moved out. He hung on, living off savings he'd never touched, until he couldn't do things for himself anymore. That's when Etta reappeared. To take care of him. He died years ago, but she's still here. She must be at least sixty by now. Ancient. But she's running for the school board. Go figure.

Her other claim to fame, which probably adds to the way

everyone thinks of her as some kind of recluse, is her dog. It's a pit bull, kind of a bronze color, named Two. Makes people wonder where One is, like Two is a distraction while One is getting ready to ambush you. But Two's reputation is that he's plenty ferocious enough; he doesn't need a One around to help him with anything, thank you very much. Etta controls that dog. That vicious, man-eating dog. He might be a medium, if she were a witch.

Anyway, there's Mr. Phinney, a vision of earnestness, eyes trained full on Mom's face, a pile of those roadside VOTE FOR signs at his feet, with CARL PHINNEY SCHOOL BOARD in that shade of red that makes your teeth hurt, it's so fake. Even from the end of the driveway I can practically see the tongue Mom's poking into her cheek. She's not big on politics, as long as they stay out of her way. Which is probably not a very sensible approach, especially in a town where positively everyone knows everyone else. It's also a little weird, when you consider that she works at the town hall, unless you know why: she wants to keep an eye on them.

I don't pay much attention to Mom or Mr. Phinney, knowing she's not putting any VOTE FOR signs in our yard for anyone, and just make my way to the back door so I don't have to be polite, so I don't get trapped into a discussion. Upstairs, I throw my books on the tiny desk that barely fits in my room with the twin-size bed, which I throw myself onto as I grab my iPod nano. I'm pressing an earbud in when Kyle darkens my doorway and glares at me.

"Shit," I say, barely above a whisper, and get up, knowing that Mr. Righteousness will be on my ass until I do the lawn.

He slaps the back of my head as I push past him. "Watch your language!"

Why do people say that? It's stupid! *Watch your language.* You can't do that unless you're writing!

It takes me seven tries to get the old mower going, and by then I'm even more pissed off than I was when Kyle hit me. I shove the rattling contraption in what's more or less a grid pattern over the front yard, beyond impatience, and it catches on every lump of dirt and irregularity, making me more and more furious. Finally, in the side yard, I step back from it and lean over, take a few long breaths, and force myself to calm down. Otherwise I'll never finish; one of us, the mower or me, will be dead before I can wrestle my way around the back of the shed.

It goes along a little better now, but I'm dripping with sweat. I keep breathing and let my mind go where it wants. It goes to trees. They're phallic; maybe that's why. But—why don't we have any trees to speak of? There are a few on the side of the yard, and one or two in back of the shed, but otherwise our old once-farmhouse sits on this big, square patch of land that has no other shape to it, nothing interesting to look at. Most of the houses on the main roads are like this, though, so there must be something to it. I suppose I could find out who owns the land surrounding our plot, but it's just scrabbly woods, nothing going on there. Ticks. Snakes. Fruitless blueberry bushes, and gray boulders everywhere, like monsters' droppings. That's about it. If we didn't have a high chain-link fence around the back, it would be hard to tell where our land ends and this semiwilderness begins.

Somewhere around the far south corner of the backyard I decide to tell Mom. I'll do it tonight. I have some homework—like reading about beetle blood—but there wasn't a whole lot assigned the first day. Yeah; tonight's the night. If I'm thinking about it all the time, I may as well get it over with or I'll go crazy.

After dinner I make sure Kyle is in his room deep into something and I go find Mom. She's sitting on the back step, smoking a cig, gazing into the sky where the sun fizzled out below the horizon just a little while ago, swatting at mosquitoes.

I plunk down beside her. "Can I have one?" I've tried smoking a few times; didn't like it much. But she doesn't know this.

She blows a stream of smoky breath, looks at me, says, "You may not." And takes another drag.

I pluck a few strands of grass growing too close to the step to have been beheaded by the mower and fix all my attention on them so that I can surprise myself when I say, "There's something I need to tell you."

"Oh? Haven't got that little witch-slash-Bible-pusher preggers, have you?"

On another day I might have snorted in appreciation of this comment; Mom thinks Jorja's harmless and doesn't mind her, but she does use her as a source of sarcastic humor sometimes. Tonight, no snort. "It's about me. Not her." I don't know what to say next. Or, really, I do. I can't quite say it.

Mom turns to look at me. "What is it, Ethan?" Her voice is soft, encouraging.

I don't look at her. Eyes still fixed on my grass, I say, "I'm gay."

She's very still. Not tense, though; calm. Another drag. Another smoky breath. I let my peripheral vision take in more of her, and she nods a few times. "I guess I can see how you might think that." She looks at me again, and I do turn to her this time. "But you're young, Ethan. Don't worry about decisions like that."

"It's not a decision, Mom. It's who I am."

"Yeah, I suppose. But look at it this way. When I was your age, I thought who I was would be a housewife. Now look at me!" She holds her arms out toward the hidden sun and then drops them. "No way."

"Mom—"

"Ethan, kid, don't worry about it. It's a natural thing for you right now. I mean, look, you don't like football, you don't like sports in general, you're not very big, you got kind of a sweet face . . . well, gentle, anyway. And so far the only girl you've hung with is this kid who actually tries to make herself look gross and probably wears a horsehair-lined chastity belt. What other conclusion are you gonna come to, I'd like to know?"

I have to say, this is not what I was expecting. I know Mom is enough of a social rebel that this revelation of mine wouldn't throw her over some edge or anything, but this? It's like she isn't taking me seriously. Instead of pointing out that maybe I'm hanging with Jorja *because* I'm gay, not the other way around, I say, "Don't you believe me?" My voice sounds whiny, and I hate it.

"Oh, don't get your knickers in a twist. It's not that I don't believe you. And yes, I've noticed how you are with Mr. LeBlanc. It's just that I expect you'll change your mind once or twice, and I want you to be able to tell me when you do, if you want. If you get yourself all locked into something, you might not wanna say if anything changes. And, like I said, you're young."

"But—what if I'm right? What if I am gay?" A cricket at my feet makes me jump.

"Can't say I'd be happy about it. I don't understand it, that's for sure. And you sure better not say anything to your brother just yet. Not until you can outrun him. But you'd still be you, right?" She swats at my head, winks, and says, "Skeeter."

It takes me a while to fall asleep that night. So I've told her, and up until I did it had seemed like such a huge deal. Now it feels anticlimactic. Like it almost doesn't matter. But it's still a big deal to me.

She wouldn't be happy about *it*. What does that mean? Would she be not happy about *me*? But she said I'd still be me. Does that mean she'd wouldn't feel any differently about me? I don't know what to do with this. I feel like I'm still in limbo.

Whatever, it doesn't seem like this is something she wants to talk about a lot. At least she didn't freak. And when there are further developments, she can't say I didn't warn her.

Chapter 2

After school the next Monday, before I step up into the bus, I hear a whistle I recognize—sharp, swooping up in a smooth slide, with a little toot at the end. It's Dad. He's standing at the open door of a Public Works truck, not his own pickup, one foot on the running board and one on the ground, one hand on the top of the door and the other hung from a finger tucked into his jeans pocket. The way the sun falls on his hair makes it look as black as mine. His sleeveless T-shirt was white once and there's a hole dead center over his beer belly. He's not fat, or anything. Just got a gut.

I wave to Jorja so she'll know she's on her own for the bus, and run toward the truck. I haven't seen Dad for maybe three weeks now. I still don't understand why he left, or why Mom wanted him to leave, whichever way it was. He hooks my neck with an arm when I'm close enough and squeezes. It presses the back of my black onyx ear stud into my neck, but I like it anyway. I can smell the sweat of his armpit for just a second before he lets go—sort of like some weird mixture of coffee and eucalyptus.

"Whatcha up to, kid?"

"Nothin' much." It's our standard greeting, and each of us

can tell by the other's tone of voice whether there's something behind it or not. Today what's there is, "I miss you." And for the first time ever, I realize that I'm not aware of anything like this ritual that he has with Kyle. No idea what that means; I'm just glad he's here for me today.

"Hey, listen, this is your mom's long day at work. What say we head out for some road trimming, and I'll pay ya a little something for helping."

"Sure." I can add this to my tattoo fund! I throw my books on the floor of the cab and climb into the passenger seat. It's a long way off the ground—a big truck that carries one of the highway snow plows in winter. "You still gonna help me rack up thirty-five driving hours so I can get my intermediate license?"

"You bet, kid."

I know Mom will never let this happen. She'll never let me drive around with just Dad supervising. If there's one thing I do know about her objections to Dad, it's that he always seems to be drinking something. Never actually drunk, as far as I can tell, just always drinking. There was one phase where he was trying to convince her he'd stopped, but she kept catching him with beer in his ginger ale cans. And there was another weird phase where he drank ginger ale from beer cans, almost like he didn't feel like a beer but wanted to start a fight. Wanted to make Mom feel stupid, yelling at him for drinking ginger ale. The whole thing didn't make any sense to me.

We drive in relative silence, manly and cool, and my eyes fall on the roaring bear head tattoo he has on his right bicep while I'm busy thinking about how I might bring up the topic of Jimmy Korbel in a way that wouldn't get Mom into trouble but that would inspire Dad to come home. But I don't think of anything before we get to where he's left the mower. He has a long stretch of fairly flat roadside to mow, the last time for the season, and there are already enough election signs poking their way along the edge that it's a royal hemorrhoid to work around them. This happens every fall when there's any kind of election, and this year there's a lot of stuff up for grabs, including

Town Council Chair. If we were a city instead of a small town, that would be like the mayor. I see Ida Mathis is running against Bob Bryant for that spot. Anyway, there's a lot of signs already. They'll multiply like cockroaches before the November election.

My job is to move ahead of the mower, pick the signs up, wait for him to mow that strip, and then while he's working on the area farther from the road to clear a little more land along the edge, I use the hammer from the truck and set the signs back up. Nobody will notice if I get them out of order. I wear his work gloves so I don't get splinters from the wooden stakes.

Dad finishes his extra strips before I'm quite done hammering signs back in, and he picks up about five *CARL PHINNEY* signs and tosses them into the back of the truck. "Stupid little prick has way too many signs out here, anyway," he grumbles.

We move on down the road a little, towing the mower behind the truck, and start the process again. I'm just about to start my work of replacing signs when an old Jeep Wagoneer, kind of a mungy brown, pulls up. Max is driving, with Sylvia in the passenger seat. I'm pretty sure he has his intermediate license already, and he's working on the one hundred eighty days before he can drive unrestricted. The Jeep stops beside me.

"Hey there, Ethan!" Sylvia's cheerful voice hails me. I guess it's okay to think of her as Sylvia out here, even though she's Ms. Modine in school. "Helping your dad?" I try to look at her when I answer, but Max has climbed out of the car and is walking toward the back. He waits there. "See you in school tomorrow," she says, and looks forward as though the truck is about to take off. I throw a glance to where Dad is, a little distance away and with his back to me, and then I move toward the back of the Jeep.

Max seems like he's not sure whether he wants to look friendly or aloof. It's awkward for a second, and my eyes fall on a silver-colored thing stuck on the brown paint above the Jeep's bumper. It's that Christian ichthus symbol, with letters in it.

Usually when you see one of these fish, if there's anything inside, it says "Jesus." But this one says "Darwin," and it has little legs. I don't have the mental focus to let this sink in.

"Hey," I say, as quietly as I can and still be heard over the noises from the idling Jeep engine and the retreating groans of the mower.

"How's it going?" he says, not really asking.

"Where you headed?"

He shrugs, looks at the ground for a second and back to my face. "Driving around, you know. Practice. Getting some cred with the folks in time to do the full license in a couple of weeks. Where are you with yours?"

"Trying to convince my mom to help me get my intermediate. I took the course last year."

"What about your dad?"

I glance that way again. The mower is now headed back toward us. "Maybe."

"Well . . . maybe after I have my full license we could, y'know, check out the sights."

My breathing shortens, and there's a sensation in my pants that would cause my right hand to . . . uh . . . stumble if I were alone. The tone of his voice—silky, suggestive—tells me he's gay, and he's betting I am, too. "Sure. I, uh, is Bangor too far?"

"What's in Bangor?"

"I was thinking of a tattoo. Something like that."

His eyes widen. "Sweet! Sure. Let's do it." He fishes in his pocket and comes up with a really cool-looking cobalt blue pen, only a few inches long. He takes my arm—which gives me shivers and makes my pants shrink a little more—and just above the inside of my elbow, in a place that won't show very much, he writes his e-mail address and his cell number.

I can hear the mower engine getting louder and louder. I'm unsure how to end this heart-pounding encounter, but Max solves it by offering me a fist bump. Most times when you do that, you pull your fist back right away; it's just a thump. But his knuckles follow mine a fraction of an inch as I start to pull my hand back. It's almost like our knuckles kiss for about one second. Then we both take a step back, he gets into the Jeep, and I go back to my signs. Though I don't even notice what names are on them now. It isn't until I get home, barely ahead of Mom, who might not like that I was out with Dad, that I realize I hadn't seen one sign with Etta's name.

Over dinner that night, which has always been a family event at our house, Mom and Kyle get into an argument over politics. Doesn't surprise me from Kyle; a sort of right-wing attitude has been growing more and more obvious in him. But Mom has a live-and-let-live approach to life, and it's only when someone steps into what she sees as her personal space, threatens her individual rights, that she gets her back up about something. I still remember her reply to some guy who came to the door a year or so ago collecting signatures against some health clinic providing abortions. Mom said, "Well, I don't think I could do that, myself. Abort a baby of mine. But I sure as heck won't try and tell somebody else what they should do. And I don't want you telling them, either." She sent the guy packing, shouting after him, "Don't approve of abortion? Fine! Don't have one!"

At first I'm not paying much attention to what Mom and Kyle are going on about, what with images in my mind of the kinds of things that could happen if Max and I drive around to "check out the sights." Eventually it gets in through my erotic haze that one of the things Mr. Phinney's campaigning for is bringing some new theory into science classes. You don't grow up around here, with about one church every mile and a half—never mind that most of them are tiny and use a prefab ranch house for a building—without knowing that just about everybody calls themselves Christian, and for most of them that means evolution might be fine as a theory but probably doesn't explain everything. But this is the first time I'd ever heard something suggested for a science class topic that sounds more like religion to me. I'm not sure I care very much; I'd rather dissect a frog than argue about that. And anyway, I don't see why it's anything to argue *about*. Kyle and Mom evidently disagree with me, because that's just what they do. Argue.

"Evolution is only a theory!" Kyle nearly yells at one point.

"Yeah, so is gravity," is Mom's rejoinder, which makes me laugh. I'd bet on Mom in a battle like this one any day; Kyle just doesn't have the balls she has. "I'm telling you, Kyle, believe whatever dang fool thing you want. That's your right. But don't try and tell me that *intelligent design*"— her voice sneers the term—"is science."

"It is so! Natural selection is a pretty poor way to make a human being. We're way too complex. ID is the only answer."

She shakes her head. "Until you can show me a better theory based on facts—"

"Facts?" Kyle's voice is getting squeaky with emotion. I sit back to watch the fireworks. "Facts? Show me facts. You want to talk about the fruit flies?"

"Fruit flies?" I venture quietly and realize my mistake immediately.

"Fruit flies!" Kyle turns his face my way, fire in his eyes. "They say that because they can get fruit flies to mutate in the lab, that proves evolution is possible. But it's the same kind of creature! They aren't making a whole new kind of bug. Only God can do that."

Mom comes to my rescue. "O ye of little brain. So tell me why God couldn't have set evolution in motion. Making only mutilated fruit flies from fruit flies hardly disproves evolution, you know. And it does prove it's possible."

"It doesn't prove it, though!"

"Dear, that's why they call it a theory. But it's a theory based on provable data. What's this ID stuff based on?"

"We *know* the Bible is true. So we don't need to *prove* anything."

Mom's face is a puzzled scowl. "Where *did* you come from?"

"More from God than from you, with your *liberal* politics." He spits the word liberal.

"Ah, but that's where you're wrong, Kyle. I'm libertarian, not liberal. I want less government, not more. Which means I do not under any circumstances want that jerk Phinney forcing his religion down my kids' throats and making me pay for the privilege."

"It's not religion! It's science!"

Mom's voice finally raises nearly to the level of Kyle's, though it's firm rather than hysterical. "If it uses the Bible for its 'proof,' then it's religion. And having some 'master intellect' or 'intelligent agent,' which this ID madness believes in, suddenly poof various forms of life into existence is the creation story from Genesis pure and simple. If you can support this ID thing with facts and evidence, we'll have something to talk about. Otherwise, it's religion. Period."

Kyle won't admit defeat, but he's smart enough to shut up. Almost. "So you won't vote for him?"

Mom snorts. "Vote for him? I'm thinking of helping Etta Greenleaf! Now shut up and finish your dinner."

I don't really think she's serious. But I see a chance to change the subject, if only slightly. "You might help her put up some signs."

Mom turns to me and blinks. "What?"

"There are lots of signs for Mr. Phinney along the highway. None for Etta."

She nods slowly. "That's true, Ethan. Though I'm not sure what good signs will do. I mean, everyone knows her."

"But do they know that she's running? And does she not want—what was it? ID?"

Mom is still nodding. "She does not. She's in this race precisely because she disagrees with Phinney. She doesn't want to run, not really, if I know her. She'd rather go on keeping to herself, like she's done for years. She just doesn't want religion in science classes." Her gaze moves away from me and into the distance someplace. "Maybe I'll call her later."

Kyle groans and pushes his plate away from him. He starts to get up.

"Young man! Sit yourself right back down there and finish your dinner. If you wouldn't be so stubborn about trying to eat everything left-handed, you'd have kept pace with Ethan." He throws her an angry look. But she's ready. "Honor your mother! Commandment number five."

It isn't just eating that Kyle tries to do left-handed. He refuses to use his right hand at all, and because he's right-handed this means he can't use a knife very well. He's been eating his corn bread with the butter perched on it in chunks because he can't hold it and spread butter with just one hand. Saving that hand for jerking off—oops—I mean stumbling, I wonder?

Jorja is starting to worry me. It's getting so it's not only that she doesn't care what other people think, but like she's actually trying to get them to think she's weird. I guess this isn't new behavior; like I said, she's always prayed rather conspicuously, which I always thought the Bible didn't really want you to do, but I'm no expert. And I can't pretend I didn't encourage standing out from the crowd, what with the journey into Goth and all.

Get this, though. We're in our last class of the day, American History. Mr. Coffin's class—he's a descendent of the tannery Coffins, and he's actually kind of cool for a teacher. Early thirties, I think, and good-looking enough. Anyway, we're going over the Constitution and how it got written, and who wrote it, all that stuff. Mr. Coffin tells us about how some of the most famous signers didn't consider themselves Christian, that they were more Deist and didn't believe in miracles or prophecy. He says Deists believe God has some kind of grand plan for the universe but doesn't get involved in the details of our daily lives.

So he's basically just told us that it wasn't all good Christians who set up the foundation of the U.S. Knowing Jorja as I do, I'm certain she's all tense and aggravated, believer in miracles and intervention that she is. But then it gets worse.

The Deist issue was just background, evidently, because what we talk about for the rest of the class is how the Constitution sets up this wall between religion and government. We go over the Establishment Clause and the Free Exercise Clause, and then the class gets into a bit of a debate about whether church property and money should be exempt from taxes at all. I don't pay a lot of attention; it's not something I care about. But I do have to know it well enough to pass the class.

In the end, Mr. Coffin makes the point that these two clauses together keep the government and religion out of each other's way and allow everyone to practice whatever religion they want, even if that's none at all. He says that the Constitution protects religion as much as it protects nonreligious people. But Jorja, who hasn't said a word yet, finally can't take it any longer. Her hand shoots up, and Mr. Coffin calls on her.

"What about our Pledge of Allegiance? It says 'under God.' "

He nods. "The original version of the pledge, written by Francis Bellamy in 1892, didn't have the phrase 'under God' in it. In fact, that wasn't added until 1954." He goes into a lot of description of the people arguing about whether it should go in or not, and then he says, "Great question, Jorja. Keep them coming."

So she raises her hand again. "In God We Trust. It's on our money, and that comes from the government."

"Yes, and again it came into being much later than the Constitution, this time in 1864 in response to the religious fervor that surfaced during the American Civil War. So both of these standard phrases, which most of us associate with our country as though they had always been there, were added long after our government was established. And regardless of what they say, where they are, and who agrees with them, they are not in the Constitution, which forms the basis for the laws governing the way we live."

Jorja stands up at this point; raising a hand is not enough anymore. "This is a Christian nation!" she shouts. "We follow God's laws!"

"Jorja, sit down, please. I'm happy to discuss this point, but we must remain calm and avoid making proclamations." He doesn't have time to say any more before she grabs her books and stomps out of the room. I sit there and watch her leave, blinking stupidly. *What the hell?* I mean, I know she's serious about this stuff, but she can't actually argue with history.

After class is over, I try to smooth things a little for Jorja. Max is watching me, probably wondering what I'll do. I walk to the desk and wait until Mr. Coffin looks up.

"Ethan?"

"Yeah, I, uh . . . I'm just thinking maybe you shouldn't be too mad at Jorja."

He smiles. "Oh, I'm not mad at her, Ethan. But we all need to understand that the founders of this country wanted us to listen to each other's opinions and discuss things intelligently, and above all to acknowledge the equality and rights of every citizen."

"Will you mark her down for leaving like that?"

He takes an audible breath. "I don't think you and I should discuss another classmate, Ethan. That said, though, I don't think this particular incident warrants any harsh action. I do hope it won't be repeated." He nods once and goes back to collecting his things.

I turn and see Max there, waiting for me at the door. He's got a really sexy half smile on his face, and I'm sure I'm blushing. If only my skin weren't so freakin' pale. . . . Max leads the way through the door and into the hall.

"Standing up for your friend is fine," he says. "But she's pretty off-base, don't you think?"

Talk about a rock and a hard place. If I agree, I'm disloyal to my best friend. If I don't, I risk alienating the person I most want to kiss in the entire world. Someone who seems like just maybe he'd like to kiss me, too. I take the coward's route and shrug. "She's pretty religious. This must have seemed like some kind of lie to her."

"Sure, but she can't argue with history, can she." It's more of a statement than a question, and he's repeated my own words, the ones I'd said in my head just a few minutes ago. We *are* destined for each other.

I say, "Still. I guess we can't expect her to give all that up in one history class."

He laughs and I find I can breathe again. He still likes me. "No, I suppose not. But she's in for another battle. I happen to know that Sylvia's going to start talking about Darwin soon."

"Christ."

He laughs again. "No, Darwin. You know, like the fish symbol on Sylvia's car. Hey, let's get a move on or we'll miss the bus. Sit with me?"

And the breathing stops again. All I can think to say is, "How come you still ride the bus at all? I mean, instead of riding with your sister."

He looks at me from under his eyebrows. "Are you serious? That would be, like, the end of my life around here. I don't wanna stick out, y'know?" He looks at me with an intensity that I know means there are a number of ways he could stick out, and he'd like to avoid all of them. Not an outlier, then. "Plus she doesn't usually leave right away. So, whaddya say?"

My feet stop moving as though missing the bus altogether is the only way to avoid making the choice he's given me. But my face gives me away.

He smiles. "You gotta sit with her, don't you."

I close my eyes for a sec and open them on his. I nod slowly. It's hard to tell whether he's in sympathy with what I have to do—sit with Jorja—or whether he thinks it's lame. But at least we walk to the bus together.

Jorja is crammed into a seat as close as she can get to the inside wall of the bus, arms hugging her ribs, glaring out the window. I settle beside her and don't say anything; give her a few minutes, I'm thinking. But we're almost to her church and she still hasn't said anything, so I do. "You okay?"

She lifts the shoulder nearer to me and drops it, still staring out. I feel pretty sure she'll get off at her church, so I have my things collected. I get up and step back, as I would ordinarily to let her out, but instead of sitting down again I follow her off the bus. Outside on the edge of the road, she glares at me. "What d'you think you're doing?"

"You're always trying to get me into that church of yours. Just thought I'd make it easy for you today. Are you telling me I'm not welcome?"

"Jesus welcomes everyone." She turns and walks into the building, and I follow, catching the message on the battered marquee as I pass: OUR CHURCH IS PRAYER CONDITIONED.

There's a Teen Meet today. There usually is; they like to have something going on after school so kids will have something to do besides drink beer, drag race, and all the other stuff we're big enough to get into and not old enough to avoid. At least Jorja sits in a chair with an empty one beside her, rather than someplace where I can't sit with her; with the mood she's in, it could have gone either way. A circle of chairs is set up in what would have been the living room of this particular prefab ranch house. Most of them are occupied by teenagers, and I know some of them from one place or another. One guy is going on about how much he wants to "be" with his girlfriend and how wrong he knows that is, and he's asking for everyone's prayers to help him remain faithful to the Bible's teachings. When he sits down, the leader—Mrs. Glasier, my school principal's wife—says something appropriate and is just starting to look around for another volunteer to confess something when Jorja waves her hand in the air.

"Yes, Jorja. I see you've brought Ethan Poe with you! How wonderful. Welcome, Ethan. Now, Jorja, do you have a challenge you're facing today?"

"Yes, ma'am. I do. I was in American History class today, and Mr. Coffin was saying that the United States is not a Christian nation. He was saying that the Constitution doesn't support God. I know he's wrong, but how can I prove it?"

Mrs. Glasier looks around the circle. "Can anyone help Jorja with some facts?" While we're waiting for someone to speak, I'm thinking that's not quite what Mr. Coffin said. But I'm not about to step into this.

One guy, whose name is Bryan, raises his hand and speaks at the same time, not waiting to be called on. "Everyone knows the founding fathers were Christian. And they put God's laws into ours."

As if that settles it, they all nod and no one else says anything. To me, it sounds just as rigid as when Kyle said, "We *know* the Bible is true."

Mrs. Glasier chimes in. "When the Revolutionary War began, probably only fifteen percent of the people in the colonies were churchgoers. If you think this conflicts with your ideas of how the colonies started, remember that they weren't all in New England and that the Pilgrims didn't spread very far out of Massachusetts. But now, there are more Christians in the United States than have ever lived anywhere before. What does this tell us? It says that Christianity is advancing, and the laws of this nation help move it forward. Onward, Christian soldiers!"

A few kids shout "Amen" and "Halleluiah." But this sounds bogus to me. I must be scowling, because Mrs. Glasier says, "Ethan? Do you have a question?"

I start to shake my head. I don't want to get into this, especially with all these Bible bangers. I don't like taking sides at any time, and it's not like I've given this topic a lot of thought. But kind of like when I surprised myself by opening that conversation with Mom about my being gay, I hear my voice say, "Well . . . I dunno, isn't it more like the laws made it possible because they stay out of your way? Does it have to be that the laws support Christianity over something else?"

Mrs. Glasier's smile makes my skin crawl. "Ethan, perhaps we need to think through this a little more. If all the laws were doing was staying out of our way, why would Christianity be the only religion growing so fast? Why would it be so predominant?"

"The Europeans . . ." I start, not quite knowing where this should lead. "I mean, most of the people who came here came from places where it was the biggest religion. Seems like that would have got things going that way."

"And they found the perfect government when they got here!" She makes it sound as though I've made her point for her, which I don't think I have.

In my head I ask, "So, where is it going?" But I must have said it out loud.

She blinks at me. "Where? Why, Ethan, all the way! It's the sacred duty of every true Christian to bring the message of salvation to all souls and bring them to the one true God. And we'll succeed!"

More shouts, and I'm beginning to feel outnumbered. Jonestown, revisited. One guy shouts, "Then we'll be a Christian nation for real!" Everyone else seems to think this would be a great thing. But in my mind—no more vocal surprises, I tell myself—I'm thinking, *What they want is a Christian version of Saudi Arabia.* That's a place where I would definitely not want to live.

I stay for a little while longer, and then one kid gets up and says she needs to leave. I give Jorja a silent salute and get up as well; I've had enough. She scowls and jerks her head toward the chair I've just vacated, but I act like I don't see. I need to get outta here. This might be fine for Jorja, but it gives me the creeps.

It's a bit of a walk home, but not unmanageable, and it gives me time to think. I'm trying to remember when Jorja got all Christian. She's been this way since we hooked up as best friends, but—was she always like *this?* I picture her family, such as it is. No siblings, just Martha and Jared Loomis, Mom and Stepdad. Jorja has told me that they don't go to church at all, and suddenly I want to ask her why she started going. All by herself. What would drive someone to do that out of the blue? I know why Kyle started going all the time, but—Jorja? At the same time, though, I feel like it's something I should have asked months ago. Like, now it's too late. Now it makes it seem like I don't know her well enough to be best friends, if I don't know something like this. So I have to pretend I understand. But I don't.

* * *

Over dinner, Mom asks me if anything interesting happened in school today. I shrug, giving myself a minute to think whether I want to bring anything up. She says, "For this I pay taxes," and turns to Kyle, who goes on about some guy who got caught cheating on a pop quiz.

I ask Mom, "What about you? Anything interesting?"

She eyes me a minute. "Why should I tell you? You haven't given me anything."

I shrug again. "Just not sure I know what to think about things."

"Well, that's interesting already. What things?"

So I tell her about Jorja leaving class and why, and about the Teen Meet. Mom lets me finish and then asks, "How does this make you feel, other than confused?"

"Confused?"

"You said you didn't know what to think. That's confused. So, how do you *feel?*"

I have this thing where I look inside my head, and I don't see what's in front of me while I do it. It's like my mental eyes take over until they see what they're looking for. What they see this time is that there are two words that pop up together. One is *Lonely*, but I don't want to say that one. I say the other aloud. "Scared." And my eyes look outside my head again and see Mom nodding.

Kyle speaks before she can say anything. "Scared of what, Ethan? All they were doing is what God wants them to do."

"Yeah, but it's like they want to take over. If it wasn't just one church it'd be, like, freaky."

Mom says, "But it's not just that one church. It's lots of them, all over the place. And far too many of them want to rule the world."

"That's not it at all!" Kyle is getting up onto his soapbox. I should never have said anything. "This is God's will! This is what Jesus commanded us to do."

"What we're talking about," Mom says, her voice tight, "is not just a case of making everyone welcome at church. It's not just living in a way that helps others. That's not all these people want to do. They're actually stomping on the rights of people who want to look at God another way, or don't see a God at all. They sure better not tell *me* what to think!"

"They're not telling you what to think, Mom. Honestly. They're telling you what to believe. And how to live."

Mom throws her napkin beside her plate, which doesn't have much effect when it's paper like ours. But that doesn't stop her. You know how when someone intimidates you, you're supposed to picture them on the toilet with their pants around their ankles to get things on a level playing field? Well, in my mind, I don't have any trouble picturing my Mom like that and *still* saying whatever the hell she wants to, to whoever she wants to say it to. So a soft napkin is hardly going to deflate the force of her irritation. Glaring at Kyle she says, "And that's better? This is a *good* thing? I repeat, they'd better not try and tell *me!*" She points a finger at Kyle for emphasis.

He's struggling not to get mad, by all appearances. Like, trying to remain calm and set a good Christian example. But he goes on for a couple of minutes about how the scriptures are very clear, quoting chapter and verse a couple of times. I can see Mom is getting more steamed. I don't want a fight here; I just want to finish my dinner and get my homework done so I can listen to some music and jerk off to images of Max's sexy smile. Kyle has just shoved a forkful of potato into his mouth, and I see my chance.

"Uh, Kyle?" Both of them turn toward me. "You're using your right hand. Just thought you might like to know."

I love Mom's laughter. It's rich and deep and honest. Kyle looks mortified, and I'm just happy I've managed to end this thing I didn't mean to start.

In my room, after my homework, I do listen to some music. And I lock my door, and I do jerk off to Max's smile. The sweetest part of it is that I know it's possible, very possible, that he's in his room right now, jerking off and thinking about me.

But as I'm lying there afterward with music thumping through my system and making my bones throb, it isn't Max's gorgeous face that hangs in my mind. Those eyes I told you about, the ones that look inward? They're seeing that fish shape with the little feet and the word Darwin inside. Like some kind of warning sign.

Chapter 3

Just like Max has said, Sylvia opens the Pandora's box called evolution the following week. It's in our book, so there's no big surprise, I suppose, but Sylvia isn't just starting at the beginning of the book and working her way through. She must have some system all her own.

She sneaks up on Darwin, though; doesn't go into the whole evolution thing yet. She gives us an out-of-book experience first, talking about his life, his family, his education, and all about how he was on some track to go into the Church of England as a career. But it seems he couldn't go on believing in a God that allowed the kind of suffering Darwin saw in the world—and it wasn't just the way people treat each other. He got obsessed with how life kills life to live.

This is a concept I haven't considered very much. I mean, I've never understood vegetarians, but it's mostly because they seem a little wacky generally. Listening to Sylvia talk about wasp larvae eating caterpillars alive from the inside out gets me thinking about killing anything. Like, how do I know whether a stalk of corn has feelings, or what it goes through when we're busy making fried chips out of its babies? Who am I to say that's okay?

Thinking about all this makes me feel kind of small. But it also makes me feel like I fit right in. I'm sitting there, watching Sylvia draw wasps and caterpillars on the whiteboard, feeling like part of the whole of nature. Feeling like maybe I'm not isolated after all, like I'm not this weird outlier. I'm not any weirder than anything else. It's almost a religious experience, really. And then it crashes when I realize that people will always make me an outlier. Because I'll always be gay. Maybe Mom didn't freak, and maybe cool people like Guy and Max are gay, but I know what happens to us, and I know why Max doesn't want to stick out. Maybe the Constitution prevents Mrs. Glasier from making me practice her religion, but if I go to town hall with Max and ask for a marriage license, not only will we get turned away, but also the government will do only so much to protect us from her.

It dawns on me at the end of class that until my mood crashed, I didn't once obsess about whether there was a good chance to look in Max's direction to see if maybe he was looking at me. Now I really want to know. How is this stuff making *him* feel? Throwing caution to the winds, I turn in my seat to where he sits, a row behind and a few seats away. And he's looking at me. And I'm sure it's not just that he saw me turn, and he looked out of curiosity or something to see why. He was *looking* at me.

This is also a banner day in American History. Mr. Coffin has moved away from the question of religion, and I would have thought Jorja had, too, after her euphoric moment in Teen Meet. Like, that vindication among her fellow fanatics would be enough. But I'm wrong. Coffin starts to go into the amendment that says state governments can't do stuff that goes against federal law, and I don't even know what it is that sets Jorja off. But there's her hand waving away again. Coffin calls on her, like a dope. And damn if she doesn't practically go word for word through what Mrs. Glasier had said.

Coffin just lets her go on right through what she must have thought would be the dot at the end. "And if that's not enough," she says, her voice pouty, "this is a democracy. And that means that the majority rule. And the majority of people in this country are *Christians*."

All eyes go to Coffin. That sounds like a good point. Will he agree? Will he let her win? Or will he say something that sends her huffing out the door again?

From behind his desk he nods a few times. "I can see you've put a lot of thought into this, Jorja. That's commendable. I hope you'll continue to do so, for if there's one thing this country needs, it's citizens who use their brains."

He moves slowly around to the front of the desk, like he's on some peaceful mission and is unafraid of any resistance that might come his way. Leaning against the desk, he asks, "Who can tell me why our government has a system of checks and balances? Yes, Max?"

Wasting no time, I turn and look.

"It keeps one area from having everything its way. It's protection. Like, the president can't have everything his way."

Mr. Coffin has a wry smile on his face. "You're right, Max. That is the concept. And within the legislative branch, we have the House of Representatives and the Senate. Which one has more members?"

I answer while I'm raising my hand; I want to be included if Max is. "The House."

"So, does the House always win?"

Silence. Then Max says, "No."

"Correct." Coffin looks at Jorja for just a second and then walks back behind his desk. He picks up our textbook and thumbs through it a moment. Then he tells us a page number. "As you'll read here, the Bill of Rights, which is the first ten amendments to our Constitution, was specifically written in a way that protects the rights of individuals against the vagaries of majority opinion or the outcome of any election." He closes the book and looks directly at Jorja. "So, you see, our Constitution protects the rights of individuals who are not Christian just as forcefully as it protects those who call themselves Christian. According to the Constitution, no religion gives any citizen more rights than any other, no matter how many subscribe to which religion." He looks around the room. "Questions?"

Silence. I risk a glance at Jorja, who's sitting to my right. She's staring at a corner of the room, jaw clenched, breathing loudly through her nose. She's furious. But she's licked, at least for now. I can anticipate what she might say at Teen Meet, where she's sure to go again today. I will not be there, though. I'm not going back to that group. Not even for Jorja.

After class, I throw a regretful glance at Max; I'd love to talk with him about this, because it gives me back that feeling from Biology where I'd felt like maybe I'm part of everything after all, that this thing that makes me so different isn't that important in the overall scheme of things. Hell, who am I kidding? I'd just like to talk to Max. Walk with Max. Be with Max. . . . But I feel like if I don't talk to Jorja, if I don't somehow rein her in a little, calm her down, she'll go nuclear. And she's my best friend. Maybe I can convince her to talk to me instead of that crowd at her church that's determined to rule the world. I have to run to catch up with her.

"Hey, you wanna hitch out to Nick's and get some pizza?" She ignores me, keeps heading for the bus. Maybe if I pretend I'm the one with the problem. "Jorja? I need to talk to you. Please?" She gets on the bus without looking at me, but I can tell she's thinking. Probably weighing my need, whatever it is, against the boost she'll get from that church crowd. When I sit beside her she doesn't turn away to look out the window, just stares blankly at the back of the seat ahead of her. So I wait. If she's heard me, if she's on board, she won't make getting-up motions near the church.

As we get near Society of Nazareth, I look out at the marquee. This time it's PUT THE U BACK IN CH RCH. Jorja doesn't budge. I take a deep breath, but I don't speak; that would kill it, and she'd be off the bus in a shot. This is how it is with her. You kind of have to walk on eggshells a little. It's almost like by the time you've gone to the trouble to make friends with her, it would be a waste of that effort not to keep going.

We stay on the bus past my house and ride to the end of the route, where it intersects with the highway. One other kid is still on the bus, a girl who used to have a crush on me. She's anything but Goth, so she's probably thinking she had a close call. She's right for more reasons than she knows.

Jorja and I must look like quite the pair to anyone driving by, two teenage kids all in black, my jeans skin-tight all the way into the tops of my Doc Martens, Jorja's long skirt with her version of a handkerchief hem—she hacked it into irregular, frayed jags herself—and huge patch pockets that have nonfunctional metal chain laces up the middle.

Most cars just drive by, but eventually we get a ride with some woman who knows us, and we have to listen to a lecture about the dangers of hitchhiking and threats about telling our parents for the four minutes' worth of road to Nick's. What she doesn't seem to understand, and I don't know how to tell her, is that hitching is half the fun of going to Nick's. One of these days I'm going to hitch someplace really far away, just for the hell of it. One day when I get the guts.

Jorja orders two slices with pepperoni, which I take to mean that she's in tough emotional shape. I get two with sausage, we grab a can of Coke each, and we slide into a red-orange fiberglass booth at the front window, where we can watch the little bit of traffic when we run out of things to say or just feel like sitting there a bit.

I've downed my first slice before Jorja says, "So what did you want to talk about?"

Oh, yeah. I told her I needed to talk. I stall for time with a few sips of soda. Finally, "Kyle tried to freeze his right hand." I've got her attention, anyway. But I don't know where to go from here. So I say, "Now he won't use it for anything."

"Anything? Is he right-handed?" I nod, my mouth full of pizza. "Must make it tough in school. How does he take notes? Or do his homework?"

I hadn't thought of this. She's right. "I have no idea. I just know he tries to eat with his left hand, and sometimes he forgets."

"But why freeze it?"

I shrug. "No idea. All he said was it was causing him to stumble. Something about cutting off members."

Her eyes widen. "You mean like in Matthew?" Was that it? I can't remember; I just nod. "What was it he did? With his hand, I mean?"

I sit back and look hard at her; do I tell her what the stumble was? I never know what she can take, what she wants to hear about, and what she doesn't. I decide on discretion. "He didn't specify."

Silence. Then, "What church does he go to?"

"The one out on Thurber Road."

"Why that one?"

"Dunno. I guess it's the one my folks used to go to."

She's quiet, but I can tell she's thinking. But when she speaks, it's a new topic. "How are you doing with your folks?"

Ah. That. "My mom's lawyer is really good-looking."

She sits up straight. "Ethan! Of all the . . . When is the divorce final?"

"No idea."

"Did they get married in that church?"

"I think so. I wasn't there."

"Then they shouldn't be getting divorced at all. Doesn't it bother you?"

My throat starts to tighten, a dangerous sign. "Jorja, what do you want me to say?"

"Oh, I don't know. Maybe something like how you don't want this to happen, like you don't want to lose your family, like your mom is really unhappy, like you're doing everything you can to get them back together again? Something like that?"

I'm shaking my head. "I can't do anything."

"Have you tried?"

"Like what? What could I do?"

"You could tell your dad that your mom misses him." I don't want to admit to Jorja—or even to myself—that ratting on Mom and Jimmy Korbel had occurred to me the other day. I feel guilty just thinking about it. *And* I feel guilty for not having tried, anyway.

Then she says, "It's not like he was hurting you or anything, was he?" Hurting me? Not past the usual stuff, spankings when I was a kid. "Or your mom?"

I shake my head. "Uh, no. I mean, she got mad at him a lot, and I suppose there were good reasons, but not that one." I need to get back to the reason I asked her on this little adventure. "Listen, I was wondering. About History class, you know. I mean, all that stuff about the Constitution. . . ."

Her eyes get all intense. "I know! Can you *believe* that? They shouldn't let that guy teach history! He has everything all wrong!"

Yes. Well. This isn't how I anticipated things going. So I try to soft-pedal the issue, try to avoid pointing out that he might know a little more than we do. "But, I mean, it's not like you're gonna change his mind. So I'm wondering if it's really a good idea—"

"You never know! Besides, I'm worried about the other kids. He's feeding them this stuff like it's gospel. Ethan, don't pretend you don't know how important this is. Don't you know the rest of the world—the non-Christian world, anyway—is at war with us? It's a holy war. And it's gonna end soon, the Rapture will happen, and anyone who's not with us, who isn't in the Church, will be left behind. They'll have the mark of the beast, they'll be tormented with fire and sulfur, and they won't be able to escape when the fires destroy everything and the sea turns to blood! Is that what you want for our classmates?"

I'm trying very hard not to let on how ridiculous this sounds. She seems to think I'm on board with this lunacy, though. Is there a good way to let her know I'm not? "Come on, Jorja, don't you think all that fire and brimstone stuff is a little . . ."

"A little what?" She leans across the table, her voice a hoarse whisper as she tells me, "Ethan. I have seen the beast. I *know* the beast. Trust me."

She's so intense it's starting to scare me. For real. All I can do is nod. Jorja leans back again, eyes closed as she takes a couple of deep breaths, almost like she's been fighting the beast right there in front of me. Then she looks at me, her eyes dull and tired. "You *do not* want the mark of the beast on you."

I'm sitting there wondering how on earth she could have got this deep in without my realizing it. I mean, the *beast?* I'm actually a little worried about her. Maybe I can find out a little more about where she's coming from with this business. "So, about this beast. Where do I look in the Bible? It's in there, right?"

"Oh, yes. Absolutely. You need to read Revelations. I think everyone should read that first, before they read the rest of the Bible. Then they'd know how deadly serious this is. Then they'd know how hard they need to work, how sincerely they need to believe. They'd know. They'd just know."

Revelations. Maybe I'll ask Kyle. Or . . . maybe not; that could take longer than reading it, and he'd be on me afterward, most likely, to test me or whatever. No, I'll just have to sneak his Bible away long enough to read Revelations. For Jorja's sake.

The next week in Biology we dissect frogs. Sylvia tells us to pair up, and Jorja gloms on to me immediately. Max is looking at me, but as soon as he sees Jorja he turns away. His body moves first, and the look he gives me cuts into me. It's almost like he's saying, "If that's the way you want it." And it isn't. But then I feel guilty; what's Jorja supposed to do if I scamper off with my new friend? She's never turned me down, never left me in the lurch.

The frog reeks of formaldehyde, which makes me a little dizzy. Jorja calls me a baby, but it's not the frog that gets to me, it's the smell. Plus, ours is a female, and she has eggs. That makes me kind of sad. I mean, okay, we have to kill something to live, but why kill something just to take it apart?

Jorja picks up on my feelings. "What's with you?"

I don't want to make a big deal out of this, so I just say, "Doesn't seem to be a very good reason to kill something. This, I mean."

Her eyes roll upward. "Oh, Ethan. It's not like the thing is human."

"It was alive. And it was pregnant."

"But it's not human."

Like that's the be-all and end-all. She's made her position clear. I'm not sure it's mine, but I don't feel like getting into it.

On the bus ride home I'm working on some convincing phrases to use on Mom to try and get her to take me out on the road, driving. If I don't get started on my thirty-five supervised driving hours, it'll be next year before I get my intermediate. But as soon as I get to the house from the bus stop, Mom captures me. "Come on, Ethan. You're going to help me with something."

I'm tired, and I just want to go jerk off and sulk in my room. "What?" My voice is heavy with sulk already.

Hands on hips, she glares at me. "Don't give me that tone! Now, come on. We have important work to do. Watch this." She picks up a hammer and walks to the front edge of our yard near the road, and now I see there's something lying on the ground there. Mom picks it up, and it turns out to be one of those election signs like the ones I'd helped Dad deal with. The kind I'd been sure she'd never agree to. The hammer comes down on the top of the wooden stake, and suddenly we have a sign in our own yard. It faces the road, so I can't see what it says. But it doesn't really matter what it says. It's one of those stupid signs, and it's in my yard. I want to hide, but that would do only so much good. Around here, everyone knows where everyone else lives.

About now I notice that our car, a rattly Subaru wagon we got thirdhand, is full of signs, all on raw wooden stakes. But these say something I haven't seen before. Some of them say, ETTA GREENLEAF. FOR SCHOOL BOARD. FOR COMMON SENSE. Another version says, GOT SCIENCE? PROVE IT. Etta's name is at the bottom of this one. And then there's RELIGION IS FOR CHURCHES. SCIENCE IS FOR SCHOOLS. Again, Etta's name. And also, DON'T PRAY IN MY SCHOOL, AND I WON'T TEACH SCIENCE IN YOUR CHURCH. All the lettering is bright green.

I'm standing there looking at them and thinking that some of them are bigger than the other signs I've seen. The average size of the others is probably around eighteen inches long and a foot high. "What am I supposed to do with these?"

"You're going to help me pound them into the dirt, that's what. This is important, Ethan. This is your brain, your education we're talking about."

"But . . ." Think fast, Ethan. "But they're too big."

"They're not! You can't get anything important into four words."

"Um, like, got-science-prove-it?"

"What is your problem?"

"Ma, I don't want to get involved in this stuff!" And I don't. I really don't. I hate taking sides about anything.

"You're involved whether you want to be or not. Do you know what will happen if Carl Phinney wins this seat? Do you?"

"I'll learn what Intelligent Design is."

"You'll be expected to take it seriously as science! It's a Trojan horse, Ethan. Do you remember what that is?"

I stretch my mind. Trojans. Condoms? No. Wait. Greeks. But I take too long.

"Get in the car."

"Can I drive?"

"Not today."

I throw myself into the passenger seat and slam the door. Mom ignores this and gives me a description of the huge wooden horse the Greeks pretended was a gift to the city of Troy during some war, and all these soldiers are inside, and they come out at night and slaughter everyone. Something like that. I've heard it before, I just forgot.

We turn onto the road, and I can see that the sign Mom planted in our yard is the *Got Science* one. And before long, I realize that we're headed in the direction of my school. "Where are we going?"

"Can't think of a better place to start than right around the school. This is an educational issue. The schools are public. They're not churches. And our government is supposed to keep the two apart. What have you learned about that in your studies?"

I do my best to shrink down so I'll be seen by as few people as possible. "The wall of separation," I mumble. "The Establishment Clause. The government can't set up a religion. The Free Exercise Clause. Worship however you want to."

"Very good. There's hope for you yet. Do you know what that all means?"

"No one can tell me what church I have to go to."

"More than that, Ethan. Sit up. No one can tell you to go to church at all. Or to synagogue. Or any place like that. But what the Carl Phinneys of the world want is exactly what the Constitution says they can't do. You heard your crazy brother last week. They want to tell you what to believe. And this so-called Intelligent Design crap is nothing more than dressing up religion to try and make it look like science so they can sneak it into the school. Not with my tax dollars, they don't!"

I steal a look at Mom from my hunkered posture. She's looking straight ahead, heaving mad, eyes blazing. Mom looks a little like Jorja when she's on her high horse. Again, like it's done a few times lately, my voice surprises me, gets away from me before I can stop it. "What makes you different from them? Seems like you're both mad as hell at each other."

"The difference?" She's practically squeaking. "The difference, my son, product of my loins, is that their rights *end* where mine begin. They want to force me into a box that doesn't fit me. I'm not trying to force them anywhere except out of my face. If they'd stay out of my business, I'd stay out of theirs." She glares quickly at me and back to the road. "They started this, sonny boy, but they sure as hell aren't going to finish it."

Hoping to calm things down a little, I ask, "Where'd you get these signs, anyway?"

She lets out a long breath. "I went to visit Ms. Greenleaf, as a matter of fact. Offered my services. We worked out the slogans, she ordered them and paid for them, and I'm putting them up. She's getting on, you know. That's why she hadn't done any up to now. But I promised to help."

"So that puts *me* on the spot?"

"Consider it a lesson in social activism. Consider it an educational experience."

Mom stops at the open field just outside the boundaries of the school property and hammers the first sign into the ground herself. She chooses *Got science? Prove it.* She says that one's her favorite. Then she sends me across the road to set some up over there. She hollers, "Not too close together. And not in anyone's yard, Ethan. Just where there's open space."

There aren't very many houses near the school, anyway. It's almost all open space. Fields of boulders with blueberry bushes going red now that it's autumn, that's the most common landscape. The edges of the roads tend to fall away from the paved surface into gullies that trap water, and they're full of milkweeds, puffed white with black-brown seeds to carry off. Twisted masses of bittersweet vines are practically choking skinny poplars. I've always liked bittersweet, the bright, hard, mustard yellow pods breaking open to expose the softer, red-orange seed head. But now as I look at them, as I see them strangling little trees, I think again about killing. It doesn't benefit the bittersweet to kill the tree it's climbing. So why does nature allow it? At least the larvae that eat wasps from the inside out are doing that to live. The bittersweet is killing the trees just because it can.

By the time I run out of signs I'm kind of far away from the car, and as I head back that way I see that there's an SUV pulled over, and someone talking with Mom. Loudly. It's Mrs. Glasier. Guess she doesn't lead Teen Meet every day. As I get closer I hear Mom's words first.

"I can put these up anyplace I want to. The side of the road is public easement. We aren't putting them in yards, if that's what you're worried about."

"Charlene, this is school property!"

"Actually, it isn't. That's the boundary, right there." Mom is pointing past her first sign. "And besides, school property is public property. Even so, that's not where I put it."

Mrs. Glasier just glares. Then, "We'll just see about this." And she marches over to her SUV and climbs in, awkwardly because of how high the thing is up off the ground.

Mom yells at the monster vehicle as it roars past. "What you'll see is lots more of these. Carl Phinney isn't the only one running, you know!"

We stand there staring at the license plate that says JLVSME, which takes me a minute to decode as Jesus LoVeS ME. Wonder what it means that the only word all in caps is ME. I figure I may as well help Mom with the last of her signs. She's on a rampage, though, slamming the hammer so hard she splits one of the stakes and has to fish out another sign. We don't stop anyplace else after that, so I guess I'll have to do this a few more times, 'cause we still have plenty of signs.

Her mood hasn't improved much by dinnertime—take-out pizza. And stupid Kyle makes things worse when he comes to the table with his right arm strapped to his side, the hand curled inward and wrapped. It looks painful. I can't imagine how he did all that with just his left hand, and maybe his teeth.

"Kyle, for God's sake! Take that thing off this minute. What are you trying to prove?"

He stands beside his chair looking all serious. "With all due respect, Mother, I can't do that."

"You *what*?"

By the time he opens his mouth and starts to form words, she's closed the distance between them and is yanking at the strips of fabric remnants that came from different sewing projects: a length of kitchen curtain gingham, some bright red from an unfortunate skirt effort, a nine-year-old piece of the racing car pattern from the construction of the bedspread that's still in my room upstairs. I'm expecting Kyle to protest, or try to get away, but he just stands there, eyes squinted shut, mouth pursed like he's some kind of martyr and Mom's striping him with lashes instead of removing stripes of random cloth. He winces as she forces his hand open, it was bound that tight. The guy is crazy. Life's weird enough without this.

Mom pushes him down into his chair, the fabric scraps in a pile at her feet. "Ethan, set the table, and give your dumb-ass brother a glass of his beverage of choice." I know it's ginger ale, so I don't ask him anything. Everything calms down a little as pizza slices find their way onto plates, and I bring mine and Kyle's to the table. Mom sits down and stares at him a minute.

"Kyle Poe, I've had about enough of this insanity. If you can't stop 'stumbling' without this idiocy, then that church of yours isn't holding up its end of the bargain." He looks at her and is about to say something. "Don't! Just don't. I've had quite enough churchiness for one day. I don't want to hear you quoting anything or praying anything. Do it in your head if you must, but don't inflict it on me."

The rest of the meal is pretty silent. Kyle's right hand might not be tied to his body now, but he leaves it hanging down, useless and pathetic.

Friday night, when either Kyle or me or both of us should have a date, we don't. I guess officially Mom doesn't, either, but at least she's going out. Another casual meeting with Jimmy Korbel. I don't have anything against him, exactly, but I can't say I want him to marry my mom. The idea of a man not my father in what I still think of as my parents' room makes me feel sick and then furious.

So there we are, the two teenage boys of the house, hanging around on a Friday evening. I've just finished washing the dishes, thinking about Max and wondering why he hasn't asked me to "check out the sights" yet, and as I hose out the sink I decide I'll watch some TV or maybe get on the computer, or both, but when I go into the living room Kyle's already on the computer, poking away with only the fingers on his left hand. So of course this is when I realize that the computer is really what I want, not the TV.

"What are you doing?" I demand.

"My business." He doesn't even look away from the screen.

"Well, you can't hog that all night just because I had to do the dishes that you can't do because you won't use your fucking hand."

Again, no turn of the head. "Don't say that word."

"Fucking, fucking, fucking." But that's not going to get me the computer, so I decide to wait him out and watch some TV in the meantime. I put the thing on mute while I cruise from channel to channel, looking for something to watch without being subjected to even a word of advertising, and before I land on something watchable I've lost out again, because Kyle's turned the volume up on the computer so he can watch a YouTube video. At first this really pisses me off, and I consider a battle of audio, figuring the TV would have to win. But then I hear recorded laughter, and then more, and I pause in my intended war of sound to see what Kyle's watching. I stand a little way behind him and watch as this clean-cut guy on the screen cracks jokes with the audience about his life, his family, about the Bible, and about science. If he hadn't finally picked up a Bible and declared that he believed it, cover to cover, I would have suspected he was a comedian making fun of both sides.

He really is funny, actually, and he seems likeable. It sure seems like he has his audience eating out of his hand. And then with no seam, no break, no "okay that's enough funny stuff we're getting down to business now," he's into his presentation. This guy is an entertainer.

He says he likes science. And then he proceeds to make it sound like he doesn't. It's clear to me pretty quickly that what he's doing is picking on some very specific things about science, lots of them decades old, and pointing out the flaws.

I creep closer—not wanting Kyle to know I'm watching this thing—to see what it's called, and I see the video title: *100 Reasons Why Evolution Is So Stupid.* This comedian-slash-whatever would seem to be Kent Hovind.

I stand rooted in place while he trashes scientific point after scientific point, experiment after hypothesis after theory after idea, keeping his audience laughing and nodding, and basically doing his best to make anyone who trusts science feel like they've lost touch with reality. As I stand there, hearing Kyle chuckle along with the others, I start to hear a voice in my head. It's saying things like, *How is he doing this? Why does what he's saying seem to make sense when I know better?*

I really don't want to get into it with Kyle. We have enough things to fight about. I back up as silently as possible, turn off the muted TV, and sneak upstairs to my room.

Lying on my bed, earbuds helping to drown out the world, I let my mind float. I don't even want to fight this battle in my head. I just want it all to leave me alone.

About four songs later, my mind starts to free itself from Hovind's fast-paced patter and the chuckles and giggles of his adoring audience. I pause the music so I can organize some thoughts.

First, his style sucks you in right away. He's a very funny guy who talks fast and keeps the jokes coming, gets everyone liking him, gets them relaxed and laughing. And nodding. Then he takes examples of science questioning itself and calls that stupid. While you're still chuckling about how silly science is, he starts cherry-picking questions science doesn't even pretend to have an answer for, and he calls science stupid. Then he points out places where science made mistakes and says "stupid" again.

What he doesn't say is what's really going on. Because what would *really* be stupid is if scientists *didn't* keep looking for better answers, and if they *didn't* admit when they made a mistake. But they do. That's how we know what the mistakes are. That's where Hovind gets them—from science itself.

Hovind says the Bible answers questions that evolution is too stupid to know. What he won't say is that we're supposed to believe the Bible is true because the Bible says it's true. He picks on science because it questions itself, because it requires proof—even from itself. What I get is that the only proof Mr. Hovind requires is the Bible's assertion that the Bible is correct.

That's stupid.

But—this isn't my battle. The thing that haunts me is that I thought Kyle was smarter than this. I wouldn't have thought he'd be so easily fooled by this guy. I mean, *I* see through him. Why doesn't Kyle?

It's only about eight-thirty or so, but I hear Mom's car over the drone of that loon Kyle's listening to. First she slams the car door, then the door of the house. I'm guessing the nondate with Jimmy didn't go so well.

Kyle doesn't have the sense to pause his video; I can still hear it going. There's enough silence from downstairs around that loon's rantings for me to imagine Mom standing there, listening, face darkening as she realizes what it is. And it seems I'm not far off.

"Kyle Poe! Turn that damned thing off this minute. Do you think I want to listen to that shit?"

"Don't say—"

"Stop it!" Her voice is high, almost frantic. "Stop it right now! I've had more than my fill of parsimonious assholes tonight. Turn that damned thing off and go to your room." There's a pause, and I can tell Kyle mumbles something. "NOW!"

I'm sorry Mom feels like this, but I'm thinking it must have to do with Jimmy Korbel, and I can't help but be happy about that. Call it unholy glee.

But I haven't heard the end of Kent Hovind. Mom wakes me up Saturday morning to ask if I need anything; she's running a couple of errands. By the time I make it downstairs, she's pulling out of the driveway and Kyle is at the kitchen table spooning milk and cereal into his mouth with his left hand.

"Still stumbling?" I plunk my own cereal bowl onto the table and settle into Mom's chair.

He swallows and then says, "You could stand a little contrition yourself, you know."

"What's that supposed to mean?"

"You know very well." He scoops another spoonful into his face.

"What if I don't? What the hell are you talking about?" Is he telling me he knows when I'm jerking off?

"Don't say hell."

"Oh, fuck off!"

"Or that." He stands, carries the bowl and spoon over to the sink. Before I know it he's back at the computer, that "stupid" Hovind character rambling on again. I can't tell if it's the same video or not, because now he's going on about sexual immorality, not evolution. I finish my cereal and chug some orange juice, planning to sneak up behind Kyle again to see what he's watching this time. But I don't get close enough to see before I hear Hovind going on about how people who allow themselves to be ruled by material life rather than God's word are automatically immoral. It takes him no time at all to get to homosexuality. Maybe when the asshole struck so close to home for me I made some noise. Whatever, Kyle turns and sees me.

He hits the pause icon. "Pull up a chair."

"You're out of your mind. That's stuff's bullshit."

"Sexual immorality? You think that's not a bad thing?"

"Sexual orientation and sexual immorality are not the same thing."

"Any sexual behavior the Bible condemns is immorality. If your orientation causes you to sin, then it's immoral."

"*My* orientation?" Does he know? Or was that a generic "you"?

"Did I say you were homosexual, Ethan?" His glance is dismissive, but then it changes, and he looks harder at me. "Ethan?"

Shit. I've blown it big-time. "Don't get your knickers in a twist, big brother. Your buddy there is just plain offensive to anyone with a brain." I turn and stomp off upstairs before he can figure out that I'm scared shitless that I've just given myself away to the person second least likely to understand it. The first is my dad.

Chapter 4

Next week, after school on Monday, Mom says I need to help her with more signs. By then, I've developed a plan. "Tell you what, Mom. I'll help you, for sure. As long as I can drive." I hold my breath, half expecting an explosion. It doesn't come. She just looks at me like she's thinking. So I prod, "Deal?"

She tosses me the keys. *YES!* Out of my back pocket I pull the folded-up pamphlet I downloaded for charting my time. A short pencil stub is in my front jeans pocket, and I get that out, too. Mom says, "What are those for?"

"I have to rack up thirty-five supervised hours, remember? So I'm gonna log how much time I drive today. And you need to initial it. I guess I can't count the time we're hammering signs." I look at her, half hoping she'll say to just clock the whole time. But she has a weird look on her face.

"I don't know about this, Ethan."

"What? You said I could drive!"

"I know, I know. It's just . . . all these rules. Instruction permit. Intermediate license. Unrestricted license. Two-year waiting periods. Honestly!"

But she gets into the passenger side, and I don't ask any more questions until we're under way. Then I say, "Is it that libertarian stuff again?"

"Yes, it is. If I were card-carrying about it, I wouldn't even believe in drivers licenses. But I guess you can take it too far. And also, I do want you to be safe. So, go ahead. Clock your minutes. And slow down."

I log fifty minutes by the time we get home. That's the good news. The bad news is that she drives me insane the whole time. *Watch out! Slow down! There's a stop sign! Little boy on a bike! Slower around curves!* And she keeps pumping the passenger brake. You know the one? It's on the floor on the passenger side. Only, obviously, it isn't. She just keeps stomping her foot on the floor.

As I'm drifting off to sleep that night I wonder if she was this bad with Kyle. She'd logged time with him; why wasn't she better at it by now? But then I figured maybe she'd just had enough. And I start remembering; yeah, she was this bad with Kyle.

Terrific.

It takes Mom and me the whole week to get all those signs in the car plastered around the countryside. It takes a toll on both of us, but she continues to let me drive, and by the time they're all placed I have about six hours of true driving time. Not much, but it's a start. Now I just have to figure out how to keep going without Mom and me killing each other inside the car, or killing someone else because we're arguing too much to see them.

But I gotta give her credit. The next Saturday, Mom says, "I've got to go up to Etta's, Ethan. Got a little campaign strategizing to do. D'you want to drive me?"

I don't stop to think what I'll do while the two of them are talking. "Hell, yeah!"

"What did you say, young man?"

"Sorry. Yes. Please."

I'd never really seen how far off the road Etta's place is. It's maybe an eighth of a mile to the house, and it's the only house out here. Must be hell in the winter. That pit bull, Two, is sitting at attention beside the steps of Etta's house. I can't tell what I think of him. Everyone knows he could tear you limb from limb, and he sure keeps an eye on Mom and me as we walk from the car and up onto the front porch, but he doesn't move. Maybe it helps that Etta is standing there to greet us. I don't look at his eyes; it seems safer. And then I see a handwritten sign next to the front door.

> *Don't touch Two. Don't speak to him. Don't look in his eyes.*

Okaaay. Not much of a pet, though.

Etta looks about the same as the last time I saw her, probably in the grocery store or something. I guess I expect her to look like some old hag, living out here all alone and hardly venturing out into the world. But she looks pretty normal. Short gray hair, suntanned face with its share of wrinkles but no more. She's kind of tall and slender, and not hideous or crazed. Clothes are pretty normal, too—jeans and a jersey camp shirt right out of L.L.Bean. She tells me to call her Etta, pours lemonade, and sets a plate of chocolate chip cookies on the table.

"Help yourself, Ethan," she says. "Take a napkin from the counter if you want to wander around. You can sit with us if you like, but that might not suit you." She and Mom have taken chairs on either side of one corner of the table, pads of paper and a few pens ready.

"Thanks." I take my glass and as many cookies as I can fit onto the napkin and make my way into the living room, where I'm very pleasantly surprised by the view from a huge picture window out across fields and toward distant mountains. I set the glass down on a soapstone coaster and look outside as I munch cookies, bending over a few times to pick up crumbs I've dropped, finally realizing that the rug they're landing on is a rich, dark, blood red rug with lots of colorful designs. I guess this is an oriental rug, but I don't remember ever being up close and personal with one before. I dig my fingers in. It's not very deep, but the pile is dense and springy.

There are bookshelves along the walls anyplace there isn't a door or a window. I down the last bite of cookie and approach a set of matched book covers that look like leather. They turn out to be all Shakespeare. One of them is on its side on top of the others, so I pull that one out and open it to where there's one edge of paper marking a place. It's in *Hamlet,* and there's writing on the paper, which seems silly because the same words are one of the pages the paper was marking. But there it is:

This above all: to thine own self be true, And it must follow, as the night the day, Thou canst not then be false to any man.

The paper seems really old, and the writing doesn't look like the sign at the door, the one about Two. I put the book back where it was and nearly knock something off the shelf in front of the other leather books. It's a dark, bronze-colored bowl with some kind of black design around the outside near the rim, and it makes a soft ringing sound when my knuckle hits it. I pick it up, feeling the slightly raised pattern of the design, and inside there's a different design, also in black. One large shape that looks sort of like a letter in some other alphabet is inside, on the center of the bottom. When I tap one side with a fingernail, that note sounds again. It really is a note, like you might sing. I set the bowl back carefully and go stand in front of the window.

Just outside are a couple of Adirondack chairs, painted dark green. I grab my lemonade and head back to the kitchen and stand there until I'm noticed. Mom looks up, and I say, "Is it okay if I go sit in the chairs out there?" I point toward where I'd seen them.

Etta answers. "Certainly, Ethan."

"Um, Two won't mind?"

Etta chuckles. "I doubt it. Just keep your head up, move forward with purpose, and follow the three rules. He might come sniff you and then sit with you, though."

Mom glares at me as I reach for another few cookies. So I say, "These are real good. Thanks." I grab my jacket and head out.

It's tempting to say something to Two, who's still sitting where he'd been when we got there. Head up, I remind myself, and he lets me pass. I walk around the house to where the chairs are, settle into one of them, and stare out across the landscape. The other chair is close by. I let my hand move a little toward it and imagine Max's fingers are waiting there for mine. We hold hands and just sit there. I feel so happy. So right. It's warm in the sun, and I close my eyes and breathe deeply.

It's probably ten minutes later when I hear Two's dog tags rattle as he trots around the corner of the house and comes right up to me. He stands there, looking up at me, mouth open in a friendly sort of smiling pant. *Head up,* I remind myself. *Don't talk, don't look, don't touch.*

But he's not following the rules. I feel his tongue on my fingers, and suddenly Max is gone. I have to force myself not to react. Then the dog lies down on the ground, facing the same way as me, like we're admiring the view together. After a few minutes, when he doesn't do anything else, it starts to feel nice with him there. And then Max is there again, and things are perfect.

Some time later, as I'm sort of dozing on and off, I hear Two's tags again, and Etta sits in Max's chair. She says, "Relaxing, isn't it?"

"Yes, ma'am."

Two gets up and goes to her, and she wraps her arms around his neck for a few seconds. He seems to be smiling. He sits beside her as she strokes his head. Guess he's a pet, after all. But just for her.

"Your mother's making a phone call, so I thought I'd wander out. She tells me you've begun your thirty-five-hour driving countdown."

"Yeah. I mean, yes, but I don't have very many hours yet."

"I've told your mother that I'd be happy to help you add to

your total. Seems to me you might benefit from a longer ride than just setting up a few signs for me. Would you like that?"

What's this, I'm thinking, payback for the signs? If so, I'll take it. "Um, sure. That would be great. Thanks!"

"And some of it is supposed to be night driving. Is that right?"

"Five hours."

"Probably shouldn't start with that, but it's been some time since I drove 201 out where it follows Wyman Lake." Mom rounds the corner and walks toward us, so she's hearing all this. "How about if I stop by your house tomorrow around eleven? We could grab some lunch in Bingham. I know of a diner that's got great hamburgers."

Mom says, "That sounds like a lot of driving, Etta."

Etta's laugh is soft and low. "I didn't say I'd let your boy drive the whole time, Charlene. We'll be fine, as long as this is all right with you."

Mom stands in front of me, arms crossed. "Ethan? Sound like something you want to do?"

"Sure does. Very much." If I'd had a little time to think about this, or if I had another option, I might not have responded so quickly. After all, we're talking about me spending, like, some number of hours with this woman I hardly know. But this is how things are. On the way back to our car I take a look at what Etta drives. It's a Subaru, too—so many cars in Maine are, what with the standard all-wheel drive and tough construction—but hers is lots newer than ours, a Forester, dark green like the wooden chairs.

That night, after Max helps me get off—he's in my mind, of course, though I really do get off—I start to think about what this excursion will be like. I've probably exchanged two sentences with Etta Greenleaf before. And we didn't exactly talk a whole lot today. I have no idea who she is, what she's like, or how weird it will feel driving around alone with her. Having burgers in a diner. My mouth starts to water as though the tang of ketchup and the salt from the fries is already in contact with my taste buds. I do have that twenty bucks my dad gave me for helping him with his mowing, if Etta isn't expecting to pay for my lunch. That might be enough. I hate that I might have to choose between getting driving time and saving for my tattoo. There's nothing for it, though.

But—what on earth will we talk about? I drift off to sleep with visions of tarmac spinning beneath me and out of sight.

Etta is fifteen minutes late, and it's kind of cloudy, and I'm on tenterhooks, thinking she's going to cancel on me, or forget altogether. But then she's there, the Forester looking powerful but not monstrous behind my mom's car. She and Mom exchange a few words that I barely hear; Mom hands me my sunglasses, her cell phone, and some money—she doesn't know about the money Dad gave me—and we head out. Etta goes to the passenger side, but she's still got the keys. When I'm settled, seat belt on, she takes me through a quiz: lights; high beams; wipers; rear wiper; defroster; hazard lights . . . it's a long list, but she's the boss right now. If I don't make her happy, the deal will be off for sure. So I take a breath and collect my patience. This is her car, I remind myself, and she doesn't have to do this. Finally she hands me the keys, and I make sure I do everything I know I should before I ease the car backward and then carefully out onto the road. I can see Mom is watching from the door, like she's afraid I'll do something wrong. I don't. At least, Etta says nothing.

I point the car west, one eye on the speedometer and one on the rearview mirror a good part of the time. Etta doesn't say anything for a while. It seems like she's mostly looking at the scenery, but I feel sure she's also watching what I'm doing, making sure I stay within the speed limit, all that stuff. Before too long, though, she starts commenting on some of the more colorful trees and pointing out patches of color on distant hills.

In a few spots we're behind slow drivers or a heavy truck that I'd love to pass. But Etta probably wouldn't want me to, so I don't. It takes about forty-five minutes to get to Bingham, and by now it's just past noon. I'm thinking this is a great time to stop for burgers, but she says, "Have you got another hour in you before lunch?"

What can I say? "Sure."

She chuckles. "Liar. Turn just up here by that gas station. In fact, let's stop and get some gas, and then we'll get lunch. The tank intake is on the right side of the car."

This is actually the first time I've had to negotiate a car really close to something solid, but I go slow and we're fine. It's self-serve, so I get out. Then I hear Etta say, "You'll need to pop the cover. Lever's on the floor there."

Oh yeah. Stupid. I bend over, see the white icon, and pull it up. Etta's hand is reaching toward me, a credit card in it. Thank God Mom has made me fill her car up more than once, so I know what to do from here. I get a receipt just in case Etta wants one and get back in the car, handing her the paper and the card.

We don't go straight to the diner. Instead, she directs me through some neighborhoods, asking me what I see. *Any children? Any dogs? Any parked cars behind which some ball and then some youngster will come tumbling in front of us?* She makes me slow down and read house numbers along one block, and what I realize is that as I'm turning to look, I sort of turn the wheel in that direction, too. She lets me realize it on my own, and it's a good lesson.

The diner is like you read about. Silver, blue trim, narrow, funky old booths with Formica tops along the windows, and a long bar with stools facing the coffee machines. Once we're in a booth Etta tells me to order whatever I want, that this is her treat. Sweet! Maybe Mom will even let me keep the bills she's given me. I get a double cheeseburger with bacon, fries, a Coke, and tell the waitress I'm going to want a hot fudge sundae. With sprinkles. And nuts.

Over the burgers, Etta asks me what I'm studying in school, and what I like—the usual. But she asks more questions than most people do when they're just going through the motions.

She's especially interested in what Sylvia's doing in Biology. I tell her about the frogs, and about Darwin's interest in how life lives by killing. This intrigues her. Not like she hadn't thought of it, more like she's surprised I did, or at least that it stuck with me.

"Have you started on Darwin's theories yet? Origin of the species, that sort of thing?" My mouth full of burger, I shake my head. "Will that be covered soon, do you think?"

"I suppose. We aren't going in order through the book."

She asks me how Kyle is doing, and from her tone I can tell she knows about the thing with his hand. Mom must have told her. I tell her, "He'll be okay. He's just weirded out 'cause of Dad not being there now. He's taking leadership a little too seriously. It's like he has to be one of those Promise Keeper types."

Etta nods like she knows what that means. I'm not sure, myself, outside of a bunch of men using a kind of Christian group-think to help each other stay on the straight and narrow.

"Ethan, speaking of promises, will you promise me that if you think Kyle's obsession is getting dangerous, you'll let me know?"

I blink at her like I'm stupid and then say, "Sure. Uh, sure." *Dangerous?* Whatever.

When my sundae arrives, Etta swipes the cherry off the top and laughs at my surprise. "I don't really like them, but I used to. And I wanted to see what you'd do."

Back in the car, with me still driving, we go to the dam at the south end of the lake. There's a place off to the side where you can sit on rocks, and look north along the length of the water. This is where Etta starts asking really personal stuff.

"I've seen you with Jorja Loomis quite a bit, Ethan," she says, loud enough for me to hear over the low rush of water. "I don't want to presume. Do you think of her as your girlfriend?"

I have to fight the urge to snort. "Um, no. Not really. We just hang together. We have a lot in common."

"Do you mind if I ask what?"

I tell her a little about being outliers. It's easy to talk to her, for some reason. There's a level of trust I didn't expect to feel, but as soon as I start to talk, there it is. It's like she's interested but not involved. Like whatever I say isn't going to rock her world. I tell her how religious Jorja is.

"And what about you?"

"Not really. I mean, I used to go to church sometimes, I guess. Not a lot. I did go with her to Teen Meet once."

"What was that like?"

I tell her what I'd told Mom, but Etta doesn't say anything. Instead, she lets silence take up a little space and then asks, "I hope you won't mind my asking, and don't answer if you're not comfortable about it, but do you *have* a girlfriend?"

She's looking at me. Not at the water. I keep my head straight ahead. What should I tell her? What *can* I tell her? And why did she ask? Is this something else Mom talked to her about, like she must have mentioned Kyle's weirdness? On one hand, telling Mom was so anticlimactic that I kind of want to tell someone else. Not sure what that would do for me, but it's there. It's me, wanting to get out. On the other hand, it's not like I want to go around telling just anybody. I say, "Can you promise me something?" It's her turn for a promise.

"Give me a hint."

"You have to promise you won't say anything. If I tell you, I mean."

She thinks for a second and then says, "As long as what you tell me isn't something dangerous for you or for someone else. Then I can promise."

Is this a trick question? "Okay, then, first let me ask you something." I turn to look at her; I need to see her reaction. "Do you know anyone who's gay?"

She doesn't flinch. "Yes. I've known a number of gays and lesbians in my time. Some of them are wonderful people, and some of them are terrible people. All of them are just people. They come in all varieties, just like nongays. Imagine that."

I turn back toward the water to let this sink in. I think she's saying being gay is just another way to be. And suddenly something in my chest is getting bigger. The feeling is kind of like that time in class, when it seemed like maybe I'm part of everything after all. I take a minute and a few deep breaths while I think. Why should I trust this woman? For all I know, she's got some ulterior motive for letting me drive her car, though I don't have a clue what it might be. Maybe she wants more help with her campaign? But that doesn't involve asking me about girlfriends. Staring sightlessly at the water, I reach out for a tall grass head and rip it off its stalk. "Why do you care?"

"One's teenage years can be very confusing. The brain is leaking hormones and bouncing between intense feelings and the numbest apathy. I know from experience that it can help if you have someone to talk to. Someone who cares without interfering. I had someone like that, so if I can help someone else, I will." Then she chuckles. "And, if I'm honest, I should tell you that I appreciate you spending time with me. I don't get to talk to many students in the very system I'm campaigning to help direct. So since you were kind enough to help put up my signs, I guess I'd like to get to know you a little, as long as that's okay with you."

I've practically already told her, anyway, so I say, "I don't have a girlfriend. I'll never have that kind of a girlfriend."

From the corner of my eye I see her nod once or twice. "I'll keep my promise. Does anyone else know?"

"My mom knows. I told her."

"What did she say?"

I shrug. "Didn't make a fuss. She's not happy about it. She says I'm still me."

"Anyone else?"

"Jorja."

"Jorja?" This surprises her. "With her attitude toward the Bible?"

"She says as long as I don't act on it, she'll keep praying for my redemption, salvation, whatever. Praying for me to change."

"Interesting. We all follow our own needs, don't we?"

"What does that mean?"

"Never mind. Nothing bad. Shall we drive some more? I think you've had enough practice on major roads for right now. Let's go north along Carry Pond, on the western shore. It's prettier, anyway."

It is pretty, she's right, driving along the water, and there's practically no traffic. At one point something flashes on the side of the road, and I brake hard, barely missing a pheasant that started up from the underbrush.

"Good job, Ethan!" Etta says, her hand at her throat. "That was a terrific save." We both follow the bird with our eyes as it flies over the water and curves north and out of sight.

Maybe a minute later, Etta says, "I've asked you a few personal questions, Ethan. Don't dredge anything up if it's not at the top of your mind, but you should feel free to ask me one or two if you like."

Wow. Okay. "Where did you live before you came back to take care of your father?"

"New York City. I was a journalist and then an assistant editor for a newspaper there."

I take my eyes off the road almost involuntarily to glance at her. "New York? Cool. I bet that was great."

"It had its good points and its bad ones, like any place else. But I loved being there."

"Why didn't you go back after your dad died?"

I hear her exhale. "You know, I've asked myself that many times. The tug was particularly strong just after he died, when I felt free again. I loved my father, but he was a cantankerous old coot. But it's not an easy thing, going back to New York when you've been away from it. The pace of my life was entirely different by then, I was several years older and didn't have a job there any longer, and I let myself get intimidated by memories of how impossible it was to find affordable housing in that city. I had friends who would read the obituaries to find out where apartments were opening up. So I ordered copies of New York newspapers, and read them and thought about it, and thought some more, and each year the thinking seemed vaguer and vaguer. The freelance writing I do now wouldn't pay for even half my living expenses in the city." Her voice kind of trails off.

"You don't even visit?"

"I've been back a few times to visit friends. They never seem to want to come up here, though." There's a humorless chuckle. "Can't think why not." I know she's being sarcastic.

I let a little time go by, collecting the courage to ask my next question. "You never got married?"

"No."

Nothing more. I suppose I could ask why not, but her "No" seems kind of final. I go in another direction. "Why are you running against Mr. Phinney?"

"I have to." The response is very quick. Then, a moment later, "Science is based on facts, Ethan. Scientists might come up with some wacky ideas sometimes, but they come up with these ideas based on some kind of evidence. Sometimes observation is enough to get them started, but it doesn't end there. They put the idea in the form of an assumption, or hypothesis. Then they apply known facts to it. They test it. They test it again. They test it until they can be sure the outcome is predictable and repeatable. When they've collected enough data this way, and they have enough tested hypotheses, they put it all together and call it a theory. If they can *prove* that it will always happen the same under the same conditions, they call that a law.

"We have to call evolution a theory, because we'd have to re-create the development of life on earth to call it a law, and also because we've figured out only so much about how to make evolution happen ourselves. But we can test it in small ways with predictable results and reasonably, scientifically, call it a theory. What Carl Phinney supports is bringing something into science class that is really nothing more than a collection of assumptions that don't even qualify as hypotheses, because the only evidence these assumptions provide is like saying, 'Life developed this way because someone designed it this way. Nothing else makes sense, so it has to be this.' They offer no facts, no testable situations, nothing scientific."

I'm busy thinking I wouldn't mind putting her up against Stupid Hovind. She takes a big breath. "That's probably more than you wanted to know. But Ethan, remember this. The testing in true science is *not* done to prove a hypothesis right. It's done to see if it can be proven *wrong*. The people who want ID treated as science aren't willing to consider that it might be wrong in any way. And that's because it's based on faith. Not science."

"So you're running because you don't like intelligent design?"

"I'm running because I value intelligence. And because I want to train students to think, not to follow something blindly, and not to swallow something that appears to make sense on the surface but can't hold up to deeper examination. You know, us old folks are going to depend on you younguns to run the show before too long. I want you *thinking*." She points to a turnoff. "Let's see how neatly you can turn around in that spot and head back."

Before I ever started driving, I might have seen a spot like the one she's pointing to and not given a thought to the difficulty of turning around there. But I've been driving just long enough now to know that she's given me a challenge. I extend my mind out to where the edges of the car are, compare that to the road and the area beside it that Etta pointed out, and just do it. It's perfect. I'm surprised, and I'm not. I'm pleased, though Etta says nothing.

Back on the road again, Etta asks, "What's your father like, Ethan? If you don't mind my asking."

I actually wish I could talk about him more, not less. I miss him badly, and Mom sure doesn't want to hear me go on about that. "We get along great. He's always finding ways for me to help him with something, and then he pays me. When I was little, he taught Kyle to ride a bike, and then he taught me. It took me lots longer to get it, but he didn't seem to mind. Kyle made fun of me about it, and Dad told him to shut up, that not everyone had to be just like him. Like Kyle, I mean. And boy, I'm not."

"Because you took longer to learn how to ride a bike?"

"Because everything. I'm not like him at all. He's all about rules and chores and stuff. He was always a little like that, always telling me what I was doing wrong, but now it's totally extreme. And then there's the church thing."

"So you still spend time with your dad?" Uh-oh. I pause too long, I guess, 'cause Etta says, "It's okay. You don't have to talk about it."

"Oh, it's not that. I—uh, it's just that my mom . . ."

Etta laughs. "I get it. She doesn't know how often you see him. Don't worry; that's something for your own family to work out. It's not my place to talk to anyone about that."

By the time we're back to Bingham, I'm chatting away about Jorja's rebellious questions in Coffin's class, about her crazy church, about helping my dad with his mowing, and somewhere in there I mention the Darwin fish on Sylvia's Jeep.

Etta says, "I guess that's appropriate for a biology teacher. When did you happen to see it?"

"The day I helped my dad. She, uh, Max . . . they pulled over to say hi." Something in my voice—or my hesitation—gives me away.

"Yes, I've noticed Max. Quite a good-looking young man." My hands jerk the wheel a little. Etta laughs again. "It would seem you've noticed him, too. That's another thing it's not my place to talk to anyone about."

I want to say *Thanks,* but that feels kind of like I'd be admitting something out loud, and I'm not quite prepared to do that.

South of Bingham, back on the highway, the skies just open. Rain is pouring down in sheets over the windshield, and I'm glad Etta made me find all the wiper speeds before it mattered. I even remember to turn on the lights. She doesn't say anything, just watches and lets me handle it. I slow down so there's more distance between me and the silver Honda sedan in front of us, knowing Etta will notice this, too, and add it to my credit. I'd like to do this again, driving with her.

I'm adding up half hours in my head to log against my thirty-five-hour total when a deer dashes in front of the Honda. The driver slams on the brakes and misses the deer, but he must have turned the wheel too sharply. The car hydroplanes all the way off the other side of the road, spins, and the passenger side slams into a tree. An oncoming white sedan misses hitting it while it's swinging over, but the sedan veers toward us, and I have to brake hard, thanking God or whoever for all-wheel drive, to avoid doing the same thing. I can't tell whether the other driver is hydroplaning, skidding, undecided, or just plain out of control. My first reaction is to stay on my side of the road and swerve to the right, but something about the way that white car is acting makes me turn the wheel to the left, where there's no traffic at the moment. As things turn out, if I had stayed right we would have hit it. We spin a little and come to a lurching halt past the Honda.

Her voice tense but not panicky, Etta says, "Pull over there, off the side. Let's see if anyone's badly hurt." She fishes her cell phone out from someplace as I find a spot that doesn't tip us too sharply into the ditch. Then she hands me the phone. "I've dialed emergency services. Tell them where we are and what's happened." And she dashes out of the car and toward the Honda.

I'm watching her as I'm trying to explain to the 9-1-1 operator what's happened. A woman from the other car runs across the road, too, so I guess she's all right. As soon as the operator says an ambulance is on its way, I drop the phone on the seat and follow Etta.

The Honda's passenger side door is buckled completely in, and there's tree where someone would have been, except the driver was alone. He's maybe fifty, unconscious, with the air bag in a sad state from where it exploded and then deflated. The seat belt's still fastened. Etta's just taking her hand away from his neck.

"He's alive, but he's not breathing. Ethan, help me get the seat belt undone. You're not really supposed to move someone who's injured, but we have to get him breathing."

We manage to ease the guy out of the seat and onto the ground. He's not fat, but he sure feels heavy. The woman from the other car says, "I've got a blanket and a tarp. I'll get them."

Etta doesn't hesitate. She lifts behind the guy's neck, pokes a finger into his mouth—I guess to see if there's anything in the way—and then breathes into him a couple of times. She lowers her ear to his chest, hand on it to see if it's rising or not. Doesn't look like it, so the guy's still not breathing on his own. She breathes in again, feels some more. The other woman is back, and she puts first the blanket and then the tarp over the guy's body while Etta tries a few more times. Finally the guy coughs, and then he groans, and then he coughs again. I can hear sirens in the distance.

Etta sits back on her haunches and breathes hard for a few seconds, watching the guy's face. He's not exactly conscious, but he's definitely alive. She says, "Thank God. I was afraid to press on his chest to help the process, not knowing what injuries he might have."

Two ambulances show up. We step back as the paramedics come over, and they load him onto a stretcher and take him away. As I'm watching them, it hits me that we're all three completely drenched. The other woman has glasses on, and I can't see her eyes. I don't know how she can see anything.

There's two police cars there suddenly, and they take Etta and me into one car and the other woman into the other. They ask us what happened, and of course they want to know all about my driving status. They grill me like I've never been grilled before. I don't know why, but my memory of what I did is crystal clear. It seems like they're trying to shake me off my story, but it doesn't work. I know exactly what I did, and I know that it was the best thing I could have done.

Etta doesn't say anything except to answer direct questions from the cop. She's looking at the one who's grilling me, like she's fine with how I'm telling the story. She's with me. We're a team.

Finally the guy who's been grilling me gives up and has to satisfy himself with making notes about Etta's license, which is in the car, and my instruction permit, which I fish out of my wallet. I'm just starting to feel like it's us, Etta and me, against them, when the cop hands my paperwork back and says, "You handled that very well, Ethan. Might have even saved lives. You should be proud of yourself." I'm blinking stupidly at him as he turns to Etta. "Are you all right, ma'am?" He waits until she nods. "You probably saved that guy's life. I'm thinking you should probably finish the trip. Driving, I mean." He hands her something with writing on it, like a card. "We might contact you again about this. Insurance, that sort of thing. When you're ready, we'll help you get your car back on the road. Keep the traffic out of your way."

Etta nods again. "Thank you, Officer."

We get out, and so does one of the cops, and we all go quickly through the pouring rain back to Etta's car. I start to go to the driver's side, but Etta catches my arm, and I remember the cop wanted her to drive now. I kind of want to. I wouldn't say I'm high, though adrenaline is keeping my pulse rate up. It's more like a sense of power. I feel strong. Like I can handle anything. But it doesn't seem like a good time to protest. The cop, in the backseat, takes some notes about Etta's license and then runs back to his car.

Etta and I don't talk at all as she eases the Forester out of the ditch. The cop cars are holding up all traffic, so we head straight across the road and back to the lane we were in before. Etta drives only about half a mile before she pulls over into the parking lot of an antique place that's closed for the season. With the engine still running, she puts the car in park and pulls the hand brake. Then she leans her hands on the wheel and her head on her hands and takes several shaky breaths. I sit quietly, giving her some space, and I see a couple of tears drop down and disappear into the rain that's already darkened her khaki pants.

Finally she sits back, eyes closed, and rubs her face. She flips the heat on high and turns on her seat heater. Seems like a good idea, and I toggle mine on, too. Another few breaths, and then she says, "I would be happy to go driving with you again anytime, Ethan."

She doesn't say anything else. She doesn't need to. We pull back onto the highway and ride in silence the rest of the way home, and I spend a lot of time thinking about what she'd done for that guy. Sure, she had a tearful moment after it was all over, but when it mattered, she didn't hesitate. Didn't panic. I want to be like that. And I think the way I handled that situation back there means that maybe I have it in me.

At home, Etta stays long enough to help me explain to Mom about our highway adventure, and I almost look around to make sure Dad is hearing this, but of course he isn't here. He's a terrific driver, and he's critical of those who aren't—like Kyle, despite his superior balance on a bicycle—and he praises those who are. I think he'd like that I'm showing signs of being like him behind the wheel.

As soon as Etta's gone, Mom wraps her arms around me. "Oh, Ethan. If anything had happened to you . . ."

I hug her back. It feels good. "I'm fine, Mom. Honest." I kind of want to stress what the cop had said, that I should be proud, but Etta has gone over all that in enough detail to pump my ego up. I decide to hoard this information against future need, in case Mom ever feels like criticizing my driving again.

But I still want to talk about it. Not to Kyle, though. I'm feeling brazen and almost unlike myself, like that sense of power is still with me. Yang-heavy in my emotional balance sheet. And like my decisions can be very, very important; after all, how many lives did I save today? I sit down at the computer in the living room while Mom's putting the finishing touches on dinner and Kyle is upstairs, probably reading his Bible, and I fire off an e-mail to Max.

> i'm catching up to your driving time mayB
> even getting a little ahead. okay, so I have
> lots more hrs before I'm at 35, but get this . . .
> today i pulled a really cool manuvr on the
> highway and missed hitting this car that
> swerved to avoid another car that swervd to
> avoid a deer . . . anyways, hope we can take
> that trip 2 bangor soon. U still up for it?

This seems noncommittal enough to keep Max from seeing me as desperate and also generic enough to keep anyone—like Kyle—from getting suspicious about my intentions. I don't have my own eddress; we all share one. I've created my own storage folder, but that's not exactly Fort Knox. I sit there as long as I can up to dinnertime, watching for a reply that doesn't come. And after dinner I check again; still nothing. I turn the PC off and head upstairs for some celebratory music to try and recapture how great I felt earlier.

I'm in the middle of some cool riff that's getting me into a good zone when the door to my room opens hard. I yank out my earbuds and see Kyle standing there looking like doom. Christ! What if I'd been jerking off or something?

"What the hell are you doing?" I demand.

He has a paper, in his left hand of course. "I want you to explain this to me."

"Duh. I don't know what it is. How can I explain anything? And you should have—"

"Here." He practically shoves it in my face. I yank it away from him.

It's from Max.

> hey charmer U can't fool me. I no ur doing
> california rolls at all the stop signs. but shit
> yeah i'm on for bangor just name the date. I'm
> be fully legal now so lets not wast any more
> time
> cul8r mm

At first my eyes catch on *mm*. Like, *mmmmm*...you know? But then I'm back in reality. All I can think to do is brazen it out, like it means nothing. "Yeah? So?"

"Who is mm? And why do they call you 'charmer' and use foul language in a message to this house?"

"None of your beeswax, bro. Just a friend from school, is all. What are you, my censor? I don't make you explain all your friends, do I?"

"That's not the point."

"Is so!" I'm shouting now. "And next time, knock on the freakin' door!"

Mom's voice precedes her from down the hall. "What's all the shouting? Kyle, leave your brother alone for once."

He turns to face her. "You should see what he's got! His friends should not be swearing in e-mails that come to this house."

She waves a dismissive hand at him. "Kyle, Kyle. Chill, will you? Ethan, what's in that message that's upset your brother so much?"

I don't exactly want her to see this exchange. Kyle hasn't mentioned Bangor, and I don't want it brought up. "Just one word, Ma. It's someone from school, and *they* doesn't have a censor to deal with. It's not like the thing is full of obscenities."

"Let me see it."

"It's a personal message! To me. Not to Kyle or anyone else. It's personal."

"Kyle? What does it say?"

"I can't repeat the word."

I chime in, "It rhymes with *shut* the door, please."

Kyle has to protest. "It doesn't rhyme with it at all!"

"I take it there are three letters in common, then," Mom says, sounding impatient. "Ethan, tell your friends to watch their language. Tell them your mother reads all your e-mails; that'll scare the willies out of 'em. Kyle, leave your brother alone." She stands there until he leaves, pulling the door shut behind her but glaring at me as she does so.

Close call. Kyle was so upset by *shit* that he forgot to mention *charmer* to Mom. Earbuds back in, I read Max's message a few times, smiling.

Charmer.

Later on, after lights out and jerking off, I'm about half asleep when my eyes open suddenly.

Jorja.

If this near-death experience had happened in August, she'd have been the first one I told. Now, it doesn't even occur to me to tell her. What kind of a friend does that make me? I make a vow to give her a really vivid description of it on the way to school tomorrow. Then I roll over onto my side and do my best to feel guilty about her, but I can't hang on to that. Instead my mind starts looking for ways to avoid depending on a shared e-mail account. If I'm going to start having boyfriends—well, at least one, maybe—I've got to have a better way to connect. Texting is what I decide on, but I need a cell phone for that. Jorja and I are about the only kids I know of who don't have one. Maybe I'll get an iPhone. I'll ask for one for my birthday! Except that's not until January. Same month Edgar Allan was born, I'll have you know. But that's too long. Hell, even Christmas is too long. I need this now. I'll have to buy it myself.

Yeah right. Like I've got a couple hundred dollars to spare. That's about what my tattoo will cost, probably. Not even with what Dad gives me for helping him can I double that anytime soon, and Mom makes me put two-thirds of everything she knows about into my college fund.

Christ! I shouldn't have to choose between these two things. They're both so important! Texting is the only way I can think of to keep my messages private, and that yin-yang tattoo is the only way I know of to say who I am. It's like a secret—but still real—way to show that I'm not all one thing or another. Ever since I saw it in the body art store window, I've been kind of meditating on it. Like it will help me bring some balance to my life. I *need* that tattoo.

I sigh and let my mind wander again, this time to how great it will be at college. No parents, no one around who knows any of the embarrassing stuff I've done growing up—'cause I'm sure not going to Orono. And best of all? Colleges have gay support groups. Which means there are gays there. Just the thought of being in a group of guys who all have this in common with me gives me—I don't know, a reason to live? It's heady stuff. I'd sure as hell be willing to give up my outlier status for that. I'd even give up my connection to the famous Poe for that.

Chapter 5

I'm seriously thinking of putting Etta Greenleaf on my shit list. The universe doesn't often conspire to get everything together at once, but it gave me the most amazing opportunity Wednesday afternoon. She calls just as I'm getting home from school to ask if I want to drive while she runs some errands, and of course I do. So far, so good. Two is in the back, his leash tied to a fastened seat belt just tight enough that he can hang his head out of the window. I'm getting used to him, I think, at least a little. Anyway, one place we stop is the drugstore. We've left Two in the car, and while Etta moves around the store following the list in her hand, I head for the sunglass display, which just happens to be across the aisle from condoms. I'm trying on some shades, looking in that teeny mirror they give you like that can help you decide what looks good on you, when I see a man reflected there, his back to me, looking over the condom selection.

It's Dad.

I spin around and stand there like an idiot, the stupid tag on the shades dangling down one side of my head, trying to decide whether to sneak away quietly so he won't know I saw him shopping for contraception when he isn't living at home or let him know I've caught him in the act. As quietly as possible, I take off the shades and try to get them back on their display perch, which of course you can't even do when you're not under pressure, and they fall on the floor. Dad turns toward me.

I almost laugh at the expression on his face. OMG comes closer than What the fuck do I do now, but they're both there, really. Needless to say, there's no *Whatcha up to, kid?* And I've just decided to kill two birds with one stone—cut him a break, and impress my car-loving father with my magnificent driving expertise that allows me to save the lives of people and livestock alike—when Etta appears out of nowhere and stops, staring at us. In another world, this might be funny.

She breaks the silence, unaware of all the unsaid swear words in the air. "You're Dave Poe, aren't you?" He says something like *Yeah,* and she stands, holding a hand out to him. "I'm Etta Greenleaf. So glad to meet you."

He says something like, "Sure, yeah, I know who you are. Right."

My fifteen minutes of fame would sound so much better coming from someone else. *Tell him!* I want to shout at her. *Tell him how great I was!* I glare at her, my eyes screaming, pleading. She sees me but doesn't quite know what to make of it.

Before anything good can happen, Dad says, "So, anyway, I gotta get going. See you, Ethan."

He scurries away like some kind of rabbit given a chance of escape from a hawk while I stare after him, forcing myself not to shout, *Wait! You gotta hear this!*

Etta says, "Ethan? Is something wrong?"

I hear the sulk in my voice. "Nothing's wrong." I bend over to pick up the shades I'd dropped and nearly break them getting the arms back into those stupid holes in the display case.

"Did I say something I shouldn't?"

I wheel on her, not knowing how to say what's really bugging me. I raise an arm in the general direction of the condoms. "Do you see where he was?"

She looks at them and back at me. "I guess he's taking the divorce proceedings seriously." I'm sure my jaw drops so low it hides my neck, but all she says is, "Is there anything you need before we leave? All I have left is batteries, and they're up near the register."

I don't say another word right up to when we get to my house. As I'm pulling into the driveway she says, "Ethan, I'm sorry if what I said sounded callous. I'm just being realistic. And when the divorce is final, that kind of scene could happen again. It's something you'll need to get used to."

As I open the car door to get out, I say, "Thanks for the driving time." I slam the door and head for the house. She thinks I can get used to my father buying condoms so he can fuck some woman? It doesn't matter that I'm pretty sure this whole thing is Mom's idea, sending him away. He's got no business being with another woman. There's something wrong with Etta if she can't see that.

But life's not all ugly. Max and I do our Bangor trip the very next weekend. He's got his intermediate license, which means he doesn't need a fully licensed adult with him. Unless, that is, he's got a passenger who isn't licensed. Like me. But he doesn't tell his folks that he's picking me up in front of Jorja's church. I don't understand my mom's politics—the libertarian angle— well enough to know whether she'd agree with the licensing requirements or not, so I tell her I'm spending the afternoon with Jorja. I feel bad about the lie, but what's a gay guy to do? It's not like Max and I can go out on dates.

Getting caught between two things is becoming a theme in my life, kind of like something we're expected to work into book reports. First I have to choose between spending my limited funds on a cell phone or a tattoo. And then Etta calls on Saturday morning and wants to go—guess where. Bangor. With Two. She takes him there sometimes to a dog park where he can "socialize" with other dogs. That's how she puts it. Seems lame to me, though maybe it's just that I'm still kind of pissed at her. But I'd love to get the driving hours in! Won't work though; Max has dibs on Saturday. I'm meeting him just after lunch. So I have to kill one thing to let the other live.

On the bright side . . . well—Max. Nothing can compete with that. Plus, I'll get my tattoo! So my next choices have to do with what to wear. Almost automatically I pick up the same black jeans I'd worn to see Guy, the ones with the huge metal teeth in the fly and no cloth cover. But then this seems too obvious, too much like I'm asking for something. I take them off and reject the black T-shirt with the strategic holes for the same reason. I try on one outfit after another, and even though I have plenty of time I start worrying that I'll be late. Rejecting Goth altogether, I settle on blue jeans, my white T-shirt with the red and white yin-yang symbol (which seems really appropriate), and white running shoes that I haven't worn in, like, forever. Because it's getting chilly, I sling over my shoulder that old black leather jacket Mom had bought for me at This Time For Sure— also appropriate, right next to the body art shop and everything.

I leave the house quietly, knowing that Mom has asked Kyle to wash the car, so they'll both be home. I don't want any questions or even any conversation right now. And I really want to avoid getting caught by Kyle in one of his dictator moods. You know, when he dictates what I'm supposed to do. Like mow the lawn, or clean out . . . something.

I'm in front of Jorja's church several minutes early. The church's battered marquee this week says, THIS IS A SIGN FROM GOD. Ha! My sign from God today is that I'm spending the entire afternoon with the love of my life. Or maybe he's just the lust of my life. Guess the options are open.

He's almost ten minutes late, and I've started to worry that too many of the people driving by will recognize me and tell my mom they saw me here. I spend the time daydreaming about what will happen when I get into the car, which in my mind is the brown Jeep. Will he send me one of his gorgeous smiles, head tilted? Will he reach a hand behind my neck and pull our faces together for some tongue action?

I adjust my jeans, which have grown a little snug in the crotch.

But the time drags, and I'm about to get really pissed off when the Modine family SUV pulls up. Not Sylvia's Jeep. It's a white Toyota Sequoia. Absolutely gorgeous. Looks like power and confidence and security all at once, and my knight, arriving on—in—a white steed. I climb in. He's got the moonroof popped up at an angle.

Max eyes me just for a second before he pulls back out onto the road. "New look?" he says, and immediately I'm thinking I should have stayed Goth. But then, "I like it. Especially the jacket."

I almost say *Thanks* but then decide to be cool and just nod. And I don't say anything about the shirt he's wearing, a nubby-textured fabric, a muted color somewhere between blue and green. No T-shirt for him. And not Goth. But I can't help stealing another glance at his profile, and that's when I take in that the seats behind us are all flattened, as though someone is about to load something large. I wait a couple of seconds and then ask, "What's with the back?"

Max doesn't look at me, but I see the side of his mouth creep up just a little, like he's trying not to let it. He shrugs. "You never know."

I want to ask, *Never know what?* but I'm still trying to be cool, so I don't.

We have to go past my house to get to the highway. The Sequoia has tinted windows, so I don't have to try and duck. Kyle is in the driveway washing Mom's car. It's almost too cold, now that we're into fall weather. I suspect Mom is asking Kyle to do things that he won't be able to do with only his left hand. He's not wearing a jacket, though he does have a long-sleeved knit shirt under his T-shirt; even so, he'll be cold. Leave it to him to make a martyr out of himself. And it's going to take him a long time, because he really *is* trying to work one-handed.

Max's head turns in Kyle's direction briefly. About ten seconds go by, and then he says, "What's with the T-shirt?"

I think he's talking about mine, of course. Today is all about me and Max, after all. "Oh, this old thing." I try to make it sound facetious.

I'm about to describe the tattoo I want when he says, "No, I mean your brother's. God Is Now Here. What the fuck's that?"

Ah. Yes. I take a deep breath. How to answer in ten words or less? Otherwise it could take a few hundred. "It's a religious thing."

Max's laugh is a snort. "Duh, I can see that. But what does it mean?"

He's made me feel like a stupid little kid. I look out my window and say, "Figure it out. There's a different sentence in the same string of letters."

"Division of labor, here. I'm driving. You do the figuring. What's it say?"

What I really, really don't want to do is get off on the wrong foot here. So I cave. "If you take out the space between Now and Here you get Nowhere." I look straight ahead again where I can gauge Max's reaction, at least in my peripheral vision. "Some argument between Bible scholars about interpreting ancient Greek."

Max's laugh now is a real laugh. "So your brother is a Jesus freak."

"I guess you could say that." Suddenly I feel defensive for Kyle. Weird. I shake it off.

"Bunch of echo chambers."

My turn to need an explanation. "What?"

"You know. Someone's an echo chamber when they just repeat everything they hear, so they'll be—whatever. Liked. Promoted. Saved. Pick one."

I don't know what to say to that, so there's maybe half a minute of silence. Then he says, "You aren't one, are you? I mean, meeting in front of that weirdo church and all."

"No." A little too hasty. Too sharp. I try to smooth it out. "No, Kyle got kind of religious after my dad moved out last spring." I'm irritated again, but I shrug it off; I'm the one who suggested the church, after all.

"Does he go to that church?"

I decide to throw in a little unwatched language. Dispel any doubt about my religiosity. "Fuck no. That's Jorja's church."

"Ah, yes. Jorja. You seem to be surrounded by Jesus freaks." His tone makes it sound like he's sneering. "What's with her, anyway? I mean, it's like she wants to rewrite history. I'll bet that Nazareth church or whatever it is teaches the same shit."

Damn it. Another rock-and-a-hard-place. I know exactly what Max means. But—this is Jorja. My best friend. I decide to let a little space go by and then introduce another topic. One that's been top-of-mind for me, anyway. "Hope we don't see any deer on the highway today."

"Could be moose. Autumn and all." He laughs. "Maybe I should have taken Sylvia's Jeep; it's ancient and already brown. If we hit a moose, big deal."

It would be a big deal; a moose will take out anything smaller than an eighteen-wheeler. Besides, he's avoiding the topic I want to get to. "I was just thinking of that deer that caused the accident last weekend. The one where I had to figure out which way to turn."

"Yeah! That must have been a real YouTube moment. Good thing you weren't on your cell. Could have been a text-ender." Another laugh.

"Text-ender?" I could sort of figure out that a YouTube moment is something that would have made a great short to put online.

He shrugs one shoulder. "Text-ender. You know. It's when you're so busy texting somebody that you rear-end the car in front of you."

Except that there was no rear end in question. What I'd avoided hitting was the business end of a car coming right at me. I can't think of another way to get back to my glory day, so I cast about for something else. This isn't feeling as good as I'd expected. I'm not sure whether to feel outclassed by all the hip terminology that Max seems to have so ready at his command, or maybe he's nervous too and is just trying too hard to impress me. I decide to believe the latter. "So what made you decide on the Toyota instead of the Jeep?"

"I don't exactly have full access to it, y'know. Sylvia doesn't even live at home. Besides, there's egg all over the back of the Jeep. Seems someone took issue with her Darwin fish. Tuesday after school when she went to drive home, the egg had been there a while, so it was all hardened. Whoever did it scrawled 666 into it while it was still wet. And they tried to pry the fish off the car, so pieces of it are missing." I'm thinking that's pretty weird when he adds, "Plus, you know, I'm not sure I want to call that kind of attention to myself."

"What kind?" Doesn't he like Jeeps?

"That fish. You know. I mean, look what happened."

"The egg wash? But—I mean, you don't think this ID stuff is science, right?"

"No way. That's bullshit."

"So, why would the Darwin fish be a problem?"

"Dude, it's a broadcast. Like telling the world which side you're on. That can be dangerous. Look what happened to the Jeep. So I got approval from corporate to take the Sequoia. Plus, you know, it's way cooler than the Jeep."

I have to agree with that. I mean, I hate getting involved in conflicts. But I don't think the Darwin fish would have bothered me. Whatever; I'm happier in the Sequoia, anyway. It *is* way cooler. I try another change of topic. "So I'm making progress on my thirty-five hours. Etta Greenleaf is letting me drive her. Mom's way too bossy, always slamming her foot on the passenger brake, you know how it goes."

Max laughs for real, and I love it. "Passenger brake! That's it. Like there's a pedal there." He glances at me, his expression pretend-worried. "You aren't looking for one yourself, are you?" I just laugh. "Wait . . . Etta Greenleaf? That old hag? You're driving her around?"

This stuns me. *Hag?* It's one thing to make fun of Jorja and her wacky religion, because she sort of throws that in your face. But—*hag?* I guess I've conveniently forgotten that I was almost surprised when she wasn't a hag, myself. I give Max the benefit of the doubt. He doesn't know her. "She's pretty nice, actually." And I see another chance to highlight my YouTube moment. "It was her car I was driving last weekend. The deer thing. Afterward she told me she'd let me drive anytime."

"Whatever."

That's not enough of a turnaround for me. I want Max to see

her as I do. "Her house is pretty neat. Not big or anything, but she's had it worked on. Views out over the mountains in the distance. Real quiet."

"So that monster of hers can hear anyone sneaking up on her?"

"Two's all right. I get along fine with him. You just have to know how."

The look on Max's face as he turns toward me briefly tells me this has impressed him. "You're okay with a vicious pit bull." He shakes his head once. "So I didn't overestimate you."

And then something fantastic happens. First, he rests his right arm on the cover of that wide compartment between the seats and dangles his hand on my side. Then he stretches his fingers and strokes my thigh. And just keeps driving. I don't know what to do. Should I touch him? Should I put my fingers with his? Then his fingers tap my thigh, like they want my attention, and I touch them with mine. They interlock just a little, and then he squeezes and pulls his hand back. It's just a moment, but—what a moment! I love the way my dick feels. I love the way my head, my chest, my ass all feel. I take a breath. *This* is what this trip was supposed to be about.

I hear the blinker. What's Max doing? He's headed for that dirt utility road over on the right? I glance at him, and his face is unreadable. As soon as we're into the trees and out of sight of the road he stops, yanks on the hand brake, and leans back, eyes shut. Then he turns toward me, and the look in his eyes is exactly what I want to see there. It's the look I've seen him leveling on me, in my mind, for weeks now as I jerk off.

He wants me.

"Ever kissed a boy?" he asks.

"No. You?"

"No."

So he's taken a chance, touching my leg like that. But—now what? And I remember all that flat, empty back area in the car. I look at him and jerk my head slightly in that direction.

He opens his door and jumps down, so I do the same. I haven't got a clue what we'll do. All I know is that I want to do something with Max. I've had all these images in my mind when I've fantasized about him, and I'd like to say they're in my mind as I open the back door on my side, but the head between my shoulders isn't getting any blood. Max is inside already, kneeling on the platform created by the backs of all the folded-over seats, his door shut. I'm torn; I want to remember this moment, sear it into my brain cells. But I want Max.

He prods. "You coming in?"

Flash of genius. "Call me 'charmer.' "

He smiles. "Get in here, charmer."

I don't hear my door slam shut; too busy wondering whether to focus more on the feel of his tongue in my mouth or to start undoing my jeans, which are absolutely positively too tight now. His hands are on the back of my neck, so I hold him the same way. It makes kissing even better, I decide. It's easier to hold your mouths together like this. Oh, *MAN* but this feels right! To hell with Jorja praying for me to change. I fucking don't ever want to change!

I know there's lots of stuff two guys can do with each other's dicks. But there's this silent agreement—silent other than heavy breathing and grunts, anyway—that we won't stop kissing. It's a little awkward undoing your pants while your faces are mashed together, but we manage. I can feel his hard dick poking at my leg. I reach for it, and he gets hold of mine. There's barely enough time to take in these new sensations before he comes. We're pressed together so hard that it gets all over my dick, and it's the greatest lube there is. I don't last more than another ten seconds.

Max throws himself down flat on his back. "Fuck! *Man!* I haven't lived until right now."

I'm panting and laughing, higher than an addict on the thought that I'm the one who gave him that feeling and that he's given it to me. I lean on my elbow beside him, facing front, breathing audibly and staring toward the woods through the windshield, focusing on nothing.

Max speaks first. "Now"—a breath or two—"maybe I can keep driving long enough to get to Bangor." He looks at me, smiling, and hands me one of two small towels he'd stashed back here, no doubt precisely for us.

I smile back. "Yeah. But what'll we do for the trip back?"

He sits up and kisses me. "We'll think of something."

Yeah. Maybe a few things. We get back into the front seat like nothing happened, but it's okay, because we both know everything in the world has just happened, and it rocks.

We sit there for maybe ten minutes, holding hands, gazing out of the windshield. Then, suddenly, there's a bird perched on the windshield wiper on Max's side. It's a cute little thing, solid dark gray back, a white underbelly like it floated on cream, and sharp, alert black eyes.

Max says, "Damn those birds. I think they're following me around."

"What do you mean?"

"Goddamn juncos. If I go outside the house and sit down anyplace, they come outta nowhere and settle around my feet. And now here's one, like it followed me." He makes a kind of snorting sound. "Sylvia says it's just that they're getting ready for winter. Juncos are ground feeders mostly. So they hop around the lawn. But that doesn't explain this one." He hits the wiper control stem and the blades sweep over and back once. The bird flies off. "And it doesn't explain why they don't follow *her* around."

He throws himself back against his seat and turns toward me. I love that smile. As he's pulling back onto the road he says, "So, this tattoo. Do you know what you want?"

"Did you happen to notice my T-shirt?"

His eyes don't leave the road as he smiles just a little. "I notice everything about you." A pause. "You mean the yin-yang symbol?"

"That's it."

"Why? You aren't Asian at all, are you? Maybe that black hair is a sign?"

"The black hair comes from Edgar Allan. My ancestor."

"No shit?"

"None at all." I give that some space. Then, "You know what

it means, right? Yin-yang? It's all about balance." I use my
hands, outlining a circle in the air, moving first one way, then
another. "Opposites balancing each other, shifting and—well,
maybe dancing, almost. That's me. A balance of male and female."

There's silence, and at first I'm worried I've said too much,
laid my soul too bare. Then he says, "Okay, maybe I actually
under estimated you."

He leaves me wondering if this is a good thing. I decide to
believe that it is, even though I feel like I've brought conversation to a halt. My eyes turn in toward my brain as I try to come
up with something to say and they land on a cell phone image.
"So, what kind of cell phone do you have?" I have to assume he
has one; anything else would be lame. Like the fact that I don't
have one.

He digs into a pocket and tosses it to me. Yup, an iPhone.
Not the latest model, but still . . . Should have known. I spend a
few minutes poking around the options, which seem endless.

"I have to get one," I say, admitting my lack. And this seems
like a good time to let him know why, so I tell him what my
mom had said.

"She saw that e-mail? Fuck!" He slams his head back, and the
car jerks a little as his foot on the gas pedal eases back and then
returns to cruising position. "How?"

"We all share the same account."

"Well . . . that's pretty lame. What did she say?"

"To tell my friends to watch their language."

"Nothing about 'charmer,' then?"

"No, but she—" He doesn't give me time to say she didn't actually see the message.

"Thank God. I don't want her knowing about us, Ethan. I'm
serious. No one can know. Are we clear?"

What could I say? "Sure." At least it was Max who brought the
conversation to a crashing halt this time, not me. It takes a
minute, but he asks about the tattoo again—is it my first, won't
it hurt, how much will it cost, what if it gets infected, does my
mom know. I don't admit that I haven't even thought about

whether it will hurt; I just say, "I suppose." It doesn't matter to me. And I don't know what it will cost; I've just pulled two hundred fifty dollars from what I had in my account after school on Thursday, hitching home from the ATM and hoping Kyle wouldn't ask why I wasn't on the bus. That's more than I've earned helping Dad in the last year, but only a little more. From my research on the Internet, that seems like what I should expect to spend on a small tat, which is all I want, anyway. Plain black ink, with my own skin filling in where the white would go. I figure, y'know, I'm pretty pale.

There's a little more silence, and then Max says, "So I was your first, right?" Half of me wants to ask, *First what?* I almost reply, but he already knows I've never kissed a boy, so I just turn toward him and give him what I hope is an impish grin. "Fine," he says, "then I won't tell you whether you were mine or not."

I don't really care, I realize with a pleasant surprise. That's not what matters. I don't know why, but I'm not worried about getting his dick into my hand again. I know it will happen. I ask, "So no one knows about you?"

"No one. Just Sylvia."

"Sylvia?"

"Yeah. She kind of . . . I dunno, figured it out, I guess. Last summer. And then she came up with all this stuff for me to read, about how it's, like, a natural way to be. There are gay animals. Did you know that?" I did not. I shake my head. "Lots of them. It's all about how we react to pheromones."

He's getting excited about this, like it makes a huge difference for him. His voice is louder, and his hands fly up into the air and settle onto the steering wheel and fly into the air again. "It's really cool, Ethan. See, I have male pheromones, but they're different from, like, my dad's, or any straight guy's. And something in my brain gets a whiff of yours and goes crazy. Much less of a reaction to your brother, say, if he's straight. And none—I mean nada, zilch, zippo—to a girl. So it'd be, like, totally unnatural for me to get off on even Miss America, you know? Wrong scent. For me. And for you."

I don't know what to say to all this, falling on me out of nowhere. It gives me a brain cramp.

"Are you getting me, Ethan?" He turns this intense gaze on me for just a second.

"Sure. I guess so."

"You *guess* so? Dude, this is huge! It's like Mother Nature is saying, 'You guys go ahead. It's the way it's supposed to be.' D'you see?" He grins.

I feel like I have to say something to show him I get it. But what had he just said, exactly? Gay animals? Pheromones? "Are you telling me that gay is natural?"

"Bingo! At least, if your brain's programmed like ours. It gets off on gay male pheromones and shrugs at female ones. I mean, lookit; just the fact that there are *gay* male pheromones should tell you something. If our pheromones are different, then there's no way we're gonna feel the same as straight guys. It's a given. And there ain't nothin' we can do about it. There's nothing we should *want* to do about it! Are you hearing me?"

He's right; this *is* huge. If I'm physically incapable of having a sexual response to a girl, and I have this huge response to a gay guy, then what am I supposed to do? I guess be gay! That is huge. But—"Why haven't I heard about this before? How do you know about it?"

"Oh, it's out there. Best place to look is online. Sylvia told me. Remember? Biology? That's her field. And that's what this is. Biology." He laughs. "First time I ever loved biology!"

"Wow." It's all I can think to say. That, and "Let's hear it for science."

"Yeah, wow. Big wow. And this is why she said something to me. Last summer, I mean, when she told me she knew about me. 'Cause she wanted me to know it's okay."

Suddenly something occurs to me. "And does she know about me?"

It's his turn with the mysterious smile, but then he adds, "For sure. She's the one who suggested I pull over that day you were working with your dad."

"Does she know where we're going today? About the tattoo?"

He shakes his head. "I didn't tell her, 'cause I'm really not supposed to have a passenger who's not licensed unless someone like Sylvia or a parent is with me. So, like, don't tell her I took you. Don't tell anyone."

"Got it."

"Especially don't tell that Jesus freak friend of yours."

"Jorja?"

"That's the one. You haven't said anything about me to her, have you?"

I'm not quite sure how to take his tone and the way he's talking about Jorja. So I just say, "Haven't told anyone."

"Why do you hang with her, anyway?"

Why, indeed. "We hooked up last winter. It's like we both suddenly realized we were outliers. It's for different reasons, maybe, but still. There we were, on the fringe. Outside all the cliques, all the little friend groups. So..." I shrug, hoping that's enough.

But he says, "Outliers?"

"Yeah, you know. Like, in a scatter chart? Where most of the dots all collect in one area, and there's only a couple of them all alone, far away from the clump. Outliers."

He looks at me, puzzled, and back to the road. "What makes you an outlier?"

"Well, I'm gay."

"That makes you an outlier only if they know. Otherwise you're still one of them." I'm thinking he must consider himself part of the crowd, which is a little disappointing, and then he says, "What else?"

I shrug again. "I'm related to Edgar Allan Poe."

"Okay, but see, that oughta make everyone want to know you. Are you, like, a great-grandson, or something?"

"He didn't have any kids. We're related through one of his uncles."

"Oh. Well, then, that's not so... you know, not as much of a draw. But still..." There's a brief silence. "That how the Goth look got going, then?"

"Yeah. Plus, you know, I look a little like him."

He turns to me again. "Really? I guess I have the wrong picture in my head. Probably from seeing old horror flicks with Vincent Price in them."

I laugh. "Yeah, that's the wrong image. Plus, those were his stories, not his life."

"So was he weird?"

"Some people thought so, I guess. Bit of a drunk."

"Gay?"

I laugh again. "Don't think so. He married his cousin. A girl."

"So there's really not much tying you to Jorja, then. Just that you're both—what, off to the side? You're not into Jesus, and you're not into girls."

"Plus, there's protection. She doesn't want boys coming near her, and I don't want everyone to know I'm gay."

He thinks about this a second. "That's an interesting ploy. Why doesn't she want boys, though? I mean, not that any of them would want *her*. Is she gay, too?"

I shake my head. "No, she can't be. And she keeps praying for me not to be. She just—I dunno, she's super-religious. Doesn't want sex before marriage, I guess. Something like that." I'm feeling rather vague about this aspect, myself; it seems a little lame as I say it out loud to Max. Lots of girls date and don't have sex. Well, enough of them. And all Jorja would have to do is send the boys away if they came on too strong. Sure, it might make her less popular, but wasn't she pretty unpopular already? There are those boys in Teen Meet, but they're too busy making sure they don't go against scripture to try anything with her. I'm glad Max doesn't press me on this; I obviously can't defend it very well.

Max throws a keen glance toward me. "You oughta get rid of her, you know."

"She's not so bad."

"She's not exactly an image booster."

I don't say anything, and we ride along in silence for a while. Then Max starts talking about some of the other kids in our class. Maybe the "image booster" phrase gave him a jumping-

off point or something, 'cause he starts talking about some kids
who he thinks are losers. "I've seen you with Kenny sometimes,
like at lunch. You probably want to start weaning him off you."

"Why?"

He makes a face as if to say that should require no explanation. "He's kind of a missing link, isn't he? And it's not just all
the hair, though I've seen him in gym. In the showers. Man, you
could stuff a pillow if you shaved his back. But he's not much in
the smarts department, either."

"He's okay."

"You and I, Ethan? We need better than okay. And why you'd
let Marra sit next to you in math I don't get."

"She's good at math! She helps me sometimes."

"She's a douchbagette, Ethan. Thinks she's better than everyone else."

I don't know what to say to this; hasn't Max just told me that
he and I need better than okay? Isn't that kind of like saying
we're better? I decide to try a little irony. "Yeah, I know what
you mean. People who think they're perfect really annoy those
of us who are."

I steal a sideways glance to check out Max's reaction. The
face he's making is kind of like, *Oh, I don't believe you just said
that.*

It doesn't stop him. By the time I have to start giving him directions to the body art shop, he's trashed about half the kids I
know, and I'm feeling totally weird. I mean, some of the kids
are losers; even I know that. But others? I don't know. Plus, why
is he hanging out with me, anyway? Does he think I'm cool or
something? 'Cause I'm not. And suddenly I don't want him to
figure this out.

It takes him a few minutes to find a parking spot on the street.
At first I'm thinking he's not real good at parallel parking yet and
doesn't want to admit it to me. He heads for where there are two
spaces together and parks the SUV on the line between them.

"What are you doing?" I ask, wanting to tease him about his
lack of parking skills but not quite sure enough of myself—or
of us—to do that.

"Don't want anyone dinging me, do I?"

I'm not sure whether this is an excuse or proof that he's rude, and I decide not to dwell on it. I reach for my jacket, glad it's the leather one. I mean, I'm going into a body art place, right?

We stand outside the shop for a few minutes, pointing at one photo after the other: a dragon tat all over some guy's back, a navel piercing, an ear with so much metal around the edge that no skin shows. Max makes a noise of gleeful disgust and points to what is obviously a woman's breast, the bar behind her nipple loaded with extra stuff so the nipple is distended and huge. Max says, "Jesus, d'you think any baby would be able to get milk outta that?"

I'm feeling more nervous by the second, and I almost want to keep looking at photos so I don't have to take the next step. But I also want to stop feeling this nervous, and that won't happen until I get this over with. Plus, I really want the tat. Finally I step back from the window, reach for the door handle, and pull.

The place is kind of small, and most of the light is artificial, what with the windows practically covered with photos. Off to the right there's a short counter with a guy standing behind it, eyes on his computer screen. I look around the room and have time to take in a few larger photos and a free-standing wooden screen blocking the back end of the room before the guy speaks.

"Can I help you?"

I look at Max, who's looking at me. This is my tat, so I move toward the counter. Hands in my jeans pockets, I shrug one shoulder. "I guess I want a tattoo."

The guy sort of smiles and shakes his head. "Well, kid, I got two things to say to that. One, there's no guessing. You'd better be damn sure. And two, you're too young. How old are you, fifteen?"

"Sixteen. Seventeen, soon."

He shakes his head again. "Gotta be eighteen. It's the law."

"Shit. I didn't know." Fuck! All the energy I've put into this, all the nervousness? And all the conviction that I need exactly this. Not to mention pulling money out of my bank account, which my mom treats like it's sacred.

The guy comes from behind the counter and I see he's taller than I'd thought. Skinny, lots of tattoos, of course. His hair is light brown, thinning on the sides of his head, and slicked back. With his eyes he takes both Max and me in one at a time, then says, "You boys together?"

I look at Max, not quite sure what the question means. There's no one else in the place, we came in together, and we're both standing right there facing the guy. Max glances at me and then quickly away. He looks like he's trying to hide something. I look back to the guy, and the way he's smiling at Max looks almost sly. He nods. "I get it. Your secret's safe with me." He rolls up one T-shirt sleeve and reveals a colored rainbow tat on his shoulder, not quite two inches by three. I take it to mean that he's gay, too. He looks at me again. "What did you have in mind, just out of curiosity?"

"Yin-yang. Just black ink."

"Size?"

"Maybe three inches across. I've only got about two hundred dollars."

He nods once. "Where?"

Feeling half shy and half flirtatious, I turn my right side in his direction and slap my ass.

Max says, "Dude, no one will see it there."

"You got it. Including my mom."

"But—what's the point?"

"The point is I'll know it's there. Like I told you, it's all about balance. Male and female. It's to help keep me sane."

Max is scowling, like he'd really wanted to be able to see it all the time. But even in this light I can see him blush when the guy says to him, "Hope you don't expect me to believe you'll never see it on his ass." The guy is grinning, teasing Max, but I can tell Max doesn't like it. Then the guy holds his hand out to me. "Shane."

"Ethan," I tell him, and I like the way his eyes hold mine.

"Who did your ear?"

I can't help feeling flattered that he noticed. "A friend put a needle through it for me."

He steps closer to get a better look, and I can feel the warmth of his body. "Did a good job. Placement, I mean." He steps back again and says, "Listen, Ethan, a tat isn't the only place you can have a yin-yang. You might not want to wear that T-shirt all the time, but look over here." He moves toward the counter, which has a display case under it.

I follow, Max close beside me, and we stand at the counter, shoulders touching. From among the paraphernalia in there— silver rods, different balls to go on the ends to make a barbell piercing, circlets of various metals and finishes, colorful stones and metal items that could dangle from some kind of piercing—Shane pulls out something silver. Picture two thin silver bands a little apart, bent into a small circle, except that the two bands bend toward each other before the circle would be complete. Between the bands, across from where they bend to join together, is a silver circle soldered in place, and inside that is a small enamel black and white yin-yang symbol.

"Ever see one of these?" I shake my head. "It's an ear cuff. Here . . ." He puts it on his own ear and turns his head so I can see it.

"Cool." I want it. I still want the tat, but I want the ear cuff. "How much?"

He takes it off and sets it on the counter. I pick it up. He says, "Well, let's just talk about that. Ordinarily I'd sell this for about five bucks. But in your case . . ." He waits until I look up and then says, "I think this special item might cost a couple hundred."

"What?"

He laughs, his eyes holding mine. "Listen, Ethan, I can't legally give you that tat. But let me ask you this. Do you trust your friend?" He doesn't look at Max, just at me, and he's serious.

I turn toward Max, who's smiling but also looking a little puzzled, his eyes on me. I smile back. "Yes."

Shane nods again and says, "Right. So if you buy this special item and then I close shop for a bit, but you just happen to be still in here, it just might happen that you walk out of here with some ink on your backside." He waits, watching my face as I get all excited. "But there's a catch. See, if I do exactly what you said you wanted when I was open for business, then even if I close up for a bit, it could be construed as fulfillment of a business transaction. Do you follow?"

"A catch? What would be different?"

"Tell you what. Buy the ear cuff. It's really only five; I just wanted to see how you'd react. Then I'll close shop for a bit and we can talk like the friends we've become. *Capisce?*"

I pull out my wallet and separate a five. "Tax?" I ask.

"You bet. Gotta do this legally."

I peel off another dollar and hand him the lot, getting my change and the ear cuff back. Shane pulls a standing mirror from a shelf behind him and helps me figure out how to get the cuff on my ear. Max is staying as close to me as he can, and I'm getting off on this—not only for obvious reasons, but also because it's almost like he's jealous.

The cuff looks fantastic. I'm still admiring it as Shane goes to the door, turns the Open sign around so it reads Closed from the outside, and locks the door. Back behind the counter, he pulls out a chart with different tats on it, all yin-yang. He points to one of them. "This is the catch. This is the tat."

It's a true yin-yang. Some of the others are really fancy, dragons around them, waves, stars, flames, just about anything. The black ink on the one he's pointing to is standard, but where the white would be—or where my skin would be, in how I've pictured it—there are lines of color, like the rainbow, only not curved. They go straight across that part of the symbol.

"See, Ethan, I've wanted to do this one for a long time. Haven't been able to talk anyone into it. And, of course, it would take a special kind of person, if you know what I mean, to wear rainbows, anyway." I start to protest, but he raises a hand. "Let me finish. I know you said you want the balance, and I get that. It's perfect. But see, what this represents is bal-

ance between straight—the black—and gay. The color. So it's
not just you. It's the whole world."

I stare at it, thinking, trying to imagine what it would feel like
to know it was on me. My original image of black ink and skin is
pretty much seared into my mind's eye. Shane moves over toward the screen and goes behind it. "You think for a minute.
I'm just checking my colors."

I look at Max. "What do you think?"

He's almost but not quite shaking his head. "I don't know
about this, Ethan. I mean, sure, you're not going around flash-
ing your ass at people, but in the locker room . . . you know?"

He's right. But at the same time, does it have to say "gay" to
everyone? If Shane hadn't said that about the black being
straight, I wouldn't have thought of the colors as gay. They
aren't in the shape of a rainbow, or anything. It's just black and
colors. And I realize I'm defending this choice, which in a way
isn't mine but Shane's. "Let me think a minute."

Max doesn't move. I close my eyes, head down, and turn my
eyes inward to picture this colorful tat on someone's ass. When
it's solid in my mind, I change the image to black ink only. It
looks dull. I feel my head nodding, and then my voice surprises
me, as it seems to do more and more lately, saying, "I'm gonna
do it."

I turn to Max and come so close to kissing him. Something
holds me back. Or, really, I feel something pushing, keeping
me just a little too far away to do that. So I turn instead toward
the screen. Shane is standing there, watching me, smiling. He
says, "Ready?"

Deep breath. Nod. Grin. Yes, I'm ready. I step behind the
screen, Max on my heels. I guess he wants to watch, and it turns
me on to know that.

Shane says, "So, are we friends, here?" He looks hard at Max.

"What do you mean?" Max looks wary, almost like he's afraid
Shane wants more than he's admitted so far.

Shane laughs. "Don't look so worried! I'm a gay man. I want
men, not boys. All I mean is that friends don't rat on each
other. Like, how this tat gets onto your boyfriend's backside will

forever remain a mystery to everyone but us three. Shake on it?"

He holds his hand out to Max, who takes it and nods. Max says, "Shake. No ratting. As long as you never mention us outside here, either."

Shane's glance is questioning. "Meaning . . . ?"

"Meaning, okay, you figured out we're together. But I don't want the whole world to know."

Shane nods. "Ashamed of being gay, then?"

"No! Just—cautious. In case you hadn't noticed, bad things can happen to gay people."

"Well, I'm not in the business of outing other people, so have no fear." To me he says, "So, gorgeous, drop trou and lie facedown there."

It takes me a minute to get into position; I'm nervous all over again. Naked from the waist down, jeans and underwear around my ankles, I bend my arms so I can cushion my head on them, then take a few deep breaths as I try to interpret the sounds Shane makes as he gets things set up. I almost wish that I'd asked for a demonstration of his equipment, but I also don't really want to know.

Max says, "Will it hurt?"

"Sure, but not so much he won't want another one some day. At least, if he doesn't get another one, it won't be the pain that stops him. Why? You want one, too?"

I strain my neck and eyes to watch Max's face.

His head makes several quick, tiny shakes. "I don't think so."

Shane just laughs, and I hear him snap surgical gloves onto his hands. I wish I could see *his* face. "First I'll shave away any hair, and then I'll apply a decal to follow as I apply the ink. Do you trust me to find the best spot, or do you want some input?"

Second flash of genius today: "You and Max decide."

Shane laughs again, and they hover over me, figuring out the best spot for ease of application and esthetics. I smell alcohol and feel something wet, and a hand presses something onto my skin. Then Shane says, "Okay, Ethan, my boy. I'll give you a couple seconds warning before I begin. It will hurt, but not horribly, and on your ass is a lot less painful than some-place with less padding. I'll be stretching the skin some to make sure I get good coverage. You ready?"

I almost say, *I guess.* But he'd already warned me about that. I need to be sure. "You bet."

"Atta boy. Okay, Ethan. Now . . . almost ready . . . Okay, two-second warning."

It hurts. It definitely hurts. I start to get worried, because it feels like he's covering a much bigger area than I'd thought. I say, "Max? Can you tell me how big it is across?"

"Maybe three inches. That's what you want, right?"

"Yeah. That's good."

It seems to take forever. By the time Shane is finished, I have to swipe at my eyes. I'm not actually crying, but stinging pain brought the tears, anyway.

Shane says, "What d'you think, Max?"

"That looks . . ." I hold my breath. ". . . That is fucking cool."

Shane tells me not to move yet. He's getting something else, I can't tell what, and I'm afraid it's going to hurt some more. But then I hear a camera lens click and see a flash. "This will be for you, Ethan, so you can see it newborn. You can get Max to take a picture again in a few weeks. Do you want to see yourself in a mirror before I bandage it for you?"

"Yeah!"

Feeling some kind of bravado, I don't bother to cover any-thing up as I kind of hobble over to a mirror attached to the wall. Shane hands me a hand mirror, and I admire the work. Max was right.

"Happy?"

I nod. "Perfect."

Shane spreads something gooey on me and tops it with what feels like gauze, taping that in place. "The spot will be tender for a couple of days. I'll give you a care instruction sheet. What you'll want to do is apply an antibacterial ointment and a fresh bandage once a day for three or four days. Then you can use this," and he hands me a small container that says *Tattoo Goo* on it. "There'll probably be some scabbing. Don't pick at it, or you'll ruin the tat. And don't soak in a hot bath or get salt on it till it heals. No ocean swimming. Once the scab falls off, as long as the skin looks healthy, just keep moisturizing it for a couple of weeks and you'll be all set."

I pull my underwear and jeans on, carefully lifting the back over the bandage. Once I'm dressed again, I look at Max and grin. He grins back. It feels so good! A little euphoric, actually.

I did it!

I pull my wallet out of my front pocket, glad I didn't have to reach into my right rear one, and start to count out some money. "How much is it?"

Shane says, "Well, hang on. Let me ask you this. If you didn't have to pay for your tat, what would you spend the money on?"

"That's easy. An iPhone."

"Basic cell isn't enough?"

"Don't have one."

There's a slight pause as he stares at me. "Buy yourself an iPhone."

I can't quite believe what I've heard. "What? You—do you mean it?"

"Don't know how you haven't been ritually slaughtered by your peers before now, kid. No cell phone? Gotta fix that." He grins at me. "This was a treat for me, Ethan. I mean, I love my work, but generally I do want to get paid. But I've wanted to paint this tat for a long time. And I think you're the perfect person to wear it."

"Wow. I—uh, I don't know what to say. I mean—thanks!"

We shake hands again, Shane and I, and I can't help feeling like maybe we really are friends. A sense of something secret is floating in my brain, like Shane and I know that whatever is between us, Max isn't a part of it. It's not sexual. It's—shit, maybe it's spiritual or something. Whatever, I really like it. I feel older, somehow. And it's not just the tat. Though, of course, that helps.

Shane hands me a piece of letter-size paper, the care instructions he'd mentioned. I fold it and shove it into my wallet. Then he heads for the front counter, camera in hand. "I'll upload this shot and e-mail it to you."

As Max and I follow, I say, "Max, can he send it to you?"

Max gets it. "Oh, shit. Right! Your mom—and I guess your Jesus freak brother—can't know about this, can they?"

"Right."

Shane uploads the shot and turns the monitor so I can see. "Still like it?"

I feel a rush of something wonderful. My eyes water again, but it's more like joy this time. "It's—it's gorgeous. I love it." I'm grinning so much my face almost hurts. Shane is smiling at me, and I know he understands. He understands completely. I want to say something to him, to let him know what he's done for me, to tell him in words that I feel the connection between us. But I guess my grin will have to speak for me.

Shane gets Max's eddress and attaches the file, and it's on its way. Then he walks with us to the door. As he's unlocking it and turning the sign back to Open, he says, "You'll have that tat all your life, unless you take very deliberate and painful steps to get rid of it. And every once in a while, when some guy tells you how much he likes it, or when you admire it yourself, just sometimes think of me."

He opens the door, we step out, the door shuts behind us, and it's over.

Max starts to move toward the car, but I'm just standing there, feeling tremendously alive. The idea of sitting down anyplace isn't very appealing at the moment, but that's not why I'm standing there. I want to hang on to this moment.

I close my eyes, breathe air deep into my body again and let it out slowly.

"Are you okay, Ethan?" Max sounds worried.

"Oh, yeah. I haven't felt this good since—well, since earlier this afternoon. With you." He smiles now, and nods. "Hey, do we have a little time? It would be great to paw through stuff in This Time For Sure. It's where I got this jacket, and it's right there." I point.

"Absolutely!"

Max has a knack for knowing what's going to look good on him. Everything he tries on works. Of course, he's gorgeous to begin with, so that helps. He hangs on to a jacket that's sort of like mine only in distressed brown leather, a wool sweater that brings out the green in his eyes, and a pair of work boots that would look like junk on most guys.

"This place is fantastic! Wish I'd known about it sooner." He leans briefly against my shoulder. "We'll have to come back."

He keeps picking through things until he's found a long-sleeved, heavy silk shirt in dusty gray-blue that looks fantastic on me. He says, "I'm buying this for you, charmer."

I look around the store, but my mind's not on the task. I don't even know what I've picked up or put down. I'm in heaven. Life is sweet, I'm in love, and I have a yin-yang tattoo.

As I expected, sitting is a challenge. On the ride home Max keeps laughing at my attempts to get comfortable. At one point he says, "You've got guts, I'll give you that. And I don't mean just the pain."

"Then, what?"

"What if you get caught? By your mom, I mean. What if she sees it?"

I shrug. "Don't know. With any luck, she won't ever find out. I guess she wouldn't kill me or anything, though. My mom's pretty cool." As soon as I say this, I realize it's true, and I also realize that I don't realize it enough. "What about you?"

He shakes his head. "Not sure what my folks would do to me if they caught me with a tat. They went spare when Mom found a half-smoked cig in one of my pockets when she went to wash them." He lifts a shoulder and drops it. "They're not horrible or anything, but I sure haven't told them about being gay. And Sylvia promised she wouldn't."

I grin at him. "They can't be too bad. They raised you and Sylvia, and she seems like she's pretty cool."

I see one corner of his mouth curl up. "Yeah, I guess. Mom's a sweetie, really. Cries real easy, whether something's good news or bad. Great cook. And my dad's okay." A couple of seconds go by, and then he glances at me, his face open and happy. "He adores Sylvia. He was totally proud when she came back home and got a teaching job here, first try."

I want to make some comment about how I'd like to meet them, but that sounds lame, almost like I'm some kind of desperate girl who isn't sure her new boyfriend really likes her and tries to seal the deal with a parental introduction. And, of course, I have met them, sort of. I mean, I'd know who they were if I bumped into them someplace. Like, if I saw Mr. Modine perusing condoms at the drugstore.

When we get back to the place where he'd pulled off the road on the way to Bangor, Max pulls off the road again. He says, "I figure, you know, what we did before didn't require you to sit down on anything, so it shouldn't be a problem now. Are you as ready for this as I am?"

Heaven.

Chapter 6

I barely remember to take off my ear cuff before Mom sees it. Or Kyle. It's not that there'd be a problem with it per se, but first I have to come up with a good explanation for where it came from. Supposedly I was with Jorja all afternoon.

And there's something else I decide to keep quiet about. The sign Mom had planted in our yard is gone. Etta's sign. I half want to ask why Mom took it down, but I don't really care. I'm embarrassed that the sign embarrassed me, but there it is. Plus I'm too high on everything that's happened this afternoon.

Over dinner, Mom says, "Ethan, Etta phoned when she got back from Bangor and asked if you'd help her put up some signs tomorrow. You can drive."

"Did you tell her yes?" As long as there isn't one in my yard. . . .

"I did. I thought that would be just fine with you. You'll have to do the bulk of the work, though."

"No problem."

"Didn't think so. Kyle, you've dropped another piece of chicken on the floor." He looks down. "No, it's on the other side." He starts to get up. "For Christ's sake, Kyle! Pick it up with your right hand!" But he doesn't. He's started wearing a cotton work glove on his right hand, probably to remind him in case he accidentally starts to use it for something. Mom makes some sound of disgust and then ignores him.

I'm feeling a little self-satisfied after my marvelous day, despite the fact that I'm trying hard not to let on that I'm leaning to the left to lighten the load on the other side of my ass. I'm also still flush—inside, anyway—with the knowledge that I've now had sex twice, and I'll bet Kyle is a virgin in any sense of the word that involves another person. I say, "Kyle, don't tell me you're still stumbling over that hand! Haven't you got yourself under control yet?" I dump a forkful of Mom's chicken casserole into my mouth and turn a smug face toward my odd brother. He doesn't reply, just keeps his head down. I can see that his ears are pink, and I have to stifle a giggle.

On Sunday morning before Mom takes Kyle to church, work glove and all—she won't let him drive if he won't use his right hand—she tells me to ask Etta for one of the signs about common sense.

"Why?"

"Someone stole our other one."

Oh, great. But—so, Mom didn't take it down herself? It was *stolen?* Weird.

When I get to Etta's, she's on the phone with someone, and the look on her face makes it seem like it's an unpleasant call. Two is standing a few feet from her in the kitchen, alert and watching her closely, on guard for some reason I can't fathom. When she hangs up the phone she looks rattled. Etta. The lady who doesn't hesitate in a crisis.

"You okay?" I ask.

"Oh, yes. Yes, of course. It's just—never mind. Listen, I've got the signs stored in the shed. It's up the hill in back a little, in the trees. Can you go up and start collecting some? I'll be up in a minute."

I head that way; I didn't know there was a shed up there. It's a lot bigger than the shed in my backyard, and it's in better shape. The door's not locked, so I open it and go in, and I start stacking signs up just outside, trying to judge how many will fit into the Forester.

As I step out with what I gauge to be the last few, pulling the door shut behind me, I'm surprised to see a dog trot around from the back of the shed, out of the woods. It's surprised to see me, too, I gather, because it stops short and stands stock still, and so do I. And then I realize that it's not a dog at all. It's a coyote.

I know there are coyotes in the area. You can hear them call sometimes, and in the spring they make really weird sounds during mating season. But I've never seen one up close and personal. And then, suddenly, there's another one. And then a third. And the way they're all looking at me gives me a really bad feeling.

Slowly I set the signs down and pick up just one of them. Maybe I'll need a shield? Do coyotes ever attack people? As I stand straight again, one of them moves to stand in front of me, and the other two start to circle around, one in each direction. They're surrounding me!

I'm thinking, you know, time to yell for help, but first I back up against the shed door; at least they can't attack me from that direction, and maybe I could get inside. I look around to see where the other coyotes are, and coming from the direction of the house I see a tawny blur practically flying toward me.

It's Two. He's silent as a ghost and, boy, does he mean business. The coyotes hear something, though, and I guess they decide I'm less dangerous, because all three of them look toward the dog. Two throws himself right at the closest coyote, but it moves just enough to avoid getting caught in those powerful jaws. There's a snarling scuffle, and the other coyotes start to move toward the fighting pair. I'm wondering if I should step in swinging my sign when I hear a loud crack.

Etta's standing about halfway between the house and the shed, and she's just fired a shotgun into the air. The two coyotes that aren't in the fight take off. Etta runs over to me and trades her gun for my sign, which she uses to separate the other two animals. At the same time, she makes this shrill whistle. Two steps back from the sign and sits down, and the coyote turns tail and races into the woods.

Two shakes his head like a boxer coming out of a tough round, and Etta and I stand there, panting, adrenaline pounding in my ears and hers, too, no doubt. We look at each other, then we look at Two, whose eyes are on her face.

She sets down the sign and works over the dog with her hands, I guess looking for damage. She doesn't find any. He's panting, too, but he doesn't look upset. He doesn't look scared. He doesn't even look angry. Just one day in the life of a pit bull, it would seem.

Etta kneels on the ground and hugs Two. I hear her voice, low: "My good boy. Good dog. Good dog."

I manage to find my voice. "I've never seen anything like that. Never even seen a coyote this close before." And, I'm dying to add, I didn't have the vaguest idea that you had a shotgun.

She shakes her head. "No. They're getting braver all the time. And three of them together is something to avoid." She laughs. "Good thing we have a pit bull protecting his pack."

"He was protecting *me*, though."

"Sure. You're in his pack now." She smiles at the expression on my face. "Okay, so let's get the car loaded." She turns back toward the house, and Two and I follow along. Just like a pack. And as of today, I like this dog *so* much better than I ever thought I would.

We drive out onto Route 154 to plant signs with Two in the back. As soon as we get to our first planting site, on the side of the highway close to Nick's, I turn off the engine and take my yin-yang ear cuff out of my jeans pocket and slide it onto the outside edge of my left ear.

Etta sees me. "Is your stud coming loose?"

I grin and turn my head so she can see; somehow I know I can trust her. "Nope. See?"

She laughs. "I haven't seen an ear cuff in years! Where on earth did you get that?"

I debate for just a second. A car goes by on the highway fast, and I feel the Subaru shift a little in its wake. "Do you remember after lunch at that diner, when we sat and watched the lake?"

"Quite well."

"I asked if you could, you know, keep a secret. You said as long as it wouldn't hurt anyone. That still true?"

She eyes me. "Yes. But I should warn you that I need to be the one who determines what harm might be done."

This gives me pause. But I can't resist; I feel like I have to tell someone or I'll burst. And in my new-slash-old leather jacket, I feel like I'm coming closer and closer to expressing who I am inside. "I got the cuff in the same place I got my tattoo." I wait.

"Tattoo. Who gave you a tattoo? You're underage."

It surprises me that she knows this. "What age is that?" I know it, but does she?

"In Maine, eighteen. I know, because I have one."

My jaw drops. "You do? Where? What is it?"

"I have the Aboriginal symbol for dingo tracks on my left shoulder. And I was fully adult when I got it." I blink; no clue how to respond to that, other than *What's a dingo?* But I don't ask, so she says, "What's yours?"

"Am I in trouble?"

She takes an audible breath. "Ethan, I certainly do not want to encourage you to do illegal things. You should not have gotten a tattoo, and no one should have given you one. But I gather you have it now. Are you taking care of it?"

"The guy gave me instructions and some goo. Plus, I searched online about it last night, and what he told me to do is what's out there."

"It sounds like this was recent. You're monitoring it carefully? And was the work done in clean conditions?"

"I'm monitoring. He used alcohol and those gloves doctors wear."

"And his equipment?"

What do I know about his equipment? "I'm sure of it." By now the whole idea of talking about it seems like much less fun than I'd thought.

"So, what is it? And where?"

"It's a yin-yang, like the ear cuff. But the white part is in rainbow stripes."

I can see she's about to grin, maybe even trying not to. "I sense a pattern. What's yin-yang to you?"

"Balance."

"Balance between extremes? Opposites? Good and evil? Earth and sky? Fire and water?"

"Um . . . I guess mostly male and female. But also not getting pulled in one direction or the other."

"Okay, I get the male–female bit. As for not getting pulled, would that be objectivity, or is it more like withdrawal?" I shrug and shake my head, and she says, "Deliberation, or cowardice?"

That gets to me. "What?"

"It seems to me that too many people take sides before they give enough thought to what's really going on. Either they can't be bothered to think, or perhaps they allow themselves to be manipulated. Or both. So deliberation is a good thing, in my book. On the other hand, once you've deliberated, once you've collected and weighed the available information and considered the results, to remain uninvolved out of cowardice is taking things too far in the other direction." She shrugs. "Some people would say that a spiritual remove, remaining uninvolved on principle, is admirable. But I think that can be taken too far, and I also think it can be like a duck blind for cowardice. A place to hide behind, and watch what's going on from a safe distance."

The longer she goes on, the more I shrink into my shoulders. I like the idea of being objective, of taking time to think about the reality of something. But I know—I know too well—that I also like the idea of the duck blind, a place where I can stand off to the side without calling attention to the fact that I'm standing off to the side. I don't know what to say.

Etta says, "It seems like you have some thinking to do about this. Don't let me . . . um . . . manipulate you into taking a stand about what your adopted symbol means to you." She grins at me for real now. "Where is it?"

I glance at her sideways, kind of from under my eyebrows. "It's on my right rear cheek."

She laughs. "That's classic. But Ethan, it's also a way to keep it out of sight. Behind the duck blind. I'm not saying you should have it on your face, and I'm not saying you chose the wrong spot at all. Just let the location be a part of your analysis when you consider what you've done and what it means."

No; not nearly as fun as I'd hoped. "So am I in trouble?"

She shakes her head. "Not from me. Who else knows? Besides whoever gave it to you."

"Max." There. That was something else I'd been dying to say. That Max is in my life. I kind of want her to ask about him, but she's just nodding her head slightly, chewing her lower lip a little like she's considering something.

She decides not to go there, apparently. I mean, to a place where I can talk about Max. "Well, if we don't get started, we'll never get all these signs planted!"

We plant the first signs near Nick's, then farther up the road and into the other towns that fall under the school board's jurisdiction. The Forester can hold lots of signs, and we plant all of them but one, which I have to save for Mom. It's not a bad day for this kind of work, actually. It's chilly but not freezing, the air feels good, and there are white puffs sailing through the blue overhead.

At the last spot, Etta takes Two on his leash for a short walk into the woods while I wait in the car on the side of the road. I watch them go down the hill from the roadside, Two pacing himself to stay at her side. They disappear into the woods, but not for long. Soon they emerge again, and I hear Etta call to me from below, where she and Two are standing. He's staring up at the car, mouth open, tongue hanging out a little.

"Ethan! Open the back door toward me." I have to get out of the car to do this, but okay. Then, "Call Two!"

Call Two? Not so very long ago, my response to the idea of calling him to run toward me would have been something like, *Oh, well, it's a good day to die.* But everything's changed between us now. I cup my hands around my mouth. "TWO!"

She releases his leash, and he charges up the hill. Suddenly I realize I'm in his path: the inside of the car. I step aside and watch the light brown streak fly past me and into the backseat. Then he turns around, panting and happy. I can't resist. I reach in and scratch behind his ears, and he laps my hand.

On the way back Etta has me pull into a Friendly's. She gives Two some water and a dog treat, and then he waits in the car while Etta and I go in for a late take-out lunch. We don't eat inside because of Two, but there are a few picnic tables in the sun, and we're already dressed for being outdoors, so we sit there with Two's lead tied to the table leg. He lies on the ground, eyes half closed, breathing through his mouth and smiling.

I watch Two for a bit while I eat one of my two burgers. He seems so unthreatening, and yet this morning he practically saved my life. "I guess Two deserves his reputation."

"What reputation is that?"

"Well, you know. Everyone says he's ferocious, that maybe he's even killed somebody."

Etta laughs. "I've had him since he was a year old. He's eight now, and in all that time he's never bitten any human."

"But—"

"He's a pit bull, Ethan. He had a reputation before he was born. And, mind you, if someone tried to hurt one of us, he'd protect us. Not just from coyotes. Even from a human. But otherwise, he's a dog. Not a monster."

"How come I'm in his pack now?"

"I've let him know that by the way I treat you. And pack members protect each other."

I stop chewing, a sense of shock coming over me that softens quickly to something warm. My eyes start to fasten on to Etta's face, but I'm not ready to respond to what she's said or to any questions about why I'm staring at her. So I stare at Two instead. The rule is not to do that, but he's not looking at me.

We're a pack, the three of us. We protect each other. That must also mean that we trust each other. And—what else? Will I be expected to do anything? Will I have to take sides?

It dawns on me that I've kind of already taken sides. Helping her put up her signs is just something I've done to get in some driving time with somebody who doesn't make me crazy in the process, but if you don't know that—or if it doesn't mean enough to you—then it kind of looks like I'm for her and against Carl Phinney in this election. And, really, I couldn't care less about the election.

"You look pensive, Ethan."

She hasn't asked a question, but that doesn't mean I can sit here like a lump. But it also doesn't mean I have to be totally honest. "Yeah. Trying to add up my driving hours so far."

"I figure you had about four hours with just me before today. You need what—35?"

"And five of them at night."

"Do you have a date for Friday night yet? Or are you planning to?"

I snap my head toward her. Is this her way of asking about Max? "A date?"

"Plans with someone, then."

I shove a few fries into my mouth and shake my head. When I can speak, I say, "Friday would be great, if you're offering to let me get in some night driving."

"You've done a lot of hard work today. I don't think you've had nearly enough driving time yet to compensate you fairly. Do you?" She grins at me.

I'm about to respond when I notice two people getting settled a couple of picnic tables away. They have hot coffee, it looks like, and as they sit down they get out cigs and light them, which they couldn't have done inside, so maybe that's why they're out here.

One of them is my dad. The other is a woman I don't know.

Dad's back is toward me. I try to get a good look at the woman without being caught staring. Etta sees, though, and she looks toward them. "Isn't that your father?"

I nod, still staring at the woman. She doesn't look anything like Mom. Blond and fluffy, though chances are she didn't come by either quality genetically. She's a little heavy, but not fat, and—well, fluffy. Pink jacket, lipstick, and her hands spend enough time flitting around that I can see long pink nails. Her voice is high and a little nasal. Definitely not Mom. And in my book, not someone Dad should have bought condoms for.

The fluffy lady sees me staring, finally, and I hear her say, "Dave, that boy over there keeps staring at me."

I drop my eyes, but I can see that Dad has turned. Then, low, I hear, "Christ. I'll be right back."

Yeah. Too late, Dad. You've been seen. He gets up and walks over, and eventually I have to look up. He says, "Hey." It's not our standard greeting, and I'm not sure how to respond. Plus, what do you say when you catch your father cheating on your mother?

Etta comes to my rescue. I'm in her pack. "Good to see you again."

"Yeah. Same here. You, uh, running more errands or something?"

I hear Two's dog tags jingle as he gets up and walks around the table toward Dad, who sees him and backs up quickly, wide eyes full on the dog.

"Please don't back away," Etta says. "It makes you look like prey. Anyway, he's tied."

Two is staring at Dad, and not in a good way. He growls. Etta turns toward him, yanks his leash sideways, snaps her fingers, and points to the ground. Two lies down again.

Wow. If I'd been Dad, I would've backed up, too. I guess Two warns people but not coyotes. He didn't growl at them.

Etta turns back toward Dad, who has stopped backing away

but hasn't come closer again. Etta says, "Ethan and I have a mutually helpful arrangement. He helps me set up signs for my school board campaign, and I help him log driving hours. It's working out very well, I think."

He looks hard at me. "Your mother know about this?"

"She set it up." *WTF? What's his problem?* Then it dawns on me. He's wondering why he isn't the one helping me log driving hours. I pray he doesn't bring it up. Then I decide to take aggressive evasive action. "Who's your friend, Dad?"

"Oh. Uh, Connie. Just a friend."

"She looks a little impatient. D'you think she wants to come join us?" I feel evil, but in a fun way. Or, not fun exactly; maybe righteous. Can you be righteously evil?

"No." Way too quick. "No, I think we won't be here much longer. In fact, I should, uh, you know." He nods to Etta. "Let me know when you need some driving time, Ethan. You know, like we talked about."

"Thanks." I watch him head back to Connie, whoever the hell she is. *Friend,* my ass. And if I log hours with Dad and Mom finds out . . . But—hell, there are so many things she'd kill me for lately. Maybe I should consider adding that one, just to get in as many things as possible before she figures anything out. How does that expression go? May as well be hung for a sheep as for a lamb? Something like that.

Etta gets that I don't really want to talk about my parental problems. She doesn't say anything about Dad or Connie or the fact that there's a flask of something he's pulled out of his pocket and is dumping into his coffee. Couldn't do *that* inside, either. He downs the contents of the cup quickly and then tells Connie to finish hers in the truck. She complains, but he's halfway there already, so she minces after him.

"So." Etta picks up pretty much where we've left off. "Friday. I would love to have you drive me to visit a friend who lives a few towns away. For dinner. We could leave early and take a circuitous route. And if you wanted to bring a friend"—she leans on the word a little—"that would be delightful. Not obligatory, of course. Any of it. Just an invitation."

This proposal takes me a little by surprise. "What kind of friend?"

"Yours, or mine?"

"Yours."

"A woman I've known for years. She lives alone, like me. She's a fascinating person. Earns her living reading people's energy." Etta smiles, watching my face. "She's also been known to do a little astrology on the side, and she isn't above telling you something she's picked up about you that she couldn't have any way of knowing."

"What is she, like, a fortune-teller or something?"

"I suspect that she'd shudder if she heard anyone call her that. I would say it's more like a psychic hit she sometimes gets from people." She laughs out loud now, no doubt at the expression on my face, which has got to be something close to terrified. "Don't worry. If I tell her you'd rather not hear any of that, she's perfectly capable of fooling you into thinking she's a completely average person." Another smile. "Ethan, please don't feel like you have to do this. It's fine; we'll come up with another plan for night hours."

The thing that got to me was the psychic part. "It's just—you know, she might say something I don't want anyone else to know."

"Well, she has quite a bit of discretion. She would be careful. But, as I said, we could—"

"I—I think maybe I'd like to." It's suddenly occurring to me that this person sounds like she'd fit right in with the whole Poe mystique. I've been wearing less Goth stuff lately, but that's mostly because I think Max doesn't like it. I haven't given up on Edgar Allan. And I'm getting an odd sensation, like what you might expect to feel if you choose to do something that's absolutely positively going to happen whether you want it to or not, and actually it's the right thing, even if you can't see that yet. Like, fate, maybe. Or destiny. It feels weird, and scary, and it pulls at me.

"Great! And is there anyone you'd like to invite to join us?"

That's not as straightforward. "Can I think about it?"

"Sure. Just let me know before Thursday, so we'll know how many to plan dinner for. Now, I think we'd better get on our way so we can get in another hour of driving before the day's over."

We drive for over an hour, and I'm able to log some good time on my chart. Then Etta asks if I'd like to come back to the house with her for some cookies. "Peanut butter." She says it in this voice that makes it sound like she knows it's my favorite. I wonder if Mom told her.

We sit at the kitchen table, Two curled up on a big pillow beside the stove. I look over at him, and he seems so peaceful, like he wouldn't hurt anybody, or anything.

"Where did you get Two?" I ask.

"He used to live with a family a little farther upstate. They went to Canada to get him for their son. But the boy was killed by a car when he was riding his bike on the highway. After that, the parents couldn't look at the dog without thinking of their son, and they couldn't provide leadership for him. A pit bull without leadership is a dangerous animal. So they started asking around, and I decided to take him. I'm the one who named him Two."

"Can I pet him?"

"Sure you can. Look how relaxed he is. This is the best time to give him some quiet affection."

I go and sit on the floor, and he opens his eyes but doesn't raise his head off his paws. He blinks at me a couple of times and closes his eyes again, and I reach out and stroke his forehead. He has funny ears, kind of like floppy triangles. I pull on one of them a little and he kind of sighs like that's just what he wanted. I run a hand down his side; the fur is a little rough, kind of stiff. It reminds me of the feel of the oriental rug in the living room.

I ask, "Don't pit bulls usually have tiny ears?"

"That's only if they're clipped. Two's ears are natural. By the way, he loves having his spine massaged."

I work my fingers into the skin around his spine, and he turns his back more toward me so I can reach it easier. Who'd have thought?

When I get up, Two does, too. Etta says, "Do you have just a little longer? It's getting cool out, but I'd love to run him a little. It's just light enough. And those coyotes will be long gone."

"Sure!" I'm not sure what she means by running him, but it sounds interesting. We go out behind the house, and Etta has this long, curved plastic stick with a kind of claw on the end. She grabs a few tennis balls from a covered bucket beside the house. Two is nearly prancing with excitement, but he's waiting for Etta. He doesn't bark or jump on her, or me, just watches her face. She puts a ball into the claw end of the stick and then flings it over her head and forward. The ball, and the dog, go flying. He looks powerful; even in the dimming light I can see the muscle definition under his hide. He comes trotting back, ball in his mouth like some kind of prize.

"Good boy!" Etta tells him. "Good boy, Two!" She holds out her hand and he drops the ball into it. She holds it out to me. "Wanna throw?"

The ball is wet from Two's spit, but I guess that's part of dog ownership. I push it into the claw and give the stick a huge arching fling.

"Beautiful!" Etta says. "You have a better arm than I have, that's for sure!"

I throw again, and again, like I can't quite get enough of it, and each time Two comes trotting back to me. I think he could go on forever, too. I love watching him run, and I love the grin on his face after he gives me the ball. Finally, he doesn't come back right away, probably because he can't find the thing in the near darkness. I'm just starting to be afraid he's met up with another coyote when he reappears, and I'm disappointed when Etta says it's time I went home. At least she lets me drive, and during the friendly silence I spend some time wondering if Mom would let me get a dog.

*   *   *

I'm sitting upstairs at my desk at home maybe an hour before dinner, trying to figure out how I can get lots more driving hours, and trying to decide whether to tell Mom about the coyotes, when there's a soft knock on my door frame. I turn and see Mom leaning there, an odd expression on her face.

"You had a few calls while you were out," she says.

Max? Did Max call? My heart gives a kind of lurch; I don't really want Mom to know how much I want to hear from him. I try to sound like it doesn't much matter. "Oh? Who from?"

"Jorja."

Shit. My lie about where I was yesterday is going to come out. I wait, and Mom goes on. "She must have called three times. Seems a little odd, given that you were just with her yesterday. Something going on, Ethan?"

I try to hide my deep breath of relief with a shrug. "Don't know. I suppose I'd better call her back and find out. Thanks, Mom."

She leaves, and I sit there staring at my driving log but not seeing it. Something's twisting inside me, heavy and dark, and it makes me want to zone out behind my duck blind rather than admit what it is.

Suddenly I feel caught again, rock-and-a-hard-place. I want to tell Jorja she's still my friend. I also don't want to call her at all, because I know I've neglected her lately. And that heavy dark feeling? Guilt. Pure and simple. And this makes me feel mad at Jorja. After all, why the hell does she have to call three times and make Mom suspicious? I'm sure Jorja's going to yell at me; it's been days since we've had anything like a real conversation. I mean, we still have lunch together and share a bus seat, but we haven't talked a lot. It's mostly my fault, what with thinking about almost nothing but Max and knowing I can't tell her any of that. But—in a way, it's her own fault. She won't *let* me talk about it.

I sigh, heave myself up and locate the phone, and carry it back to my room. Then I lie on the bed to try and pretend this is all cool and casual, that everything's perfectly normal, like I haven't practically deserted my supposed best friend, my best friend who doesn't want to know about the love of my life.

The first thing she says is about what I expect. "Oh, it's you."

"Um, yeah, like, hello? You called me three times today."

"Was it three? Whatever."

"You got a cold or something?"

Silence. Then, "No. Why?"

"It's just—you sound stuffed up." Then—has she been crying? Surely not about me. There's more silence, so I break it. "What's up?"

"What d'you mean?"

I heave a sigh. "Jorja, in case you've forgotten, you called me. Three times."

"Yeah. So? You weren't there. You expect me to remember what I called for?"

Okay, not making sense. "Are you okay?"

"Fine." But she doesn't fool me. She sounds like she's about to start crying again.

"D'you wanna come over for dinner?"

"What for?"

What for? WTF? It's part guilt, part remorse, part pity maybe. "I've got something to show you."

"What?"

"You have to come over to see. We'll probably eat around seven."

More silence, and then, "Fine. I'll see you at six-thirty." And she hangs up without saying good-bye.

Mom gives me a dirty look when I tell her there's a guest coming for dinner. "You could tell a person, Ethan. What if there wasn't enough food?"

"You're doing a roast chicken. There's always enough."

"Not the point. Next time, ask me first."

Jorja is fifteen minutes late, and I've been on tenterhooks trying to decide whether to show her my ear cuff or my tattoo or both. By the time she gets there, time's too short to do either. I let her in.

"You're late." She just shrugs. "I'll have to show you after dinner."

"Whatever."

I don't get it. If she's mad at me, why did she even come over? Just so she could rub it in? But she helps me set the table, and then I call Kyle down from his lofty tower of a bedroom. He's still got the glove on.

Jorja is hardly the most tactful person in the world. "What's with the glove, Kyle?" He glares at her and doesn't speak. She turns to me. "This the offending right hand you told me about?"

That gets to Kyle. "You told her? How dare you talk about it!"

Mom plunks a bowl of gravy onto the table. "Kyle, for heaven's sake. If you wear that glove to school, you can hardly keep it a secret."

After dinner Jorja helps wash up, and then she and I go upstairs to my room. Mom eyes me as we head toward the stairs, like she's not sure what to say but feels like she ought to warn me about behavior in some way.

Once we're in the room behind the locked door, I say, "Ever see one of these?" And I dig the ear cuff out of my pocket. She takes it and shakes her head. So I demonstrate.

Her voice tells me I've broken through the apathy of earlier. "Wow. That's cool. Where did you get that?"

It feels like we're friends again, so I decide to go all the way. As it were. "Turn around for a sec."

I turn my back to her as well and pull my jeans and my underwear down enough to let me expose the right side of my ass. I pull the bandage off and peer over my shoulder to watch her reaction. "Okay, look. It's not all healed yet."

She turns, and her eyes and her mouth open wide. Anyone else would have said, *OH, MY GOD!* In a harsh whisper she says, "Ethan! Where did you get that?" I wait, and she walks over to it. I can tell she wants to touch it but doesn't quite dare. I'm wondering if she'll get the rainbow implication and point out the sinfulness, and I'm all ready with an answer that should satisfy her: It's where no one can see it, so it's like being gay without acting on it.

I let her stare for a few more seconds and then pull myself together again. "Same place I got the ear cuff."

"Man! Would they . . . d'you think they'd give *me* a tattoo?"

Okay, that's not quite the reaction I expect, though I probably shouldn't be surprised; she's even deeper into Goth than I am. At least she hasn't picked up about the rainbow, and that makes me feel a little calmer about the locker room at school. "I don't think so. They weren't even supposed to give me one. You're supposed to be eighteen. And they made me promise not to tell anyone where I got it."

"You could ask."

"Maybe. I'll see." Truth is, I don't really want to. I like the specialness I get from being the only kid I know with a tattoo. Plus, I'd led the way into Goth, and Jorja had followed and then outdone me. The last thing I want is for her to get a tattoo someplace where it shows and get all the attention for it, when it was my thing first and I can't show mine.

We chat for a while, and I'm sort of waiting for her to say something about why she'd called me three times, but she doesn't. I mention that I'm going to get an iPhone, and I come *so close* to telling her I'm in love. It's right there, so many times, just waiting to be said. But I don't. Instead I tell her I'm going to meet someone who reads energy and gets psychic hits off of other people. I'm half thinking maybe I'll invite her to go with me on Friday. But she ruins that idea.

"Ethan, don't do it! Those people are in league with Satan. Where do you think they get those powers?" Right; I almost forgot. The beast again, no doubt. "God doesn't give powers like that to anyone."

But that gets to me. "What about the prophets? What about Isaiah and maybe half of the Old Testament?"

"That's different."

"Why?"

"They're telling us how to prepare for what God has in store, obviously! Like the coming of Jesus."

"Wouldn't it be just as useful to know about specific bad stuff that's coming?"

"That's in the Bible, too, you know. Have you read Revelations yet?"

"No."

"Read it. You'll see. And stay away from that person, Ethan. I mean it."

I'm thinking that she must not know anything about the origins of the yin-yang symbol, or I'd have gotten a lecture on that.

When she leaves it's almost like we're friends again. Almost. Mostly it's like she thinks we are.

Mom and Kyle are in the kitchen, arguing as usual these days. I start to head upstairs, but then I catch just enough that I want to hear more. I hear Mom's voice say, ". . . tomorrow morning. I have the distinct honor of meeting with you and Mr. Glasier."

"What? What for?"

"What do you think? It's that stupid hand of yours. Evidently your left hand hasn't learned to take notes or write essay exams very well yet. Don't pretend this is a surprise to you, young man." Kyle mumbles something I can't quite hear, and then nothing.

Jorja had asked about taking class notes that day we hitched out to Nick's, as soon as I'd mentioned the hand. It's something I hadn't even thought of, and now here it is for real.

After school the next day, as I head for the bus, all thoughts of Kyle and Mom's appointment with Glasier evaporate when I hear Dad's whistle. I look around for a truck, either his or one of the town's, but I don't see one. Then I see him waving an arm at me, standing beside a black Chevy Camaro, obviously several years old but in great shape. It has a cowl induction hood with the raised center portion tapering to three points a little above the front end, making it look like a black panther with flared nostrils. I stand there like an idiot, wondering where the hell it came from, and then I wave to Jorja and trot over to him.

"Whatcha up to, kid?"

I grin. "Nothin' much." This time our message is *Yesterday at Friendly's didn't happen. We're cool. And something different and fun is about to happen.*

"Get in." He gets behind the wheel while I throw my pack behind the passenger seat and climb in. "Thought I'd give you a taste of real driving. Bet no one's given you a taste of a stick, have they?" He bounces a hand off the knob while I struggle not to think about what else a taste of stick might mean.

As I watch his hand lift up before slapping the stick head again, I see it has a silver wolf head against black. Custom, obviously. Whose car is this? But I don't go there. "This is standard transmission?"

"Yep. Sure is. Six gears. I'm gonna teach you how to drive like a man." His legs move as he works the pedals, the engine guns, and suddenly I'm pressed hard against my seat back. I *know* we leave a trail of black on the pavement behind us. As we head down the road, too fast for the legal limit, I test the air to see if I can smell booze. Nothing. Maybe he's actually totally sober today. For me. My throat tightens a little.

He pulls into a parking lot behind some storage buildings, the place where they keep the equipment for mowing beside highways and plowing roads in winter, practically deserted today, between seasons. Then Dad shows me a side of him I didn't know was there.

From a dead stop, he guns the engine a little and then takes off fast; ho-hum, he'd done that at the school. But then he scares the willies out of me, heading right for a machine storage building and cutting around the corner so close I can feel the wheels on my side lift a little, and I think I'd have lost a hand if it had been hanging out of the window. By the time we get to the opposite end of the long wall, we're going so fast I don't dare look at the speedometer, or at anything other than the side of the building only a few inches to my right. We take another heart-stopping turn and head into the open parking area, nothing in it but us, the car, and the exhilaration we get as

Dad does figure eights and tight wheelies and hellishly fast ac-
celerations. It's almost as good as sex.

Finally he pulls calmly toward a corner, turns the car around
in less space than I would ever have thought he could, and
turns the engine off. He looks at me with an expression I don't
remember. "Your mother used to love that. When I met her.
Don't let her tell you otherwise." He lets out a breath that's almost a sigh and says, "Okay, kid. Switch places."

Behind the wheel, I have to pull the seat forward a little, and
then I play with things. It's all got a totally different feel from
anything I've driven before. The steering wheel is wrapped in
black leather, and the dashboard has only basic instrumenta-
tion on it—none of it digital. Everything you can adjust has
knobs instead of push buttons.

"Cool," I say, feeling something like power run through me.
Dad's left arm is draped onto the back of my seat, and he's
watching me. I know this response is what he wants, and I don't
mind giving it to him.

"Nice jacket," he says. "Where'd you get it?"

"Bangor. Mom and I went to a used clothing store." I love
that he's noticed.

"The pedal on the far left is the clutch," he tells me. "Press it
down with your left foot."

"It feels weird."

"Yeah. Not used to using that foot to drive, are ya? Better get
used to it or you'll strip the gears. And this ain't my car, kid."
He laughs, but I can tell he's a little nervous about what strip-
ping the gears would mean. It occurs to me on some almost
subconscious level that he's put a friend's fancy car at risk to
give me something Mom and Etta can't.

He brags about the car a little, almost like it's his: eight cylin-
ders, six-speed transmission that's evidently some big advantage on the highway, some huge number of horsepower. I nod
like I know what the hell a drag launch suspension is, and I can
sort of get the importance of not having a fuel limiter. And I'd
noticed the twin exhaust already.

"Before you turn the key," he says, "let me tell you a little about what makes this kind of driving so fantastic. When you're idling, and you step the clutch all the way to the floor and put the stick into first, you control everything. You control how much gas to give it—okay, that's not new. But you can give it all the gas you want as you ease the clutch out. The more gas, the faster your start. Like I did back at the school. And once you're in motion, you can run the engine up hard before you shift up. Most of the time you won't do that. It's hard on the transmission. But there are times . . . Ethan, my boy, you're in control. Nothin' else like it."

"What do I do first?"

He walks me through the motions, all with the engine off: clutch in, shift gear, clutch out, speed up a little, clutch in, another gear, clutch out. We sit there for maybe ten minutes with him telling me everything I know I'll forget once the engine is running. But I'm loving just sitting here with him, knowing he's sober, knowing all this is for me.

Finally, "You ready to try it?" I grin and nod. "We aren't going onto the road. Like I said, it's not my car. But I want you to know what real driving is, so when you get your own car you make the right choice."

"You think I should get a standard?"

"I think you should get the car that makes driving feel good. And how will you know what feels good if you haven't had a baby like this in your control?" He jerks his chin toward the ignition. "Clutch in. Right foot on the brake. Fire it up."

My dad's not right about everything, but he's sure right about this. I won't pretend I didn't stall the thing out once or twice, but I was pretty quick to get the hang of releasing the clutch and stepping on the gas and at getting moving from a dead stop. I really love shifting up, and I sure as hell love accelerating. Shifting down is trickier, but I get much better at it before we're done. And I've made the gears grind only a little, and only a few times.

After Dad has me do a few tight turns and some unusual reverse patterns, he makes it clear he thinks I've done as well as I think I have. "I knew you'd be good at this, son."

I'm almost glowing as he drives me home, and I can't help working my legs with him, imagining the feel of the clutch and the gas working together to create that sense of power that's nearly intoxicating. I laugh out loud; maybe Dad doesn't *need* a beer when he has a Camaro!

"Did you enjoy yourself?"

"For real. That was great." I grin at him. "Thanks, Dad." He reaches over and ruffles my hair. It feels good and sad at the same time.

The trip toward home, quiet other than the old rock numbers Dad is playing on the CD player, leaves me feeling like I still have a dad after all, even though somewhere in my head reality is lurking. But today has been fantastic. I shift a little on my ass, relieving my right side of some weight. The tat feels pretty good today, not too sore, though I remind myself I have to re-bandage it when I get home. The one from this morning came off in the locker room after gym class, which actually was pretty cool, 'cause I got all kinds of cred from the other guys when they saw the tat. Didn't seem to me anyone thought the colors meant anything gay. I really don't think they picked up on that. So I just nod my head to the beat of Dad's old music, window down and my elbow on the door, and drum my fingers on the Camaro's roof. It's a good day.

As we get close to the house, I'm deciding to count this time against my total on the driving hours log, feeling cocky about any protest Mom might make about it. He pulls over to the side of the road, just out of sight of the house, and lets me out.

"No point in asking for trouble, eh?" he says.

"I suppose not." I'd almost hoped he'd go right into the driveway. "Thanks!" And I pat the warm hood of the car once as he starts to move away.

Our boring car is in the driveway already, so Mom's home. This might mean I get a chance to test my resolve right away. The bus would have got me home much sooner, so obviously I wasn't on it. And, sure enough, as soon as I open the door, I hear, "Where have you been, young man?"

Mom's stopped in the middle of the living room, where she must have been pacing, a lit cig in one hand. When I take the time to turn and shut the door all the way she says, "Well?"

Her voice sounds more than just mad at me. There's something dark in it, like fear.

I shrug. "Just out getting some driving in."

She blinks. "With Etta?"

"No. Dad."

"What?" Now it's anger.

"Look, he showed up at school. He wasn't drunk. Didn't smell like it at all. And I didn't even drive on the road. Just in the parking lot at the municipal storage area." I decide against mentioning the Camaro.

Her expression changes a few times, like she's trying to find fault with that and can't quite land on anything worth yelling about. But her face settles on something kind of distracted, like she has bigger things to worry about.

"Did you know what your brother was doing?"

I have no idea what she's talking about. "Doing . . . ?"

"Doing to his hand."

"Other than his usual weirdness?"

She starts to say something that would probably have been *Did you know about it or not?* But instead she says, "He's been cutting himself. Digging things into his hand. That's why he's been wearing the glove."

"Oh my God."

"Damn right, oh my God." She takes a deep drag on the cig and paces back and forth a few times. Then, "How could we not have known this? Your principal pulled that glove off him when we were in that meeting today. Said it was time Kyle stopped the nonsense and used his hand like a normal person, and before Kyle—or I—knew what was happening, he got up and yanked the glove off."

I just stand there, feeling like someone's punched all the air out of me. *WTF?* I can't get my brain to settle on anything other than that: *What the fuck?* For a couple of minutes there are no other words in the universe.

Suddenly she pulls me into a hug, swaying back and forth, smoke drifting around our shoulders. I can tell she's trying like hell not to cry. She says, "Ethan, promise me . . ." She has to stop for a second as her voice catches, and I wait. "Promise me two things. One, that you'll never, ever do anything like this to yourself! And two, that if you ever find out your brother is doing this again, or anything else like it, you'll tell me immediately." She pulls back and swipes at her eyes with the heel of her cig hand. "Promise."

"I promise, Mom. Really."

"He's in his room now, asleep. Knocked out, actually. His hand's all wrapped up. I've searched his room for anything he could hurt himself with. We both have to keep an eye on him; I can't take everything pointed or sharp out of the house. And I'll need your help making sure he takes the antibiotics they gave him, for the next ten days. Can you do that?"

"Sure. Of course." I have no idea what it will mean to help with these things, but how can I say anything else? Then I realize it might mean being around the house more than I have. "Um, is it okay if I go out Friday night?"

"What?"

"I mean, do you need me to be here, or can I go with Etta to visit a friend and get in some night driving? I'll stay if you need me to. I just have to let her know." *Please say you don't need me. . . .*

"Oh. Right. I forgot. She told me she was going to ask you. That's okay, Ethan. I'll be here Friday. You go." She hugs me again. "Listen, do you mind going through his room again? Boys might be more creative than I am about doing damage."

I nod. "I'll take a look. I won't wake him up."

I don't find anything she hasn't. She's even taken all his clothes off the wire hangers they'd been on and folded them into piles on the closet floor, and there are now no hangers anyplace. The lamp on his desk isn't the one that used to be there; it had a glass shade. The one there now is cloth or paper or something. Did she think of the lightbulb and decide it's a risk we have to take? It makes me wonder what he's used on himself—not to mention why. This has gone beyond just stupid and weird and into fear and danger. I don't get it at all. And as I'm looking under his bed I remember that Etta had asked me to let her know if this got worse. Out of hand, as it were. I think it's crossed that line.

Before I leave I stand by the bed and look at him. He's on his stomach, definitely down for the count, facing me. His right hand, on the pillow beside his open mouth, is covered in so much gauze it looks like he's holding a swaddled kitten.

The only thing I take with me when I leave is Kyle's Bible, the only one in the house, so I can read Revelations and see what's going on with Jorja. Honestly, people are falling apart all around me. It hits me what a rock my mom is, and this physical wave of love washes over me, leaving a little water in my eyes. I drop the Bible in my room and head downstairs.

Mom is on the back step, smoking, wrapped in the shearling coat she'd bought at This Time For Sure. I put my leather jacket back on and go out to sit with her. I say, "He's still asleep. And I didn't find anything, unless you count the lightbulb in the desk lamp. Good idea about the hangers."

She picks up a glass with something amber colored in it and takes a gulp. "Thanks. I didn't think about the lamp. There's an overhead light; maybe I'll take the lamp out of the room."

"What about matches? And your lighter?"

She rubs the bridge of her nose a sec. "You're right. I'll have to think about that. Thank you, Ethan. Keep thinking."

"Um, Mom? I had, you know, I had mentioned this thing with Kyle's hand to Etta. That day we drove out to the lake and nearly had that accident?" I wait for her reaction, but she just takes another drag. I sort of know she's already said something to Etta, anyway. "She told me to let her know if it got worse. Is it okay if I do that?"

Mom turns toward me. "Why? What's she going to do?"

I shrug. "Dunno. But she seemed serious. Almost like she knew something."

Mom stubs out the cig on the cement step and gets up. I follow her into the house, where she picks up the phone.

"Etta? Charlene Poe. Listen, sorry if this sounds odd, but Ethan just told me that you had asked to know if anything happened with Kyle. His hand, I mean." Pause. "Yes, it has." Mom's voice nearly breaks a few times as she tells Etta what's happened, and when Mom hangs up she says to me, "She's coming over."

"Really. What did she say?"

Mom shakes her head, a few quick shakes like she doesn't know what to say.

Etta shows up maybe half an hour later with three pizzas, various toppings, and some soda. "I figured you probably didn't feel much like getting dinner on the table."

I go check on Kyle, who's still out cold, and then we sit at the kitchen table, pizzas and soda spread around. This would be fun under other circumstances.

Etta breaks the strained silence. "The reason I asked Ethan to let me know if things got worse is because I've seen something like this before. There was someone I used to work with, in New York, who had to quit work because of damage to his lower leg. Damage he did himself. Eventually it got so bad they had to amputate it. He had something called body integrity identity disorder. BIID. It's when people truly believe that a part of their body shouldn't be attached to them, and they'll go to extreme lengths to get rid of it. Most commonly it's the lower leg, but it could be a finger, a hand, an arm, whatever. As far as I know, it's a psychological disorder, and I don't know of any cure. If Kyle has this, you need to find out. He should see a therapist."

This is too weird. I say, "He said it was causing him to stumble. I think he just meant he was using it to . . . you know . . . um . . ."

Etta smiles. "That may have got him started thinking his hand was his enemy. But it's far beyond that."

Mom rubs her face a second. "That's what he told the doctor this afternoon. He kept quoting Bible verses."

"That's only what gives him permission, Charlene. It's the disease that makes him do it."

"So the Bible's like a duck blind." My voice surprises me.

"What?" Mom's voice is exhausted, like that mental stretch is more than she can handle.

Etta nods. "I know what you mean, Ethan. The religious aspect is obscuring what's really going on."

We sit there a minute, and then Mom says, "Therapy. I wouldn't know where to start."

"I can help. Talk to a couple of people, get some references. Will you let me do that?"

Mom covers her face with her hands, fighting sobs, and Etta gets up and holds her shoulders. She says, "You're not alone, Charlene. It might feel like it sometimes, but you're not."

I don't know what to do. So I just sit there. Maybe it's enough.

Chapter 7

The rest of that week is totally weird. I'm almost afraid to go to school, and Mom takes sick days from work to stay home with Kyle. Meals are pretty quiet, with no one wanting to call attention to Kyle's left-handed struggles. I don't even know if it's okay to ask something like, *How's the hand today?* And for sure no one feels like talking about cheerful things. The noncheerful thing sitting at the table with us is sucking out everything else. It's not like Kyle and I were ever close, really. Only now—now, we're in different dimensions.

He doesn't fight taking his meds, at least, so I don't feel like I have to do anything about that. He notices right away that his Bible is missing, though, and has a fit.

"I'm reading Revelations," I tell him. This stuns him.

"Well...give it back and you can take it when you need to." None of the lecturing I'd expected. Nothing that smacked of smugness or *I told you so.* If nothing else convinces me that he's in trouble, this does. A month ago he would have been all over me, telling me it's about time I came to my senses, stuff like that.

When I finally get to it, I find out that Revelations is like somebody on shrooms. If the rest of the Bible stretches credibility, this part breaks it. I don't even make it all the way through before I give it back to Kyle for good. And now I have confirmation: Both my brother and my best friend are going quite literally bonkers. What the hell am I supposed to do with that?

The only good thing that happens that week is Tuesday evening. Mom had told me to be home right after school because she had errands to run, and when she gets home afterward she hands me one of the shopping bags. It's from an Apple store. I just look at her.

"I think you'll like that," she says.

It's the newest iPhone. Just like I'd wanted. "How did you know?"

She just smiles. But then she says, "I figure I might need to reach you in a hurry." I know she means because of Kyle, so I don't reply.

I get up and give her a big hug. And then I spend the rest of the time before bed getting it set up. I text Max. He texts me back. He calls me charmer and sends me the shot of my tattoo.

Max doesn't want to come with me to visit Etta's friend. He calls it lame. On Wednesday I've finished lunch with Jorja, and Max and I are hanging around outside waiting for the next class to start, shivering in our leather jackets. I'm thinking it must be about time to start wearing my new-slash-old pea coat. That's when I invite him.

"Why would I want to go with one old lady to visit another old lady who sounds like she's off her rocker?"

"Gee, I don't know, maybe because you'd be with me?"

"That's not how I want to be with you. In fact," and he lowers his voice and looks around, "I'd like to take another drive to Bangor on Saturday. What do you say?"

Maybe this thing with Kyle has me too on edge, or maybe my reaction is what it should be, but something in me snaps, and Max and I have our first fight. Quietly. Right here in front of the school.

"Y'know, Max, it's really not cool with me the way you talk about Etta."

"What'd I say? Jeez!"

"Let's see. You've called her a hag, and you use the term 'old lady' like it's an insult, and you say spending time with her is lame. I got news for you. I *like* spending time with her. And if you think that's lame, then you must think I'm lame, too."

I stop long enough to take a breath, but I'm on a roll. "And you can stop saying mean things about Jorja, too. D'you think I don't know she's weird? But she's my best friend, and she can't help it that she's so scared of life that she needs the Bible to lean on." *Where did that come from?*

I stare out toward where the highway runs in front of the school, my eyes catching on the last orange berries of the bitter-sweet vines that are strangling those baby poplars. What will Max do? Is this, like, the end of us?

He looks off to the side, away from me, for a minute. Then, "All right, all right. Don't be so prickly. Christ. Sorry if I hurt your feelings."

I turn toward him. "It's not my *feelings,* Max. Etta is a terrific lady who's helping me, and Jorja is a sad person who needs a friend. They're . . . they're my people. You gotta get that." I wanted to say they're my pack, but it seems odd to say that about Jorja.

"I get it, okay?"

There's about two minutes of painful silence, and then we go back inside.

I'm worried all afternoon. I know I did the right thing, but being with Max feels like the right thing, too. I leave History class with my head down, moving toward my locker like some automaton. I'm standing there, barely able to focus on what to leave and what to take home, when I hear a voice in my ear.

"I really am sorry, Ethan. That I said all those things." I turn to look at Max, and he shrugs. "It's just . . . I dunno, sometimes I'm just not sure what to say around you." I feel my face soften. Then he says, "So, are we good? And what about Bangor again?"

I haven't told Max about Kyle, and I'm not sure whether Mom will need me to stay with him. All I can do is tell Max that yes, we're good, but I have to get back to him about Bangor. I do my best to convince him that I really, really want to go, and I think he believes me.

What I don't say, about that trip to Bangor, is that there had better not be any more talk about how much better Max thinks he is than people I care about. If he cares about me, he cares about them. It has to be that way. I steal a sideways glance at his gorgeous face and silently ask the universe for the courage to stick to these convictions.

Mom drives Kyle to Bangor on Thursday afternoon for an evaluation with a shrink. Kyle is very subdued at dinner that night, more even than he's been all week. It's like it's hitting him that there's something really screwy going on in his head and he's just realizing how bad it is.

After Kyle goes up to bed, early for him, I bring my homework downstairs so Mom won't be alone. I'm at the kitchen table, iPhone at my side in case anyone (read: Max) wants to get in touch, and she's watching something on TV. When I finish I go sit in the chair beside her. She's watching something really stupid, some show she doesn't even like, and I realize it doesn't matter. It's just noise to drown out what else her brain would be telling her. I decide this might be a good time to ask about Saturday, and I'm not going to lie to her again.

When I've got her attention, I say, "I know I'm going out tomorrow night, so if you need me here on Saturday I'll do that. But it'd be great if I could spend the afternoon with a friend." I wait; will she ask for details?

"Can the two of you spend it here?" I'm straining my brain, trying to think how I can let her know that won't work, when she shakes her head. "Never mind. I can see that's not what you had in mind. I can go to the grocery store on Sunday. Who is it, Ethan?"

Nanoseconds pass like minutes. "Max Modine."

"Max? Sylvia's brother?" I nod. "What are you going to do?"

"Maybe drive around, get a burger. You know, stuff." Will she ask about his license?

She takes a hard look at me. "You like this boy, don't you, Ethan."

I look down at my hands, clasped together tightly between my knees. "Yeah." And I wait.

Finally, "I need another promise from you." I look up at her. "Promise me that you won't let anyone—and I mean anyone, I don't care how cute he is—get inside you." I feel my body jerk and find myself sitting up straight. "You look shocked; good. I'm hoping that means it hasn't already happened."

I can't speak, but I manage to shake my head.

"Promise me."

Swallow. "I promise." God, I haven't even thought of that! At least, not seriously.

"I don't want to run your life, Ethan, but I know something about young boys. I was young once, and I was no angel. But I can't face *both* my sons getting sick. I just can't...." Suddenly she's on her feet and out of the room and up the stairs. I hear her bedroom door shut.

I sit there maybe twenty minutes, watching and not watching the same stupid program that's still on the TV, before I fish out my phone.

I text Max, *we're on for sat afternoon that still cool w you?* Within minutes I get, *fab! same place?* And I reply *no my house 1:00 ok?* Then I see *fur sur but no blabbing ok*

It takes me a few seconds to realize that he means he doesn't want my mom to know who he is to me. Too late for that. But I reply, *k cu* and sign off.

Etta picks me up at five on Friday. It feels weirder than our other times together, a Friday night date with an old lady, even if that's not the insult Max made it sound like. I've dressed more Goth again for tonight; it seems appropriate, going to have dinner with someone who practically tells fortunes for a living. Looking at myself in the mirror before going downstairs, I see wrinkles in the cloth that wouldn't have been so bad a few weeks ago. My Goth stuff has found its way toward the bottom of my drawers lately.

Etta comes into the house briefly to see how Mom is doing. I know they've been on the phone already about Kyle's therapy appointment yesterday, which I gather was not particularly encouraging. He has another evaluation, different therapist, on Monday. Etta is living up to her promise.

Two is in the backseat again. I have to chuckle at the picture in my mind of either Max or Jorja sharing that space with him; maybe this is better with just me.

This time of year it's getting dark by five, or close enough, so when we finally leave the house I have no trouble promising myself to log all driving tonight in the "night" category. Etta tells me where we're going but then says we'll take the long way to log more time. She gives me a few directions, I put on my ear cuff, and we're off.

"Do you have anyone you can talk to about what's happening with Kyle?"

This throws me. In fact, I've been looking forward to *not* talking about him, not having him a couple of rooms away, not having that darkness over my head. "I don't want to talk to anyone about it. I haven't told any of my friends."

"Even so, I want you to know you can either talk to me about it or not. It's up to you, and I'm glad to hear anything you want to say. Or say nothing. But I think you should talk about it. Do you have a friend in mind?"

I don't bother to go over the list out loud. There are a few kids I call my friends. There's missing link Kenny, according to Max, anyway, and (per Max again) douchbagette Marra. And of course Jorja, the Jesus freak. But Max isn't wrong about that label. Even so, if I can talk to any of them about this, it's Jorja. Maybe. And "maybe" is all I say to Etta.

"School counselor?"

That wouldn't have occurred to me. "I'll think about it." My mind goes instead to Sylvia Modine. Could this be called science, in a pinch, if Etta's diagnosis is right?

"What about your father?" I stare at nothing for a second. *Does he even know?* She must take my silence for a *No way* 'cause before I can think how to respond she says, "Can you talk to Max?"

"About that? God, no!"

"And that's because . . ."

"That's just not the kind of conversation I want to have with Max, okay?" Only after I say this do I hear how angry my tone is. And I don't even know why. We're both quiet for a minute, and then I say, "Sorry."

"That's all right, Ethan. You're going through a very difficult time right now. I won't pester you. But I do hope you talk about this, and I hope you choose the right person. So. Is there anything else you'd like to know about where we're going?"

"I can't think of anything. Can I just drive?"

"Of course. Do you mind some music?"

"That's okay." I'm sure she'll put on something I don't like, but it's her car.

She plays with the CD changer for a minute and then the car fills with the richest, most intense voice I've ever heard. It's a woman, but her voice is kind of low. The songs are fun or sad, full of love or pain, it doesn't matter. I could listen to her forever. She pulls at something in my gut, and it's both beautiful and wrenching. When it's over I ask, "Who's that?"

"That was k.d. lang. Did you like it?"

"Yeah. Do you have any more?"

"At home, not in the car."

"Can you play that one again?"

She does. Doesn't say a word, just starts it again. And as I'm listening it occurs to me that one of the things I like about Etta is that she doesn't overreact. She doesn't make me feel silly or too young to be taken seriously. She's never treated me like anything other than another person whose life is just as real and just as important as hers. Like I'm part of her pack.

We don't talk at all after that except when Etta has to direct me. And just before we pull into the driveway I realize there is something I want to know.

"Um, what's your friend's name?"

Etta laughs. "I guess I didn't tell you, did I? It's Heidi Wolcott. I'm sure she'll prefer it if you call her Heidi."

The house is pretty far away from any neighbors, set back from the road behind some trees. We park next to a beat-up, old blue Volvo, Etta puts Two's leash on him, and I follow Etta and Two along a path of wobbly flagstones that winds every which way toward the porch. It's dark for real now, and the season for most everything but pumpkins is over, so I can't tell what *was* growing beside the path. All I can see is that there are dead plants everywhere.

There's a soft light coming through the windows, and as we step up onto the porch I try to peek inside. But the porch light is dim, and there's so much stuff scattered all over the place that I have to watch my step as we make our halting way down the long porch across the front of the house toward the door. I see what looks like a bronze moon crescent dangling from within another circle that's got spikes on it, and then I realize it's the moon inside the sun, and the whole thing is suspended like a mobile from the porch ceiling. There are flowerpots and planters all over the floor, some with dead stuff still in them, others empty and stacked into crooked, unstable columns on a bench beside an old wooden rocking chair.

Something catches at my hair and I say, "What the . . ." But it's only a fake spider web, and as I look up I see a huge fake spider with a Day-Glo green spot gleaming on its belly. I'm just wondering what I've got myself into when the door ahead of Etta opens. A large woman appears, in silhouette because of all the light coming from behind her. I can make out only her rounded shape and the long, loose hair all around her head and shoulders. She says nothing, just wraps Etta in a long hug. Then, "Is this your young friend?"

I step into a room scattered with stuff that's different from what's on the porch, though the flavor is the same. Moons and stars and suns and masks are on the walls or decorating flat surfaces everywhere. There are a couple of what I guess are tapestries, one with faces all over it and the other with some kind of symbols I don't recognize. Everything about the place strikes me as the exact opposite of Etta, and I wonder how they met and how on earth they can be friends.

We go through the introductions, and Heidi tells me to call her that, just like Etta had said. Two sits quietly at Etta's feet de-

spite the fact that I see at least two cats, one with orange stripes
and one with lots of tiny black and orange freckles, walking in
curls around table legs and anything else that's on the floor.
Heidi notices that my eyes are darting everywhere, and she
laughs.

"I can see the room is distracting you, Ethan. Come, let's
move into the kitchen. Though please feel free to explore in
here as much as you want."

Yuh. It would take some exploring. But the kitchen is or-
derly, even if it has ancient fixtures and wallpaper I wouldn't
choose on a bet. And it's huge. At the far end it opens up into
another space where there's a large wooden table, chairs all
around it—each one different from the others, but all wood—
and beyond that is this ginormous fireplace with all kinds of
tools and pots and things around it. I turn back to the kitchen
area to make sure there's really a stove, and there is. Not a new
one, for sure, but at least Heidi doesn't cook everything in that
fireplace. Though it looks like she could.

The whole time I'm looking around, Heidi is talking. "Don't
let the porch and the parlor fool you, Ethan. I mean, I had lots
of fun hunting down all those things that play off of what people expect to see when they come here. Don't get me wrong; I
love them all. I'm sure Etta told you that I do astrology readings, and I take our cosmic environment very seriously. But I
also like to have fun with it."

One phrase stands out for me. "What do people expect to
see?"

"Why, all that kind of stuff that you found so distracting. I do
readings, like I said, but not just astrology. I also work with energy, helping people figure out where theirs is stuck or dark or
too intense, and then helping them shift it or release it. I have
a room where I work with my clients, and it's not cluttered with
whimsy and paraphernalia, but people who come for my services expect to see that stuff. Or most of them do. Some of
them get the joke. They know it's for show, and that it's fun.
But a lot of people ask about some of the objects in these
hushed, serious tones. Sometimes it's everything I can do not

to laugh! But that wouldn't be fair when, I mean, after all, I tempted them. I set them up."

In the light of the kitchen I can see her hair is dark brown shot through with silver threads, and there's a shock of solid silver hair falling in waves beside her right eye. Somewhere in the wavy strands are dangle earrings of multicolored glass beads; it's hard to make out what the design is. And she's dressed in what I guess is a caftan, lemon yellow background with soft orange and dark red designs all over it. A few fingers and one of her thumbs have silver rings on them, different styles. My ear cuff fits right in here.

There's a sudden noise from the front room, followed by the sound of dog nails on wood floors. Etta sets a bowl of dog food down in the corner. "Sounds like the cats are keeping Two in line." And sure enough, Two comes trotting in, a look on his face that says, *Cat? What cat? I didn't see no stoopit cat.*

I'm confused. "But—he's a pit bull. Wouldn't he just eat one of the cats for dinner?"

"He does and I'll eat him tomorrow!" Heidi is grinning, but I think she's half serious. "Ethan, Two is well trained. He knows curiosity is one thing, but killing something is another matter. He's not the pack leader. Etta is. She's One." She gives Etta a look I can't quite interpret, and I'm feeling like an idiot for not having figured that out already. "Shall we sit down? I think everything's about ready."

There's a lot of food, but most of it doesn't look much like what I get at home. And it smells different, too. Etta says, "I didn't warn you, did I? Heidi is a vegetarian. But wait till you taste everything. Very unusual."

So much for her threat of eating Two. Heidi gives a brief description of each dish before she offers it. The only one I turn down is something with okra in it. I'm willing to try new things, but I have my limits. In the end, I think my favorite is something I have three helpings of—this eggplant bulgur casserole with cumin, a flavor I don't remember having in any of Mom's cooking.

Heidi asks me a bunch of questions about school, especially

science. But, really, they're more like questions about the other kids in class.

"How many of them do you think reject evolution the way your friend Jorja does?"

The fork I'm lifting to my face hangs in midair. "What do you know about Jorja?"

Etta says, "I hope I didn't break any confidences, Ethan. The only thing I said was that Jorja is staunchly evangelical Christian and that she was having a hard time accepting secular realities."

Heidi nods. "It might surprise you, Ethan, but a lot of people are concerned about the rift developing in your town. There's some conflict in the other two towns the school board serves, but for some reason it's worse where you live. And Jorja seems to have been the canary in the mine. An early warning sign. A lot of people know about Jorja's reaction in your American History class, and Mrs. Glasier's teens have been quite active."

I'm blinking like a dolt. "Active?"

Etta says, "You haven't noticed?" I shake my head, and she laughs. "Ethan, I know you're a little, um, distracted lately, but—really."

I assume she means Max, but then there's Kyle, too. "Why? What have they done?"

"Well, for one thing, they had a sit-in at Bob Coffin's house. Your history teacher. They sat around his house just outside the property line all last weekend, taking turns, reading scripture and holding up signs that say things like, 'Dead atheist: All dressed up with no place to go.'"

Last weekend . . . I'd been with Max on Saturday, out all day Sunday. She'd called me three times Sunday afternoon; was she trying to get me to join the sit-in?

Heidi says, "I expect it won't be long before they turn their attention to the house where Sylvia Modine is renting an apartment. And she's been such a help to you, Etta! She's talked an awful lot of folks into putting signs in their yards." She turns to me. "And I hope you'll be willing to help Etta replace some of those roadside signs someone's been stealing."

"Stealing?" This was news to me. And, really, I should have

noticed this; I mean, not only did one of them disappear from my own yard, but also there probably isn't one sign with Etta's name on it that I didn't have something to do with, as long as it's not in someone's yard. And Sylvia's been helping? "How have I missed all this?"

Heidi shakes her head. "I couldn't tell you that, but I can tell you that you won't be missing it much longer."

"What d'you mean?"

She looks at me a second, like she's trying to figure out what she can say. "I don't have any specifics for you. But I can tell you that you're going to find yourself in a place where you'll be pulled from both sides, and you'll have to figure out how to go up to get out of the tension."

"How . . . how do you know that?"

Etta starts to say something, but Heidi touches her wrist and says to me, "I see two poles, deep in the ground, with you in between. Around your waist is a long, tough elastic that's wrapped around one pole, and from the other direction there's one from the other pole around you. The closer you get to one pole, the tighter the pull gets back to the other one. Both poles are wrong for you. And you'll have to go up—escape from them—to find the right place for you."

Everyone has stopped eating. As soon as I can break my eyes from Heidi's intense gaze, I look at Etta. Has she told Heidi about the duck blind? Does Heidi know that I don't want to be pulled anyplace, by anyone?

When I look at Heidi again, she's frowning. "Ethan, you have a brother?" Well, this she could have heard from Etta, or from anyone. I nod and lift one shoulder. "Is he going through some trouble right now?"

Etta says, "Ethan, I said nothing about Kyle to Heidi."

"I'm sorry." Heidi shakes her head. "I have no right to question you. It's just that suddenly there was this kind of dark feeling."

I ask, "Is it gone?"

Heidi closes her eyes, waits briefly, and says, "No."

"Excuse me a sec." I get up and go into that front room with all the weird stuff where I have some privacy, I fish out my iPhone, and I call home. Mom answers. I can hear the TV in the background. I say, "Hey. Just thought I'd call to see how things are."

"No change as far as I know," she tells me. "Why? Do you know something I don't?"

I don't know what to say to that, and she says, "Hang on. I'm going upstairs." She keeps the phone with her, and I can hear her feet landing on the stairs and her breathing; she's in a hurry. Then there's silence, and a weird sound. It's Kyle's voice, sort of. Then I hear Mom again. "Kyle, what are you doing?" It sounds like she sets the phone down.

"Mom?" I nearly shout. "What's going on?" But she doesn't answer.

I can hear her voice and Kyle's, but I can't quite tell what they're saying. Then I hear her say, "And don't do that again! How do you expect the thing to heal?" Silence. And then, "Are you hearing me, Kyle?"

"I hear you."

It sounds like she picks the phone up. "Now get up off the floor. Maybe you should just go to bed now." There are sounds I can't quite make out, and I yell into the phone. Mom says to me, "Yes, Ethan, I hear you." There are footsteps, probably as she heads for the stairs. "It's just your brother, on the floor in there, chanting some nonsense. Bible verses."

"What about his hand?"

"He was holding his right arm up in the air. Don't know how long he was like that, but it wasn't easy for him to let it down again. Hang on; I'm just going to make sure he got up." I wait, and then, "Yeah, he's okay. He's lying on his bed now."

"Mom, do you need me to come home?"

"And what would you do, I'd like to know? Sit there and watch him? Don't be silly. Enjoy your evening. You can tell me all about it when you get home."

"K."

"Ethan? Thanks for calling."

I stand there a minute, staring around the room at colors

and shapes and clutter, seeing nothing except Kyle's back where he sits on the floor of his room, his bandaged right hand held high in the air.

When I get back to the table, Etta and Heidi are talking about a town hall meeting that I didn't even know about, with both Etta and Carl Phinney. "Whose idea was that?" I ask.

Etta answers. "Mrs. Glasier's, it seems. I didn't want to accept, but I'm afraid that if I don't people will interpret it as giving up on the election. Even though it's not true, it would have the same effect. So I'll have to do it."

Mrs. Glasier. The one who'd told Mom, *We'll see about this.* "When?"

"Wednesday."

I nod; my usual thing would be not to go, but I feel pulled, just like Heidi has said. I look at her. "Is my brother going to be okay?" I feel my throat tighten, and I'm angry with myself for feeling weak, for asking the question. I feel like a helpless little kid, and I hate it.

"I'm afraid I can't tell the future, Ethan. Not exactly. And I can't even get impressions by looking for them. They come when they're ready. When I'm ready. Etta told me a little about his situation while you were in the other room. Is he all right at the moment?"

I'm thinking about just saying, *Yeah, he's fine,* but somehow I think she'd know I was lying. "He was sitting on the floor in his room with his hand stuck in the air. Mom made him lie down. Wait . . . how did you know I called home?"

Heidi and Etta exchange an odd look, and then Heidi says, "It seemed likely."

I decide that wasn't too big a leap and chalk it up to putting two and two together. Plus, they could probably hear me shouting *Mom!* from the other room.

Dessert is great; it's dark chocolate pudding in these tiny little dishes, with whipped cream. Etta tells me Heidi isn't vegan, so I guess the cream is okay. When Heidi puts the little pot down in front of me I'm thinking, *Wow, that's not much.* But it's rich, so when Heidi offers me thirds I have to say no, thanks.

Heidi smiles at me for nothing that I can figure and goes into another room. Etta gets up to clear, and I start to help, but she says, "Stay put, Ethan. Heidi has something for you." She's still in the other end of the kitchen at the sink when Heidi comes back. She has a toy stuffed animal with her, a bat. It has an oblong gray body, slightly plush, and long black wings made out of felt or something. Tiny black felt ears are sewn onto the head, and the eyes are thick knots of black threads. In the middle of its back there's a black loop, like you could hang the thing from the ceiling. Heidi sets it down on the table, facing me.

I stare at it. "What's this?"

"Your bat. It's for you. We could meditate to see if a different animal comes to you—usually the power animal comes to you, not the other way around—but I feel strongly that Bat would be very good for you right now. As a power animal the bat represents adaptability, helping you take stock of your surroundings and figuring out the best direction to go in. With its power, you'll be able to identify barriers and dangers that might not be immediately obvious, the way the bat uses echolocation to avoid hitting what it wants to miss and finding what it needs to eat. And it knows how to go up." She stops and looks at me.

I don't know what to do with this, so I just say, "Thanks."

She laughs. "I can tell this is the first time you've heard of power animals. Am I right?" I nod, and she says, "Shamans, or people like me who make connections between the physical and spiritual worlds, see everything as having life, power, and wisdom. Power animals represent sources of help and strength, using their own characteristics to support and protect us. You might have more than one power animal at a time, but I think that right now, Bat is for you, Ethan. This is a pivotal time for you. I sense that you're about to go through some kind of transformation, and you'll need to use senses you might never have used before to figure out the best way through it. The beauty of a power animal is that it helps you get through difficulties and come out the other side even more truly yourself than when you went in."

Etta comes back to the table, wiping her hands on a towel. I ask her, "What's your power animal?"

"I've had a few animals help me in my life, but the most consistent has been the dingo. The Australian wild dog."

"What does it do for you?"

"The dingo is bold but also suspicious, or wary. It's independent, and it uses instinct to find the best path and make the right decisions without giving up its intelligence. And it has the power to adapt well to changing situations. Remember I told you that I have dingo tracks on my shoulder?"

"Oh, right! Your tattoo." She nods, and I look at Heidi. "Do you have a power animal?"

"Oh, Lord, yes! I've been so lucky, and many animals have traveled with me. But like Etta, I have a predominant one. The fox. It's helped me learn to be less blunt, more subtle in the way I approach things and people, in the way I speak." She laughs. "I'm afraid I need more lessons there, though! The fox knows how to use the shoulder times, dawn and dusk, to assess things from a position of camouflage, figure out which way the wind is blowing and who else is on the move, and make creative decisions that help shape what happens."

And because Max spends so much time in the front of my mind, I ask, "What about the junco? Can that be a power animal?"

"It can, indeed. Why do you ask?"

"A friend of mine says juncos are following him."

Heidi blinks at me. "Really? My. Well, the junco has powers, but if it's forcing its way into your friend's life it may be trying to warn him. With the junco, I think the warning would be to take stock of the way he's expressing himself. Warning him that perhaps he's talking just to hear himself speak, or that he's using words—chatter—to disguise his true nature. Perhaps even from himself."

I pick up my bat and examine his ears. Each one is sewn in a little curl, very neatly done. Focusing my eyes on the shape, my mind is trying to focus and trying *not* to focus on what the junco might be telling Max. What is there about his true nature that he'd want to hide? Being gay, or something other than that? And are words Max's duck blind?

Etta says, "I've got to get this young man home. Ethan, would you call Two into the front room and put his leash on him?"

"Won't he follow us out to the car?"

"There are coyotes in the area, and I don't want to take any chances that he'd go after them."

I grab my bat and slap my thigh, looking at Two where he's curled up in a corner on a large, flat pillow that looks like it's there just for him. He gets up and follows me to the front room, and I put his leash on him. He looks up at me like he's smiling, eyes half shut, mouth open and tongue hanging out. I rub the fur on his head and behind his ears, and he grins even more. I chuckle; some holy terror he turned out to be.

In a couple of minutes Etta and Heidi come into the room. Heidi gives me a long hug.

"Thanks for the bat, and for dinner," I say when she lets me go.

She smiles at me. "The bat has another power I think you're going to need. He'll help you face your fears. And because he isn't fooled by what things looks like, he'll be able to help you determine the real nature of something that looks huge and fierce but that might not be as bad as it seems."

Etta takes the leash, and as we head back to the car I watch for coyotes. Don't see any.

On the drive home, I ask Etta about the town hall. She says, "I'm not looking forward to it. I mean, it makes sense on the surface of things. But this issue is even more divisive than I thought. I'm a little afraid of what I'll face from the audience."

"What are you afraid of, exactly?"

"I think I'm afraid because I don't know how bad it could get, so I don't know how to prepare myself. I've been getting the most horrid letters. People I've known for years, people who've been cordial or even helpful to me, are writing the most awful things. And there have been phone calls."

For a second, as I picture her standing in her kitchen on the phone and looking distressed on that day the coyotes appeared, I almost forget I'm driving and that I have to pay attention to the road. "Like, who? What are they saying?"

"I'm not sure I should tell you who, Ethan. That wouldn't be fair to you. But some of what they're saying . . . Most of them are just stupid, as far as I'm concerned. Plagues from God, hellfire, that sort of thing. One person called me Satan, which I took as a compliment. Without Satan, man wouldn't know good from evil, because he'd never have eaten from that famous tree. But a few of them have sounded a little violent. One was actually a death threat, though of course I don't take it seriously. It's disturbing, all the same."

Again: How have I been missing all this? "Wow," is all I can say.

"Don't let it worry you, Ethan. And no one has mentioned you at all, by the way."

I'm about to ask why they might, but then I realize it's because of the signs I've helped with, and maybe some people know she's been helping me rack up driving hours.

We're going back the long way, just like we came, and I've just rounded a bend on the narrow road when the headlights catch on something that looks almost bright against the blackness of the country night. I brake, and suddenly Two's head is practically on my shoulder—not because of my stopping short, but because of what he sees. Maybe a hundred feet in front of us there are about seven coyotes, spread out enough so they're taking up the whole road. They don't move. And they're staring at the car like they're considering tearing it apart for fun.

"Go forward slowly, Ethan," Etta says. "Don't turn the wheel, just go straight. They'll move out of the way." Her voice is calm, but Two answers her with a long, deep growl. I can sense how tense his body is without seeing it.

It's not like they can hurt us, inside the car, I tell myself. I ease forward, and they give way grudgingly, like they want to let us know they aren't afraid of us. Two, still growling, moves around the backseat to look out first one window and then another, like he's making sure they stay outside and he's prepared to make them.

As we get through the pack I check them out in the rearview

mirror. They've turned so they can watch us. They haven't moved otherwise. I pick up speed, glad to leave them behind.

"Wow. Now I see why you wanted to make sure you had Two on his leash."

"They're amazing animals, but I can't say I like it when they act in such a brazen way."

"You didn't shoot the one fighting with Two."

"No. I would have, if I'd had to, but I really don't want to kill them."

"Are they a power animal, too?"

"A potent one. They represent a kind of balance, too, though not quite like the yin-yang. They are deadly serious, and they're also tricksters. They remind us of the karmic nature of the universe: what you do to others will become yours."

"What goes around, comes around?"

"Something like that."

Suddenly it surprises me how seriously I've taken Heidi's power animal theory. "Do you buy that stuff?"

"Yes and no. What I see is that the power we ascribe to these animals is directly in line with how we perceive them. But if we focus on the characteristics we see in them, it can benefit us just by virtue of us reminding ourselves what will help us."

"So why are juncos following Max?"

"So it's Max, is it? I thought it might be. That question I can't begin to answer."

I'm thinking she might ask me why *I* think they're chasing him, based on what Heidi has said about them, and while I want to talk about Max I don't want to focus on that question.

She doesn't go there. "Did you enjoy meeting Heidi?"

"Sure. I love that front room. And she sure is a good cook."

Etta laughs. "I was sure you were going to take a third chocolate pot de crème."

It's nearly eleven by the time I get home. Etta drops me off and tells me to say hi. Mom is half dozing in front of the TV, an ashtray full of cig butts and an empty pretzel bag on the table beside her. "Did you have good time?"

I grin and hold up the bat. "Meet my power animal." I toss

him toward her and then, oddly, regret it. Like I've treated him too lightly, Coyote's warning in my mind: What I do to others will be done to me. And if Heidi is even half right about the bat's powers, I need them all. "I'm thinking his name is Edgar."

Mom looks at him a second and tosses him back. I try to hide the fact that I stroke his head in apology. Mom says, "What's that for? Did Etta give you that?"

"Her friend Heidi did." I sit in a chair and tell her a little about power animals, but I know I don't have her attention until I mention the coyote pack.

"Honestly! Those things are getting entirely too bold. I'm not one for slaughtering wildlife just because it's inconvenient, but those creatures worry me. I heard about someone walking his dog in the woods who was followed for nearly half a mile by a pack of them. He had to head toward a major road to get away from them. He was terrified. So was the dog."

I'm glad I never told her about Two protecting me from them. She has enough to worry about. "How's Kyle?"

She looks at her watch. "As of twenty minutes ago he was snoring lightly. I left the door open some, so be quiet when you go up."

I nod. "Um, did you know Etta was getting hate mail?"

Mom sits up straighter on the couch. "Yeah. She mentioned it and asked me if I'd rather she didn't take you driving anymore. Concerned for your safety. I told her not to worry. That okay with you?"

"Sure."

"I've known most of these people all my life, Ethan." She sighs. "I can't believe any of them would hurt you. But I also can't quite believe they'd write those letters. Did she tell you what was in them?"

"A little. They don't mean anything though, right?"

She smiles, but it seems fake. "Let's hope not! Why don't you get ready for bed now, honey." *Honey.* First time she's called me that in a while. "What time are you and Max getting together tomorrow?"

Max. My pulse quickens just hearing his name. "He's coming by around one."

"He's driving?"

"Yeah." I wait. Will she put her foot down?

"I looked into this, Ethan. If he gets caught, you don't suffer; it's all on him. That is, as long as you aren't driving, which I *know* you won't do." She gives me a heavy look. "But tell me this, and tell me honestly. Do you trust his driving?"

I think back to our drive to Bangor. "Actually, yeah."

"So you've gone driving with him before?"

Trapped. I shrug and grin. "Once. He didn't pull any stunts, or drive fast—nothing like that."

She gets to her feet; it looks like an effort. "Good. Just leave your phone on in case I need to reach you. And remember your promise of the other day. Now, good night. Give me a hug."

Before I head for the stairs it hits me that I haven't seen her do anything fun lately. I wasn't that wild about her going out with Jimmy Korbel, but at least she went out. Maybe she's having second thoughts about kicking Dad out? If so, she needs to take action, or Connie will move in. I decide I have to ask. "You haven't seen Jimmy again, have you?"

She plunks back down onto the couch. "Mr. Korbel and I do not see eye to eye, I've realized. Mind you, I could have tolerated the difference of opinion, but he, evidently, could not."

"What opinion?"

She looks at me like she's wondering if I've lost my head, but she just says, "He can't tolerate that I'll fight to keep people from bringing the Bible into the classroom."

I blink at her. "And . . . he doesn't want to see you anymore because of *that?*" As much as I'd rather have my parents together than not, this seems crazy to me.

"Not only Jimmy. It might have escaped your notice, what with all the goings-on with your brother, but Nancy Hyde won't speak to me. Or Jeannine Stevens, either. Seems my letting them know that Etta could use their support stretched a lifetime of friendship too far." She takes a shaky breath. "So it's good that you're going out with friends, Ethan, because you're the only one who seems to have any right now."

She turns away from me like she's looking for the remote control, but I'm sure it's so I won't see her face. Nancy Hyde has been Mom's best friend since, like, high school. I can't believe this stupid ID stuff would make Nancy turn against Mom! ID. That's part of BIID. Which makes you want to shed something that really belongs to you. With you. Like best friends.

I want to say something, like, *How can she do that? Doesn't she know how much you need her right now?* or *How could she let something like this come between you?* or *Some friend she turned out to be!* But I'm afraid that would only make things worse.

Instead of any of that, I ask, "Does Mrs. Hyde know about Kyle?"

Mom won't look at me. I'm sure she's either crying or trying not to. "Yes. Go to bed, Ethan."

I head for the stairs and climb slowly, racking my brain for something comforting to say, working through wild scenarios where I go to Nancy Hyde and confront her. I can't come up with anything sensible, except that I wish I'd mentioned Etta when Mom said we have no friends. Etta is definitely a friend. At least, I think of her that way, and I feel sure Mom does, too. But that won't quite make up for Nancy.

I peek in at Kyle's room. The light from the hall is just strong enough that I can see what Mom probably saw the last time she checked. I head to my room and nearly jump as my phone beeps at me. I tuck Edgar under an arm and pull the phone out of my pocket as I close the door to my room behind me.

Max! Of course. It says, *can u chat? have u heard the news?*

I respond, *chat yes news no what is it?*

rocks thru all windows sylvia's apt 1 with note

saying?

go back to city take darwin with you

Well, this is creepy. It's just like Heidi said. I type, *man, weird. she ok?*

yeah shaken up staying with folks for now just wanted u to know cu tomorrow

And my stroke of genius: *dream of me*

always do

I'm in love. I'm definitely in love. And my sheets could have told a tale that night.

Chapter 8

Saturday morning I wake up to the sound of Kyle and Mom arguing. What else is new? They're in the bathroom, where I gather she's changing the bandage on his hand. He's complaining that he wants to do it, and Mom's refusing to let that happen.

I get up and move silently toward the open door; I haven't seen his hand, just bandages. And after I peek around the corner of the door frame, I wish I hadn't. You can tell it's a hand, but just barely, through the bruises and dried blood where unhealed wounds have bled a little. I see puffy skin around what look like deep cuts, and dark spots where he must have stabbed it with something. The whole thing is swollen and misshapen. I have to step back quickly and lean on the wall for support, trying not to gasp loudly enough to let them know I saw. I couldn't say why, but it occurs to me that it's easier for Mom if she thinks I don't know how bad it is.

The image of that mutilated hand stays with me through breakfast so that I'm almost glad to go up to my room and do a little homework. Kyle is in the living room at the computer, supposedly doing some of the homework the school is sending to help him stay with his classes, while Mom runs a short errand. Even though I know she won't be gone very long, I keep tiptoeing to the top of the stairs, creeping down just far enough so that I can see Kyle's back where he sits at the computer, pecking at the keyboard with the fingers on his left hand. For all I know, there's not much that would stop him going for kitchen knives and doing God knows what to that offending member he's so convinced is causing him to stumble.

BIID. I can't remember what that stands for now, but I sure as hell remember what people who have it do to themselves. My stolen sight of his hand will make sure I don't forget *that.*

Nothing horrible has happened by the time Mom gets back. I go downstairs when I hear the car, and she comes in with stuff from the pharmacy—probably more bandage material. She throws her coat—not the shearling, not cold enough for that yet—at the closet door, obviously furious about something.

She looks right at me. "Did you know what happened to Sylvia Modine? To her windows?"

"Max texted me late last night. She's staying with her folks for now."

"Were you going to tell me?"

I shrug, not sure why she's mad at me. I counter, "Were you going to tell me about Etta's signs getting stolen, and the hate mail, and the town hall? I wasn't hiding anything. It just happened last night, and I found out after I went upstairs."

She takes a few audible breaths. "I'm sorry, Ethan. It's just that it's all so stupid."

Kyle, who has moved quietly toward us, says, "It's not stupid. They're just expressing their opinion. They're allowed to do that."

Mom wheels on him but then forces herself to speak calmly. "Kyle Poe, shame on you. That's violence, not 'opinion.' They threw rocks through every last window in the place Sylvia Modine calls home. She had to leave. If someone did that here, would you defend them as 'expressing an opinion'?"

Kyle turns away and goes back to the computer.

Mom turns her glare back to me, but it's not at me any longer. "And that's not all! Did you see—what did I do with it— have you seen any of these?" She bends over to dig in her coat pocket and comes up with a crumpled red paper. "It was on my car windshield." She shakes it in my direction. It has a crude drawing of what is probably supposed to be Etta's face in thick black lines, and underneath is a lot of typing, also in bold black. I take it so I can figure out what it says. It's something vague about how by supporting evolution, Etta is by some association that isn't clear to me supporting the ACLU, which according to this, supports NAMBLA, which it says is the North American Man / Boy Love Association. I can feel my face crumbling into confusion before I even look up at Mom.

"Can you *believe* that?" she squeaks. "Of all the confounded, idiotic, asinine—words fail me."

"What's NAMBLA?"

"It's a sick group of people who think it's okay for adult men to have sex with young boys. That's not the point. The point is—the point is that there is no point! How in God's name they made that connection has got to go into the *Guinness Book of World Records* for the most labyrinthine logic of all time."

I decide not to ask what "labyrinthine" means. I can sort of work it out. But she's really upset. "Mom, do you want me to stay?" And, surprising myself, I actually mean it. Much as I want to be with Max, right now I don't know whether I'm more worried about Kyle or Mom. She can't do this alone, and right now all she has is me.

She wraps me in a hug that lasts maybe ten seconds. Then she pats my arm, not looking at me, and says, "Ethan, you go. Have a good time. Just don't drive, and keep your promise. Come back to me whole and healthy." Still keeping her face turned away, she picks up her coat, hangs it in the closet, and then goes upstairs with the plastic bags full of gauze and antibiotic ointment.

Max is late. Again. At first I'm wondering if this is going to be a thing with him, but then I think maybe today it has more to do with what happened to Sylvia. Even though I want to support Mom, just sitting in the house waiting for Max gets on my nerves too much. I put on the silk shirt Max bought me on our last excursion, and then my black leather jacket, knowing the pea coat would be better for hanging around outside waiting but wanting to be in the leather for Max. I walk up and down the driveway a few minutes and then my iPhone rings. It's not a number I recognize, but I answer, anyway. It's Max, saying he'll be another few minutes. I could go back in, but I don't want to. And then I get an idea. I punch some numbers into my phone. My dad answers.

"Whatcha up to, kid?" I don't make my usual reply, so he says, "Ethan? You okay?"

"I'm fine, Dad. I just didn't know whether you'd heard about Kyle. Has Mom called you?"

Slight pause. "No. What's wrong with Kyle?" He sounds both angry and anxious.

"I guess they're still trying to figure that out for sure, but he might have this disease." He doesn't speak, just lets me explain as much as I can.

When I fall silent he says, "How is he now?"

I take a deep breath. "Um, well, his hand is pretty bad. He has to keep it bandaged. Mom does that. And he's taking antibiotics. He saw one therapist last week, and he'll see another this week. Kind of evaluations, like. You know?" I keep hoping something fatherly will kick in and he'll take over the conversation, but there's more silence. I imagine him grinding his jaw.

Finally he says, "Ethan, thank you for telling me. Are you sure you're all right?"

"Yeah. Fine. I mean, it's weird, and I'm trying to help Mom, you know. But I'm okay."

Another short pause, and then, "Okay. I gotta hang up now."

I say "Bye" into a hang-up click.

Now I'm a little scared. Mom hadn't told him, and I'm sure I've just made things worse between them. But—damn it, he should know! If I had something wrong with me like Kyle does, *I'd* want Dad to know!

I think.

Anyway, he knows now, and Mom's going to tear me a new one when she finds out. Which will probably happen while I'm out with Max. Fortunately I don't have to stand there shivering and getting more terrified by the second for very long; the white Sequoia appears like a glorious steed. I slide my ear cuff on, get into the car, and Max whisks me away.

I'm thinking we should kiss or something, but Max just smiles and then backs out of the driveway again. Once we're on the road he says, "Bangor again?" and gives me this sexy look. "Same detour?" I've noticed already that the back of the car is prepared.

I'm amazed and a little ashamed at how easy it is for me to respond to this suggestion. The first response is purely physical, and I nearly have to adjust my jeans. "You bet." Then, when I've given that some space, I say, "How's Sylvia doing?"

"She's being Sylvia. Which is to say she's acting like she wasn't scared shitless last night, which she was. She's all furious now, going on about how she'll show them they can't frighten her, on and on. My folks are still scared, but she refuses to be. My dad took her to go get some more of her stuff. The window repair will have to come out of her security deposit, if that even covers it all, and meanwhile it's cold as shit in there."

His iPhone rings, and he fishes it out of his pocket. It's not the same one he'd had just last weekend; this explains the number I didn't recognize. He doesn't say much, and when he hangs up he says, "The folks want me back by five." He sort of chuckles. "We'll see."

"New phone?"

"Yeah. You should save the number I called you from earlier. This is the latest phone, probably just like yours. Did a hand-me-up with the old one."

"You mean hand-me-down?"

He looks at me like I'm an idiot. "No, dummy. There's no one I'd hand it down *to*. I let Sylvia have mine. She didn't have a cell at all, and with things like they are she might need one."

Here we go again. I want to ask, *Is this chatter? Are you hiding behind all this hip talk? And does it make you feel good when you say things I don't get?* Instead I say, "Seen any juncos lately?"

He turns to me for just a sec, something like fear in his eyes. "How did you know about that?"

"You mentioned it last week. They came and sat on the car after . . . you know. Have there been more of them?"

"For real. I went out onto the back deck this morning to get away from the tension in the house. There were no birds there when I went out. And suddenly there's all these juncos. And they're all males. Even Sylvia thinks it's freaky now."

"D'you have bird feeders?"

He shakes his head. "Haven't put them out yet. My folks always wait until Thanksgiving for that. Something about not wanting to convince birds to stay if they ought to migrate, but the ones that stay will need food. I don't know why they care. So, anyway, these little gray birds appear, one or two at first, but then it's like Hitchcock. They flutter down to the floor of the deck and peck at nothing, surrounding me. I shooed them away once, but they came back. That's about when I decided to go back in."

"They didn't peck at you or anything though, right?"

"Just hopped around me. Anyway, d'you wanna go back to This Time For Sure? Maybe there'll be another one of those silk shirts." He jerks his chin toward my chest. "I see you're wearing the one I got you last week. Maybe in black this time?" His grin makes me forgive him for any amount of making me feel dumb. "You would look fabulous in a decent black shirt."

We take the same detour as last time. Max leaves the engine running so the heat stays on, and we get into the back again. I come first this time, then him, but then we don't get back in the front seat right away. Instead, he has me lie down on my stomach, ass exposed, while he runs a finger softly around my tat, which is essentially healed now.

"Gorgeous," he says quietly.

"Looking great, isn't it."

He chuckles, low and sexy. "Yeah, but that's not what I was admiring."

The next thing I know, it's not his finger on my tat, it's his mouth. The contrast between his tongue and his teeth, first one and then the other and on and on, makes me hard again. He's kneading the other side of my ass with his hand, and pretty soon I can't stifle a groan. He laughs again and turns me over.

Now, mind you, I'm already well aware of that thing I've heard called a taint—that strip of skin behind my balls. But this is the first time anybody else has touched it. Max grabs a towel just in time, laughing in what sounds like delight. And then he's kissing me.

We lie there like that for a long time, touching each other everywhere, kissing and kissing. Max starts to doze a little at one point, and I watch his face, the beautiful mouth, the soft hair at his temples. Then there's an odd shadow overhead, and I see a small bird has landed on the glass of the sunroof. Then there are two of them, their creamy underbellies giving away that they're juncos. A few of them must be landing on the hood, judging from the sounds I'm hearing.

I shift my position a little to try and see the hood, and Max wakes up. He shouts, "Fucking birds!" They all take off at once. "Did they crap on the car?"

He scrambles into his jeans and shoes and jumps out of the car, walking around it, examining the finish. Doesn't look like he finds anything. Back in the car he grins at me. "Hold me, charmer. I'm freezing! Warm me up."

I have to undo his jeans to do the job right.

Back on the road, I tell him about my dinner with Heidi and Etta. I'm just about to get to the part where Heidi seemed to know something was wrong at home when I realize he's not really listening. I back off of what I was going to tell him about power animals. I need to make sure he heard me the other day, about my friends being my friends.

"Etta's helping me, y'know. It was great night driving time. I logged maybe half of what I need."

Silence for a second, and then, "That's good."

I guess I have to give him credit for trying. I try a change of topic. "Hey, did you hear about the sit-in at Coffin's house?"

"Of course. That's old news."

Another step disappears out from under me. "Not that old."

"Your mascary friend Jorja was the ringleader."

"Mascary?"

"Um, sorry if that came out wrong. It's like way too much crap around her eyes."

Can't exactly argue with that, but the other accusation isn't true. "It wasn't Jorja. It was Mrs. Glasier."

"Not what I heard. Oh, the Glasier witch was there, all right, but Jorja led most of the chanting. Shouted loudest, is what I heard."

"Anyway . . ." I can't think of anything to say next.

"No biggie. Coffin can take it. At least they didn't smash his windows."

"You going to the town hall meeting?"

"You kidding? Why? Who wants to see a couple of people yell at each other about some school election?"

"Etta's been getting hate mail."

This gives him pause for a second or two. "Really."

"Death threats, some of them." For some reason, I want to impress him. I want him to know I'm not a dope, that I'm up on what's going on, too.

He says, "So, is this the same thing as with Sylvia? I mean, dogma versus Darwin? Evolution? All that?"

"Must be. Phinney wants ID taught in science class. Sylvia's not exactly for that, is she?"

He gives a kind of snort. "Don't get her started. She might throw rocks, herself. Drives my folks a little batty, talking about it all the time; they just want this whole mess to go away."

"Etta's on Sylvia's side, you know. She says she wants intelligence in the classroom, not religion."

"Sounds like Sylvia, all right. Maybe they should get together."

I decide not to tell him that this has already happened, like a little secret piece of news I know that he doesn't. It occupies me a good deal of the rest of the ride to Bangor.

Max finds another double space. I don't say anything this

time, but it still seems wrong to me. Then he wants to go right
to This Time. I want to go to Shane's place first, but I don't say
anything. I just open the door instead of walking past. Max is
surprised, but he follows me in.

Shane looks up from the counter and grins at me. "Hey,
Ethan!"

"Hey."

Max comes up behind me. "What would you do if we walked
in when you were working on someone?"

"I always lock the door when I'm doing a tat, if my business
partner isn't here. Can't risk being interrupted." He looks back
at me. "The cuff looks great. What can I do for you boys today?"

"I have a friend who wants a cuff, too. And I might buy another one."

"What kind of friend? What do they like?"

"She's . . . well, she's kind of Goth, but she's also Christian."

Max says, "Jorja? You sure you want to buy stuff for her?"

I ignore him. Somehow, this place is mine, not his. I don't
think too deeply about it, but I feel it deeply just the same.
Plus, on some weird level I'm thinking maybe if I'm nice to
her, she won't be such an activist. Maybe she'll stop shouting at
people. Maybe I'm trying to buy her off with gifts, but it's
worth a try.

Shane has pulled out a silver cuff with an ichthus in it where
the yin-yang is in mine. He sets it on a black velvet pad. I'm
nodding, and Shane is searching for something else. He comes
up with this plastic zipper bag that has something metal in it,
flashes of silver and blue shining from it. Then he gets out a
Styrofoam hand form stuck onto a metal bar that holds the
hand pointing up. By the time he gets the metal thing on the
form, I already know Jorja would love it.

Shane says, "Maybe the Goth side of her would like this
slave bracelet. I have a few designs, and this one also comes in
purple."

My eyes must have lit up when he said "purple," because he
grins and reaches for another plastic bag. He puts away the

blue one, and once the purple one is on the form I can't stop looking at it. Between the silver rings around the wrist and the silver ring on the middle finger is a diamond pattern of purple links and black beads. I've never seen anything like it. It's exactly up Jorja's alley, and it'll make me feel better for not wanting her to get a tat and compete with me. A sticker on it says it's twenty dollars. "I'll take it."

Max surprises me. "What other ear cuffs have you got?"

Shane narrows his eyes and looks at Max like he's thinking. Then he pulls out a plastic bowl with a bunch of cuffs and gives Max another black pad. I help him sort through them, though I sneak a gaze into the display case, wondering what else Shane might have pulled out but didn't. What I see tells me Shane has pegged Max as less daring, maybe; the cuffs Shane gave him are all pretty tame. No beads or crystals or dangles, like some of the stuff he didn't pull out.

There's one in the case that looks like it might be a spider web curled so that it would be the cuff part, with a long, thin chain down to a silver spider that must be a stud to go through a pierced lobe. I almost ask about it, but Max distracts me before I can get up enough nerve. He picks up a silver band, a narrow, shiny center going around the cuff, with tiny silver dots in a line on top of the band and below it, like margins. Shane sets the mirror near him. It takes Max a minute to get the thing on. He admires himself in the mirror and then turns to me.

"You like?"

I'm tempted to kiss him, but somehow I think he'd freak. So I just grin and nod at him. To Shane I say, "Um, what's in that other bowl?"

Shane picks up the bowl with the spider in it, and I hear Max say, "Now, that's weird stuff." But I ignore him. I reach for the spider, but just as I'm about to pick it up I see a bat. Like the spider, the bat is a stud. As I pick it up I see there's a long thin chain on this one, too, falling in a big loop to the stud from a silver cuff, which is carved to look like a tree branch. Shane sets the spider on the black pad, and I set the bat next to it.

Max says, "You're not serious."

I pick up one and then the other, and I look at Shane. He's watching me closely. Then he says, "The bat."

Something that I didn't even know was there lifts off my shoulders. I feel light, and both excited and peaceful.

Max makes a scoffing sound. "How much is that one?"

Looking at Shane, I say, "I don't care."

Shane grins at me, and I know for sure now there's some connection between us, something Max doesn't see and wouldn't understand if he did. I pay for the lot, including Max's cuff.

At This Time, Max buys himself some brown leather gloves to go with his jacket, but we don't see a whole lot more today. Or maybe we're both so focused on what we got at Shane's that we can't spare any imagination for clothes. No black shirt today, but that's okay.

We're at the counter paying for Max's gloves when the little bell over the door tinkles. I look up kind of automatically and nearly lose my balance. It's Guy.

The place is dark enough that someone just coming in has to adjust their eyes, so he doesn't see me right away, thank God, because I must have looked like a dorky little kid. By the time he's fully inside and sees me, I've recovered as well as I can.

"Ethan!" He comes over and offers his hand to shake. I'm busy taking in the jacket he's wearing, black leather but definitely not something he bought here. It looks like black butter, soft and smooth. No suit jacket under that, for sure. It's Saturday, after all. "Good to see you. I was just catching up on some work at the office. This is one of my favorite places." He barely touches the arm of my jacket. "It looks like you've shopped here before."

I'm trying to come up with something—anything—to say, when I feel Max shove me a little. "Oh, um, Guy, this is my friend Max Modine." To Max I say, "Guy LeBlanc. My mom's divorce lawyer."

I catch the look on Max's face. He's impressed. Maybe too

impressed, like he'd rather be with Guy than me. But I decide not to worry about that.

"Glad to meet you, Max." He tilts his head, sees the ear cuff. "That's unusual."

"It's an ear cuff. I have one, too," I say, immediately regretting it. Stupid, needy little kid.

Guy looks at me. "So you do! I didn't see that ear very well. Where'd you get them?"

Max says, "The tattoo parlor, next door."

I *am* irritated now; Guy is *my* find, and so is Shane! So I say, "If you stop in, tell Shane Ethan sent you."

Guy laughs, showing a gorgeous set of white teeth. "I'll do that." He starts to back away. "Say hello to your mom for me." A wave of his hand, and he disappears into the racks in back of the store.

The sound of the tinkling door, muffled behind us as we leave, follows me down the sidewalk toward the car.

Max breaks the silence. "Man, what a dick magnet! How long were you gonna keep him a secret?"

This stuns me. "Secret? There's no secret. Anyway, he's too old for us."

"Hardly!"

I don't like the direction this is going—never mind that I'd lusted after Guy myself—so I say, "Maybe he'll go looking for an ear cuff, and he and Shane will hit it off."

Max laughs. It's not a fun laugh. He's laughing *at* me. "You gotta be kidding, Ethan. Shane is *totally* not in this guy's league. Don't be a dork."

I stop in my tracks, wishing I could think of something to say to this. *Dork?*

The look on my face must tell Max he's gone too far. He wraps an arm around my neck and squeezes. I'm hoping he'll follow it up with a kiss—a quick one to the cheek would be enough—but I guess that's too daring for him.

On the way home, Max pulls into our spot again. I'm trying to sulk; I'm not real happy with him right now. But he's too gorgeous, and he has no trouble getting the right kind of rise out of me.

He's left the engine on again to keep us warm. Afterward, I'm on my back, groggy and watching the sky slowly turn to dusk. Max's hand rests on my chest. His fingers start to move, and as he walks them over to one of my tits he starts giggling and then pinches me hard.

"Hey!" My voice is soft; I don't really mind. I grab his hand with one of mine. "What's so funny?"

He frees his hand and wanders back to tender pink skin. "If there's an intelligent designer, why do men have tits?"

I strain my neck so I can look at his face. "Is there an answer, or are you saying there's no designer?"

"Oh, I think there is, actually. But the ID side won't like it." He lifts his body up and kneels as well as he can in the confined space, one leg on either side of my hips. "It's so gay guys have another body part to play with."

He proceeds to play with mine, and before long we've both come again, and I'm feeling kind of sorry for straight guys. I mean, there can't be a girl alive who would know how to get to a boy like another boy does.

When we get back on the road, I start noticing the election signs. Maybe it's because this is the first time I've been up so high on this road, in this huge vehicle, while not either gazing like a puppy at Max or trying to watch him in my peripheral vision. Anyway, there are signs for a lot of things, not just the school board seat. Just as I'd predicted, they've multiplied like roaches. Town council, state representative—everything you can think of. They look unstable on their rough-cut, raw pine sticks, even mine (I mean, Etta's), impaling the ground insecurely and tilting each at a different angle as they march in irregular formation along the scrabbly roadside. Uncut grasses and the heads of dead weed flowers crowd the sticks and partially obscure the signs.

Closer to home, where there are more houses, I see two or three signs in the front lawns. Some have Etta's name on them, and I feel an odd pride: someone else supports her enough to put up a sign in their own yard. Then I see something that makes me tell Max, "Stop!"

He brakes and turns toward the side of the road. "What? What's the matter with you?"

I throw the door open and trot to a yard maybe two hundred feet back, Max right behind me. "What is it?"

I point. There's an Etta Greenleaf sign, the one that says, RE-LIGION IS FOR CHURCHES. SCIENCE IS FOR SCHOOLS. And right next to it there's another one, looking like the people who live here made it. It says, STEAL THE SIGN AGAIN AND IT'S $50 MORE TO GREENLEAF.

Max says, "Yeah? So?" He just doesn't get it. I turn and head back to the car. "Ethan, what's with you?" Both our doors slam at about the same moment. "Well?"

I look at him, trying to figure out the best thing to say. "You know, I've been helping Etta put these signs up. People are stealing them. *Stealing* them! What the fuck do they think, that's going to make a difference?"

"Well . . . you didn't put that one up, did you?"

I heave a weary sigh. "No, of course not. It's in someone's yard. But they've been stealing them from all over. Even from our own yard."

Max looks confused. "Dude, this is just some erectoral vote, isn't it?"

"What?"

He pulls back onto the road. "You know. It doesn't mean dick."

"Ha! Ask your sister."

"Not askin' her nothin'. She's off the deep end at the moment."

"I thought you cared about this. Science makes *us* okay, remember? And religion doesn't?"

He shrugs. "I guess. Maybe I'm just getting kind of tired of hearing about it."

I'm thinking, *That's too bad, because it ain't over,* but I don't say it. I glance at the dashboard for the clock. Just after four. And suddenly something I've been pushing to the back of my mind since Max picked me up earlier crashes to the front with a painful thud. I fully expect that Dad has let it be known by now that he doesn't appreciate being left out of Kyle's life—and out of this problem that might even threaten that life. And I fully expect that Mom is going to take it out of my hide somehow that I told him.

On top of that, despite the way something delightful jumps from one part of my body to another every time I so much as glance at Max, we just don't seem to be on the same wavelength in some areas, and it's spoiling the euphoria. So what I do say is, "Listen, I should probably get back. And it's almost your curfew, too."

He lets a few seconds go by. "I was kinda thinking we'd go get a soda or something."

Maybe this would be the time to let him know what's going on; I haven't wanted to before, but it seems more serious now. To get things going, I say, "I think my mom probably needs me."

"For what?"

We're maybe four minutes from my house at this point, not enough time to tell him before we get there. "Maybe a quick stop."

We share a large order of fries with our drinks. Max gets a Diet Pepsi, which takes me a little by surprise, but I don't say anything. I mean, around here girls drink those, but not boys mostly.

I open. "So, the reason my mom needs me right now. These days, I mean." And I stop. Max, sucking on his straw, waves a hand in a circular motion, like *Go on*. I take a deep breath. "I have to ask you not to talk to anyone about this. Promise?"

He swallows. "I guess. I don't know what it is."

"It doesn't affect you, really."

"If it takes you away from me, it does."

Sometimes the wavelengths flow together. . . . "Yeah, but—hell, it's my brother. Kyle. We just don't want it spread around, you know? He has this problem." I start with the ice bag in the shed and go through all the weirdness with the fabric ropes and the work glove right up to when I saw his hand this morning. Max's eyes get wider with each new aspect of this weirdness. For my finish, I say, "So we have to keep an eye on him. And now that my dad's not around anymore, it's just Mom and me, and she can't do it all the time. She's already, like, fried. Exhausted. And it's why she got me the iPhone. So she can reach me if she needs to."

Max looks stunned. It takes him a minute before he says, "Wow. Man." And then, "Shit."

I stare down at my fingers, playing with a soggy fry, eyes focused on the spots where the grease soaked in. Somehow even telling Dad about Kyle hadn't felt quite as overwhelming as telling Max.

"Is there, you know, anything I can do?" His voice is soft.

I look up at him; he's serious. Not like it's just something you say. "I guess just understand that I need to get home. That I can't leave Mom alone too long."

He nods. "K. I'm done here. You?"

Max backs the Sequoia into my driveway. "This way no one from the house can see through the tinted glass," he says just before exploring the inside of my mouth with his tongue. God, but I could *live* in this mobile white castle with him. Then he asks if he should go in and say hi to Mom.

I don't think this is a good idea; I expect there will be yelling, at me, as soon as she hears the door open. "Maybe not today. Another time."

He makes a quick grab at the side of his head and pulls his ear cuff off, I guess so he won't be seen wearing it at home. Then he gives me one more quick kiss and I'm out. I watch him drive off, feeling lonely and scared like some little kid, knowing that inside my house a monster waits. Maybe two different monsters, if you count Kyle. And yet I have no place else to go. Just to be on the safe side, and maybe to eliminate another thing to set Mom off, I take off the bat stud and cuff and shove them into the bag in my jacket pocket.

Be with me, Edgar, I think to the bat Heidi gave me; *help me face my fears.* I close my eyes, navigating by echolocation, touch the door handle on the very first try, and open the door.

I see Mom through the doorway into the kitchen, paperwork on the table in front of her, smoke curling upward from an ashtray. She doesn't even look up. I know, somehow, that this is even worse than yelling. I stand there a minute, not knowing which direction to go in, caught between knowing I have to let Mom yell at me and being pulled upstairs as though it's a sanctuary, which it isn't really. Heidi said I'd have to find a way up to escape the elastics that pull me back and forth. I don't realize I'm staring at Mom until she turns her head. Her eyes are puffy, but the expression on her face isn't sadness. It's cold fury.

The way up, Edgar whispers to me, *is to know that what you did was right.*

I hang up my jacket, head into the kitchen, and sit down in the chair across from her. I'll let her make the first move.

She stubs out her cig. "Aren't you going to ask how your brother is?"

I know this isn't really what's on her mind; she's just trying to put me in the wrong before we even start. "Did something change?" That's as much as I'll give her.

She stares at me for a few seconds while I remind myself that if I speak first, I lose. Then, "If there's a change, it will be for the worse. And Kyle has you to thank for that."

"That makes no sense."

She stands up so fast the chair falls over behind her with a sharp thud, wood on wood. I jump just a little. She paces the kitchen once or twice and then stops a few feet from the table.

"Do you give me any credit, Ethan? Any credit at all?" I shrug; probably not the smartest move, but I don't know what she's talking about. "No? I guess I'm not surprised, given that it never occurred to you that perhaps, just maybe, there was a very good reason I wasn't bringing your idiot father into this situation with Kyle. More than one, in fact. But you don't even give me the courtesy of asking me! You don't even mention that you're going to talk to him! You just blab the whole thing. And do you know what he does? Do you?"

Her voice has been rising through this speech. I glance toward the stairs, wondering if Kyle should be hearing this.

Her voice dripping sarcasm, Mom says, "Oh, *now* you're concerned about Kyle. *Now* you're thinking maybe we should be doing what's best for him. He's out cold. I gave him a sedative. I had to. All because you couldn't keep your fucking mouth shut!"

This is too much. "What are you so mad about?" I'm about to go on, but she doesn't give me a chance.

"What am I so mad about? I'll tell you, since you're too stupid to figure it out for yourself." She paces again, hands flying through the air as she talks. "That bastard of a father of yours showed up here, unannounced, and just marched in. Didn't even knock. 'Where's Kyle?' he says. 'I want to see Kyle!' Took way too much time and way too much of my patience—something I don't have in abundance these days—to calm him down even a little. And then he hikes up the stairs and yells at Kyle, telling him what an idiot he is, telling him he's a disgrace and he needs to pull himself together and not be such a baby. Shouting at him to be a man and stop all the nonsense. In other words," and she stops and stares at me again, "he does everything the therapist said we're not supposed to do. He does it all wrong. Exactly as I knew he would."

Any confidence I have in my decision to tell him is waning fast. "What did Kyle say?"

She shrieks at me. "What do you *think* Kyle said? He went into that mumbo jumbo of his, quoting Bible verses and defending his actions with scripture. Which is exactly what the therapist said was the problem. Kyle's been using the Bible to justify these actions, which have a psychological source he isn't seeing. And all your bastard father did was push him further into his corner, while I'm paying through the nose to coax him out of it." She turns away from me, and when she turns back, her eyes are shining with tears. "Ethan! How could you *do* this?"

"I . . . I didn't know."

"Didn't know *what?*"

My breathing is odd, noisy in and out of my nose. "Look, you didn't tell me any of that. You didn't talk to me about the therapist and what he said. You didn't tell me not to tell Dad. Kyle is his son, too, you know!"

Mom picks up her chair and sits down hard on it. "Ethan, do you have any idea why I told your father to leave here in the first place?"

"He drank too much." It's the best I can do; this question takes me by surprise and I'm not sure how to respond.

"That was such a small part of it. Maybe it was the easiest for you to understand." She rubs her face with both hands. "Your father is an emotional child. He sees everything only as far as it relates to him, which means he can't put himself in someone else's shoes. He can't put his own needs or his own feelings aside long enough to consider that someone else's need might be more important right now."

"You married him."

There's a silence big enough to fall into. Finally Mom says, "You have no idea how much I regret that."

Now I'm not breathing at all. She's telling me she wishes she never had me, or Kyle. She would change her whole life if she could, and I wouldn't exist. And that would be the way she wants it. I launch from my chair and run for the stairs. My room might not be a real sanctuary, but it's sure as hell better than where I am right now.

I lock the door, even though I know she's coming after me as fast as she can, and I throw myself on the bed. She knocks quietly and says in a hoarse whisper, "Ethan! Come out. Please. You're taking that the wrong way."

I lift my head off the pillow long enough to shout, "Go to hell!"

I can hear her pushing something into the lock, trying to break in. I jump up and throw myself against the door just as she starts to open it.

"Let me in, Ethan. We need to talk. Calmly."

I struggle to keep my voice low and still make it sound ugly.

"There's nothing to talk about. You got the really shitty end of the stick, didn't you? A bastard lowlife for a husband, a psycho freak for one son, and a faggot for the other. It sure sucks to be you, doesn't it?"

The door eases shut as she controls her release of pressure on it until it closes quietly. I can barely hear her walk away and back down the stairs.

Back on my bed, staring at the ceiling and breathing deeply to fight off the tears stinging my eyes, I consider my options. Maybe I could go live with Etta. I'm part of her pack, after all. It's better than running away altogether, and better than trying to live with Dad in his one-point-five rooms over somebody's garage. And I could still be around if Kyle needed me, though obviously I'm as bad as my father as far as Kyle's concerned. I mean, didn't I just do exactly what Mom accused Dad of doing? Didn't I just decide on my own that I wanted Dad to know this, not at all considering what it could mean to Kyle or to Mom?

I squint my eyes shut and roll onto my belly. How was I supposed to know what Dad would do? How did I know he would make Kyle worse? No amount of thinking about this from Kyle's or Mom's point of view would have made me do anything else.

Would it?

Christ!

I curl my arm toward my face, and without meaning to I bring Edgar toward me like I'm hugging him. Heidi said the bat would help me through times of trouble in a way that would also make me more truly myself.

Suddenly I want my bat ear cuff. I need that feeling I got when Shane said, "The bat." It's in my jacket pocket, and that's downstairs. I stand at my door, ear to the crack; where's Mom? Can't tell, so I open the door slowly and listen again. I think I smell fresh cigarette smoke over the aroma of lasagna cooking, but I don't hear the TV, so maybe Mom's back in the kitchen, which means she'll see me. I decide not to hide, though I don't know how convincing my attempt is to move casually down the stairs and over to the closet like nothing's wrong. I don't look in any direction other than the closet door, and then at my jacket, and then at my wrist as my hand disappears into the pocket where my package is. Just as I'm turning to head back upstairs, Mom calls to me.

"Ethan. Come sit. We need to come to an agreement."

But I've already decided I'm not doing any more sitting or talking until I'm truly myself. "Just a minute." My voice sounds tight, not natural at all. She doesn't protest. I take the stairs two at a time, go into the bathroom, pull out my bat cuff, and put it on. I allow myself maybe twenty seconds to admire it in the mirror before tossing the bag with the other stuff onto my bed and heading downstairs again.

I sit in the same chair as earlier and wait. When she looks up, she opens her mouth and then pauses, staring at my ear. Then she says, "New jewelry, Ethan?"

"Max and I went to This Time For Sure. Got this at the body art place next door."

She glares at me from under her eyebrows. "Body art? You didn't get a tattoo, did you?"

"It's illegal. I'm underage." She looks unconvinced, so I add, "Mom, believe me, I didn't get any tattoos today." Partial truth is all she's going to get.

"What did Max get?"

"A plain silver band ear cuff, and he's now the proud owner of a brown leather jacket from This Time. No tattoo." Okay, so I'm not being totally honest about timelines, but, it's the best I can do. The best I'm *going* to do, anyway. I decide against mentioning her divorce lawyer.

But she's not done. "Any more piercings?"

"No."

She takes another drag on her cig, exhales, and looks hard at me. "Ethan, you and I have got to make an arrangement. We have to be a team and work together to pull your brother out of this chasm he's fallen into. And I'm sorry, but we have to leave your father out of it."

I want to ask why, to challenge this exclusion I don't really like. But if her description of what happened while I was out is at all accurate, I don't need to know more. But there's more to say. "Then you have to let me fully into it."

"What do you mean?"

"I saw you and Kyle in the bathroom this morning. I hadn't seen his hand outside of bandages before. You didn't tell me it was as bad as that. You called Dad a stupid idiot, but you called me that, too."

"When did I call you that?"

"You said I was too stupid to figure things out for myself. Y'know, I didn't hear anything the therapist said, and you haven't told me anything other than a few bare facts. You told me I had a fucking mouth." She starts to say something, but I drown her out. "And you regret having both me and Kyle." Silence. "So I guess I know where I stand on this team."

I can see tears pooling in her eyes, and it hurts. I want to feel vindication, and righteous anger. I don't. I can't.

She gets up and walks to the back door, staring out through the nine panes of glass separated by narrow strips of wood and taking a few shuddering breaths. It's maybe a full minute before she wipes her hand over her face and comes back to the table, and I know she's not crying to make me feel sorry for her. If she were, she'd have cried right there at the table. But I feel bad all the same.

"I'm sorry I said those things to you. But I'm not sorry I had you. You've always been my sweet, sweet boy. I haven't called you that; I don't expect most boys want to hear that from their mothers. But that's what you are. I don't regret for one second that you're my son. All I regret is what I had to do to get you."

She rubs her face again and I take advantage of the moment to swipe quickly at my own eyes. Then she grins at me. "I love the bat."

It's the best thing she could have said, really. That is, once she's told me she doesn't regret me. And I believe her about both things.

She takes a deep breath. "If I've kept things about Kyle from you, it was to protect you. So you need to let me know how much you're willing to hear. What would you like to know?"

"Is he going to be okay?"

"I don't know."

"That's not enough."

She sighs. "You know he's seeing another therapist next week. The first one would like to treat him, but that consists mostly of standard talk therapy and keeping him away from that church crowd. I don't know whether they've made this any worse, but they sure as hell can't make it any better." She sighs. "Evidently there's no medicinal treatment anyone's found that does any good. There are a few other kinds of therapy that have been tried, but their track records aren't any better than standard stuff."

"Is there anything special about the therapist next week?"

"She combines standard therapy with something called EMDR. I forget what it stands for, but it means she does something to make him move his eyes back and forth for half a minute a few times during the session. It's supposed to help him make cognitive connections with whatever is causing the irrational behavior."

"But . . . that doesn't work, either?"

"From what I can tell, the only thing that really works is amputation. And I've already asked about that. No one is willing to do that unless the limb is so damaged that it threatens the patient's life."

"Does this threaten his life?"

Another deep breath. "They're talking about infection. But . . . it's not unheard of for BIID sufferers to commit suicide."

We just stare at each other. Then she leans on the table, lowers her head to her arms, and sobs. I pull a chair close and do my best to hug her, but I feel so fucking helpless.

What *is* this thing my brother's got? No one will do the one thing that would make him stop hurting himself, and other than that there's nothing that will make him stop wanting it? *Fuck!*

Rock-and-a-hard-place is something I didn't really understand until this very moment. Kyle is between a rock and a hard place, and there's a pendulum swinging over his head.

I want to ask Heidi, *Which direction should Kyle go in? What's "up" for him?*

Kyle's still groggy when dinner's ready, so Mom takes his dinner up to him and stays while he eats it. Then he goes back to sleep again. Over our own dinner, Mom and I don't say much. The one thing that stands out is when she says that Kyle can't go through the rest of his life sedated. I don't say that it looks like just about the only option at the moment.

Around ten, I get a text from Max. *u ok?*

bout the same

hang in there

Chapter 9

Sunday morning Etta calls and asks if I'd like to drive to the dog park in Bangor, and Mom reminds me she needs to go to the supermarket later, so I shouldn't stay out too long. I nearly forget to put on my new bat ear cuff.

Etta notices it right away and laughs, not at me, but because she likes it. "Ethan, you do have an interesting esthetic." Two leans forward from the backseat and licks that ear.

I've never been to a dog park before, so I don't know what to expect. It's a bit overcast, with a chilly breeze. Not many leaves are still on the trees. Etta has Two on his leash as we approach the gate to the open area, and she makes him sit down quietly before she leads him in. She makes him sit quietly again inside until he looks up at her, then she rubs his head and takes the leash off.

I have to say, if I'd been there with my toy poodle, or my collie, I'm not sure I would have been thrilled to see a pit bull. Some of the smaller dogs could have been appetizers for Two. But I watch him trot forward and exchange sniffs with a few dogs, and then he's off, dashing around, playing with the other dogs—laughing, as far as I can tell.

I look at Etta, who's smiling fondly at her monster. I ask, "So, what does it mean to a dog? Socializing, I mean. That's why you bring him, right?"

"It is, though I enjoy it too. Sometimes there are other owners I know here, and I do a little socializing myself. But a dog that doesn't live in a pack of dogs needs to be reminded every so often how dogs behave. The more like a dog he acts, the easier it is for me to manage him, because he's more predictable. And a pit bull takes some very deliberate management, or he'll take the upper hand. That's not a good thing."

I watch Two's dense bronze body running, even jumping, he's barking happily, and it's hard to remember that he has the potential to be dangerous. He looks like just a dog out there, having fun being a dog. At one point, he sits down, panting, and looks around for us. When he trots over to us he sits down beside me, almost on my feet, and looks out across the park.

"Is he tired?" I ask.

"Probably. That's a lot of running for a dog built for power rather than speed."

I look down at the top of his head, his ears in floppy triangles bobbing with his panting. "Can I sit next to him?"

"Certainly. Let's both sit for a minute."

As soon as I'm on the ground, Two turns to me and laps my face. It makes me laugh, and without thinking I wrap my arms around his neck and hug him, just for a few seconds. Then he's on his back, paws in the air, grinning at me.

"Rub his belly. He loves that."

He sure does. I rub and rub, and he squirms and makes puffing noises that aren't quite whines and aren't quite barks. Before long, we're wrestling on the grass, this dangerous dog and me. Etta laughs, and it hits me that I love being in this pack. I get peace, and relief, when I'm with it. Finally we lie still, my head and Two's touching, and through half-closed eyes I watch the clouds move across the sky, letting my heart and his rest together as close as our heads.

I want a dog. Actually, I want this dog. I close my eyes and let the image of my tattoo lend sweet balance to this feeling of peace.

A few minutes later Two jumps up, checks with Etta, and then trots over to be with the other dogs again. We wander around, not quite following him, and from time to time he bounces over to us and then races off again. Etta and I don't talk a lot; it doesn't seem necessary. But I do decide to tell her how bad Kyle's hand is, partly to see if she already knows, if Mom told her and not me.

"I saw Kyle's hand without the bandage yesterday," I open.

She looks at me. "Oh?" And when I don't go on right away, she adds, "Is there something you want to say about it?"

"It was bad. Did Mom tell you how bad it is?"

"No."

I describe it a little, realizing after I've started that it hurts me to talk about it. Not because it's Etta listening, but because it's my brother's hand. And he did this awful thing to himself. My voice kind of tapers off, and I'm almost dizzy. Then I feel Etta's arm around my shoulders. She doesn't say anything, just pulls me to her side a little, and after a few seconds lets go.

On the drive home, Two lies down on the backseat and promptly falls asleep. He has a gentle snore that suits him somehow, and the inside of the car feels like home, or someplace safe and warm.

But I know it's an illusion. I'm beginning to think there is no place that's safe enough or warm enough to offer any real protection from the world. Mr. Coffin's house, and Sylvia's place, should have been safe for them. And Etta gets letters delivered to her house, and phone calls to her own phone, threatening her life.

My voice says, "Why is it only the ID side that's doing things?"

"Doing things?"

"You know they threw rocks and broke all Sylvia's windows, right? And there was the sit-in at Mr. Coffin's, and you get those letters."

Etta lets out a long breath before she speaks. "Sometimes people believe in something desperately. That means there's fear there. When that happens, anyone with another point of view is dangerous. The believers get scared, though they might not see it like that. They'll try to fight with words, but if they meet too much resistance, or if they meet resistance that takes the power out of their beliefs, they might pick up a weapon instead.

"When these beliefs revolve around God, people can convince themselves that anything they do to preserve their beliefs is actually something they're doing for *God*. And this makes them feel like they have permission to do almost anything, because they're convinced God is working through them, and it's not just them doing it."

"Kind of the opposite of saying, 'The devil made me do it,' right?"

Etta chuckles, but there's no humor in it. "To me it's exactly the same, anytime someone does something violent or that doesn't come from love. Helps me tell the difference between a disciple and a partisan."

Disciple I'm pretty sure I get—like the guys who followed Jesus around. But . . . "Partisan?"

"Someone who follows something—some idea, or someone—blindly, without thinking, no questions asked, without stopping to see if the path they're on actually makes sense."

This sets my mind into gear, and I picture Jorja going on about the mark of the beast, and all the other crap in Revelations that's more like a bad horror flick than anything I would think God wants associated with his name. It's like the ID Christians are afraid that something about evolution will kill them, so they try to kill it first. And I don't see a way to show anyone that evolution won't kill anyone.

I'm quiet for so long that Etta finally says, "I can smell the wood burning, Ethan. Thinking about anything you want to share?"

My thoughts are so scattered I don't know where to start. But I manage to ask, "Doesn't it bother you? All the hatred? And the letters and calls? Aren't you worried?"

"Sure. It's scary, even though I try hard to convince myself that no one would really do anything truly violent. This is a small community, Ethan, and most of us have lived here all our lives, give or take a few years. I can't believe that they'll forget that, for all their threats. They're just afraid."

"But so are you!"

"Yes, but I know my fear is greater than the actual threat. And even if I'm wrong, what they're afraid of is so much less identifiable, so much bigger and scarier and vaguer, that they're at more of a disadvantage."

I'm not sure I agree with her assessment; if someone threatened to kill me, maybe that's not vague, but it doesn't get much scarier. But I decide against saying anything that might make it harder for her. I have to ask this, though: "Why don't you drop out of the race? You don't even really want to be on that stupid committee, do you?"

Another long breath. "Have you studied much about Nazi Germany in school?"

"Enough to know what it is."

"Did you learn about how the Nazi movement indoctrinated the young people? They taught them hatred and prejudice very deliberately, very early, and they recruited them into youth armies, doling out rewards and praise when the children exhibited blind allegiance to Nazi principles. If one of the children in Hitler's youth army heard or saw something from their own parents that seemed even remotely sympathetic to the Jews, that child would turn his parents in to the party authorities.

"To me, inculcating school children with ideas based on specific religious doctrine that leaves no room for any other viewpoint is very nearly the same thing. Furthermore, teaching it as *science* could damage your ability to perform true analysis and arrive at valid understanding of so many other things about life. This isn't just a question of Intelligent Design versus evolution. It's a question of how we teach children to think. Or, no, actually it's *whether* we teach children to think."

"Jorja believes she's met the beast in Revelations."

"Met the beast? What do you think she means?"

"Um . . . I don't know. I guess she means what she says."

Etta's quiet for a couple of minutes. "Is she all right? I mean, is there anything difficult going on in her life right now?"

"Not that I know of." And my mind goes bouncing off again, revisiting recent conversations with Jorja. Not that there have been very many of them. And again, there's that nagging guilt, that I haven't exactly been her friend lately. I try to shake it off and just drive.

At home that afternoon, after a yelling match between Kyle and Mom because she wouldn't let him go to church, Kyle wanders in and out of the kitchen and the living room, like he can't decide what he wants to do. He sits down at the computer for a bit, pecking with the fingers on his good hand, while I do homework and try to time my computer needs in between Kyle's assaults on the keyboard. At one point I send Jorja an e-mail to let her know I have something for her.

Sometime around three, just after Mom gets home, the doorbell rings. Kyle jumps up from the computer like it's shocked him and runs upstairs; not many people know how bad his hand is. I go to the door.

It's Jorja. "So? What have you got for me?" She looks like she's trying not to seem interested, but I can tell she is.

"Come upstairs. I'll show you."

On the trip up she says, "What's that on your ear now?"

"Just wait. You'll see."

In my room, she examines the bat closely. "Cool. When did you get this one?"

"Yesterday. And"—and I open the package and pull out just the ear cuff first—"here's one for you."

"An ichthus!" She grabs it and dashes to my bureau to watch herself put it on. I start to tell her how, but she shushes me and manages to get it on by herself. "Thanks, Ethan!" She's actually smiling.

"That's not all."

"Oh?" And as she's turning toward me, I lift the sparkling silver, purple, and black mass up and hold it aloft. Her eyes get

huge as I drop it, link by shining link, onto her palm. I have to
help her put it on, though she'll be able to do it herself next
time. She turns her hand one way and then another, holds it
up, turns it again, her whole face kind of glowing. Then she
turns toward me and wraps me in this bear hug.

"Ethan, Ethan! They're *gorgeous!* Both of them. Thank you
so, so much." She lets me go so she can admire the slave
bracelet again. "I'm never taking this off!" She's practically
skipping around the room by now. I put some music on, not
too loud, and she plops herself onto my bed.

"I thought you'd like that. They had a blue one, but—"

"Oh, no. Purple's *much* better." She grins at me and then
says, "So, how's Kyle doing? How's his hand?"

I sit on the end of the bed, sorry that the euphoria has to
end. "Not great." I look at her; how much should I say? "How
much do you want to know?"

"You mean, like, how badly, or how much information?"

"Both, really."

She changes position to sit cross-legged. "Tell me."

Where to start? "Okay, but don't let on to Mom that I told. I
don't know how much she wants me to talk about. And you
have to promise not to say anything to anybody."

"I'd swear on the Bible, if you had one."

"We do, but it's in Kyle's room, and so is he right now, hiding. I'll trust you." I rub my face with both hands. "Okay, here
goes. He has this thing called BIID. Some psychological thing
about body identity. He thinks his right hand shouldn't be part
of him anymore, and he's damaged it pretty badly. Cuts, punc-
tures—it's hideous."

Jorja's eyes are big again, but not in a good way this time.
"Are you serious? What does he think that's going to do for
him?" I shrug, and she adds, "Of course, if it's still—what was it
you said?—causing him to stumble, then I guess if it's damaged
enough it won't be able to do that. Did you ever figure out what
he meant? What the stumbling part was?"

"Not entirely," I lie. Sort of.

"Gosh. Well . . . who's helping him? What are you doing for him?"

"He won't really talk to me or to Mom, except when we do something he doesn't like. He yelled and screamed today when he couldn't go to church."

"Why couldn't he go to church? That's exactly what he needs!"

"No, Jorja, listen. He's got this disease, right? This disorder? And he's using scripture to make himself believe it's the right thing to do. But it isn't, obviously. So as long as he's focused on all those scriptures that tell him to cut his hand off, that helps him think he has to do that to make God happy, or something."

I pause; Jorja's scowl tells me she's thinking hard.

Finally she says, "Well, you know, Christians are also supposed to let Jesus's love for us teach us how to love ourselves."

I blink at her. That's nothing like what I thought she'd say. "Are you learning to love yourself?"

She looks away and then down at her hands. "Sort of."

"Can you help Kyle?"

She takes a shaky breath. "I doubt it. But, listen, that doesn't mean there isn't someone in the church—his church, or someone else's—who couldn't. Maybe you just need to look for someone."

I give a kind of snort. "You mean like Mrs. Glasier?"

"I don't know, Ethan. This isn't my area. But have you tried?"

I haven't. We haven't. And I don't have a lot of hope that it's an idea Mom will embrace enthusiastically. Didn't the therapist say no church? "I'll think about it."

We listen to some music for a bit, talk a little about school—staying away from touchy subjects like science and history, talking more about the other kids. Once or twice my mind lands on what Max has told me about Jorja's part in the sit-in at Coffin's, but I don't let it stay there. That would not be a productive discussion. And she never mentions it.

At about four-thirty she looks at her watch. "Can I stay another half hour or so?"

I shrug. "Sure. You wanna see my iPhone?"

Her eyes light up. "You have an iPhone?"

"Mom knew I wanted one, and she figured she might need to reach me because of Kyle. So instead of just getting me a boring old cell, she got me this." I pull it out, and we spend about forty minutes playing with it. I have to grab it at one point to avoid letting her see my messages from Max.

By the time she leaves, slave bracelet still on her hand and her quiet parting words—*I'll pray for Kyle*—echoing in my mind, it kind of feels like we're best friends again.

Almost.

Kyle has dinner with us tonight. I make a few attempts to talk to him, but his responses are minimal. It gets my goat, and my voice gets away from me, words getting out before I know what they're going to be.

"You know, Kyle, Jesus is supposed to help you learn to love yourself. Why don't you try focusing on that part of the Bible?"

He freezes, and Mom says, "Ethan!"

"What? It's true!"

"Stop it!" Her hands are wrapped in fists around her knife and fork, leaning hard on the edge of the table.

Kyle mumbles something about having to go to the bathroom and gets up. Mom glares at me before following him, and then I hear her voice saying, "Don't lock that door, Kyle. I'm waiting out here."

They come back down in a few minutes, where I'm in a black sulk. Mom says, "Ethan, apologize to your brother."

"For what?"

"It seems to me you just told him he doesn't love himself. You don't have the right or the knowledge to say that. Now apologize."

I let out a long breath through my nose. "Sorry."

Kyle manages a few bites of dessert before he heads back upstairs. "I've got some more homework to do." I don't know for what; he's not going to school again yet.

While Mom and I wash and dry the dishes, she lectures me

about how to talk to Kyle. "I just told you yesterday that he needs to stop focusing on religion. That's what got him into this mess. So don't you do anything to lure him back in again."

"I was only trying to help. He needs to see the good side—"

"Ethan!" Her voice is a hoarse whisper. "There *is* no good side to religion!"

So much for trying to find someone helpful from any church to talk to Kyle.

Mom collapses in front of the TV, and I settle at the computer and do some research on BIID without finding out anything more useful than what Mom has told me. Every so often I feel the slender chain on my bat where it dangles against my ear, and suddenly I'm searching the Internet for power animals. Maybe because it's close to the front of the alphabet, Cat stands out right away. I keep looking, but I also keep coming back to Cat.

There are so many things about the cat's powers that seem like they're exactly what Kyle needs. They see in the dark, so they're not afraid of the same things people fear. Their energy moves in the opposite direction from a human's, so if someone's energy is going wild the cat's can neutralize it. They help us see that the physical and spiritual worlds aren't separate, because they're both very sensual and very mysterious. And they can act as guides on a journey that takes you into self-discovery, helping you find your way in the dark. Some of these things, I notice, are in common with what Edgar is supposed to do for me.

I almost don't want Kyle's power animal to be Cat; it seems so ordinary. Mine's Bat, after all, and Etta's is the Australian dingo. Even Heidi's Fox seems more interesting than some old cat. But the more I read, the more magical Cat seems.

When the phone rings, Mom and I both jump out of our skins. I get there first. It's Sylvia Modine.

"Ethan, great! Just the young man I wanted to talk to."

"Really? Um, how are you? I mean, after they broke all your windows. I'm really sorry that happened to you."

"I'm managing, thanks. And that's not exactly why I'm calling, but it's related. Listen, do you mind if I come over for a few minutes?"

I glance at Mom, who's watching me. "Now? You want to come over now?" Mom sits forward on the couch.

"If it's okay. I'd like to talk to you and your mom together, if she's there."

"Hang on." I don't want to make this decision, so I tell Mom what I know and hand her the phone.

"Sylvia? What's this about? It's been kind of a tough weekend for us." I wait through Mom listening to Sylvia talk. Then, "Well, I can't answer for Ethan. But why can't you talk to him tomorrow?" More listening. Then, "All right, since time is so limited. See you when you get here."

"What's up?" I ask.

"Sylvia wants to ask you a favor. I'd better let her describe it. But I don't want you to feel pressured to do it. I'll support you if you do, but do it only if you really want to."

Well, that's mysterious. I try to get more out of her, but it doesn't work. So I'm kind of nervous by the time I hear the Jeep pull into our driveway. Mom turns the TV off, and then I hear voices—Sylvia's and Max's. I have the door open before they can knock, reminding myself that Mom isn't supposed to know about Max and me, knowing that Sylvia does know, and feeling a little panicked about how this will all work itself out.

We all sit kind of formally around the living room, though it doesn't take long for Sylvia to get to her point. "Well!" She glances around, hands propping her up from where they press against her thighs. "I have a very exciting opportunity for you, Ethan. Did your mother tell you about it?"

"Not yet." I'm already not feeling great about this. When someone in any kind of authority role says they're excited about something they obviously want you to get excited about, too, that's usually a bad sign.

"Okay, well, you know about the town hall meeting this week, right? And, I mean, the whole subject. The whole idea about bringing religion into science class by calling it 'Intelligent Design.' You've heard all about that?"

"I've heard a lot, sure."

"Max tells me you've helped Etta Greenleaf put up campaign signs. Can I assume that means you'd be against ID?"

I give myself enough space to consider how much intelligence could have gone into the design that makes Kyle want to remove part of himself, or how intelligent it is that best friends cut each other off. "I guess. I'm not really taking sides, though."

This stops her, but just for a nanosecond. "I think what you'll hear at the town hall—you are going, right?—is that it's going to be pretty difficult *not* to take sides. There's going to be a pitched battle, Ethan. I don't like it, but there it is. What happened to my windows proves it, and so does the sit-in at Mr. Coffin's house. You heard about that?" I just nod, deliberately not looking at Max, who's deliberately not looking at me. "So, if you don't like taking sides, then you probably don't want this battle, either. So help me neutralize it."

"What? How?"

"I think that if we could just present the facts to enough people, they'd understand why ID isn't science. They'd understand what a true scientific theory is and why ID is an idea and a belief, but not much more. We need to present these facts, and they'll understand. It's the only logical approach." She stops long enough for the silence to echo before she goes on. "I'm not talking about denouncing religion, in case you're worried about that. What I want to do is make it really, really clear to everyone what science *is,* so they can understand what it is *not.*"

I look at Mom. She's watching me, but I still don't know what Sylvia wants. I say, "So, why are you here?"

She grins and sits up very straight. "I want you to captain a team at school that will debate another team. Your team will support evolution. Theirs will support ID. The topic is, 'What Science Is.' "

I'm shaking my head before she even finishes talking. "Oh, I don't think so. I told you, I don't like to take sides. I don't think I'd even want to be *on* that team, let alone lead it."

"Before you answer," she says, as though I didn't just do exactly that, "let me tell you what it would mean. I'd coach you and the evolution team. Mr. Ivers, the geography teacher, has agreed to coach the ID team. Max will be on your team, and there will be a few other students, and all of us will research the topic, collect salient facts on both sides, and you—as captain—and I will prepare our position. Our team members will practice by debating each other, taking turns arguing each side, so we can be prepared to respond to what the other team might say. At the debate itself, as captain, you would speak first for the team, but the rest of the team will participate. It won't all be up to you."

I rack my brain for a way out, and my glance falls on Max, who looks almost as excited as Sylvia. But—hadn't he just called the school board campaign an "erectoral vote"?

"Why doesn't Max captain the team?"

"That would look like nepotism."

"Who's captain of the other team?"

"That's still under discussion. But decisions will be made by tomorrow. We have to move quickly if we want to have the debate before the election, which is a week from this Tuesday. The debate will take place a week from tonight, next Sunday."

I just stare at her. Then Max says, "What if Ethan and I go up to his room to talk about it? Give him a chance to breathe."

Mom gives me a stern glance. "For a little while." Her voice is prickly with warning.

I'm not even sure I want to go, given what Max wants to talk about, but he stands and heads toward the stairs. I look at Mom again and follow reluctantly, making sure the music Kyle's playing in his room is loud enough to cover at least some noise from mine.

Of course Max is all over me as soon as the door is closed. I try to enjoy this, but I don't know what's coming afterward. Somehow I pull away and sit at my desk, so it's harder for him to influence me physically while we talk.

He sits on the bed and grins at me. "So, will you do it? Say yes."

"Why do you want to do this at all? I thought you didn't care about this whole thing. You're not even going to the meeting on Wednesday."

He waves a hand, dismissing my point. "I changed my mind about it. Sylvia and I were talking this afternoon when I helped her bring some more of her stuff over to the house. She says if we can get people focused on science, on facts instead of gut reactions, it'll help us, too. I mean, guys like us."

I blink. "You mean . . . gays?"

"Yeah. Look, people who don't like us don't have any valid reasons. It's just gut reaction. If they thought about it scientifi-cally, if they knew the facts, they could get over it."

"I don't think so. And, anyway, you don't even want anyone to know you're gay!"

"Duh. Of course not, not when they're still allowing their gut reaction to rule their minds. This will help!"

I'm convinced he's repeating Sylvia's phrases; *allowing their gut reactions to rule their minds* doesn't sound like Max. "But this debate isn't about being gay. It's about evolution."

"Yeah, I know that. But if we can get people over ID with sci-ence, we can get them over us, too. Don't you see?"

"I must be missing something, here. How's it going to do that, exactly?"

"Don't worry; it'll all come out in the research. I have it all planned." He gives me his sexiest smile. "Do this? Please? For me? No, wait—for us."

I'm squirming, inside and out. "Why can't I just be on the team? Why do I have to be the captain?"

He looks disappointed, and I feel like a shit. "It would be so much better if the captain is gay. That way you'd understand the whole picture, not just the evolution corner of it." He waits, but I just sit there. "Okay, how about this. Just say you'll be on the team. We can decide about the captain a bit later. Will you do that much?"

My right heel starts to vibrate up and down. I see Edgar be-hind Max, next to my pillow, and it seems like my brain is a bat, but not in a good way. It's trapped inside the room, and it's flapping around frantically trying to find an escape route, using senses that aren't adapted to this kind of situation, like I can't even tell what escape *looks* like. *Up?* What good is that here? The only Up I see is not to get involved at all, but that's what Max won't let me get away with. Maybe I should join the other team? I waste a few seconds considering that before Max decides to bring the walls of my trap closer.

He stands and moves toward the door. "Fine. You won't help. You know, this is really important to me. It doesn't feel very good that you—"

My kingdom for a duck blind. "All *right!* All right."

He turns back. "Really? Oh, charmer, I knew you would!" And he lifts me into a bear hug. The kisses are not from a bear, though. With the decision made, for good or ill, I allow myself to enjoy Max's attentions now.

Before we go downstairs we've managed to sneak in a quick hand job each without fully undressing. I offer my pillowcase for cleanup, giddy that I'll have that to enjoy later.

Max gets into the living room ahead of me and announces, "He'll do it!"

And before I can say that all I've agreed to do is be on the team but not the captain, Sylvia extends her right hand, a huge smile on her face. "Congratulations, Captain! Welcome to the good fight. We'll knock 'em dead!"

After Sylvia and Max leave, Mom gives me a long hug. She says, "I'm so proud of you, Ethan."

Despite the pillowcase, I don't sleep very well.

Chapter 10

This is the week. The week for origin of the species. I remember when Etta had asked me over lunch at the Bingham diner about what we were studying in Biology, Sylvia had talked only about Darwin's life by that point. Now, it seems, we're plunging ahead. The class is mostly silent as Sylvia tells us what chapter to open our books to, because she gives not only the chapter number but also the title, which includes the word evolution.

For a while, silence rules, except for Sylvia's lecture. It's like no one wants to say anything about this topic, and I'm guessing it's because anyone who speaks will be seen as being on one side of the issue or the other, and most of us aren't ready to do that yet. Hanging in the air for me are images of Sylvia's mangled Darwin fish, the sit-in at Coffin's, and Sylvia's stone-shattered windows. And I wonder whether anyone in here, or any of their parents, could be responsible for the threats Etta's getting.

It becomes evident to me now why Sylvia hadn't just gone through the book in order. Before she started down the origin of the species path, she made sure she had presented us with a picture of nature's diversity without any particular order to it. Now she's ready to reorder it, pulling in stuff she's already gone over about a number of species so that we can see a progression from the earliest fossils to man.

Every so often I steal looks at some of the other kids in class. Most of them seem like they're trying not to make it obvious whether they're buying into the science or are thinking evil things about it, but there are a few kids who are not hiding their perspectives. And the facial expression and body language of each of these kids tell which perspective it is.

It isn't until close to the end of class that someone—Jorja, of course—has the guts or whatever to challenge what she's heard. Kyle would have been proud of her. "Everything you've said makes no sense if you take the most important thing out of the picture."

Sylvia, like she doesn't know what Jorja's going to say, asks, "What's that, Jorja?"

"If you don't have God watching over this process, bringing intelligence into it, all you've got is some weird idea that fish *chose* to go blind so they could live in an underground cave where there's no light. They're not going to do that."

"That's putting the cart before the horse, actually," Sylvia says. "What happens in cases like that is that the fish who don't rely on vision survive when they end up in total darkness, where sighted predators can't find them. They're genetically blind, and because they stay alive, that's the genetic material that they pass on to their offspring."

Jorja doesn't wait to be recognized again. "That's crazy! It would take forever for genetic traits to become standard if they're only good in total darkness."

"Don't forget that evolution, through natural selection, has been progressing for billions of years—"

"Wrong! Six thousand!"

I hold my breath, but Sylvia heaves a long-suffering sigh. "No, Jorja, I'm sorry. I know that some religious beliefs hold the earth to be only that old, but we can prove it's far, far older than that." Jorja glares at Sylvia and starts stacking her books. "Jorja, you can't win an argument by leaving in the middle of it."

Over her shoulder Jorja says, "I don't need to win any arguments. God will do that."

I turn toward Sylvia. Will she take steps Coffin had not? Now that Jorja's making a habit of this, will there be consequences? All Sylvia does in front of us, though, is assign some homework that, unfortunately, seems to involve thinking.

Sylvia has moved very quickly, it seems, with this school debate idea. By afternoon study hall she's already got permission to pull out a few kids we might want on our team. She says she and I will caucus (her word) after this interview session to select the ones we want. So I sit in the science classroom instead of study hall, watching snow pour down on the other side of the windows, half listening to Sylvia grill the other kids in the room, the thinking part of my brain focused on who I might be able to talk into being captain. I settle on Marra Whitfield, the girl Max had called a douchebagette because she thinks she's better than everyone else. Her attitude could play to my advantage; it could make her want to put herself forward as captain if she's given half a chance. She's really smart, and she's not afraid to say whatever she thinks to whomever might be in earshot. Seems like a natural.

Even though Sylvia has said she and I would "caucus," it turns out to include Max. I guess I'm not surprised. Perhaps he's really the de facto captain here, anyway, which could help explain why Max wants me in that role so badly. Sylvia agrees with me about having Marra on the team, even though Max tries to keep her off. But when I suggest her as captain, Sylvia shakes her head.

"Ethan, the captain isn't necessarily the loudest mouth on the team. The captain is someone who knows how to take a more balanced stance, to think of the team *as* a team, and do what's best for the team's objective. Marra has lots to offer, but leadership's not on the list."

I heave a sigh. I'm going to be the most backseat captain I can be, that's for sure.

Our team ends up being me, Max, Marra, and a guy I don't

know very well, Gregory Pines. Max says he's a "good hang," which I take to mean Max approves of him generally. We'll meet every day in here during study hall, which bums me out because eliminating study hall means I'll have to do all my homework at home, cutting into my free time in a big way. Then Sylvia announces we'll go as a team to the school board town hall on Wednesday. I'm in it now. Nothing I can do.

The atmosphere in American History, my last class, is full of static. Part of it might be the dry, cold air brought by the snowstorm, but there's a tense undercurrent that I'm thinking must be coming from the fact that the ID team also just finished their own selection process. Jorja won't even look at me. I don't know why.

By the time we get outside after school, there's about half a foot of wet snow on the ground. I nod to Max and then look around for Jorja, thinking maybe I can get something out of her on the bus ride home, which is sure to be a long one through all this snow, but I don't see her. Then I hear what sounds like kids shouting. I step away from the clutch of kids at the door, dodging flakes that hit me, anyway, and see what looks at first to be a good snowball fight. I'm not the only one interested, and other kids step away from the building to watch.

One of the snowball throwers, a guy in a lime green parka, gets hit hard on the side of his head. Then I see blood, and the guy collapses. I stand there like an idiot, not knowing what to do, expecting that the fight will stop. But it only gets worse. It's the worst kind of snowball fight, where they're packing snow around stones. I start backing toward the building as the throwing stops and the punching begins. Pretty soon there are maybe seven guys at each other, with more approaching to join in. I turn and run into the building to find someone who can help stop this, because I sure as hell can't, but I don't get very far before I see Mr. Glasier and a few other teachers, including Mr. Coffin, running toward and then past me to get to the fight. I follow them out and watch, a painful tension in my chest, as they wade through the snow and into the fray. Sylvia goes around to all the bus drivers, telling them to wait.

Mr. Coffin is the first teacher to head back toward the school, an unconscious Gregory Pines in his arms. The blood streaming from his head and the lime green parka tell me he was that first casualty.

Sylvia comes over to me. "Ethan, do you have a cell phone on you? Mine's inside." I nod. "Call 9-1-1 and get an ambulance over here. Maybe two. Tell them there could be a few injuries."

I'm cold standing out here in just my leather jacket, but that's not why my hand shakes as I dig out my cell and call in an emergency for the second time in only a few weeks. As soon as I end the call I see the person I'd been looking for earlier. Jorja. She's coming away from the crowd that was rooting for the kid who threw the rock at Gregory.

Suddenly Max is beside me. "What did I tell you."

For the first time, Max and I sit together on the bus, which finally leaves the school grounds almost an hour late. I've already phoned Mom to let her know what's going on. She wants to come get me, but I tell her no, stay with Kyle, I'm fine.

As I expect, it's a long ride home. I won't pretend I don't like the way my thigh and Max's press together, or that I don't feel tingles just thinking about how close his face is to mine, but even so the nearly silent bus ride is eerie. The worst part is that the bus seems divided down the middle, not just by the aisle between the rows of seats. It's also divided by this chasm, this crack in the earth between the kids who had been with Gregory and the kids Jorja had joined. Max and I are on Gregory's side of the bus, even though he's not here. There are kids who aren't obviously on one side of the debate or the other sitting wherever they end up, but the rift for the rest of us is pretty clear.

Jorja is a couple of seats ahead and across the aisle. The crack. The chasm. She's sitting with Naomi Fallon, something I wouldn't have predicted in a million years, even though I'd seen Naomi at that one Teen Meet I attended. But I guess now they have even more in common. Now they hate us.

I'm in the aisle seat, and I'm looking at Jorja when she turns and gives me this ugly look. She stares at me as she takes the slave bracelet off, and even in the gloom of the bus I see flashes of light from the black and purple links as the sparkling mass falls to the floor.

I can't take it. I get up, ignoring the frantic grasp of Max's hand, and pick up the bracelet. "What's going on?" I ask Jorja.

Through gritted teeth she hisses, "Don't talk to me. Go back to your *friend.*"

Louder this time, "What's going on?"

She turns to me sharply, glaring. "You know very well! How can you do this? You've betrayed me!"

"What the fuck are you talking about?"

"Bad enough that you're even *on* that heretic team. But you have to be captain! And now"—she gestures toward Max in a way that's nearly obscene—"you're with *him.* I can't believe I was ever friends with you." And she turns away again.

The hand that's holding the bracelet coils into a fist. There's a corner of my brain that wants to protest, that wants to say I got roped into the debate, that I looked for her today, and that if she hadn't walked past me I'd be sitting with her now. But there doesn't seem to be any space to say these words into.

I don't remember getting back to my seat, my mind struggling to figure out how anyone could have figured out already that there even *are* teams, let alone who's on them or who's captain. I drop the bracelet in my pack and pull out my iPhone and text Max. I don't feel safe talking aloud to him. I say, *how do they know already*

In return, *they started it*
started what
the debate thing they had thr team since last wk
what???
it's true
is jorja on it
not sure but we know who she cheers for
i thot this was sylvias idea did ivers start it
not sure how he got involved but sylvia agreed to do it if old lady glasier isnt the other coach

shes not even a teacher!

exactly

so how could she be involved

dude i dont know all the details ask s

The bus slows to a halt, maybe at a stop or maybe because of the snow, and Max and I look out the window beside him just as a small bird with gray feathers and a creamy underbelly crashes into the glass and falls. A junco.

I barely hear Max say, "Jesus Fucking Christ."

As we pass Jorja's church, several of the kids get up and the bus seems to lean sideways because so many of them were on one side. Through the flakes I can see that the sign today says DON'T PUT A QUESTION MARK WHERE GOD PUT A PERIOD.

As soon as I get home, Mom is full of questions. I do my best to answer, but I don't know very much. Kyle is at the computer, and I know he's listening intently. When I've said all I can, Mom hugs me and then sends me out to shovel.

"But it's still snowing!" I protest. "I should wait till it stops."

"Etta's coming over for dinner. I'm helping her prepare for Wednesday."

I let my dark mood override the fact that Etta is probably my best friend right now. "Why is she always coming over here?"

"Ethan, you know very well. I'm the closest thing she has to a campaign manager. Now please, go shovel."

Wanting nothing more than to go upstairs and use music to calm me down, I make sure I'll at least have the music. I grab my earbuds, put on some boots and that old ratty parka Dad left behind, and go out to shovel. It's frustrating work, because the snow's wet and heavy, and as soon as I get one area of the driveway clear and turn to the next bit, there's more snow behind me. Plus the plows keep going by on the road, and every time they leave more of this gunky, icy, heavy berm of crud that's hell to shift. The music isn't helping enough.

Everything is ganging up on me lately, and I'm getting angrier by the shovel. It sucks that I have to do this at all, and it's a shitty job, and all of a sudden I have to do it because Mom chased Dad out. On top of all that, Kyle can't help because he's taken himself off the chores list by hurting his hand. Where's the justice in life? He's the one who created the fucking chores list! And the kids at school are at each other's throats, and Jorja won't talk to me because Max and Sylvia talked me into this stupid debate thing I didn't want to do in the first place.

So I have a boyfriend who's terrified of anyone knowing that, and who practically withholds sex if I don't do what he tells me to, like being on this fucking debate team. Damn Max, anyway. What makes him think he can sway people's thinking about gays if he won't even admit he is one? Why should they listen to someone who lies about himself?

But I can't say it's like I've made any announcements about myself over the PA system at school. Mom . . . Etta . . . Heidi? . . . Sylvia . . . and Max, of course. That's everyone who knows about me, unless you count Jorja, who was stupid enough to think I wouldn't do anything about it. But I didn't freak when I found out Max had told Sylvia, and he *did* freak at the idea that Mom might maybe know anything.

I throw the shovel as another big plow goes by and dumps more icy crap at the end of the driveway. *Where the fuck is my father?*

Finally the snow lets up enough for me to call the driveway done and to trust that the street plows won't be creating too much of a berm for Etta to get in with her Forester. I'm calmer now but still not any too happy with my lot in life. I take one more glance around before heading back to the house, and I realize that I can't see that second Etta Greenleaf sign Mom had made me plant. At first I'm thinking, you know, it's getting dark. But I have to admit that it's not so dark that I shouldn't be able to see the thing against the snow.

I don't want to walk through the snow in the yard, so I go out to the road, make sure there's no traffic, and trot to about where it should have been facing the street. I have to step up onto the berm along the edge of the road to be sure it's gone, but it's gone. It wasn't in a place where the plow would have covered it in snow, either. It's gone. And I ain't sayin' nothin' about it.

Mom's waiting for me inside. Before I can even get out of the parka or let her know what a huge debt she has on her account with me at this point, she's holding the phone toward me.

"You need to call your father."

I glare at the phone and then ignore it long enough to hang up the parka and take off the boots, tossing them into the plastic milk crate beside the door to dry. "Why?"

"Etta can't get out. The guy who usually plows her out didn't show up."

Yeah, like our plow guy didn't, thanks to you? "Maybe he's, you know, busy?"

"Don't be a wiseass, Ethan. She called him. He won't do it."

"Why not?"

Mom exhales, looking like she's holding in the language she'd really like to use. I just glare at her; she *really* doesn't want to know what *I'm* not saying right now. "It's because of the election." I just blink stupidly at her, so she shoves the phone at me again. "Call your father and ask him to please go plow her out. She'll pay him, of course. Otherwise she'll be trapped up there for days."

Dad's sure to be out someplace right now, plowing away. I dial, thinking, *Sure, now you want him for something. And you even make me be the one to ask him. We didn't have to choose between paying someone or making me do the shoveling last year.*

Dad picks up on the third ring. "Ethan? Everything okay?" I can hear the truck engine behind his voice.

"Yeah, we're fine. But, um, I need a favor for a friend. Her usual plow guy can't get to her, and she's old. She won't be able to get out of her long driveway. She'll pay you. Can you do it?"

"Who is it, Ethan?"

"Etta Greenleaf." Truck engine is all I hear for maybe twenty seconds. "Dad?"

"I guess I can use the money. Who's her usual plow?"

"Don't know. How soon, do you think?"

"Is there a rush?"

"She's supposed to be here for dinner."

More truck noise. Then, "I'll try to get to her before seven. That'll have to do. How's your brother?"

I glance at Kyle, who's trying to ignore me from his perch at the computer. "Great, all things considered. Nothing to report."

"K. Ethan, I'm counting on you to keep me informed. Consider it a return favor for plowing out your friend."

"Thanks, Dad," is all I say before I hang up.

While Mom calls Etta, I stare at the side of Kyle's head. He glances at me and then back to the screen, fingers of his left hand poking at the keyboard. I try to feel that anger again, like outside when I was furious that he wasn't out there helping me, but it won't come. I go in and pull a chair over beside Kyle at the computer.

"How'd it go today?" I ask, referring to his second therapy evaluation, which was this morning before the snow got bad. He turns a blank face to me. Can't really blame him; it's not like I've gone out of my way to ask about much of anything. So I prod. "Did you like this person you met with?" I want to ask if he thinks she can help, but it's not clear to me that he sees himself as needing this kind of help.

He shrugs. "She's okay, I guess. This whole thing isn't my idea." We both give this some space, and then he says, "Why are you doing this debate thing? What are you trying to prove?"

"I'm not trying to prove anything." I can feel myself getting defensive. *Breathe, Ethan.* "It wasn't my idea, just like this therapy wasn't yours. I think we're both getting pushed into something we don't really want."

"Wanna trade?"

It's the closest thing to humor I've heard from Kyle in, like, months. I say, "Sure."

"Anyway, I wish you wouldn't. It's not the way to do it."

"Do what?"

"Here," and he moves the mouse around the screen; he's gotten pretty good with his left hand. "I've bookmarked some sites that talk about ID so you can see it for yourself. You can see how much sense it makes. But even if you don't see that, a debate . . ." His voice trails off and then picks up. "A debate is just going to make things worse. Wait till you see what happens on Wednesday."

I'm feeling an odd mixture of concern at what sounds like a warning and respect for what sounds like an insider's knowledge. "What's going to happen Wednesday?"

"It will end up like at school today."

"How do you know what happened at school?"

"Don't be stupid. I've heard Mom talking to people, and I'm online. You think I'm completely out of touch just because I'm a prisoner here?"

I let this sink in. Then, "Do you know who's on the ID team at school?"

"Sure. Naomi Fallon, Cathy DuFresne, Bryan Galway, and your friend Jorja Loomis."

Wow. So she is on it, though whether we're still friends is debatable. "Who's captain?"

"Naomi."

It hasn't occurred to me to consider Kyle a source of information about anything, but I'm trainable. "So what do you think will happen Wednesday, really?"

"It'll be a free-for-all. That's all I'll say."

"Um, Kyle, you know, I'll be there, and Mom. If you know anything . . ." I let that hang in the air without asking outright where his loyalties lie.

"Hey, I'll be there too." He kind of snorts. "She can't find anyone to babysit me. But that's all I'll say. It'll get ugly, though, you can count on that." He gets up. "Anyway, I won't be joining you guys for dinner tonight. Consider it a political protest. You should check out those ID sites."

I watch him trudge up the stairs and then I take the chair he's vacated. Maybe I should check this stuff out, if for no other reason than so I can prepare myself and my team for our debate. If I can't get out of this thing, at least I don't want to get slammed. So I surf around, reading bits here and there. A few statements stick out, because most of them sound like pure fanatical lunacy.

Take this one: *If natural selection is a universal rule, molecules would have to find ways to live on the surface of the sun.* Ha! *That's* stupid. All physical matter is made up of molecules. So the sun itself is made up of molecules, dope. And, anyway, who's to say there couldn't be living organisms on the sun? Just because we can't see them with our limitations doesn't mean they aren't there.

Or this one: *Archaeologists who say civilizations were already flourishing 6,000 years ago are basing their conclusions on man's idea of time. If you start with the idea that the earth is four and a half billion years old, that's twisting things to fit man's idea of time.* Again, ha! We aren't starting with a number bigger than 6,000 years. We started with things we can get our hands on today, and then we figured out how old they are.

But this one scares me: *Would you prefer a God you can trump intellectually? Or would it be better for God to be superior to you—intellectually and otherwise?* The flaw, of course, is that it assumes everyone wants a God. It assumes there *is* a God. So the scary part is this: Does arguing the evolution side of this debate put you in the position of saying that there's no God?

I do a little more surfing, and before long I come upon an article on the *New York Times*'s site about some guy named Jonathan Wells who asks ten supposedly science-based questions designed to support ID. The article also shows the answers from the National Academy of Sciences, supporting evolution. It sure looks to me like the Academy wins. I send the article link to Max and tell him to show it to Sylvia.

With Kyle upstairs, it feels safe to talk to Mom about this whole thing while I make the salad for dinner. I know she and Etta will be talking about this stuff, anyway, so I put aside how angry I was outside and just launch right in.

"Mom, do you believe in God?"

She doesn't look up from the ground beef she's pushing around in a pan. "Define God."

Well, this stumps me. I'm silent so long she looks up at me. "Sorry, Ethan. I didn't mean to be so abrupt. But, see, everyone has their own idea of what God is or might be or should be, so just asking it like that isn't something I can answer. Ask me differently."

"Okay." Thinking . . . "Does believing in evolution mean you don't believe in God?"

"No. Not at all." She sets the wooden fork down and turns toward me, hand on her hip. "I don't hate God. I just hate religion. See, this is a really nasty point the ID side will try to make. They want to say that you can't believe in science and still have faith in spiritual things. Many of them will say that a belief in science makes people immoral. Bunch of b . . . Bolshevik." She picks up the fork again and stabs at the helpless pink mass.

I stifle a giggle; she doesn't want to deny being immoral and then polish it off by saying the word bullshit. I clear my throat. "So, are you saying you have some kind of belief in God, as long as you're allowed to define God?"

"Ethan, everyone who says they believe in God defines God in their own way. Many people won't admit that, but it's true." I stand there staring blankly at her for half a minute, then she says, "The fact is that it's none of their business whether I believe in God, or what religion I do or don't belong to. And they don't have any more right to define God for me than I have to define God for them. And that's at the heart of *my* position. So if they try to bring their idea of God into the science classroom I'm paying for, the one my kids attend, I draw the line. Hard."

At around seven-thirty, I hear a car, and when I run to open the door it's Etta. She has Two with her, bundled into a black and green plaid doggie sweater. I sort of half laugh at the sight of a pit bull dressed up in kilt fabric.

Etta grins at me as she takes it off him. "It's Black Watch plaid, a very famous Scottish clan pattern. I like these colors, and Two was born in Nova Scotia."

"Well, it's not just the plaid. I mean, you know, you think of pit bulls as being these tough dogs, and here he can't go out into the world without a doggie coat?"

This makes her laugh out loud. "I see what you mean. But, really, dogs with short hair and not much in the way of blubber for protection get cold very easily. Also, if you have any doubt about the ferocity of the Scottish warriors who wore plaid kilts into battle, you should have a little chat with Mr. Coffin." She folds it and sets it on top of her boots, which she's traded for loafers. "Where's your mother?"

"She's taking Kyle his dinner upstairs. I guess he doesn't want to be a part of the enemy's strategic planning."

"That's too bad. I was hoping to see how he is. Can you tell me anything?"

I head toward the kitchen, and Etta follows, Two's nails clicking softly on the wooden floor. "He had his second therapy evaluation today, but he doesn't want to do it at all. I don't think he sees himself as having a problem."

She nods. "That's very much like what I remember about the person I knew."

"You said he had his leg amputated."

"He did, but only because he damaged it so badly it got infected. They *had* to take it off."

"Was he, like, happy after that?"

"For a while. Then he started looking askance at his other leg." She stops, but I want to know more.

"What happened?"

She watches my face. "Eventually he killed himself. But, Ethan, that's unusual. It's more common for people like him to feel normal once the first limb is gone, and not very many people go on to target other body parts."

"They won't take Kyle's hand off."

"No. Not just because he wants them to."

"Unless he damages it so much it gets infected."

She sits down, points to the floor near her feet, and Two lies down, head on his paws. "Thank you so much for having your father plow me out, Ethan. He said you had called him."

Guess she doesn't want to talk about BIID any more. Neither

do I, because the answers get uglier the more I ask. "The other guy won't come because of the election?"

"That's more or less what he said."

"Kyle says the town hall is going to be ugly."

"He's probably right."

"There was a bad fight at school today."

"What? What happened?" I tell her what I know, and she pulls out her cell phone. "I'm going to make sure Gregory's all right." It sounds like she's talking to the hospital, and then to Gregory's parents. When she hangs up she says, "It's a minor concussion. They're keeping him overnight for observation. Was anyone else hurt?"

"Not like that. Not that I saw."

"Do you know what started it?"

I shake my head. "All I know is that it's about this debate at school."

"What debate at school?"

Wow; she hasn't heard much. She listens as I fill her in, and what I see in her face tells me she's thinking something she doesn't want me to know. When I finish, she beams at me.

"Ethan, I'm so proud of you. I know it's not easy for you to take sides, and captaining the team is making a statement. But I think this fight today should remind all of us that it would be easy to descend into physical attacks. You and I, Ethan—we have the hard work. We need to do everything we can to help the others remain calm and discuss the truth about all the is-sues, not the emotional effects they have on us. Unfortunately, too many people on the other side of this fence will do every-thing they can to whip up dangerous emotions."

Mom comes in, carrying a tray with used dishes. "Sorry to be late. I decided to watch Kyle eat. The last thing we need right now is a hunger strike from him."

Etta asks, "Is he getting harder to deal with?"

"Just stoutly refuses to see either therapist again. But he's going to. I've decided on the one we saw today." She stacks Kyle's dishes and wipes the tray off with a sponge. "At least Dave's offered to help pay for it."

My head snaps toward her; no one has told me that. I decide to make a point. After all, Mom and I agreed to be a team on this project. "Why didn't I know that?"

She takes the phone out of her apron pocket and thunks it back into its cradle. A sharp edge to her voice, she says, "Maybe because I just talked to him?"

Fine, but she doesn't have to be so nasty. I can speak in edges, too. "So maybe it's good that he knows, after all. I guess he's good for some things."

Into the silence, Etta says, "If tonight's not the best night—"

Mom waves a dismissive hand. "No, no. There are not enough more nights, and this thing with Kyle isn't going away anytime soon. We're still working out how to get through it together, that's all. Ethan, will you help me serve? Etta, has Two had his dinner?"

Etta puts some water down for Two, who has in fact had his dinner, and it's nearly eight before we have our own. This is unheard of in our house, and I'm famished. I shovel food into my mouth as Mom and Etta discuss their approach. It's all based on just what Mom said earlier, that the real challenge will be to fight the perception that all scientists are atheists, knowing the opposition will push things that way no matter what the topic is supposed to be.

My own voice surprises me, like it does so often lately. "Can you prove they're not all atheists?"

Mom and Etta both sit back, and then Mom looks at Etta like she's stumped. But Etta isn't.

"Have you heard of Dr. Francis Collins?" Mom and I both shake our heads. "He was the lead scientist for the Human Genome Project, mapping out the genetic blueprint that makes humans human. He's a born-again Christian. I read his book, *The Language of God: A Scientist Presents Evidence for Belief.* His point is that faith in God is actually supported by what science teaches us. God works through science." She shrugs. "What I see is a long line with a movable point on it. The line itself is God. Toward the left is science, and toward the right is faith. Centuries ago that movable point was pretty far over to the left, so the science portion to left of it was pretty small and the faith part was pretty big. Over time, that point has moved toward the right as we learned more about science, so we needed faith a little less. I doubt that we'll ever be so smart that the faith part will disappear entirely, but even if it does—the line itself is still God. Science will never replace God."

Again, my voice from nowhere: "So you believe in God?"

Etta smiles at me. "I do, although it might not look like the kind of God you're used to hearing about. Your friend Jorja would probably not recognize my belief as belief in her God at all." She leans back, looks down briefly at Two, and says, "I will probably be asked that question Wednesday night, Ethan. I would be very grateful if you would spend a few minutes right now asking me questions you think I'll hear from the opposition. I'll write them down and work on my responses at home. Will you do that for me?"

"Sure. Hang on." And I go to the computer and print out the ten questions—and answers—about evolution and ID. I hand it to Etta. "This is a good start."

Mom gets up and reads over Etta's shoulder. Etta says, "Ethan, this is very useful for discussions with people who try to attack the science of evolutionary theory." She sets it down next to her placemat. "I'm also looking for the kind of question you asked me a few minutes ago. Do I believe in God, and how can scientists believe in God. Most of the audience on Wednesday will not be asking these ten questions. They'll be asking really personal questions, and making accusations, based on their own feelings and fears. What would be really helpful is if you can pretend that you're one of those people. Can you do that?"

"Give me a few minutes," I say, and go into the living room. I sit at the computer, half listening to Mom and Etta as they talk about the town hall, and pretend I'm Jorja. I open a blank file and start typing. Maybe half an hour later I've got a whole page full of questions. I go back to the top and read, and I have to admit that the first few are kind of mean-spirited, because I've been pretending I'm Jorja, and I'm mad at her. But after about the fourth question they start to get more realistic. At the end I even throw in one I've seen online someplace: *How can homosexuality be natural when it doesn't have any evolutionary advantages?* To be honest, that one troubles me a little. I carry a printout into the kitchen.

Etta takes it from me, reads through it nodding and smiling, and then she gets to that last one. She frowns a little and looks up at me. "Ethan, do you have reason to think people will bring up homosexuality?"

"You never know. Max wants to prepare our debate team to respond to that kind of question. Plus Mom got a paper left on her windshield that says you're connected with—what was that organization, Mom?"

Etta says, "NAMBLA. Yes, I've seen that. You're right, ludicrous though that whole string of illogic is." She looks back at the page. "This question assumes there's a scientific basis to say that it *is* natural. I wouldn't know what to say to someone who says it isn't. At least, not from a scientific perspective."

I tell her what Max has told me, what Sylvia has told him. Her eyes get big. I ask, "Do you want me to look that up on the computer?"

"Yes, please."

It doesn't take me long, and I print out a few pages about the pheromone studies. I even find a site that shows all the animal species that have homosexuality, and it goes on and on. I do a screen dump of a couple of pages just for examples. As I'm waiting for the printouts, I can hear Etta talking about the guy who wouldn't plow for her tonight. Mom asks who it is.

"Lowell Galway. I've known him for years. He's been plowing the driveway since before I came back from New York. He plowed for my father."

I'm thinking that's probably Bryan's father when Mom says, "Lowell Galway? The guy who keeps a shotgun in his truck?"

"Does he? I didn't know. Guess I've never had occasion to see it."

By the time Etta leaves, she's got a whole pile of stuff to read. Mom and I stand near the door as Etta puts on her boots, and I remember the sign I saw Saturday.

"Listen, you know how your signs are getting stolen? I saw one the other day in somebody's yard, and next to it there was a sign that said if anyone steals the sign again it's another fifty dollars to Etta Greenleaf."

Mom laughs, and Etta stands up straight and stares at me.

I go on. "So I was kind of thinking, you know, we could plant some of those other signs beside the regular ones. It would make it look like you've got all kinds of support."

One boot on, the other foot still in just her sock, Etta reaches out and hugs me.

I'm most of the way up the stairs after she leaves, on my way to my room so I can finish my homework, when the phone rings. It's kind of late, which of course makes me think something's wrong somehow, and I listen as Mom picks it up. Her voice sounds hesitant but not irritated as she says, "Dave."

It's Dad. She talked to him already once tonight. Is he okay? I sit on a stair just far enough down to be able to hear without being easy to see and listen shamelessly to the half of the conversation available to me, filling in the other half as I sense what's going on.

"Yes, thanks for doing that. I really appreciate it. . . . Well, I guess I'm kind of her campaign manager. Ethan's been helping her put signs up. . . . You knew? How?"

Shit. Dad! Shut up about things I haven't told Mom! Like, that I've seen you at all.

"He didn't mention it."

I'll bet Dad's wishing he hadn't said anything, about now; he probably doesn't want Mom to know about fluffy Connie. Maybe he just wants to make sure I haven't ratted on him.

She listens for a couple of minutes, and since Dad's not really talkative I'm thinking she's giving him a chance to hang himself by tripping over his own words. I know, mixed metaphor, but I'm tired. But when she does speak, her voice is almost sweet.

"I know, I know. It's been really hard on all of us. I'm sorry I didn't tell you. I know I should have. I'm just trying to cope."

So the part I fill in for myself is that Dad is apologizing for flying off the handle after I told him about Kyle, and Mom's letting him. She's forgiving him.

Maybe there's hope for them. As I move silently toward my room I rest my hand on my ass, willing the tattoo to send balance into my parents' marriage.

Chapter 11

Jorja walks right past me on the bus Tuesday, even though I'm sitting against the window on "her" side, in the seat we've normally shared in the past. I don't turn to watch, so I don't know where she ends up after rejecting my offer of a truce. Max gets on at his stop, and his eyes widen a little when he sees what side I'm sitting on. He rejects me, too, even though I'm wearing my cool new-slash-old bar code pea coat for the first time, and sits on the other side, a few rows up. I'm sure that's as much so we won't be seen sitting together again as it is that I'm on the "wrong" side. And I'm beginning to feel creepy enough over here that if he'd sat in an empty row I would have got up and sat with him. But he didn't. It's actually a little scary that I feel like I have more guts than he does. And even scarier that I might have more guts than is good for me.

No one sits beside me all the way to school. And the chasm, other than my tiny little statement, is still there. To try and make myself feel a little better about my isolation, I remind myself that I'd started this year being proud—or at least pretending to be proud—of my outlier status. So even now that I've essentially declared a side, I'm still an outlier. Life's a funny thing.

Philosophizing about my isolation isn't enough not to make

me feel creepy. There are twinges in my stomach from that kind of low-level anxiety that you can't really do anything about. I need a distraction. I could, of course, pull out a book, but that seems kind of desperate. And then I realize I have something much better. My iPhone.

I pull it out and start cruising on the Internet, nothing particular in mind, and I end up on iTunes. In the back of my mind someplace I know there's some music I had wanted to download, if I could just remember what it was. I browse aimlessly, stretching my mind back over the last week or so, and then it hits me: k.d. lang. By the time I get to school, I'm stocked up on about three albums, nearly blowing my whole month's allowance on Mom's credit card.

When I get to my first class, the chasm has followed us all from the bus. We don't have assigned seats, but usually most kids sit in the same seats out of habit or something. Not today. And it keeps going throughout the day. There's some number of kids, how many I can't tell, who look kind of bewildered and don't seem to understand what's going on or what they're expected to do about it. This keeps me—and probably anyone else—from being able to get a sense of which camp outnumbers the other. But one thing's for sure: Each camp is much bigger than either debate team.

Jorja isn't in Biology. I don't have a clue where she is, but I'm positive this is some kind of protest on her part. As for me, the stuff I'd been looking up last night for Etta gave me lots of great fodder for my homework, and it's kind of fun to hand it in.

More Darwin today, or at least his theories. And today there are more comments from the kids. I'm guessing that somewhere between Jorja setting the stage yesterday and the thinking Sylvia had us do for homework has made some of the Teen Meet kids bolder. They start asking questions that have a lot in common with those ten I'd given Etta, the ones that almost make scientific sense. It seems I'm not the only one who found them. Max must have passed them on to Sylvia, or maybe she already knew how to respond to them, because she holds her own, for sure. The only thing she can't win against is when someone starts quoting scripture. And this usually brings out protests from kids on the other side of this issue. Like Marra, and Max. But others, too.

After about five of these Bible references, Sylvia's impatience starts to show. "Everyone, please. This is Biology. Science. Just saying something is true without providing sound data, repeatable tests, and conclusive results isn't science. Scripture is about faith, not facts. If you don't have facts to talk about, you aren't talking about science."

We could almost start our debate right here. Either that, or another rock-ball fight. Max is scribbling furiously, and so is Marra, no doubt taking notes to use in the debate. They're obviously much more into this controversy than I am. I just want it to be June so we can call the school year over. June is "up" for me right now, I decide. Bats hibernate in winter around here.

The debate meeting is weird because of Gregory not being there. Marra, of course, already has some research material in multiple copies for us, and she doesn't even show it to Sylvia before she hands the copies out. Sylvia gives us all copies of the ten questions article I'd sent to Max, and Max has some papers he's not sharing. I assume they're about homosexuality.

Sylvia says, "Okay, let's take a moment to skim over what I've handed out—thank you, Max, for finding it—and then we can look over Marra's material."

Max? Those questions were *my* find! I glare at him, but he's not looking at me. I decide to give him the benefit of the doubt; maybe he just forgot to tell Sylvia that I sent them to him.

Marra says, "Ethan hasn't brought anything."

Max still won't look at me. I glare at him again, not sure whether to stand up for myself here or not. Then I remember what Etta had said about those questions, so I use that as an excuse to claim them. "I found those ten questions last night. But I think that kind of argument is the easiest to be ready for. We also need to be ready for a different kind of opposition."

Sylvia says, "Like what, Ethan?"

As I tell her about some of the other things I'd found last night, I consider giving Kyle the credit. But this doesn't seem like a moment for irony. Then I repeat what Etta said, about how emotional some people will get.

There's silence for maybe five seconds, and then Sylvia says, "Ethan is absolutely correct. The position the ID team will come from will not be directly from scripture, because the proponents want to deny that their position is inherently religious or specifically Christian. So we must remember that the debate isn't about the Bible. It's about what *is* science and what is *not* science, and why. Also, remember that the audience will not be all classmates. It's on Sunday evening, and there will be lots of different people there, not just students who've been studying science recently. We must be ready to spot arguments that come from emotion and not facts."

So I've just helped keep us on the same track as Etta. Maybe I'm not a bad captain after all.

By the time we get to American History, Mr. Coffin has obviously had to deal with the opposing camps in his other classes, and he's not taking it lying down. As we come in, he hands us each an index card with a number on it. I look at mine: seven. Max, behind me, gets eighteen. Coffin tells everyone, "Sit at the desk with the matching number. I will be checking."

The numbers on the desks are in order, and they start at the back of the room and go across, so I'm nowhere near the front. Everyone is really quiet, almost like we're afraid to talk to each other. Coffin leans against his desk at the front and looks all around the room.

"It's the year nineteen fifty-five," he says, "and those of you with numbers nine and lower are black citizens. All others are not." Kids look around; I try to see if all the newly black kids are on the evolution side of things, but we're not. Coffin has really mixed it up. "The non-black citizens are convinced that black people are less intelligent, less industrious, and somehow less worthy than they are. They believe the issue of black versus white is understood only by those who know that blacks are inferior. They believe this in their gut. And they believe they're using their brains as well. It's obvious to them; why else would God have made blacks so obviously different?"

He pauses, then looks to us in the back. "So, all of you back there, smarter people than you have decided you're not worthy of the good things in life, that you need to accept the position we're convinced you belong in. This isn't a problem for you, right? Because our gut tells us that we're right. What your guts tell you is irrelevant, because our guts are worth more."

Dead quiet now. Really awkward. I look around again to see who else is black. There's Jorja, at the other end of the row, and Marra, who must be apoplectic at the idea that anyone would think she's anything other than the best of the best.

Coffin's voice breaks the painful silence. "Good news for those in back! Between nineteen fifty-five and the present, we've figured out and proven that there is no support for this belief about black people. You are every bit as capable at intellectual and industrial achievement as anyone else. And, today, there are not many people left—black or white—who cling to the fallacy that black people are inferior. And yet fifty or so years ago, many white people were willing to defend that fallacy with everything from discrimination to violence to murder."

He turns suddenly. "Jorja Loomis." From the corner of my eye I see her jump. "In what year did the black woman Rosa Parks refuse to give up her seat to a white person on a public bus?"

"Um . . . I—I don't know."

"Max Modine?"

"Nineteen fifty-five." Clever, to figure out that it was the year Coffin already gave us. But then, Max is sitting toward the front of the room, so he's one of the smart people.

"A peaceful march from Selma, Alabama, to Montgomery ended only six blocks from where it began when local law enforcement troops committed immensely violent acts upon the marchers, severely wounding large numbers of people. This is known as Bloody Sunday, and it occurred on March seventh of what year? Naomi Fallon?"

"Um . . ."

Ha! She's in the very front row, but she didn't know.

"Anyone?" Silence. "Nineteen *sixty*-five. Take these down; you'll be tested."

He goes to the whiteboard and starts scrawling things down in a table. *Year* is one column, *Event* is the other. "When did the National Voting Rights Act outlaw discriminatory practices that disenfranchised black citizens?"

More silence. Coffin starts filling the columns. Kids start to take notes, but there's some hesitation, like they're not quite sure they're gonna like where he's going with all this. I look around for Jamal Mason and Monique Burns, the only two real black kids in the room. Monique, in the second row with the white crowd today, looks nervous; Jamal at number nine looks defiant, his sexy good looks forming a scowl somewhere between fear and anger.

Finally Coffin puts down his marker and faces the silent class again. "You'll see that the time between these events begins to compress in the nineteen sixties, and multiple events are noted in each year. The violence of the early events helped garner support for the movement as a whole. More people came to see the injustice. And over time, more people just grew accustomed to the idea of treating blacks equally."

He walks back around to the front of his desk. "The black citizens who were degraded, who were ridiculed, defiled, and killed, were treated like that because non-black citizens were terrified. They were terrified that the life they had always known, the life they believed was God-given and righteous, the life they knew *in their gut* was the life they deserved, was being threatened. People they believed to be not only inferior but also dangerous were demanding to be treated with the same degree of respect and allowed the same rights as their superiors. A change like this threatened everything they knew. They were convinced it would turn their world upside down."

He looks around again, taking everyone in. His next words are heavy and slow. "They were terrified." Another pause. "And terror often begets violence."

A dropped pin would have seemed loud at this point.

"Until nineteen sixty-seven, when the U.S. Supreme Court finally stepped in to stop the discrimination, it was illegal in most states for a black person to marry a non-black person. While there are still some people today who think interracial marriage is necessarily bad, most of us know better. So how come most of us feel differently today? What changed? Where did all that terror go? Why did U.S. citizens stop killing each other over this issue?"

My voice speaks for itself. "They got used to us."

Coffin turns toward me. "Us?"

I hold up my card. "I'm black today." I'm kind of getting into this now; maybe Max is right about bringing homosexuality into the debate, because what's really going through my head is not that I'm black but that I belong to another category that terrifies people. I'm gay. Maybe all this is connected somehow.

Coffin says, "So you're saying that the sky didn't fall. Black people came into restaurants and buses and schools and neighborhoods, and some of them married white people, and nothing bad happened. Is that it?"

"Bad things still happen today." Jamal's voice is almost a growl. All eyes turn toward him.

"Yes, they do. Jamal is correct. But it isn't happening to the non-black people who were so terrified of the change. In fact, it's coming *from* those who didn't want to accept black people. So, Jamal, why do you think that is?"

"They won't learn."

Coffin looks around the room. "What won't they learn?"

"That it's okay to be different," my voice says. "That not everyone has to be just like everyone else. That we don't all have to look alike or think alike."

"What does learning something require?"

Max speaks up. "You have to have brains."

"True. What else?"

Marra looks at Jorja and says, "You have to be willing to *use* your brains. You have to open your mind."

"And what do you think keeps people from being willing to open their minds?"

Jamal again: "Fear."

"Precisely! Fear of losing status and privilege. Fear of uncertainty. Fear of not being right, of not already having everything figured out. Fear of change."

Coffin lets this sink in as he goes to the whiteboard, and on the side across from his list he writes FEAR. He turns back to us. "Yesterday someone threw a rock at the head of Gregory Pines. Fortunately the injury was not worse than a minor concussion, and I know that he was released from the hospital early this afternoon. But someone threw that rock at him with the intent to hurt someone. What was the fight about?"

"God." Jorja's voice, dark with hatred.

"Stupidity," is Marra's suggestion, and she glares at Jorja.

"Unwillingness to learn," says Naomi.

"Learn what?" Coffin asks.

She replies, "That Intelligent Design is science."

"Wrong." Coffin's reply is quick and hard.

Someone's voice says, "Anger." Coffin ignores that.

Monica speaks, finally, and quietly. But we all hear her. She says, "That it's really about fear."

On the whiteboard, he underlines FEAR. Then he draws an arrow to the right and writes, VIOLENCE. He says, "People who run out of discussion points often resort to violence." He looks around the room, marker in hand. "What do you think was causing that fear?"

Toward the end of class, he's listed reasons that each side of the ID versus evolution issue might be afraid. The only one I remember about why anyone fears ID comes from Max, who says he's afraid taking ID seriously in a classroom will force everyone to follow its religious rules. I know what he means. He's afraid the religious rules he'd be forced to follow would deny his right to be who he is. It would deny mine, too. In fact, it could easily mean going back to a time when it was illegal to be gay. That feels like ancient history to me, but I know it was true once upon a time.

So I don't remember a lot of specifics. But I remember this: It seems like there's a lot more fear on the ID side. And I remember asking Etta why so much violence was coming from that direction. Now it's making sense to me.

Discussion peters out, and Coffin points to the list and asks, "Do you think anyone with any of the fears on this board will have their minds changed because someone in the opposing camp threw a rock at them?" He pauses, just for a second. A few hands go up, but he ignores them. "For tomorrow's class, type a five-hundred-word paper in the first person. You're George Washington just *before* December twenty-fifth, seventeen seventy-six—and for anyone who's forgotten, that was the date on which he led the ill-prepared, nearly starved, frozen, ragtag group of colonists, only a semblance of an army, across the Delaware River. Write as General Washington, and explain why even a total defeat by the British wouldn't make you believe that you should want to be a British colony under King George III. Tell me why the worst beating they can give you won't make you change your mind. And don't assume that using words like 'liberty' and 'freedom' will be enough to meet this assignment. Give me your personal reaction to violence from those who oppose you, who tell you you're wrong."

The bell rings, partially drowning out the groans and protests around me, and as we stream out the door, kids clump together according to which side of the ID issue they're on. I could be making this up, but it's looking like now there are more kids in the evolution crowd than the ID clump, and not as many bewildered as before.

I dawdle at my locker. In a way, I'd like to sit with Max on the bus again, but I'm not very happy with him right now, and something tells me he won't let it happen again so soon, anyway. It seems to me that what should happen is that kids shouldn't be so much on one side of the bus or the other, and that maybe I should sit on the ID side again, but I don't quite have the guts to do it the way I did it this morning. Instead, I want to see who else might do it. If someone else crosses the aisle, then I will, too, but I'm not gonna be the only one again. So I don't want to get on the bus too soon. I end up sitting alone again, on the evolution side.

As I get off the bus I see that we now have three signs in our front yard. There's the slogan about having science and the one about common sense, and there's one like what I'd told Etta about, saying stealing the sign means money for her. Approaching my front door I can hear Mom yelling. I stand there, hand on the knob, not sure whether to turn it and go in or turn around and go—where? I go in.

Kyle is standing halfway up the stairs, his face red with fury, his right arm looking weighted down with the amount of bandaging at the end. He doesn't look at me, just yells, "You never even asked me! You never gave me a chance to say anything! I live here, too!"

He turns and stomps upstairs, slamming the door as Mom shouts, "Get back down here, young man!"

I'm slowly taking off my coat and hanging it up, not wanting to get involved in whatever is going on. Mom wheels toward me.

"Did you know who was taking down our signs?" I shake my head. "It was your brother! Of all the damn fool things."

"Kyle?"

"How many brothers do you have?"

"Hey, don't yell at me!"

"Sorry. I found them in the shed when I went out to see if we had any salt for our walkway. So I decided to make one of my own."

"Yeah. I saw." My voice must have sounded as embarrassed as I felt, and maybe even as ashamed of being embarrassed as I felt.

Mom looks at me like she's trying to figure out whether to yell at me again, but finally she just says, "It will be a riot sitting with him tomorrow night, but there's not much choice. He has to go, or one of us has to stay home. And that's not going to happen."

"About that . . ."

"Ethan, you are going! Don't—"

"I never said I wasn't!" We stare at each other, and I take a long breath. "I have to go with our debate team. We're having dinner at Sylvia and Max's house and then going over together. Sylvia says we have to take notes as prep for the debate."

Mom nods and says "Sorry" again. "I'm just on edge, Ethan. So many things seem to be happening at once. Any word about Gregory?"

I tell her what Coffin said and then take a chance. "Um, do you know if Kyle actually *wants* to go to the town hall?"

She stops in her tracks and turns toward me, frozen in place. Then she closes her eyes and looks a little like she's trying not to cry. "It has come to my attention that I'm not treating Kyle like a person. I'm treating him like an invalid without normal mental capabilities. I didn't give him a chance to weigh in about the signs, and I haven't even asked him whether he wanted to go tomorrow night. But what would we do if he doesn't?"

"Okay, so don't take my head off here, but maybe Dad could stay with him. He's calmed down, right?" I don't dare say too much, or I'll have to admit that I eavesdropped.

"I'm not crazy about that idea, Ethan. But Kyle shouldn't be forced to go if he doesn't want to, so if that's the case we'll have to think of something. Do you mind asking him while I work on dinner?"

Not my first choice, no. But I trudge upstairs. His door is shut, of course. I knock.

"Go away!"

"It's me, not Mom."

He opens the door. "What do you want?"

"First, I think you made your point about the signs. I don't know what will happen next, but I think Mom heard you. But about tomorrow night. You said something last night that made it sound like maybe you didn't really want to go. Do you?"

He leans against the door frame looking skeptical and challenging at the same time. "Who wants to know?"

"I do. So does Mom."

He watches my face for a second. "What if I want to go but I don't want to sit with you guys?"

"Well, I'm being forced to sit with my debate team, so you wouldn't sit with me, anyway."

"I want to sit with people who are on the right side of this issue. I want to sit with Mr. Phinney's supporters."

"And if you do that, you'd still go with Mom, right?"

"You mean, in her car? Duh. How else would I get there?"

"Look, don't give me any grief. How do I know you haven't already been online with your friends arranging rides and stuff?"

He lifts his head in acknowledgment but doesn't respond to the question. He just says, "I want to be there. And I want to sit in the Phinney group. Even if that means I have to arrive and leave with the enemy."

"Kyle, you know Mom's not the enemy."

"She's mine."

"I don't think so. She wants you to be okay, and she doesn't understand what's wrong."

Our eyes lock for a second, like Kyle's trying to figure something out, or make some decision. Finally he says, "I'll be all right as soon as I can get rid of this offending member." He holds his right arm up, the bandage looking heavy and unnatural.

My stupid voice says, "Why will that help?"

He blinks at me. "I thought I'd made that obvious."

I shake my head. "No. You haven't. Not to me, anyway. If you need to stop . . . you know, stumbling, there's lots of ways to do that. But you want to cut off your freakin' hand. Why?"

He clenches his jaw, and I realize suddenly that he and I have never talked about this. Teeth still nearly grinding, he says, "It's not a valid part of me. It fooled me for years, but there was a demon growing in it all along and now it's strong enough that I can't control it anymore. The only way to get rid of the demon is to get rid of the hand."

It occurs to me to suggest an exorcism, but Mom has already yelled at me for saying anything to Kyle that smacks of religion.

It also occurs to me to ask if he's considered what his life will be like if he loses the hand, and whether the demon might not just go inhabit some other part of him. All these ideas that even my dumb-ass voice doesn't dare say out loud are floating around my head, and I can't think of anything that I can actually say.

My lack of response gets to Kyle. "You think I'm crazy, don't you?"

His eyes look deep and very, very sad. I've never seen him like this. I say, "I guess I don't understand. I can't imagine not having my right hand."

"I'll bet you also can't imagine you could have the mark of the beast on you."

We stand there staring at each other, and then Kyle steps back and slowly closes his door.

As I'm lying in bed that night, holding on to Edgar instead of jerking off to a mental picture of Max's face and other body parts, I think about something I'd looked up on the Internet earlier when I was trying to come up with an opening for my George Washington paper. It was another power animal. As much as I like my bat, I'd been thinking that my power really ought to come from something even more Poe-like. *Quoth the Raven,* all that good stuff. So why not the raven?

What I'd found out is that Raven is just too much for me. Most of what I find says Raven is always a she. That's not much of a problem. But she's supposed to keep universal secrets, she understands magic and mystery and multidimensional existence, and she's a shape-shifter. There's something about how she's connected to "the void," whatever that means. There's stuff about transformation and spiritual awakenings, and worst of all it says she helps us eliminate inner demons. All in all it's clear to me why Heidi didn't give me a raven.

When I saw the part about eliminating demons, I'd wondered about Raven for Kyle. But then I'd looked up Cat again and was even more convinced it would be exactly what Kyle needs.

Kyle and I have never been what you'd call close. We're too

different, and always were, even before Dad left. But I don't hate him, and he's my only brother, and the stuff Etta said about her friend has really scared me.

So I lie in bed, hold on to Edgar, and try to focus on Cat. I close my eyes and lie very still, willing myself to concentrate on Cat, picturing Kyle holding on to Cat's tail with his possessed right hand through a darkness that blinds him but not Cat. As they move, slowly and in a kind of winding pattern, I imagine Cat absorbing the negative energy that's in Kyle's hand or his brain or wherever it's coming from, and neutralizing it. The last thing I see is Cat leading Kyle out of some thick blackness and into a place where he isn't insane anymore.

But when I fall asleep, it isn't these animals that come into my dreams. It's Coyote. Only instead of representing anything good or useful or mystical, Coyote gets its front paw caught in a trap and chews it off to escape, dripping blood behind it. I toss and turn, unable to stop seeing things I don't want to see: reddish black drops of blood on white snow, and the mutilated mass left behind in the trap. It's not a paw. It's a human hand.

Chapter 12

On the bus Wednesday, I sit beside Kenny, the kid Max called a missing link. He's not a big talker, and that's kind of what I want today. I close my eyes at first, but I have to open them so I'll stop seeing the blood and the hand. I've just started to wonder when Kyle will ever go back to school when the bus passes the white farmhouse, a lot like my own, that serves as the Brearly family home and Mrs. Brearly's yarn shop. The sign out front about the shop has been pushed over and kind of battered with something heavy, or maybe run over by a truck, and the front door is in the middle of a gigantic spray of red paint that says SATAN. There's more red paint on the clapboards and even on the windows, but I can't tell whether it's supposed to be letters or just a mess. The bus slows down, probably expecting fourteen-year-old Missy Brearly to come dancing down the stairs as usual, but she isn't there. We stop, and everyone gawks at the house while the bus driver makes up her mind what to do. She beeps the horn, waits maybe half a minute, and then moves on.

There's a quiet buzz of conversation on the bus, and I listen hard, finally piecing together enough whispered phrases to figure out that Mr. Brearly had gotten into a shouting match last night when Mrs. Robichaud at the convenience store next to Nick's Pizza wouldn't sell him any beer because he'd made a face at something religious she had plastered over a big American flag behind the counter. Mrs. Robichaud evidently called him on it, and they fought about the town hall tonight. So the rumor working its way through the bus is that Gus Robichaud, her oldest son, is the one who sprayed the red paint. Gus is a year older than me and always hangs out with his buddy Mitch Dalton, who usually drives both of them to school in his high-wheeling, four-wheel-drive black pickup. If Gus is involved, Mitch must be as well. And I know I saw Mitch with the kids who threw the rock at Gregory.

Before I can figure anything out, Gregory gets on the bus, his head bandaged to cover the area beside his left eye. The skin around the bandage is bruised and puffy. From my side of the bus, a lot of kids clap and cheer. Almost immediately, some kids across the aisle yell "Boooo!" and "Get off the bus!" Gregory looks like he's trying to dissolve into the nearest open seat on my side, and I feel myself shrinking as kids around me respond to the jeers.

The bus has started to pull onto the road again, but then it stops, and Mrs. Wallace, the driver, stands up and faces us, hands on hips. She's a large woman, tall and broad, navy blue windbreaker and work boots all she needs to keep warm. Her voice is as big as she is.

"Hey! All of you! Knock it off!"

Most kids settle down, but not all, and Mrs. Wallace thunders down the aisle, slapping at a shoulder here or the side of a head there. Back at the front, she faces us again. "If I hear one more peep out of you kids, I'll start taking names. You don't want to know what I'll do with them."

One more heavy glare and then I feel rather than see her land in the driver's chair. The gears grind a little, and we go on in silence.

I allow myself to breathe at this point, glad Kyle is still at home for this, glad Mom isn't here, glad Etta didn't see the

Brearlys'. We're at the school before I realize Jorja isn't on the bus.

And at school, there's more upheaval. The teachers try to keep kids in homeroom classes so we won't see, but the buzz is too loud and we all follow in the general direction of the loudest noise. Someone, or some group of someones, has trashed everything they could damage in Sylvia's classroom. Ripped-up books are thrown everywhere, her see-through plastic insect and animal bodies with colored organs are in shards where they landed after being heaved at walls, and the whiteboard is covered in meaningless scrawls of black paint. The desk itself is tipped up on its end, black spray paint around the edges marks a crude outline of a gravestone, and slanting from top left to lower right in black is the word WITCH.

Sylvia herself is there, and she must have had time by now to decide what her response will be. She's watching the janitor sweep up the mess, arms crossed on her chest, jaw set and eyes glaring. I'm watching from just outside the door, peeking around heads at the mess and wondering what Sylvia will do.

"Coming through," I hear behind me, and the assistant principal goes in carrying metal easels, and behind him is Coffin with some of those large pads of white paper to go on the easels. Looks like Sylvia will be holding class as usual. I have to admire her guts.

Principal Glasier's voice comes over the PA system.

"All students proceed to your first-period classes. Repeat, all students proceed to first-period classes."

It takes some time, but we eventually settle into chairs, and it's a little less obvious to me who is in which camp today. I don't understand this, but it's true.

By the time I get to Biology, just before lunch, things have been put into some semblance of order. The desk is where it's supposed to be and we can't see the paint on top of it. The black-scrawled whiteboard is still there, but in front of it are three easels with the big paper pads. They'll probably have to just replace the board. Sylvia looks grim and determined. Max looks nervous; so do most of the kids.

"Welcome, class. Welcome to all of you, even those who might have some sympathy for what happened in here last night."

She walks slowly back and forth in front of her gravestone desk. "This is Biology, a subject that is important to each and every one of you. It's important not only because you need to pass the class to graduate, but also because each of you is living inside a biological structure. Everything about your life is biological. Biology rules how you sleep, how you wake up, how you eat, drink, eliminate waste, walk, see, hear, and think. Yes!" She wheels on us, knowing someone is going to protest. "How you think! Your brains would not function if there were no activity across nerve synapses, and all that happens because of enzymes, hormones, molecular movement—all of it dictated by biology. And all of it"—she glares around the room—"existing as it does today after roughly four-and-a-half billion years' worth of changes that took place very slowly, with many failures along the way."

Naomi waves her hand in the air, and Sylvia calls on her. "That's not the only way it could have happened. It could be that we're all here today as humans because this is the way it's supposed to be." She stops, flushed and breathing loudly through her nose.

Sylvia calls on Marra next. "You're assuming you know how it's supposed to be."

Naomi is looking rather like one of those blind fish, mouth in an odd O shape, eyes looking sightless and weird.

Sylvia says, "Evolution progressed without regard to whether one mutation was right or wrong. Each change either enhanced or prevented survival and integration into the physical world at that time. Blindness in birds, for example, would be something that would severely discourage survival. But then we have bats, which are nearly blind. How do they survive, flying as birds do, avoiding collisions with trees and buildings, finding food? Ethan?"

Yes, my hand goes up. How could it not? Bats . . . "Echoloca-tion," I nearly shout.

"So bats see in a different way, and over millions of years their ability to detect things in this way allowed them to avoid competing with birds that are dependent on daylight, and it allowed them to have nearly sole hunting rights for nighttime insects and to avoid the crowds at the fruit trees. They survived, their genes were passed on, and their numbers increased."

Bryan's hand shoots up. Guess everyone on the debate teams is getting in a little practice. "But it doesn't make any sense that all that happened without a plan."

Sylvia: "Why not?"

"It . . . it just doesn't!"

"If that's true, Bryan, then let's put together a hypothesis around it. What you're saying is that somewhere there's some intellect we can't see, hear, feel, or touch, and that this intellect made countless decisions about how every form of life would be formed. Do you know how many kinds of insect species there are?"

"No; we haven't figured that out yet."

"Correct. But we've discovered massive—and I mean massive—numbers of species so far. There are more than three hundred and fifty thousand different kinds of beetles alone. Each species is different from each of the others in many, many ways, and decisions would need to have been made about each of them. And not just decisions as to what the differences would be, but decisions as to *why* each difference exists."

"And you'd need to be pretty intelligent to do that!"

"Well, it seems to me that the huge numbers of species and differences are more easily explained by a process like evolution, where changes in environment and survival techniques correspond to the differences, but that's my subjective perception. And so is your position that it would require intelligence." She looks around; no more hands. "I've been talking all week about the data, tests, and proof around evolution. Your turn. What data do you offer to demonstrate the presence of this intellect that's making all these decisions?"

"Just look around you!" Bryan shouts.

"I am not saying, Bryan keep your tone reasonable please, that an intelligent plan is out of the question. But until and unless we can provide—broken record, here, but you need to get this—until we have data, repeatable tests, and consistent, predictable results, it's not science. It's faith. So I encourage any of you who subscribe to the intelligent design idea to keep working on it. You're not there yet, though, so I won't present it as a scientific theory."

Max tries to come to her rescue. "If this design is so intelligent, why do men have nipples?"

I'm blushing, stifling laughter, unable to look at Max, so I look at Sylvia, who also seems to be smothering an impulse to chuckle. She clears her throat.

"That's a good question, Max. And I'd also like to ask this agent why we have tonsils, and appendices, and why whales and snakes have vestigial legs that make sense only if they evolved from some animal that had them, or if they evolved into an animal that could use them."

In the silence I know the ID kids are trying to come up with some denial to that. I decide to change the direction with something Etta said. "When science does its testing, isn't it trying to prove an idea wrong? I mean, to make *sure* it's right?"

"Yes. That's an excellent point. Does everyone know what Ethan means? When I give you your first big test next week, I won't be trying to prove that you've paid attention. That will be your job. I'll be trying to *disprove* it. And this approach is essential for science to be science. If you want to prove a plan exists, your tests should be designed to *disprove* that it exists. If you can't disprove it, and your data-driven tests keep proving that it *is* there, then you have science."

Someone behind me says, "So scientists have tried to prove evolution is *wrong?*"

"Absolutely. And because we haven't failed at this, we call it a theory."

That seems to silence them all, at least for now. Plus, the bell is about to ring, which usually brings discussions to a close, anyway. Sylvia assigns some homework that doesn't sound like it's specifically around evolution, and I feel a huge relief.

At lunch I look around for Jorja, wondering if maybe she came late and cut Biology deliberately, but I don't see her. I get corralled by Max and Marra, anyway, and led over to where Gregory is sitting, off to the side, and M and M compete with each other for who can recount the most points that we'll use at the debate. Gregory and I are just chewing and swallowing, and I wouldn't be at all surprised if he feels kind of like I do. There's no way we're going to prove anything to anyone by having a debate. Even though I see more clearly every day why the debate exists, even though I understand so much better than I used to why each side thinks it's right, there's not going to be any resolution. No one is going to win the debate. Kyle is right.

I'm still feeling like this when I get back to Sylvia's room for our debate meeting, and I don't contribute very much to the discussion. Gregory doesn't look good; his face is almost gray, and his eyes are at half-mast. Max and Marra pretty much run the session, and Sylvia keeps closing her eyes and breathing deeply. I guess it's been a pretty intense day for her, too.

Marra tries taking me to task. "Ethan, will you show some leadership? You've hardly said anything!"

Sylvia sticks up for me. "I don't think he can get a word in edgewise, with you two." She looks at Gregory, kind of slumped over, eyes fully shut now. "Gregory, I want you to go to the office and have them call someone to come get you. Now. Ethan, walk with him, will you?"

It's a slow walk. We don't talk at all, just shuffle along, and I start to worry about the guy. But at the office, the nurse says it's just exhaustion, and she takes him off my hands. I make my way to American History, wondering what drama will occur in there today, wondering if I can take any more.

Outside the classroom, I watch for Naomi to ask her about Jorja. I can't say why I'm worried about Jorja. God knows she's not likely to be worried about me for any reason. And I'm still mad at her for dropping that slave bracelet on the bus floor. I try to tell myself she just has a cold. Once upon a time, though, she would have described her suffering to me in painful detail on the phone the night before, or these days she might have left, like, seventeen messages on my iPhone. But lately she's not speaking to me. I have no reason to think there's anything serious. Like I said, I don't know why I'm worried. I just know I am.

I see Naomi from a distance, and she sees me. She walks right up to me. "Ready to capitulate?"

I just blink at her, and only after I ask her my question do I realize she means the debate. "Do you know why Jorja's not in school today?"

"Nope. But I do know she just got replaced on the ID debate team. We don't have time to wait for people who don't even let us know when they're not coming. So now it's me, Cathy, Bryan, and Monique Burns."

This stumps me. "Monique? But she . . ." My voice trails off.

"She what? She's black, so she can't be smart enough?"

"That's not what I meant!" Naomi circles around me and into the room while I stand there trying to juggle too many thoughts at once. Jorja is out, and we don't know why; she's been taken off the ID team, and she probably doesn't even know it; Monique has taken her place; and Monique, because she's black and because of all the stuff Coffin told us about this week, should understand that being on the side of believing someone else is wrong just because you believe it's wrong is like believing black people are stupid just because you believe that.

It occurs to me that I need to devote some gray matter to this last point; maybe Monique doesn't *realize* that she thinks ID is right just because she wants to believe it. But my brain is broken from everything that's happened today, and all I can focus on is that I'm still worried about Jorja.

I move rather mindlessly toward the empty seat beside Max, kind of automatically gravitating toward something that feels right, but he looks up at me intensely and, just barely, shakes his head.

Christ. I don't even have the energy to be pissed. I move forward a few seats and fall into a chair. I manage to take a few notes during class. Coffin is going on about the assignments we've handed in, about why the Brits couldn't have beaten us into thinking we were wrong even if they'd won the war, raking through some of the rational and some of the irrational things kids said in their papers, without naming names. I perk up at one point when he says something good about something I know I wrote, but then I'm back into my stupor again. I'm just starting to wonder whether concussions are contagious when the final bell rings.

I make sure I leave the room beside Max. "Sit with me on the bus, at least?"

"Dude, be real. It's bad enough we're both on the debate team. I'll be sitting with you tonight, okay? Don't call attention. Anyway, Sylvia's looking for me."

I shake my head. Whatever. Maybe this is just his way of dealing with the stress, but I don't much like it. I get on the bus and sit squarely in the middle of the side most of the non-ID kids will sit on and lean against the wall below the window. I'm watching through some kind of haze as kids pour out of the school doors, my gaze fixed more on the white lines between the red bricks than on the people. It's occurring to me, not for the first time, that this relationship with Max is not turning out quite like I want it to. I mean, okay, I get that he doesn't want to advertise that we're together. I don't either. But he's, like, paranoid about it. We should be able to sit together on the bus sometimes, and the fact that we're both on the debate team should give us an *excuse* to sit together, not cause suspicion when we do. And even when we're alone, he says things that make me feel stupid. So things are cool with us only when we're alone in the *back* of his parents' Sequoia? And it's all about sex?

Don't get me wrong; it kind of *is* all about sex. But—there's more, too. Or there ought to be.

Mrs. Wallace, at the wheel, is making noises like she's getting ready to pull the bus away from the curb. I haven't been watching who got on, and I gaze around just to see if Max is sitting with anyone at all. I don't see him. Maybe he's behind me someplace, but I don't have the energy to turn around and look. Eyes back on the school doors, I see nobody at them except some kid who looks like Gus Robichaud hanging out over to the side. All the other buses have left already; Mrs. Wallace must realize she's missing a few kids, and she's giving them more time. But Gus is the only person she can see. She calls to him.

"You getting on?"

He shakes his head.

Okay, so he's riding with Mitch. But where is his partner in crime? As the bus starts moving, I do see someone inside the school, heading toward the doors to come out, and I can tell it's Max, alone. He's going to miss the bus, but—to hell with him, anyway. He can ride with Sylvia. I'm not going to yell to Mrs. Wallace that he's there. *Don't call attention, right, Max?* Out of the corner of my eye I can see his arm start to rise, trying to get Mrs. Wallace's attention, but she's already got her eyes on the road. And then I see another motion. Gus pushes away from the wall he's been leaning against and heads toward Max. And then there's yet another motion. From the other side, where I hadn't seen him, Mitch is moving toward Gus. Toward Max.

Fully alert now, I twist so that I can watch. I can't see out of the dirty windows very well, and the bus is pulling away and distorting the scene, but I can see well enough.

"Hey! Stop the bus! Stop the fucking bus!"

"Young man!" Mrs. Wallace shouts back.

I'm out of my seat, dashing to the front. "Stop! Goddamn it, stop!"

Christ, but everything is happening so slowly! I can see that Mrs. Wallace is looking in her outside rearview mirror, which is capturing a clump of three bodies engaged in something decidedly wrong. She gets up, throws the handle to open the door, and she and I kind of tumble out together and run toward the clump. I see Max's face for a microsecond, twisted in fury and distorted with effort.

Mrs. Wallace, still moving forward, has grabbed my arm. "Get inside. Find help." She pushes me to the side just before we get to the battle, and she wades in. I'm thinking that Gus and Mitch will certainly stop now, and I turn toward the doors to do as I've been told. But then I hear a sickening thud and a groan, and I turn to see that one of the guys has slugged Mrs. Wallace, and she's down.

I can't say what it is, but either the sight of a woman struck to the ground or the idea of Max being slaughtered, or both, snaps something in me. I turn back to the battle and hurl myself onto Gus's broad back. I grab his ear and hang on even as he throws me off of him, and he yells and falls sideways to avoid losing that ugly flap of skin. I dig my fingers into his hair, pulling hard and holding on until he manages to get his hands around my neck. At this point I figure all bets are off. Fighting the urge to grab his hands, which I know won't get him off me, I grab his body with my hands and plunge my knee into his groin. Hard. He screams, falls, and rolls helplessly on the ground.

This is when I notice that kids from the bus are gathered around, and some of them are grabbing at Mitch while others circle Gus. Max is standing to the side, hands on his knees, panting and watching me. He says, "You okay?"

From my hand I shake some loose hairs that I pulled from Gus's scalp, massage my neck a little, cough once, wondering whether I can speak. I try, and "I will be" comes out convincingly enough.

There are now about seven teachers with us, and Glasier is bending over Mrs. Wallace, who is now sitting up. I can see that Coffin is on a cell phone, no doubt calling for yet more ambulances. They should just leave one stationed here.

Sylvia rushes over to Max and says all the usual things, examining his face, which looks a little battered but not bad. Still gorgeous. He'll have some bruises and scrapes, and the way he's standing tells me there are no doubt bruised ribs in there.

She hugs him, tears on her face. "This is my fault. This is all my fault. I'm so sorry, Max."

I want to ask why it's her fault some Neanderthal slugged her brother, but then it comes to me that these lunks were probably not happy that she wasn't sufficiently intimidated by the damage to her classroom, and rather than attack her they jumped Max. Coffin comes over to me to ask if I'm all right, and I nod. Something in my face makes him ask, "What is it, Ethan?"

"Somehow they knew Max would be alone. They were waiting for him."

"How do you know?"

"I saw it from the bus. Gus was over there, and Mitch was over there"—I point—"and the bus was pulling away just as Max got to the door from the hall. He was going to miss the bus, and they knew it."

Coffin and I both look around, at the door, at where the boys had been waiting, at Max and Sylvia, at the bus.

And then it hits me. "Max told me Sylvia was looking for him. Maybe she wasn't really."

Coffin heads toward them and I follow. He says, "Max, did you stop to talk with Sylvia before heading for the bus?"

Max looks a little dazed. His face will be rather purple tomorrow. He glances from Coffin to his sister and back. "I had a note. Meet her in the cafeteria because it wasn't safe in her room, but she wasn't there. I waited a few minutes, gave up, didn't see her in her classroom either, so I headed out here."

Sylvia says, "I didn't write any note, Max."

Coffin asks, "Do you still have it?"

Max fishes in his jacket pocket but finds nothing. I look around, and there's a crumpled white paper on the tarmac off to the side. Coffin says, "Don't touch it, Ethan!" He comes over, gloves on his hands, and opens it carefully. It's a typed note, and it says just what Max had said. No signature, just Sylvia's typed name at the bottom.

I hear the wail of sirens, and this time two ambulances and

three police cars arrive nearly at the same time. I figure, you know, time to tell Mom I'll be late. Thank God for this iPhone.

This time she does come to get me, and Kyle stays in the car. Since I'm the one who saw it start, and then I got involved in the fight, there are lots of questions for me from the police. They also ask me about the bus ride this morning. They already know about the classroom, but they ask me, anyway.

Mom stays with me through all of it, glancing from time to time toward Kyle in the front seat of the car. She acts pretty much like Etta had, the day of the road accident, which is that she just lets me tell my story. She doesn't prod, she doesn't say anything to the police, she's just there. For me.

When they finally let us go, I see someone I hadn't expected. Etta. Mom must have phoned her to tell her what was going on. She comes over to me, and as she's hugging me she says, "Glad you're on my side, Ethan."

Just before Mom and I get into the car to leave, Sylvia comes over to me. "I'm going with Max to the hospital to make sure he's okay. But I need to tell you something. I've talked with Mr. Glasier and Mr. Ivers, and we're canceling the debate. I'll let the others on our team know."

I glance at Etta, and she's nodding like she already knew this. I wonder if she might even have been the one to suggest it. I ask her, "Is the town hall meeting still on?"

"At this point, yes. Though I'm pretty sure there will be some police presence. If there's a change, I'll call."

I look around for Carl Phinney, and there he is, moving from parent to parent—a number of them have shown up by now— and generally behaving like some rabid politician.

Mom and I climb into the car, and I'm thinking there'll be no debate team dinner tonight. This suits me fine, but I would like to have sat with Max at the town hall. Now he probably won't even be there.

Kyle's in front, so I get into the backseat, and as Mom's pulling onto the road she asks, "Ethan, why do you really think those boys attacked Max?"

I glance at the rearview mirror, and the expression on her

face tells me she thinks it might have something to do with being gay. She doesn't want to say this out loud in front of Kyle.

I hold her gaze for just a second, to let her know I understand. "It's just that he's Sylvia's brother. I'm sure, that's all." And I am sure, actually; I don't think anyone has a clue about Max.

Then Mom surprises the hell out of me. "How would you kids like to have some burgers tonight, and have Dad join us, before we head over to the meeting?"

Kyle turns a puzzled face toward her, and I decide to speak up. "Yeah! Great!" I'm thinking, you know, maybe Mom has decided to keep Dad up to speed on what's going on with his sons. Maybe that's why she's suggesting this get-together.

"Ethan, why don't you phone him now? That way if he can join us I'll stop and get stuff at the market."

Dad tells me he's glad I called. "I almost came over to the school. Heard something about what was going on. Just didn't know if you'd still be there. Called your mom and got no answer."

"She probably had her cell off. We were talking to the police for a while. Anyway, you'd need to come early for dinner, 'cause then we have to go to the town hall meeting. Are you going to that with us?" I glance at Mom; she hasn't said anything about that.

Dad doesn't seem too sure about it, either. "We can talk about that over dinner, Ethan. What I want most is to see you kids and find out all about what happened."

Mom leaves me in the car with Kyle when she stops at the supermarket. I understand why, but there's an odd silence between us that I don't like. I'm remembering his response when Mom and I talked about the people who threw rocks at Sylvia's house. He'd said they were just expressing their opinion. So I'm biting my tongue now; otherwise my voice will escape and say something like, *Which opinion were they expressing today, do you think?*

So we don't speak at all, just sit there and wait as it gets darker slowly. Sightlessly my eyes follow cars coming in, people walking into the store, coming out, on and on in this irregular but predictable mosaic pattern. I imagine what it would look like from above, and how you can't tell by looking at any of these people which opinion any one of them might want to express about this debate, which seems to have spread everywhere. Etta's signs get stolen from people's yards. She gets hate mail and death threats. Lowell Galway won't plow Etta's driveway for the first time in, like, decades. Coffin gets called an atheist by a crowd of people camped outside his house. Sylvia's home is wrecked. The Brearlys' place is trashed. Have I left anything out? And that doesn't include all the stuff at school: Gregory hospitalized overnight and still weak today, Sylvia's classroom, the fight today, Mrs. Wallace getting slugged.

And then something sneaks up on me from the back of my brain. It moves forward like it's on bat wings, silent and sure in the darkness. In that whole laundry list of violence, I can't come up with one thing that didn't start in the ID camp.

I let my voice out. "Kyle? Still sitting with Phinney tonight?"

He takes a minute, breathes audibly, then, "Don't think I want to go."

"Why not?"

"This isn't right. This isn't how it should be. I know what it's going to be like, and it's wrong. This isn't how God wants it."

Wow. I wouldn't have given him that much credit. I decide he deserves a little more. "You were right. About the debate. Fortunately they've called it off."

"Good."

"But you'd still, you know, if you could vote, you'd still vote for Phinney?"

"Of course. As far as I know, he hasn't hurt anyone, and he's still right."

I shrug. "You're entitled to your opinion. And I'm entitled to mine. Guess we'll have to agree to disagree."

"Guess so."

Truce. I might actually like my brother. What a concept.

I see Mom leave the store, and her path to the car takes her across the path of a woman going in. I see Mom freeze in her tracks and look at the other woman. It's Nancy Hyde. Nancy's head turns just enough to see who's standing there, and then she looks back toward the door she's headed for. She doesn't say a word. Neither does Mom.

I want to run after that bitch and shake her so hard she bites her tongue.

I notice there are no signs in our front yard when we get home. I'm pretty sure that this time Mom took them down.

Dinner is short but kind of fun, because Dad can't get enough of my story. I'm sure he wouldn't have used my techniques—ear pulling, hair yanking, groin kneeing—but he loves that I jumped in when Mrs. Wallace got slugged. He's proud of me, and he says so. The day is still a dark cloud, but I do get some silver lining.

Then I ask about the town hall. I know now that Kyle doesn't want to go, so I'm unsure who will go and who won't. I kind of don't even want to go at this point. I'm thinking maybe Mom and Dad could go together, and that might actually be good. But Dad says he doesn't want to go. Doesn't want to get involved. I cringe a little; it sounds like me, and I don't like it. I decide suddenly that I do want to be there.

This is when Kyle says he doesn't want to go, and Mom looks at him, surprised. "I thought you wanted to support your candidate." She actually gets up and walks over to him, places her hand on his head, and says, like it's a joke, "You aren't sick or anything, are you?" But then her smile fades and she says, "You do feel too warm, actually."

He shakes his head, picking through the pile of loose ground beef mixed with onions and ketchup that Mom gave him so he can use only his left hand. "I still support Mr. Phinney, because I still think evolution without design is wrong, but I hate all this violence. It's wrong, too. And there'll be more tonight."

Mom looks at him for a few seconds before she sits down again. "I expect you're right. Ethan, I'm going to ask you to stay home with your brother. You've had enough excitement for one day, and there's no debate assignment now."

I'm trying to weigh the need to watch Kyle against my decision to support Etta when Dad says, "I can stay with Kyle, Charlene. If Ethan stays home, it'll look like he's scared after what happened at school today. He'll look like a coward."

"He'll look like a sensible person!"

They can't argue; I won't let them. But I don't want to lose Dad's pride in me. "Okay, okay. Look, Mom, you shouldn't go alone. Kyle's right, this will be ugly. I'm okay, y'know. I didn't get hurt today. And Dad can stay with Kyle." I know she doesn't like this idea, but for reasons surpassing understanding, Dad's been great ever since he got here. Having him stay here with Kyle isn't quite as good as having my parents do something together, but it would keep him involved with the family. Finally, I add, "I want to support Etta."

Mom scowls, looking like she's trying to come up with a good reason why this won't work. Evidently she can't. She also can't deny that Etta deserves support.

We get the dishes stacked up, and Dad even says he'll wash them so Mom and I can head over. Like, wow. Kyle goes into the living room and turns on the TV. I stand in the doorway to the kitchen where I can watch Kyle and hear my parents.

"Dave, I can't have you talk to him like last time—"

"I know, Charlene. I won't. I was just pissed that you hadn't told me. I know more about it now. It'll be fine, I promise."

"What have you had to drink today?"

"Nothing but coffee and soda. As a matter of fact, I haven't had a drink in over a week."

There's a pause, like Mom is taking this in, and counting in my head I wonder if that flask he poured from at Friendly's was his last. Then, "You have to watch him. He does things like sit in his room, chant Bible verses, and hold his hand up in the air to deny it nourishment." Dad nods, but I can see he's taken aback by this. "If he goes upstairs, you'll have to keep going upstairs to check on him. And take his temperature; he felt too warm to me. Give him some ibuprofen if he's over ninety-nine."

"Got it."

Dad sees us to the door, and he surprises me. "Be careful, you two." He watches as we drive away.

The meeting is at one of the other schools that the board represents, in the auditorium. I'm glad it's not my school; there's too much tension there already.

We're not the first ones there, that's sure. Etta's there already, and Carl Phinney, onstage and discussing the speakers' chair placement, water pitchers, who knows what else. She sees us and waves. Mom puts a hand on my shoulder and moves us toward a position near the front but off to the side Etta is on, near the emergency exit door.

I watch as other people mill around, choose seats, chat with each other. So far, so good; I don't see any signs of trouble. But then people carrying homemade signs start to show up. They stand in the back, on the Phinney side of the house. They're quiet, but their signs are not.

BLESSED IS THE NATION WHOSE GOD IS THE LORD

This is the first one I notice. I point it out to Mom, and she snorts. Into my ear she says, "As opposed to which other God, I'd like to know?"

Some of the other signs are even sillier:

SCIENTISTS ARE THE PAGAN PRIESTS OF ATHISM!

NO GOD = NO GUILT = NO MORALITY

GOD'S CHILREN ARE NOT MUD AND OZE!

IN THE BEGINING, GOD CREATED. THAT'S ALL I NEED TO KNOW.

CREATION IS FACT!

DON'T VOTE GOD OUT OF TOWN!

There are more, but I can't bring myself to read them all. I want to laugh at some of the misspellings, except that I don't want to laugh at all. To Mom I whisper, "Sylvia thought the ID side would deny that ID is religion."

"Guess some of them have decided to be honest about that,

at least. But that's good; it should make it easier to put ID in its place."

I shake my head; I'm not so sure. It seems to me that if two words tell someone everything they need to know, they're not likely to even see that there *is* any place other than theirs.

I see Mr. Coffin come in and sit a few rows behind us. The Glasiers settle in on Phinney's side, but they seem to want to distance themselves from the signs. Then I see Mr. and Mrs. Modine. They don't have Sylvia or Max with them; I'm not sure what that means. They sit in our row but toward the middle.

Mom says to me, "That takes guts. I admire them for that."

I crane my neck to see everyone I can, seated and coming in. No sign of Jorja. Sylvia does appear, finally, and sits with her folks. I look hard at her, wanting to ask about Max. She turns to me, smiles, and I see her mouth say, "He's fine." So he's not coming. Just as well, I suppose.

Before long there are no more seats. It's not a huge auditorium, but it's big enough, and it's standing room only. More signs have appeared on the Phinney side. I strain to look around to the back of my side, Etta's side, and there are no signs at all. I wish I knew what that means. I also wish I could tell for sure whether there's overflow from one side to the other. I mean, with no empty seats, I can't tell if ID has more supporters, and they just had to sit on our side, or if it's the other way around.

I'm just about to turn back to the front when I catch sight of a woman with long frizzy hair who's wearing something billowy in greens and blues. It's Heidi Wolcott, maybe four rows behind us. She sees me looking at her and waves, smiling broadly. I don't know the woman she's sitting with, but I make a mental note to introduce Mom to Heidi when this thing is over.

Etta had been right about the police presence. There are men and women in blue standing at attention all along the walls, with one at either end of the stage, hands crossed before them, eyes in motion around the room. This makes me feel creepy, and I look at Mom. She looks at me, and I use my eyes to indicate what I'm noticing. She nods and whispers, "Government is good for some things, Ethan. I'm not against keeping you safe, y'know."

This makes sense to me. I gaze back toward the stage. Etta looks calm, but lonely.

The school board president, a Mrs. Chamberlain, stands at the podium and hits it lightly with a gavel, but not many people hear that. She taps a finger on the microphone, and the room quiets down.

"Good evening, everyone. I think we all know why we're here, so I won't spend a lot of time on introductions. Please remember that you must be recognized by me before you address either candidate, and I reserve the right to dismiss any question that I deem unproductive to the discussion. Also, I want to stress that all speech must be respectful, and all behavior must be civilized. Nothing else will be tolerated. Are there questions before we begin?"

There are one or two folks who don't understand the protocol for asking questions, so she goes over it. Then someone else wants to know why the police are there, and Mrs. Chamberlain says something vague about a recent disturbance. Then she says just a few things about both the candidates' qualifications. Phinney's all seem to be things like selectman, that kind of experience. Etta's surprise me. Evidently she's done quite a bit of work with different political agencies in New York, which sounds impressive, though I expect Phinney will get more credit for having done his work locally.

The first question goes to Etta. Someone wants to know more about her experience that would qualify her for this post. I listen, but I have to say it doesn't mean a whole lot to me. The questions after that stay pretty tame for a while, with Phinney taking every opportunity to point out how much more specific his experience is for the school board seat. What worries me most is that he also seems more human, or more easy-going, something like that. Etta doesn't look nervous, exactly, but she looks a little stiff. And I don't fool myself that people won't let this difference matter when they decide how to vote.

Then things start to heat up a little when someone asks Etta whether she believes in God. I half expect her to look at me, but she doesn't. Mrs. Chamberlain says that's not pertinent and recognizes someone else, but the second person says they won't vote for anyone if they don't know what that person's religion is.

Mom whispers to me, "That's unconstitutional. You know that, right?"

I nod, vaguely remembering Coffin talking about that kind of thing in a previous lifetime, which is about how far away the Free Exercise Clause feels about now. Etta says she'll respond, if Mrs. Chamberlain will allow, and she gives an answer that's not quite what she said to me. Obviously she really did work on those personal types of questions I gave her, and she says something vague enough to be true but specific enough to get by.

This pacifies folks for a little while, and Phinney fields a few more questions. Finally someone brings up ID, which no one has mentioned by name until now. Phinney gives a few reasons why he supports it and says he would take steps to make sure it receives appropriate recognition in science studies.

And, just like this afternoon when Gus put his hands on my neck, all bets are suddenly off. And so are the gloves. The next question comes directly out of Sylvia's classroom. Some woman says, "My daughter tells me that she learned in *science* class," sneering the word, "that bats are not birds. That's crazy!"

Mrs. Chamberlain says, "Are you addressing a candidate?"

"That one!" And the woman points at Etta.

Mrs. Chamberlain responds, "Ms. Greenleaf is running for school board, not for science instructor. Your question is not relevant."

Mom whispers, "Relevant, no; insane, yes. What is *wrong* with people?"

Etta doesn't say anything about taking that question on, and the next question comes from the guy holding the CREATION IS FACT sign. "Ms. Greenleaf, how can you say you believe in God and then deny his intelligence and his design?"

"I deny neither of those things." Etta seems to be coming to life at last. "There is nothing about evolution that denies God in any way."

"Liar!"

Mrs. Chamberlain bangs her gavel. "Speak only with respect! Ms. Greenleaf, do you have more to say before we move on?"

"Yes, thank you. Relying on the methods at our human command to verify the physical world around us is using the tools God gave us. We have the best brains on the planet, and we've used them to examine our surroundings. If you believe we have God to thank for our own intelligence, then you will recognize that using it to the best of our ability is an expression of gratitude. We use science to follow the clues left for us. Intelligent Design as a discipline does not follow the scientific method. It is therefore not science." She has to speak loudly to be heard over the crowd grumbling. "I am not calling it an invalid approach to understanding the nature of God. I am saying only that *as it has been presented,* it is not science."

It takes several bangs of Mrs. Chamberlain's gavel to get folks quiet enough to go on. "Let's have a question for Mr. Phinney, please. Anyone?"

I'm thinking this might calm things down a little, but the question comes from Sylvia. "Mr. Phinney, what data can Intelligent Design provide to help us apply scientific methods for testing it? Please be specific."

He starts out looking sure of himself, but after he rambles on for a bit he starts talking in circles. In the end he says stuff kind of like what Naomi and Bryan had said—not that different from "Just look around you!"

Mrs. Chamberlain lets Sylvia ask a follow-up. "You're basing your support for ID completely on observation. What about scientific methods, though? I didn't hear you respond to that."

Mom whispers, "She's trying to push them into admitting that this is all religion."

I whisper back, "How can they deny it? Look at those signs!"

Phinney looks like he's trying to come up with something to say, but before he forms words there are people shouting from his own side, more at Sylvia than anyone else.

"God's word provides all the data we need!"

"Read your Bible!"

"You can't even prove evolution!"

That's about all I can make out before it gets so noisy in the back that I have to look away from the stage and at the crowd, wondering how long it will be before they charge. The cops on that side have moved forward, and I see a couple of them touch the shoulder or the arm of someone who seems to be over-excited. There's a lot of anger over there.

Anger. That's what someone in Coffin's class said, just before Monique said, "Fear."

Maybe I'm having a PTSD moment after my difficult day, but I'm starting to get nervous. I look at Mom; she doesn't look nervous at all. She's starting to look angry, though. Her jaw is clenched, eyes narrow—the classic signs. I look down at her hands, and they're clasped together hard, like she's trying to stop herself from hitting something. Someone.

Some guy in the row behind us stands up, and I hear him shout, "Will you idiots shut up and listen to someone make some sense?" I turn to see who it is, and my jaw drops. It's the guy whose life Etta saved, the driver who missed the deer and hit a tree. When he turns to sit down, shaking his head in disgust, he sees me. I smile, and he smiles and nods. He never actually saw me that day, so he probably doesn't know who it is he just smiled at, but maybe he knows what Etta did for him. It's a good moment.

Gavel banging is having no effect at all at this point. Even Phinney can't be heard; he's standing now, his arms held out to the crowd like he's trying to calm them down. One of the cops on the stage steps forward and blows hard on his whistle. The room settles down a little, and he moves to Mrs. Chamberlain's microphone.

"If we can't have a peaceful meeting, I'm going to have to clear the room." He stands there, glaring at everyone, until it gets quiet. He steps back.

Mrs. Chamberlain, looking nervous herself now, comes forward again and recognizes Mrs. Glasier.

"Mr. Phinney, I want to know where you stand on prayer in schools."

. "I would like to see prayer allowed everywhere, Mrs. Glasier." He stops, like that's enough.

Etta says, "May I respond as well?" Mrs. Chamberlain nods. "Prayer is already allowed everywhere. There is nothing stopping any child from praying in school today. What's prohibited by the U.S. Constitution is the leading of prayer by—"

"Liar!"

Again with that? The gavel bangs, and an officer steps forward toward the shouter, who had stood up and now sits down again.

Mrs. Chamberlain recognizes Mr. Coffin. He says, "Mr. Phinney, I'm sure you're aware of the damage done to a science classroom in our district last night, and of the violent activities committed this afternoon related to it. I feel sure *you* don't support this violence or this destruction. Is there anything you can say that will help prevent further . . . um, disturbances?"

Mom whispers, "Very clever. He's pointed the violence right at Phinney's supporters without actually saying it."

Phinney seems happy to accept the spotlight on this question, at first. But even as he states how deplorable he finds violence, I can see it's dawning on him that it's his side doing it, and that he's just accepted that blame along with the responsibility to stop it. He sits down as soon as he can.

There are another couple of questions for Etta, one from our side and one from theirs, and the shouting starts again. This time it's worse, and the sign holders start to pump their arms—and their signs—up and down. I have to say almost all the noise is now coming from one corner of the room, over near the signs. Most everyone else on the ID side is sitting pretty still, staring either at the signs or toward the stage. The police move around again, and the crowd gets just quiet enough so that we can hear the guy holding the sign calling pagans atheists say, "Professing themselves to be wise, they became fools."

Mom pops up out of her seat, turns in that direction, and shouts, "Professing themselves to be Christians, they commit violence!"

And all bets are off again. The sign holders start to move forward in the room, the police surround them, and for a few seconds it's hard to tell just how bad things might get. Two officers position themselves behind Etta, and two of the cops along my wall move, one to stand at the center of the aisle near Sylvia, and the other close to Mr. Coffin. Mom does look a little nervous now, and just before I think she's ready to grab my arm and head for the emergency exit door, the police whistle sounds again from the stage.

"I want that corner of the room cleared now." The officer at the podium points to the signs. We all watch in relative silence as officers escort the most vocal people out of the building. I can hear the crackle of police radios as the cops outside keep the one on the stage informed about the departure of the troublemakers.

The officer at the podium gets everyone's attention again. "In the interest of protecting the peace, I'm calling this meeting over. I want the people on this side"—his arm indicates the ID side—"to file out of the auditorium quietly and in single file, please. One row at a time. The officers will direct you. Then get in your cars and go home."

The people on my side start talking suddenly, and they start to get loud, so the officer blows his whistle again. "Please remain quiet. We'll be moving you out in the same manner shortly." I hear someone in the back say something that sounds like "police state."

I watch Etta. She looks nervous but not scared, hands folded in her lap and eyes forward, watching the room. Phinney is pacing slowly on his side of the stage, one hand behind his neck.

Mom gets the attention of one of the cops. "Is it all right if I speak for a moment with Ms. Greenleaf?" I can tell it irritates the hell out of her to have to ask for permission to talk to her friend. There's a signaled communication between our officer and the guy at the podium, and they let Mom go to the foot of the stage. I can't tell what they say, but the discussion includes one of the cops behind Etta. Mom comes back.

"I asked her if she'd be all right alone at home or if she wanted to stay with us. But those two officers are going to see her home and then stay there."

Now I am scared. It hasn't occurred to me that Etta really might not be safe in her own home. *Feeling* safe was over a while ago, but actually not *being* safe is too much. Two might protect her from coyotes or a burglar, but what can he do against all this? I look up at her, thinking of the death threats she's received, and she smiles at me. I can't quite tell how real the smile is or how much fear is behind it.

It strikes me that there's fear that creates violence and also fear that results from it. I'm starting to see why violence is such a bad idea.

Mom and I file out when the cop near us points to our row. I'm thinking I'd like to talk with Sylvia, maybe see how Max is doing, and there was that idea of introducing Mom to Heidi. But there are more police officers outside, and they keep us all moving toward the cars. Guess I'll have to text Max later.

The drive home is silent. I'm sure Mom just doesn't dare speak or she'll start shouting or something. The only good thing I can think of at the moment is that it's only a few more hours until tomorrow, until this horrible day is over. Of course I have no idea what will happen tomorrow, but it can't be worse than today.

As we approach our driveway, there's a rectangle of yellow-orange light where the front door is standing open, and I can hear shouting. I strain my eyes toward some motion, and it looks like Dad is running across the front yard toward two people. Our headlights catch the face of one of them. It looks like Fred Kilburn, a kid in my class. We've never liked each other, but there hasn't been any real trouble between us since we were, like, ten, maybe? What's he doing in my front yard?

Mom pulls to the side of the road so the headlights show more of what's going on. I can't tell who the other kid is, but now they're both running away, and I can see they were setting up some kind of pole that they couldn't quite get into the ground. It's on its side now, and Dad goes over and lifts it. If the kids had managed to get it in place, it would have been as tall as Dad. He stands it up to see what's attached to the top, and the headlights fall on this hideous, witchlike scarecrow with long dark hair. It's hung from the top of the pole by a rope around its neck. On its white T-shirt are two red letters: CP.

Charlene Poe.

I'm out of the car before I know I've opened the door, running down the road, shouting at the top of my lungs. "You assholes! Fuckers! Shitheads!"

I can hear Dad's voice behind me, calling my name, but I ignore him. I run until I fall into what's left of the snowbank, banging my knee on something hard and scraping my chin on the icy crystals of the berm. Scrambling up, I don't even know I'm crying until I lose my footing again on the slippery clumps of icy snow and fall once more. I lie there until Dad catches up with me. He pulls me to my feet.

"It's okay, son. It's all right. Come back, now."

"I hate them!" I'm helpless, impotent, useless. "I hate them!"

"I know, I know. Come on back, now. I'll get rid of that thing."

Mom's parked the car, and she's standing beside it. In the darkness I can't make out her face. Dad shuts the car door and takes her arm, still holding mine with his other hand, and we all go inside. Kyle is just inside the door, looking scared.

There's a look on Mom's face I've never seen before. It's not fear, exactly, and it's not quite anger. I guess confusion comes closer than anything else. Dad takes her coat, and she just lets him. I hang mine up and go into the kitchen to wash my chin and wipe my eyes. When I get back to the living room, Kyle is watching our folks, who are sitting next to each other on the couch. Mom looks dazed, and Dad has his arm around her shoulders.

Christ! Why couldn't this happen for a *good* reason?

Dad says, "Ethan, would you make a pot of tea for your mother?"

I look at her; she doesn't respond at all, so I go into the kitchen, put the kettle on, dump a couple of tea bags into the teapot, and go back to the doorway while the water heats. I can hear talking, and I want to know what's being said. I get there in time to hear Dad say, "I think I should stay here for a while, Charlene. You and the boys shouldn't be here alone. I, uh, I can sleep on the couch."

And the unthinkable happens. Mom closes her eyes and leans against Dad's shoulder.

Yes!

Kyle and I look at each other. I can't read his expression, but I have a cautious grin on my face. If nothing else good comes out of this terrible day, let it be this!

Chapter 13

The divide on the bus Thursday is bigger than ever. But I can tell the lines have shifted, because even though all the ID kids are on their side, they take up only about half the seats over there. It's obvious that everyone else on that side is now with my group, whatever "side" that is. Max surprises me by sitting with me. I had texted him last night, to see how he was and to tell him about the scarecrow, though I couldn't bring myself to call it what it really was: my mother hung in effigy. But I've told him my dad is back in the house. I'm hoping this will even help Kyle get better. It's hard to keep my hopes in check.

I give Mrs. Wallace a lot of credit. She has a whopper of a bruise on her face, but she's here, driving the bus just like always.

"You okay?" I ask Max, keeping my voice quiet and trying to sound as casual as possible.

"For sure. I'll get out of gym for a few days, though. Cracked cheekbone, bruised ribs." He shrugs, and then winces like he forgot that was going to hurt.

"How's Sylvia?"

"You'll see for yourself. She's definitely teaching today, even though Mom tried to talk her out of it. Gutsy. Or stupid."

We ride in silence a few stops. Then he says, "Where's your friend Jorja?"

Right. Jorja. We'd passed her stop, and her church. (This week it's T.G.I.F. THANK GOD I'M FORGIVEN. I'm thinking they sure need forgiveness, with what some of them have done this week.) There's no sign of her. "Don't know. Second day, now, at least if we count only full days. I should've called her. It's just been so crazy."

I'm expecting him to tell me to forget it, to forget her, but he doesn't say anything.

The whole day is weird. People are going around acting like everything's normal, only everyone knows it isn't. Some kids don't show up for Biology, like Bryan and Naomi. Religious grounds, maybe? Monique is there, and I look at her, wondering what she makes of everything that's going on. She's always seemed kind of shy, withdrawn. But she was ready to be on the ID debate team. She catches me looking at her, and her eyes fall immediately. Guilty conscience?

At lunch I pull out my iPhone and call Jorja's house. No one answers, so I leave a vague message about calling me back. Now I *am* worried. I call home to see how Mom's feeling today, after that ugly thing last night, wondering as I do whether she'll ever go back to work. She'd taken a leave of absence or something to take care of Kyle, but sitting at home is not good for her. There's no answer there, either.

Why would Mom and Kyle not be home? They don't have another therapy appointment until tomorrow. I suppose it's possible she had to go to the store, and of course she'd have to take him with her. But up to now she hasn't done that—she's been keeping him from having to face people or answer questions about his hand—so . . . The only reason I can think of is ugly: Kyle's done something else to hurt himself. For some reason, instead of calling Mom's cell, I decide to call Dad.

"Hey, Ethan." No standard greeting. Tension in his voice. The world is not right.

"Dad, there's no one answering the phone at home. Do you know where they are?"

He clears his throat, seeming to search for words. "I think they're over at Etta's."

"Etta's?" Dad says nothing else, so I add, "Maybe I'll call her cell."

"No. Um, no. Uh . . ."

Around the lump in my throat I say, "Dad? What the fuck's going on? Is it Kyle?" My eyes fall on Fred Kilburn across the room, laughing at something. He's with Craig DeYoung, who might well have been his partner in crime last night.

I hear Dad exhale. "No. Kyle's fine. They're both fine. Listen, kid, if I come get you, can you miss the rest of your classes today? You don't have some big test or anything, do you?"

"No test," I lie, knowing I'm not ready for that exam in math, anyway. And, again, "What's going on?"

"I'll be there in ten minutes. Be out front."

Christ! I look around for Max and see him at a table with some seniors I don't know very well. Probably showing off his battle scars after yesterday. I stand there a minute, thinking maybe I'll text him; I really don't want to go over there, upset like I am, and say anything in front of that crowd. It's just that I want to talk to someone, and I want it to be him. Damn him, anyway! Why can't he at least treat me like a friend, if he won't admit to being my boyfriend?

I ditch my tray and nearly capsize Sylvia as I leave the cafeteria.

"Ethan? Everything okay? You look—upset."

I stare at her a minute. "I don't know."

"What is it?"

"Dad's coming to pick me up," I manage to say, my voice getting squeaky as my throat closes in panic.

She takes my arm. "Where's your locker?" She goes with me to get my coat, the long funky pea coat, and I can't even enjoy it. Then she takes me with her to get her parka, and we stand out front together.

She's perfect. She doesn't say anything. No assurances, nothing about being sure "everything is fine." No attempts at small talk. No mention even of the town hall last night.

Dad pulls up in his pickup, and as I climb in Sylvia asks, "Mr. Poe, is there anything I can do?"

He shakes his head. "That's nice of you, Sylvia. We'll let you know."

She backs away and I slam the door. I can barely hear her say, "Call me, Ethan, will you?"

I nod, and Dad pulls away from the curb. He's not tearing up the pavement or anything, so maybe things aren't actually falling apart.

"So will you tell me now?"

He takes a deep breath. "First, your mom and Kyle are fine. It's not them."

"You said that already. So what the hell is it?" This is the second time in half an hour I've sworn in his presence, and he doesn't even seem to notice.

He opens his mouth, closes it, opens it, finally manages, "I don't even know how much this will upset you, Ethan. Your mom seemed to think you'd be torn up, but..."

"*What?*" I'm shouting at him now, and he doesn't even protest at that.

"It's Etta's dog."

"Two?" What the ... what's he talking about?

Another deep breath. "When she got home last night, with the policemen, they found him. He ... he'd been shot, Ethan. He's dead."

I turn my face to look out the side window. So many questions fly into my brain, but they can't make it out of my mouth. I almost can't breathe, and I sure as hell can't see through all these tears. But I don't want my dad to see. So I just stare out the window and let the salty water run down my face. If I wipe at them, Dad will know.

Two. I see his smiling face, broad and dense and powerful, looking up at me from the grass in the dog park, begging to have his belly rubbed. Then I see intense determination on that same face as he hurtles toward me, outnumbered three to one by wild coyotes, intent on protecting his pack. To keep Etta and me safe. To throw his power, his ferocity, and possibly his life into the fray for us.

Two. *How can Two be dead?* Two is invincible!

Eventually I unclench my jaw and manage to ask, "Who shot him?" I'm still staring out the window.

"Lowell Galway's truck was tearing ass out of Etta's driveway just as she and the cops got there after the meeting last night. One of them chased him down, and his shotgun was warm. And the dog was shot with a shotgun."

I swallow a few times. "So Mom's with Etta?" I try to sniff while Dad's talking; maybe he won't hear it that way.

"Yeah. She's probably on her way home about now, with Kyle; Etta's friend is going to stay with her."

"Heidi?"

"I think that's her name, yeah."

I've managed to wipe away the tears, unobtrusively, I hope. "What about Two?"

"I dug him a grave up behind the house."

My head snaps in Dad's direction. "You've buried him? *Already?*" I won't get to say good-bye! I won't get to stroke my hand down his side one last time, or tweak a triangle of ear, or—anything! "God! How could you do that?"

Dad looks confused. "Well . . . he was dead."

I try to do what everyone else seems to be doing lately. I try to use anger to hide what's really going on inside. I grit my teeth and pound on the dashboard and swear a blue streak. But it doesn't help. And it doesn't last. Before I know it, my screams of obscenity turn to sobs, even the foulest words fail me, and tears are streaming down my face. I don't care anymore that Dad will see. I don't care about anything.

The next thing I notice is that Dad seems to be heading home. I've stopped crying, but my voice sounds dead as I say, "No. Take me to Etta's."

"Ethan—"

"Take me to Etta's!" I don't mean to shout, but getting there is imperative. If I have to, I'll walk. But Dad heads that way. I want to feel bad that I yelled at him, but I can't.

The drive to Etta's is a total blank. I wouldn't have noticed the cop car at the end of the driveway, but Dad waves at it. Without registering it on any level of reality, I see Heidi's Volvo beside Etta's car. I'm out of Dad's truck before he can even roll to a stop, the only thing in my head an image of Two in front of the house, facing the intruder ferociously, fearless and determined to protect his world. I know this is where I'll find his blood.

Someone tried to cover it over with snow, but I find it easily. A dark stain is soaked into the dirt where death found him. Death by hatred. Death by stupidity. Death by anything except God. I dig my fingers into the spot, but the earth doesn't yield, and all I get are a few grains of grit. I look up at the door, but no one has opened it, so I walk around the building to find the grave.

Etta must have told Dad where to dig. The spot is a little distance from the house, next to a huge boulder poking out of the earth, overlooking the distant hills. From the Adirondack chairs, the grave is directly in the sight line to the distant horizon. I don't look at the hills. I look only at the mound of dirt, where someone has placed pebbles to form the shape of a heart. I guess this is instead of a cross, which of course would be all wrong here. I suspect Heidi.

Kneeling beside the grave, I'm vaguely aware of Dad standing at a distance, no doubt wondering what to make of this scene, of his son's fury and tears. But I have only about a second of attention for him. From inside a pocket, my iPhone makes its text message sound. It's probably Max. I ignore it.

I sit fully on the ground and try to think of some symbol of my own to leave, something appropriate to share with this creature who balanced power and loyalty so beautifully, and of course my yin-yang image comes to mind. But I can't bring myself to draw it, or form it with stones, or even hold it in my head. I feel no balance here. I can't believe in balance at all.

There's nothing but loss and pain. And for some amount of time I lose track of, that's all that exists in the world.

I'm almost unaware that someone's hand touches my shoulder, and a woman is crouching down, about to sit beside me. It must be Etta. She feels this pain, too, and we can mourn Two together. I turn toward her.

But it's not Etta. It's Heidi. I blink stupidly at her, registering on some nearly subconscious level that I can't see Dad anymore.

Heidi doesn't say anything. She takes my hand and looks at the warrior's grave, and I see tears on her face that she doesn't even try to wipe away. We sit there until we're both shivering with cold, and then we sit there some more. Finally, teeth chattering, I ask, "Where's Etta?"

Stupid question. She's inside, of course. But what I mean is, *Why isn't she with me? Why is it you and not her holding my hand out here in the freezing cold?*

Heidi interprets my question correctly. Through her own shivering, she says, "I've never seen her so upset. She's lying down, doesn't want to talk, won't eat anything. I don't know that she's had anything other than water since last night."

Some sense returns to me and I get up, slowly, feeling like an old man with stiff, aching joints and a heart that has little life in it. My voice sounds like a stranger's. "You should go inside. Do you know where my dad is?" I help her to her feet.

"I think he's in his truck, waiting for you."

We look at each other a moment, then down at Two's grave. I ask, "Can I come in and see Etta?"

"Oh, Ethan . . ." I turn, and Heidi's face looks sad and maybe a little afraid. "I don't think that would be good for you right now."

"For me?"

She takes my arm and moves toward the corner of the house. "I'll explain another time."

At the truck, Dad rolls down his window and hands Heidi a thermos; she must have made hot coffee or something for him while he waited for me. How long was I out there? "Thanks for that," he says to her. "I'll take Ethan home now."

I climb in, hoping I won't have to talk. And Dad seems to know this; he says nothing all the way home.

We're pulling into the driveway, and finally my voice wakes up. "I'm sorry I swore at you."

He nods. "Unusual circumstances. I know you won't do it again."

Mom is waiting inside the door, and before I can even take my coat off she's in front of me, then hugging me, holding on hard. If I let this go on I'll cry again, and I don't want to do that. So I push away a little and she takes the hint. At least she knows better than to say anything like how sorry she is, which would only make it worse for me. I slough off the coat, hang it up, and trudge upstairs to my room. As soon as I lie down on the bed, my iPhone goes off again. I pull it out of my pocket and don't even look at it before I toss it onto the desk. Edgar seems to come toward me under his own steam somehow, and I hold him and roll onto my side, a huge, dull ache where my chest should be.

Through layers of thick air I hear the house phone ring, and then Mom's voice low with the words indistinguishable. Sometime later it rings again, and then she knocks on my door. I don't respond, just lie there facing away from the door, and Mom cracks it open.

"Ethan, honey? It's Max on the phone."

"I don't care."

There's a second or two of silence, and then, "I'll tell him you'll call back later."

"Tell him whatever you want."

My brain feels dead. I don't care about anything. Mom and Dad getting back together, Kyle's hand, the election, Max my almost-boyfriend, the missing Jorja, even Etta, who evidently doesn't have space for me in her life right now. I feel a few tears seep from my eyes when I think of Etta, the only other person who would understand this loss. Of everyone I know, she's the only one I want to be near. But she's shut me out when I need her most, even though we could divide this pain between us, make it a little less overwhelming. She's cut me off.

I didn't hear a car engine, but I do hear the knock on my door, and then, "Ethan? Ethan, I'm coming in." It's Max.

I want to yell, "Go away!" but I don't have the energy. I'm still lying on my side, eyes closed, Edgar where my heart should be. The door opens, shuts quietly, and I hear the desk chair being moved over beside the bed. There's a soft touch, and then Max's hand is kneading my shoulder, my arm, my neck.

"Hey, bud. I know what happened. Sylvia called and got the story from your mom, and when you wouldn't talk on the phone I had to come see you."

His touch feels good, but it also makes me want to cry. To fight that, I don't respond at all. He moves to sit on the bed and strokes my hair and then my back. He bends over and kisses my temple, and then he tries to hug me. But I'm still curled around Edgar, and Max can't wrap his arms around anything. So then he climbs onto the bed and spoons me, and that feels so good that I do let a few tears sneak out.

We lie there like that for a while, and then he strokes my hair again. "Ethan, I had no idea this dog was so important to you. I mean, I know you'd figured out how to, y'know, be with him without getting hurt or anything. I'm not saying this right. But I guess the point is—"

"The point is you just don't know me very well."

Okay, that is not a door I want to open right now. Damn that stupid voice!

Max sits up. "Dude, I've licked your dick, okay? Don't tell me I don't know you."

Suddenly I'm in motion, and then I'm sitting up, too, glaring at Max's gorgeous face. "Dude? Really, Max? *Dude?* I'm not just one of those guys you sat with at lunch today. I'm not just some kid on the bus you sat next to so you wouldn't be seen with your boyfriend."

I'm on my feet now, and Edgar lands on the floor. "Christ! Jorja's supposed to be my best friend, but she won't let me be who I am. You'll let me be who I am, but only if that doesn't reflect on you." I slap my ass, hitting the yin-yang hard. "Some balance I've managed to bring into my life! What a fucking joke this is."

The door hits the wall behind it as I fling it open. I charge down the steps, grab my coat, yank at Mom's car keys on the hook near the front door, and I'm out of the house. The white Sequoia blocks the Subaru in the driveway, so I back and fill until I can drive over the lawn, crunchy with leftover snow, and hit the road. By this time Dad's been at the door, yelling something at me, but I ignore him. He'll probably be after me in the truck in very little time, so I gun the engine. I have no idea where I'm going until I realize I'm on the road to Bangor.

Another time I would have spent a few gray cells wondering what it is that's pulling me to Bangor, and I probably would have come up with an image of Guy LeBlanc. And I would have been wrong. Because where I'm headed, without knowing it until I get close, is Shane.

He's inside the shop and just coming toward the glass door as I approach, probably to close up shop for the day, and I can tell that he's surprised to see me. Or maybe he's surprised at the look on my face, which has got to be somewhere between fury and pain. He opens the door to let me in, closes and locks it, and turns the sign to Closed. Standing in the middle of the room, nothing but his face in my vision or my mind, I let him approach me, wrap his arms around me, and stand there with me, swaying gently back and forth in silence until I hear my sobs start.

He says nothing, just lets me sob and moan and drip tears all over his shoulder. When the sobs turn to sniffles and hiccoughs, he takes my head in his hands and looks into my eyes. "You're in bad shape, boy. Wanna talk about it? Come over here."

He leads me to the back of the shop, toward a table pushed against a wall. There's a sink and just enough counter to hold a coffeemaker and some odds and ends, along with a box of tissues that Shane plunks onto the table next to me. "Do you drink coffee, Ethan?" I blow my nose and shake my head. "You do now." He gets a fresh pot started and points to the one chair at the table. I sit and listen to the sounds of him dragging a wheeled chair over from behind the front counter. "So. Talk.

I'm not gonna assume it's about that other kid. . . . What was his name? So I'll just let you tell me."

This almost makes me laugh; Shane can't even remember Max's name, and yet somehow I feel sure he knows me better than Max does. "Not exactly. I suppose he's part of it."

"Part of what?"

"Part of everything that's wrong."

"Tell me."

So I tell him. Sipping hot, strong, black coffee, grateful for the strangeness and the bitterness of it, I tell Shane about my parents splitting up, about Kyle's sickness, about Jorja's obsession and refusal to accept me, about Max's aloofness everywhere except the back of his parents' SUV, about all the terrible things that are happening to people in my school and my town, about Etta and how she's let me be myself while I learn about k.d. lang and power animals and fear and the dark side of religion, and dogs . . . Dogs. It takes all that time for me to get to dogs. To Dog. To Two.

I have to swipe at my eyes a few times as I talk about that supposedly terrible pit bull, about his sweet nature and his contagious grin, about his power and strength and loyalty and determination, about his joy in being with Etta and with other dogs—and with me. I describe lying on the ground with him at the dog park, the soft clouds flying by overhead, and the two of us head to head in peace and companionship. And I tell Shane about the gun, and the hatred, and the death.

And I tell him how Etta won't see me. And then I'm about out of steam.

Shane pours both of us more coffee but he doesn't speak, and half my replenished coffee is gone before I do.

"Why?" I'm pleading with him.

"Why what? Why was Two killed?"

"Oh, no, I *know* why that happened. That was fear and hatred and assholes. Why does it hurt so much?"

Shane leans back. "You're not wearing your bat."

"What?"

"Bats are special to you, right?"

"They're supposed to be my power animal."

He nods. "I wondered if you knew that. Who told you?"

"Heidi. Etta's friend."

"Friend?" His voice gives the word an odd inflection I can't interpret. And then he says, "Heidi Wolcott. Of course."

I don't know what this means, either. "Yeah. She's into, you know, energy, and power animals, that sort of thing. But what's the bat got to do with this?"

Shane's laugh is friendly, gentle. "Ethan, your power animal has to do with everything. But that's another topic. I was just trying to find out if you'd heard about the concept. Because the dog is a power animal, too. And the powers it brings have to do with healing emotional wounds, and with unconditional love." He takes a sip of coffee. "I'm going to say that last bit again, because I want it to sink in." He pauses and makes sure my eyes are on his. "*Unconditional love.* Do you have any concept of what that is?"

It's a term I've heard before, sure, but any deep meaning isn't all that clear to me. "I guess not really."

"It means there is no condition, no situation whatsoever in which that love would go away. There is nothing you could do to lose it. There's nothing you can do to get it, either; it comes to you or it doesn't. And you are one lucky son of a bitch. You had it in that dog. And the fact that that particular dog could just as easily have ripped your throat out is huge. So you were given unconditional love from an animal with healing powers who could have had you for breakfast. Most people never get it anywhere. You were damn lucky to have it, but that makes the loss just about the worst thing in the universe."

He shrugs. "Lots of parents think they give it to their kids, and I'm sure many of them come damn close. Still . . ." He shakes his head and sips again, and in the silence I hear my mother's words: *Can't say I'd be happy about it.* And I can't even imagine what my dad would say if I told *him* I'm gay.

I fill my mouth with bitter coffee and swallow hard. "I sure as hell don't get it from Max."

"Oh, you'll never get it from a lover."

This stuns me. "Why not?"

His empty mug makes a loud thud on the wooden table. "You're not giving it to him, either. All he has to do is not sit with you on the bus and you don't love him as much. And when he expresses confusion over why Two's death is so hurtful for you, instead of telling him why, you fly into a rage because he doesn't know you well enough. Lovers make lots of demands on each other. That makes it conditional. And that's the opposite of unconditional love."

I stare into the total opaqueness of the inch or so of coffee still in my mug. Blackness. Obscurity. And suddenly I wish I had my bat ear cuff, and I feel horrible guilt at having allowed Edgar to get kicked under the bed when I flew into a rage at Max.

Shane's voice seems to come from a distance at first. "So you lost your heart to Two. But you hold him in your heart, too." He laughs at the word play. "You could consider paying him a special kind of tribute."

I blink at him. "What are you talking about?"

"I have a template for a pit bull face." He watches me while this idea sinks in. "You don't have to decide right away. In fact, you shouldn't. And of course, I never suggested it, just like I don't know anything about the ink you already have. But think about it. You might get your own dog someday, and it might be a poodle instead of a pit bull. The tat would pay honor to Two but it would represent not so much him as that love that only Dog and God can give you." More word play, but he doesn't laugh this time.

My brain is no longer dead. It's firing all over the place. The only words I have are, "Tats are a lot more important than I ever thought."

"Lots of people get them for the wrong reasons, Ethan. I see all kinds in here. But when they're done right, and for the right reasons, tats are an expression of who we are. They're not the way everyone wants to express themselves, and that's cool, but they work real well for some of us."

"Etta has dingo tracks. That's her power animal."

"Does she, now?" It's almost like he already knows this. "By the way, I hope you can give her some space around this. I know you feel kind of betrayed, but try to think what she's going through. That dog would still be alive if Etta hadn't joined the race for the school board seat."

He's right. I hadn't thought of that. And I'm not real happy about the way I treated Max, either. He shows up at my house, which was brave to begin with, and even in front of my dad he comes upstairs to me and shuts the door. He did everything he could to comfort me.

Even when things in my life are really bad, I have to stop thinking it's all about me.

Shane takes my mug, dumps the dregs in the sink, tidies up the counter. "You should probably get on home, now. I'll bet they're worried about you."

I reach for my iPhone, thinking I should call and let them know, especially if Dad's out driving around. But it's not there; it's on my desk at home. "Shit."

Shane gets it immediately. "You can use the store phone at the desk if you want. Here, take this chair back with you."

Mom's not any too happy to hear from me. "Ethan, for God's sake! This is the last thing we need right now, you chasing off to no one knows where in some kind of fit. And your phone is upstairs? Why? We heard it ringing when I tried to reach you. I've been worried sick!"

She's about to go on, but I interrupt her. "I know. I'm sorry. I'll be home in less than an hour."

"An hour! Where the hell are you?"

"See you then." And I hang up before she can rant at me anymore. There'll be plenty of time for that when she has me in the same room.

Shane's at the front of the store, waiting for me to leave. He probably just wants to get home, away from the whiny little kid who barged in here unannounced and after hours. But he gives me a long hug before he unlocks the door. "You're gonna be fine, kid. You have all the power you need, and you know how to find it."

I pull away. "How do I find it?"

"Well, you came here. That's one way. Now go find some others. May the Bat be with you." He squeezes my shoulder and opens the door. We don't say good-bye, or good night, or anything. It's not necessary.

I'm halfway home when I wish I'd asked what Shane's power animal is.

Chapter 14

Mom says she has a good mind to ground me, but she doesn't say more, probably realizes there's nothing much to ground me from. She finally satisfies herself with, "And don't you go anywhere without that phone I bought you! Why do you think I got it, anyway?"

At least Dad is still here. He looks pretty pissed; he drove around for a good hour before he gave up looking for me. Even went back up to Etta's. That would have been a good guess, actually, except that she's pretty much withdrawn from the world.

Mom wants to put me to work in the kitchen to help get dinner ready, but I need just a few minutes first. I dash upstairs, give Edgar a kiss and restore him to his place near my pillow, and pick up my phone. There are those two text messages from Max, each one more intense, and a voice mail from Mom when she must have thought I had the phone with me on my flight to Bangor. I call Max's cell but get no answer. So I try the Modines' number, and Sylvia answers.

"We're in the middle of dinner, Ethan. Can Max call you back?"

"Will you just tell him I'm really sorry? I acted kind of bad to him. I wanted to apologize."

I'm waiting for her response, but Max must have snatched the phone. His voice is harsh. "You're a little shit, Ethan, you know that?"

"Yeah. I'm sorry. I know I was awful to you. I'm really sorry."

I can hear breathing, like he's trying to control his anger. Then, "All right. I guess you were in pretty bad shape. But Christ, Ethan! I felt like an idiot, going downstairs after you stormed out. How could I explain that to your folks?"

Good point. "What did you say?"

"Just that you were real upset. What else could I say?"

"I'm still upset, but I was wrong to put it on you like that."

Two beats go by. Then, "So what's with this dog, anyway?"

I take a deep breath and send a silent thank-you to Shane. "It was like he gave me unconditional love, you know? When he could have ripped my throat out. We got really close." I can feel my throat closing up against tears, and I think Max hears it too.

"I get it. That makes sense. I just wish you had told me."

"We need more chances to just talk, Max." Will he get the hint?

Silence. Then, "Yeah. I know. We need to work this out." I hear a voice calling to him, and he says, "I gotta get back to the table."

"I gotta help my mom with dinner here."

"K. See you tomorrow." And then, so quiet I nearly miss it, "Kiss."

"Kiss."

Life's not *all* bad.

After dinner I spend the time at the computer, ignoring the TV and trying to find out from some of the other kids what I missed in school this afternoon besides the math test. Kyle sits at the kitchen table, reading his Bible, an untouched glass of orange juice and two ibuprofen tablets in front of him. Guess he's still running a fever. Every time I hear a noise from in there I worry that he's getting a knife or something to hurt himself with.

Later, just as I'm getting into bed, reaching for Edgar, I get a text. It's Max.

hey charmer glad we talked. sit with me on the bus?

To which I reply, *U bet.*

There's still this heavy lump in my chest, because Two is still dead, but Shane has helped me understand where the pain is coming from. And Max has helped me believe it will pass.

Before I leave the house Friday morning, I get onto the computer and look up the junco as a power animal. I cut and paste the most interesting points and print it out before I dash out the door.

As soon as I settle into a seat against the window and plunk my bag into the other half to save it for Max, I wonder if this will be the day Jorja reappears. It would be just my luck that she'd want to sit with me like everything was cool between us. But no Jorja. This has gone on too long. I call her house, but again there's no answer. Again I leave a general kind of message.

Max gets on and grins at me. "This seat taken?"

I grin back, pick up my bag, and hand him the printout.

"What's this?" And he reads. I've printed that the junco brings the ability to move easily from one environment to another, that it brings activity and opportunity, and—most important to me—that it teaches lessons about equality and communication. He finishes and looks up at me.

I ask, "Juncos still following you?"

"The usual. What's a power animal?"

I stare at him just long enough for several thoughts to flash through my brain. He doesn't know about power animals. I never told him about them. I never told him about my power animal, or anyone else's. He's not the only one who needs a lesson in communication. Maybe the juncos were coming after *me?*

"Power animals are really cool. Every different kind brings different powers and strengths, and usually one at a time comes into your life when you need it. Some people have the same power animal all their life."

He cocks his head at me. "What's yours?"

"Bat. It isn't afraid of the way things look, because it doesn't use its eyes, and it can move around safely even in darkness. And it knows that sometimes going up instead of just back and forth might be the best way to get out from between a rock and a hard place."

"Up, huh? So, what's 'up' right now?"

"I need to give that some thought."

"The ear cuff helping you?"

"And Edgar. Remember that friend of Etta's I went to visit? She's the one who told me about power animals, and she gave me a stuffed bat. A toy, you know. I named him Edgar."

"And that's because . . ."

"Edgar Allan Poe?"

He nods, but his face looks a little odd. I'm beginning to think I'm throwing too much at him all at once, so I shrug to relieve some of the intensity. Can't tell him everything about me in one bus ride to school, after all. He looks at the paper again. "So you think the junco is my power animal?"

"Maybe. You said they were following you around. Anyway, if you want to, you should look online. There's lots of info about what animal has what power, and you can compare that to what your life is like and what strengths you need. Who knows if it helps, but it's kind of fun."

"So this isn't, like, some kind of religion for you or anything."

I laugh, even though he's not that far off. "No. It's just kind of cool. Etta's power animal is the dingo, the wild Australian dog, and she has a tattoo of dingo tracks on her shoulder." I decide to add, "So she says; I've never seen it."

"Hmph. Ought to be a pit bull." I decide not to respond to that. Max looks around. "No Jorja again. What's she done, emigrated someplace?"

"Not sure. I probably oughta figure that out." I don't want to dwell on that, so I change the subject. "Ever listen to k.d. lang?"

"Who's that?"

I punch up one of her albums on my iPhone and hand him the earbuds. He listens the rest of the way to school while I sit back and close my eyes, and in between our thighs touching with the motion of the bus, I feel sad that Two is gone and Etta is hiding. Some folk singer once sang something about not knowing what you have until you don't have it anymore. She was right. I didn't know how much of a place in my life Etta and her dog had.

There's a lot of talk around me all morning about how Etta Greenleaf's dog was shot. In the hallway between second and third periods, I hear some jerk say something about how that monster should have been shot long ago. I drop my books and shove him hard, and before he can recover his footing there are about five other guys standing with me. He scrambles to his feet and walks away fast. Things here have definitely changed for the better.

At lunch Max and I sit with Gregory Pines, whose head is pretty well healed. He says he's glad the debate was cancelled. I agree; I've had enough commotion around this whole issue to last me a lifetime, and all I want is for that election to be over, whoever wins, so we can put this behind us. Maybe even find some balance. I think Max feels the same way, despite the personal agenda he wanted to pursue.

Marra, on the other hand, is still ready for a fight. "I heard you shoved Derek Johnson in the hall, Ethan. Way to go!"

"Man, word gets around fast." I'm not sure I want to be known as a shover.

"I think Etta's got this thing in the bag. Have you noticed how many kids have come around to reality in the last couple of days?"

Max says, "The kids aren't voting."

This doesn't faze Marra. "No, but they're a reflection of how their parents will vote."

Max shrugs. "Whatever. I guess we'll know Tuesday night."

"I'm having a victory party at my house Wednesday. Do you guys want to come?"

Max again: "I think they call that counting your chickens while they're still eggs."

"I'm telling you, there's no contest! It'll be a landslide."

"And then what? You've seen what some of these idiots will do when it's just a campaign. What do you think they'll do if Etta wins?"

I haven't really thought about that. What *will* they do?

Marra won't let go. "But there's fewer and fewer of them all the time! They're like coyotes. They travel in packs, and if the pack gets too small they lose courage."

And *I* can't let *that* go. "I wouldn't underestimate coyotes."

Gregory chimes in. "Anyway, I think jackals would be a better description." And this makes me wonder what the jackal represents as a power animal.

But, really, I'm just thrilled to be sitting with Max at lunch, whoever is around us and whatever they're talking about. He doesn't sit with me on the bus ride home, but he sends me a text.

loved kd. wanna hang out tomoro nite?

Saturday. Date night! *4 shr!*

But that doesn't happen.

Saturday afternoon Mom wants me to go with her on a couple of errands, which include buying me and Kyle some socks and stuff. I try to protest; I'd rather be fresh for my evening with Max. But no.

"Ethan, you know how fussy you are about your underpants!" I cringe. *Underpants.* But she's right. And maybe I'll see a really nice black shirt; Max said I'd look great in one.

We leave Kyle at home with Dad on orders to make sure he drinks orange juice, takes ibuprofen, and rests in his room; Mom says his fever isn't getting better, and she's going to call the doctor on Monday. This plan seems terrific to me; she's trusting Dad, and he's getting back into the routine of home more and more with every day. He's still sleeping on the couch, but I'm thinking that won't last much longer. At least that's what I want to believe.

Anyway, shopping or no shopping, I'm kind of high all afternoon, after Max texted me in the morning about our plans. I just need to get to his house, which I know I can count on Mom for, and Sylvia will bring me home—not breaking any driving rules tonight—and we'll spend the time in his room watching DVDs and doing whatever comes naturally, as long as we're quiet and quick. I haven't kissed that guy in way too long, and I can't wait to see what that will lead to. Hey—maybe we'll actually talk and get to know each other better.

But when Mom and I get home, there's an ambulance in the driveway, and the paramedics are loading Kyle into it. Mom stops the car where she won't block them, but she doesn't even turn her car engine off; I have to do it. She races over to Kyle.

"Oh, my God! What's happened? What's going on?"

Dad's standing there, and I run over so I can hear what he says. "He was in his room, Charlene. He was reading the Bible. I checked at least four times."

"What did he do? Dave! For God's sake, what did he do?"

"I heard this banging, you know? He was pounding the desk chair leg onto his hand on the floor."

Mom climbs into the back of the ambulance, despite the paramedics' protests. "I'm staying with my son!" Her voice is frightened and frightening all at once.

Dad is standing there looking like he doesn't know what to do. I go into the house and grab his coat, and the ambulance is on the road when I get back to him. "Here." I shove it at him. "Get in the car."

I still have the keys, so I head for the driver's side, and he doesn't say anything. The siren and red lights on the ambulance make it easy to follow.

Dad tries to explain what happened, sounding confused and more frantic by the word. "He was fine, Ethan! He was fine. Just sitting up there reading his Bible. I checked and checked, even though I couldn't imagine what he might get into. I was downstairs, watching the game, you know? And I heard this pounding. So I went upstairs, and your stupid brother is on the floor, his right hand flat, and he's lifting the wooden chair up with his other hand and banging the chair leg down onto it. I—I didn't know what to do! How crazy is that? God!"

He takes a few breaths, and I'm trying not to yell, *Don't call my brother stupid!*

"So I grab the chair and haul him to his feet. He was crying. It must have hurt like hell. But that's not the worst of it. Do you know what he'd done?" I venture a quick glance, and Dad's eyes are huge with horror. "He was pounding, all right. He was pounding something into the wounds. It was shit! Ethan, he was pounding shit into his hand!" And Dad throws himself against the seat back, rubbing his face.

This news is almost too much for me. I'm having trouble focusing on the road, and all I can do is watch the red lights of the ambulance ahead while I blink like mad to keep away tears of something I can only call awe.

"Ethan, why would he *do* that?" Dad's practically yelling at me now. "You've been at the house this whole time. Was it ever as bad as this?"

I cough to clear my throat. "No. This is new. A whole new level." We drive in stunned silence for a minute, and then it occurs to me what Kyle must have been thinking. So I tell Dad what I know about BIID, and what Etta had said about infection. "He must have been trying to infect his hand."

Dad doesn't respond right away. When he does, his voice is quiet and slow. "He's not going to get better, is he." Not really a question. Good thing, because I don't have an answer.

The drive could have lasted five minutes or fifty. I know now it was about thirty. Somehow I manage to park, and inside, Dad and I find Mom by her voice as she tries to explain to the medical staff what's going on with Kyle. They've heard all they need to, I guess, because they push her toward us as soon as they see us.

We sit in the waiting room, silent as doom for longer than I think I can stand. Finally I get up and look out the window. It's getting dark. Shit! I have to cancel with Max. I pull out my iPhone, start to dial the number, and realize I don't want my folks to hear me talking to Max. Not even Mom. And certainly not Dad. I could go someplace, but what if someone comes out to talk to us when I'm not nearby? So I start texting.

"Ethan! Put that damn thing away!" Mom hisses.

"I have to cancel my date," I say before I can form different words.

Dad sounds confused. "You have a date?"

"Not anymore." I don't want to go into it, and I don't want to lie.

mm sht hit the fan cant do 2nite

Thank God, Max answers. *what sht?*

Problem w / kyle. at hospital now.

There's a moment of dead air, and then, *do u want me to come?*

Yes! But . . . *no. bad scene here. i'll txt later.*

k. I'll be here.

I don't know whether to be happy that Max is telling me he'll be there for me or angry because Kyle has fucked up what would have been a really great time. It helps to remind myself how fucked up Kyle is, but only so much. I'm still staring at the last part of Max's message when I hear someone say, "Mr. and Mrs. Poe?"

There's a woman in a white coat talking to my folks. I move closer so I can hear her explaining that they've cleaned out the wounds and that he'll need reconstructive surgery for the bones he's damaged. I almost ask if it isn't time to cut the thing off. It would solve so many problems.

Mom asks, "When will we be able to take him home?"

The doctor's face looks odd. She asks, "How long has he been running a fever?"

"A few days, since Tuesday or Wednesday. But it was low last time I checked, maybe ninety-eight or nine. I've fed him ibuprofen and orange juice."

"Well, it's one hundred two point six now. Any idea why there are marks on his wrist beneath the bandages?" Mom looks at Dad; they both shake their heads and turn back to the doctor. "It looks as though he might have been wrapping something around it to cut off the circulation to the hand."

Mom reaches behind her for a chair, and Dad helps her sit down. I ask, "What does that mean at this point?"

"It could have helped worsen his current condition. The fever, along with his heart rate, blood pressure, and breathing pattern, indicated he's in sepsis, and blood tests have confirmed it. We've put him on intravenous fluids and antibiotics in the intensive care unit. We have to watch for organ failure and be prepared to step in quickly. We're seeing signs of possible kidney malfunction, and he seems agitated and confused, which could mean his brain is being affected as well. I'm afraid I won't have any more specifics for you until we've stabilized his condition. If we can stabilize him, we'll assess the options."

"If?" Mom's voice is nearly a whisper.

"We're doing everything we can to clear the sepsis. But if we can't stop it, or there's too much organ damage, it will be very serious."

Dad's voice is a little stronger than Mom's, but not much. "How serious?"

"It could be fatal."

Mom covers her face with her hands, and Dad looks stunned. I ask, "How soon will you know something?"

"It's touch-and-go at the moment. Once we've replaced enough fluids and the antibiotic has a chance to work, we'll know more. If you want to see him for a minute or two, go in now. After that there's nothing you can do until we see what progress is made."

Mom stands up again; she seems like she's determined to be strong. "I'll stay here tonight. Dave, you take Ethan home. I'll call if there's a change."

I say, "I'm going in to see him first."

"Ethan, don't make trouble. You and your father—"

"It might be the last time I see him alive." I don't know where I get the strength to say that. I should be feeling weepy and scared, and that's all in me someplace, but right now I want to see Kyle.

The doctor says, "This way," and we all follow.

Kyle is hooked up to more tubes than I would have thought

a person could tolerate. His eyes are closed, and I can't tell whether he's aware of us or not.

The doctor says, "We gave him a mild sedative. This treatment is invasive and frightening. He may not respond to you."

Mom stands by the bed and takes his left hand in hers. "I'm right here, Kyle. I'm not going anyplace." She stops to regain some composure; her voice is tight and ragged. "We're all pulling for you."

I move forward. "We'll pray for you, Kyle." Mom looks at me, but I can tell that she can't speak without sobbing. She just nods. And then we all stand around like dopes for maybe half a minute before Mom heaves this big sigh and heads for the door, Dad right behind her.

She turns in the doorway. "Ethan?"

"Be right there." I want some quality time here. Not sure why. Not sure what I'll do with it. I can't think of anything to say, so I just stand there listening to the beeps and gurgles all that equipment is making trying to keep Kyle alive.

He wanted to lose his hand. That's where all this started. He couldn't see that it was really a part of himself, valid, alive, useful. In his mind it was different from him, somehow, so it seemed wrong. He tried to kill it so he could live. And just might have killed himself in the process.

I focus on the mechanical sounds, letting my mind zone out. And then, even though I'm still standing beside Kyle's hospital bed, I'm also starting to float upward in the room, and it actually seems like I'm looking down on Kyle and me standing next to him. It's a totally different perspective. I've gone Up, I guess, but I don't know what to do with it. I close my eyes and call to Edgar.

Before I can even try to convince myself that Bat is with me, I'm scared shitless by sudden loud noises all around me. Kyle's machinery is going berserk, and I barely have time to realize that a sharp smell is my own fear before people come running over. Someone shouts "Coding!" and pushes me out of the way. Mom tries to get to Kyle, but they stop her. Dad and I stand off at a distance and watch helplessly as people in white and blue surround Kyle so that we can't see him. I don't know exactly what they're doing, but one thing's for sure: If they don't succeed, Kyle will die.

Someone draws a curtain across to hide where Kyle is, and now all we can do is listen. The only thing I remember is "Clear!" and a loud pop. And then again. And again.

And then nothing.

The doctor's voice says, "Damn it! I will *not* lose this kid!" There's one more *Clear!* And another pop, and then a wave of something rolls over me, and I know they've saved Kyle before I hear the electronic heartbeat sound start up. Dad helps Mom over to a chair in the hall, and I have to lean against the wall or I might fall. My brother just nearly died a few feet from me.

A nurse peeks out to make sure we know Kyle's pulled through. "The doctor will be out in a minute to talk to you." And she disappears again. My eyes stare at the place where she was standing, and my ears hear Mom sobbing behind me.

I'm still standing there when the doctor pulls the curtain aside. She nods to me, her face looking tight and strained, and I follow her to where my folks are waiting. Dad's sitting beside Mom, holding one of her hands.

"We managed to pull your son through that crisis," she says to my folks. "But it's my opinion that we don't have very long before the next one. The sepsis is starting to clear, but it damaged his kidneys. They're just about gone. Dialysis will help temporarily, but he needs a transplant. I can't pretend that kidneys are easy to get, and of course we need a donor who's a good match. In any case, we need to finish clearing the sepsis first."

Dad asks, "What options do we have, then?"

"It's possible that a family member could be a good match. If so, we could take just one kidney and give it to Kyle. Both Kyle and the donor would need to be monitored after that to make sure all is well with the one kidney, and both people will need to avoid extreme activities, but these cases are usually very successful. If we have a good donor, his chances of survival increase dramatically. But I must warn you that there's still a chance we'll lose him. His blood tests show that his liver is in good shape, considering his general condition, but it could go next, or something else could fail before his system is clear." She glances at her pager, which has gone off. "This isn't about him. I'll let you talk about this for a few minutes. Page me when you're ready to talk about how to move forward." She nods at each of us and heads down the hall.

Mom looks up at me. "We all need to be tested, then. Any objections?"

I swallow. This isn't something I've ever considered. Obviously. I have no doubt that donating a kidney, or anything that deeply buried inside you, would be a painful ordeal with a lengthy recovery period. And it sounds like it would change your life. It's not something I've been planning on.

But Kyle is dying.

Poles. Always those fucking poles, bouncing me back and forth.

I barely hear Dad's voice say, "Charlene, yes, of course. But Ethan should be the last one considered. If one of us can do it, I say we should."

Reprieve? Maybe? I'm ashamed that my mind goes next to what the testing will be like, if it will be painful. All I can do is nod.

When the doctor appears again, Mom takes over. "We'll all be tested. Ethan is our last choice, but if he's the only match, he'll do it." I haven't *exactly* agreed to this, but this doesn't seem like a good time to protest. "And when you give Kyle the kidney, I want you to take off his hand."

"That might not be necessary. He'll certainly lose two of the fingers, but there might be enough viable tissue—"

"I'm going to say this again, and it's not up for discussion. Take the hand. You know very well he has BIID, and you know very well that he'll keep damaging that hand as long as it's on his body. We'll be back here in a month, he'll be in worse condition, and the donated kidney will have been wasted because Kyle will die. The hand comes off."

Dad moves to stand behind Mom and a little to the side, like they're forming a wall of resistance in case the doctor protests again. I move so I'm on her other side. We haven't talked about this at all, but I know Mom is right. I know this is the only way to go.

I can tell the doctor wants to argue, that she wants to try to save most of his hand. But she only said it *might* work, and she must realize that hand will kill Kyle. Because finally she just gives one quick nod.

They herd us off to take blood samples, which isn't too bad. We'll have to come back tomorrow for more testing: X-rays, EKGs, CT scans—all kinds of crap. At least it doesn't sound painful.

The ride home is silent. I don't dare ask if I can drive, and actually I'm kind of glad to be alone in the backseat, anyway. There are so many things bouncing around inside my head that my brain hurts. I don't even want to call Max and tell him what's going on. Not yet. I'll do that later. Right now I just want to be left alone.

I might lose a kidney. They might cut me open, cut out one of my kidneys, and sew it into Kyle's body. Just the *idea* grosses me out, and yet I know I'll do it if I have to.

I think.

We all move around like zombies at home. I help Mom make tuna sandwiches for dinner, and she makes hot cocoa, which I love. I can barely taste it.

When I go upstairs, the first time since Mom and I got home and found an ambulance in the driveway, I see Kyle's door has been broken down. He'd probably locked it before he started pounding shit into his hand, and Dad had to force it open. It's too dark to see inside. I sniff experimentally but don't detect anything nasty. It's too much for me, just the same; I turn away and go into my own room and call Max.

He picks up immediately, and his voice is serious. "How's your brother?"

"It's an ugly situation." I tell him the first part of the story. It just tumbles out. He's quiet, listening, saying *Holy shit* or *Oh, my*

God from time to time. Then I get to the worst part. "Kyle coded. They had to do that electric thing to get his heart started again. And now he's on dialysis. Kidney failure. I might... one of us might have to give him one of ours."

"Holy shit! Oh, man, Ethan. I—that's beyond fucked up. I don't know what to say."

"No one does. It's like a cemetery here. No one's talking. My dad says if he or Mom can donate, they'll do it, so it's me only if they can't. But we all have to do the tests. They took blood today, and we have to go back tomorrow morning for X-rays and shit. They'll know by the end of the day who it's gonna be, and they'll do the surgery Monday."

"What if it's none of you?"

Ah, that. I knew there was something we'd all been avoiding. No wonder no one wanted to talk in the car, over dinner, after dinner. I don't respond, and finally Max says, "Sorry. Bad question. One of those bridges you don't want to think about crossing."

I nod, like he can hear that. "Also, Mom's making them take his hand off."

It's Max's turn to be silent. And, really, there's no good response. *I suppose that's for the best* doesn't cut it somehow. Neither does *That's a terrible idea.*

Finally Max says, "Well at least he won't be trying to hurt himself anymore, right?"

"Right." Unless he decides some other body part is possessed. But that's not a place I want to go right now. Or ever.

"How did it get this bad? You didn't see any of this coming?" I have to bite my tongue to stop a sarcastic comment like *Sure we did; we didn't do anything because it was kind of fun to watch.* The fact is, I'd been wondering the same thing. Why didn't we see this getting so bad? Why didn't anyone tell Mom to watch for a fever? Should she have called a doctor as soon as she knew he had one? Could just a couple of hours today with something tight around his wrist have done enough damage to matter? If not, why didn't anyone see the marks before, or if they did, why didn't it ring any bells?

I'm so busy biting my tongue I don't respond, and Max says, "That was a dumb-ass question, wasn't it? It does seem like it got super-bad super-fast."

He's right about that. But there's more to this. "Yeah, but you know it's been a hell of a week. Mom knew he had a fever, but it wasn't much, and what with the damage at Brearlys' and at school, and the guys beating us up . . . well, beating you up, and the town hall and Mom getting hung in effigy and Two getting shot. . . ." My voice trails off. It really *has* been a hell of a week.

"Hey, I'm not saying it's anyone's fault."

"I know." There's silence. Then, "I miss you."

"I miss you, too, charmer. Say, is it all right if I let Sylvia know what's going on?"

"Why?"

"You're gonna need an advocate at school. D'you think your classwork isn't gonna suffer, whoever gives up a kidney?"

"Good point."

"Hey, maybe if you miss some school, I can bring stuff over, help you with homework. Sound like a plan?"

"Sounds like the only good thing I've heard all week."

"What else can I do?"

I nearly lose it. I have to press the phone against the bedspread for a couple of seconds so I can get everything under control again. "Just be there. I, uh, I'll call you as soon as I know what's going on." We listen to each other breathe for a second. Then I say, "Max, I'm sorry. I mean, you know, you didn't bargain for this. You shouldn't have to deal with this."

He gives a kind of snort. "Hey, dude, don't go getting all wimpy on me. I don't deal with anything I don't want to. I figure you're worth it. I'll let you know if I change my mind."

This makes me smile; not sure why. "Deal."

"Call me when you know more. Or if you're up for a little phone sex."

My smile gets bigger. "You bet." Then I say out loud something I once texted. "Dream of me?"

His response, thank God, is the same: "Always do."

I lie there for maybe fifteen minutes, thinking of Max, being glad he's in my life. It amazes me how much better I feel than before I called him. I suppose some of that is just from talking to someone not in the thick of it. But a lot of it must be him. Eventually I go downstairs and sit with my folks for a bit, watching Dad cruise from channel to channel, not caring what's on.

The first part of Sunday morning is pretty much a blur. At the hospital, they tell us that the sepsis is clearing nicely, so a new kidney is the next step. We all go into separate rooms, this guy asks me a lot of questions, makes me fill out a lot of forms, and just before he gets ready to start with the X-rays he examines me all over for whatever. Skin cancer, maybe? Anyway, that's when he finds my tattoo.

He freezes, and maybe five seconds later I hear, "How long have you had this?"

With everything that's happened lately, I haven't really thought about my tat in a while, so it takes me a minute to get what he means. "Oh. Um, I think . . . maybe a few weeks ago?"

"Okay. Get dressed."

I pull up my underwear and pants first and turn to face him. "Does it make a difference?"

He nods. "Sure does. You're not exhibiting any symptoms, and no infection showed up in the blood tests. But there's no point in any other testing. You can't donate."

I'm working my sweater on over my head when I hear him say that I'm out of the running. I'm glad he can't see my face, which probably looks wildly relieved. But then another thought occurs to me. "You, um, you don't have to tell my folks why, do you?"

"They don't know about this?"

"No. And this seems like a bad time to spring it on them. Can't you just tell them you saw stuff in the blood test that means I can't be a donor?"

"You don't think they'll want to know what?"

"They don't want me to donate if one of them can, anyway."

"But until we know, they'll want you to go through the rest of the tests. We're not going to do that now. They're very expensive. And I'm not telling your parents there's something wrong with your blood when there isn't. You're the same blood type as your brother, and there were no other contraindications."

Fuck. Shit! "But they don't need this right now!"

"They don't need any of this. But they've got it. Don't you think they'll be a little more focused on your brother than on the fact that you have an illegal tattoo? I suggest you tell them yourself. You might get a little credit for that. If I tell them, it could even add embarrassment to their list."

He's right. But—shit.

"By the way, do the rainbow colors mean what I think they mean?"

Suddenly it's hard to get a breath. "Which is . . . ?"

"That you're gay?"

I shrug to hide how nervous I am. He won't lie about the blood tests. What will he say about this? "My mom knows."

"Does your primary MD?"

"No."

"You should fix that at your very next appointment. Seriously. It's very important for you. And now that I know, I can give you a choice. You say your mother knows you're gay. If your father does, too, then you can avoid revealing the tattoo. Legally we can't even take blood from gay males, let alone an organ. *Does* he know?" I shake my head. "Then you have a choice. You can decide which would be more difficult to do. Tell both your folks you have a tattoo, or tell your father that you're gay." He waits, and I don't say anything. "So, who's talking to them?"

"I am." My voice sounds small and frightened.

"And you're telling them what?"

"About the tattoo." At least Dad might see a tattoo as a "guy" thing to do. He has one himself, after all. And I'm just not ready to tell him anything else.

"A suggestion? If you tell them in a relatively public place, like a hospital, it might be less dramatic." He ruffles my hair, which surprises me. "Okay, Ethan. We're done here. But take this." He fishes in his pocket and takes out a business card with his name and number. "Talk to your MD, seriously. And if you'd like to talk to someone else as well, give me a call. We play for the same team." He slaps my arm and leaves me here, staring at the door he closed behind him.

Life's a funny thing. They send me in here with a male nurse or whatever so there won't be any perception of foul play, and it turns out we're both gay. Go figure.

It's a little while before I'm in the same place as my mom and dad at the same time. We end up in a waiting area around eleven, after everyone's initial exams.

Mom says, "So the other tests are all this afternoon, and then I guess we wait for the results. I'm going to go see how Kyle's doing."

Dad says we should all go, and I spend about a nanosecond debating whether to tell them right now or wait, and maybe tell them in Kyle's room, or maybe look for a place to pull them aside, and a nanosecond turns out to be too long. Before I know it we're all standing around Kyle, who's still unconscious. I don't know if this is a good thing or a bad thing. The nurse tells us he was awake for a few minutes earlier, and that was a good sign, but that he needs to rest as much as possible. So we don't talk, and we don't stay long. As we leave, I get up the guts to say something. For once my voice doesn't get ahead of me. I'm right with it.

"Mom? Dad? I have to talk to you about something."

Mom says, "We have some time. Let's go to the cafeteria." Of course Mom wants me to start talking on the way, but I say we should get our trays first and sit down. She stops walking and looks at me. "This is something serious?"

"Not necessarily. Can we go?"

I probably should have just blurted it out. By the time we get sandwiches and follow Dad into a corner where he can sit with his back to the wall and watch the room, my whole body feels prickly.

Mom shakes a sugar packet and tears it open. "Okay, Ethan, out with it."

"I can't donate a kidney."

"Why not?" She stares at me. Maybe glares is a better word. "You're the same blood type. How do you know already? What's wrong?"

I take a breath and try not to let it shake on its way out. "Evidently if you got a tattoo recently, they can't use your organs for someone else. And . . . well, I have a tattoo."

All motion ceases. Dad's no longer interested in his sandwich. Mom's coffee could freeze for all she cares. She sits back hard in her chair. "I do not need this, Ethan. I do not need this. What kind of damn fool—"

"Charlene." Dad's voice is heavy, solid. Mom and I both look at him, and she falls silent. "Ethan, where did you get a tattoo?"

"It was a few weeks ago." I can't tell him where, though it occurs to me with a fright that Mom will figure it out. But I promised Shane, so I give Dad what I can. "It's a yin-yang symbol. For balance."

Mom snorts. "And it's worked really well, hasn't it."

I know better than to respond. "I'm sorry. It means I can't help Kyle. I would have, you know that." Safe enough to say that now, of course. "But how was I to know he was gonna need a kidney?"

Mom's not swayed by this logic. "You know damn well you shouldn't go around getting tattoos!"

"Charlene, it's done. Ethan, they took blood tests, didn't they?"

"Yes. Nothing else, though. No point."

He turns to Mom. "If the tattoo caused any problems, we'll know." He glares at me now. "And young man, don't try and tell us you didn't know better. Where did you get the money?"

This is not a question I had anticipated. I could lie and tell him I'd saved it up. But I knew that would put an end to any further spending money. "They, um, they didn't charge me."

"What? Why not?"

"I'm underage."

Mom can't stop herself. "So they shouldn't have given you one at all!" So much for the protection of a public place. She's practically shouting. "I have a good mind to have them arrested!"

Shit. She knows. She remembers the shop next to This Time For Sure. Again, I try for distraction. "Look, I'm really sorry. I only got it because everything seemed so out of synch. I felt like everything was all mixed up, all moving in different directions." I work up a little self-righteous indignation as ammunition. "First you guys get separated, then Kyle starts treating me like some kind of slave, then he starts with the hand, then all that shit with the election and school, and then Two got killed and now this! I needed balance."

Dad says, "Ethan, half that stuff happened after you got the ink."

"Not all of it! I'm telling you, I felt like everything was spinning."

Mom's not sympathetic. "And you thought a tattoo would help how, exactly?"

"Not just because it's a tattoo. It's balance, and it's part of me now. It's permanent." She does not look convinced. "Look, I don't need this right now either, you know. I was gonna tell you about it. Just not yet." And my voice, harsh and sounding almost like I don't mean it, adds, "I'm sorry, okay? I'm really sorry!" And I leave my sandwich and my soda and my parents where they are and practically run out of the cafeteria, my mom's voice calling my name behind me. I head for the nearest men's room and hole up in one of the stalls, arms around my ribs.

My brother is dying, and I can't help him. I can't help my parents help him. I can't do anything except upset everyone. I may as well have told Dad I'm gay. Couldn't feel any worse if I had. I couldn't feel any less trapped, any less helpless, any less like a stupid little kid.

My voice surprises me. "It's not all about you." Thank God I'm alone in here or they'd lock me up in the psych ward.

It's not all about me. What does that mean *this* time? My brain is a complete and utter blank for about five seconds. Just try that. I'll bet you can't get there. And then my eyes look inward.

What I see is how my dad might have reacted if I'd told him I'm gay instead of confessing to the tattoo, and it's not pretty. I don't think he'd kick me out of the house or anything, but I don't really know that. And he might get really crazy right off the bat and do or say some things he might not be able to take back, or that I might not be able to get over even if he tries. I think I was right, based on his relatively calm reaction to the tattoo, that at least he gets the idea.

But my being gay? Not so much. Telling him he has a gay son would not have gone over well at all. I guess this was a lose–lose proposition. Pole–pole. I had to choose, and I chose, and it's done. At least this way they have someone to blame, even if they never actually go after Shane. With gay, they have no one to blame unless they blame me or themselves. And right now I think it's probably a good thing for them to have someone outside the family to blame.

So maybe I did the right thing, for them. But for me? I'm not sure there was a right thing.

"Ethan?" It's Dad. He's found me.

"In here." I flush the toilet like that's the only reason I'm hanging out here.

When I come out of the booth Dad wraps his arms around me. "Things will get better, son. I promise." He pushes us apart but holds on to my shoulders. "Now you promise. No more tattoos until you're over eighteen." I take it that he's managed to calm Mom down.

I nod. "Promise." So much for the pit bull head. But Shane said not to do anything right away, anyway.

While my folks finish having their tests, I wait in a chair next to Kyle. He's still unconscious, so I pull out my iPod and earbuds and let music wash over me for a while. At one point a nurse comes over to check on him, and after she leaves I watch his face for a couple of minutes. I hardly recognize it, and not just because he's lying there nearly dead. It's been a long time since I really looked at my brother. If I ever did. He seems almost like a stranger to me. And yet I have more in common with him than with anyone else in the world, on so many levels.

In between the beeps and the boops of everything attached to him I remember the promise I made him yesterday. I can't quite bring myself to kneel, not here at least, but I sit up straight in my chair, hands in my lap, and close my eyes. And I whisper.

"Okay, God, it's been a really long time, I know. You probably don't know who I am anymore. But you know Kyle, because he's been talking to you, like, nonstop, for months. You're not much of a God if you don't know he's in trouble, but it's supposed to help things if people pray for someone in trouble. I don't understand it, but Kyle thinks he does, so I'm praying for him. Please don't let him die. And don't let him blame some other body part, okay? Otherwise he's just going to do all this again."

I'm about to say *Amen* when something else occurs to me. "And please help my mom and dad get together again. They really need each other." And then, "Be nice to Etta, will you? She doesn't mean to cut me out, she's just hurting. I'd ask you to make sure she wins the election, but I don't really know what she wants at this point." And finally, "One more thing. Can you make sure this thing I have going with Max works out? I know the Bible isn't real friendly about us, but somehow I don't think we're understanding it right. I don't think you'd make us gay just to make us miserable. That doesn't make any sense. So. Amen."

I sit there another minute or so, trying to see if I know how to meditate, until some noise just down the hall startles me. And now I'm feeling weird about praying. Who am I kidding? Won't God see it as totally hypocritical?

I only wish I knew whether it could actually help.

As soon as we get home, Mom goes up to Kyle's room and cleans up whatever mess is in there. Makes me wish I'd done it last night when I'd thought about what it must be like in there. I feel guilty, and I'm mad at Mom for making me feel that way. Talk about not making sense.

Dinner is pretty silent again, partly for the same reasons as last night and partly because Mom is still pissed at me.

Balance. I want it so much! Here we are, the three of us, and we should all be pulling together for the same thing: Kyle's recovery. But Mom and I know something about me that would *totally* blow Dad's mind in a very bad way so he can't know, and Dad and I have this simpatico thing going on around the tattoo while Mom fumes and has to force herself not to yell at me about it. So we sit there in silence.

Is this a kind of balance, only not the kind I want? Is this one of those *Be careful what you wish for* moments? Christ!

We get a little relief around eight when the phone rings. Dad answers it and then hands it to me. "It's Etta."

I stare at the thing. What the hell am I going to say to her right now? But I take it.

"Ethan, I just wanted to see how you're doing. Heidi told me how upset you were. I'm sorry I couldn't talk to you myself. It was just too overwhelming."

Two. She means upset about Two, not Kyle. "Um, okay, I guess. I, uh, I talked to a friend who helped me get a handle on . . . you know. How I felt. But . . ." I don't know what to say next. She knows what's been going on with Kyle up to now. Should I tell her more? I decide yes. "Did you know Kyle is in the hospital?"

She didn't. I give her an update, and her reaction is all Etta. She wants to know what she can do to help. Of course I can't come up with anything, so when I run out of news she asks for Mom, who asks Etta to make sure I get dinner Monday night, and then she says something no one has told me. Mom and Dad are under strict orders not to eat or drink after midnight, because in the morning they'll know if one of them is going under the knife. She doesn't say anything to Etta about why I'm not a donor, but listening to this conversation is the way I find out that I'm expected to go to school tomorrow and probably stay here alone tomorrow night. Whichever parent doesn't donate will stay at the hospital.

I consider protesting at how all these decisions are being made not only without my agreement but also without my knowledge. I consider it. But I don't do it.

*   *   *

Monday morning before it's even light I watch my folks drive off in the Subaru. I can't exactly participate in what's going to happen today, but I don't much like being so completely left out, waiting for someone to call with news. At least Mom seems like she's forgotten all about the tattoo. She has other things to worry about today.

Mom calls me while I'm on the bus, sitting with Max. She tells me they're taking one of Dad's kidneys. Mom's not a match, and of course we'll never know about me. There's a new doctor, someone from Portland who specializes in this sort of operation. Evidently they're all worried about Kyle pulling through, he's already so weak. A local surgeon will amputate the hand if the other surgery is going well.

"I asked them about your father's liver. In case you were wondering. You know what alcohol can do. But they double-checked those results, and it's fine. I'll call you when I know more, Ethan. It'll be a long surgery, if everything goes well. So hope for that." I tell her I will, and then she says, "Ethan? I just want you to know I love you."

"Me too, Mom. Call me." I'm dying to say, *So Dad wasn't drinking as much as you thought, huh?* But this is really not the time.

It's a long surgery, all right. I make sure all my teachers know I'm waiting for an urgent family call, 'cause I don't know when it will come. Mom calls once or twice when I'm in class, and I jump each time and run into the hall. But there's no real news until midafternoon. Mom sounds like she's trying not to cry, but the news is good.

"They're fine, Ethan. It's just seeing your brother's right arm . . . I can't look at it."

"They took the hand, then?"

"Yes. Thank God."

I couldn't agree more, and yet I totally get what she means about seeing it. As soon as I hang up, my whole body kind of slumps. I didn't know until that moment how much I've been holding myself in all day, how stressed out I am. I've left History to take the call, and I don't go back in right away. I lean against the wall for a few minutes, eyes closed and watering a little. Then I walk up and down the hall, my mind empty of words but full of images of handless arms. When my dream image comes flying into my head—the one with the human hand in the leg-hold trap—I decide it's time to go back to class. Max is watching the door from his chair, and I half smile and nod once. I can see his body slump a little, too, in relief. He really does care about me.

Within minutes my phone rings again, scaring the bejesus out of me. Did something go wrong? But it's Etta's number on the display. I go into the hall, anyway, and Max follows me. I can't quite believe that he'd do that, but here he is.

I answer my phone, sort of at the same time telling Max it's not the hospital. His turn now to slump against the wall.

"Ethan, your mother's just called to tell me how things are. It sounds really good. She's staying at the hospital though, as you know. So I'm thinking it would be great if you could come here for dinner tonight. Heidi's cooking, but if you want some meat I can make sure you get some. Shall I pick you up after school?"

Most of this sounds fine. I'd like to see Heidi again, and it sounds like she's still spending time with Etta, like she's been doing since Two was killed. But I'd kind of hoped to spend a little time with Max. "Can you hang on a sec?" And I ask Max about his after-school plans, totally and completely shocked when he suggests that we both go to Etta's, at least for a little while. He says it's about time he got to know her better, since I seem to like her so much.

"Etta? Listen, do you mind if my friend Max comes, too? He can't stay for dinner, but—"

"Of course! I'd be delighted. I'll pick you both up, and then I can give him a ride home later."

This day didn't start so great, but it's turning out all right after all.

Heidi is out grocery shopping when we get to Etta's. I give Max a tour of the cottage, which has only three rooms, and since we came in through the kitchen, a tour means I show him the living room. We're alone there, so after I point out where Two's grave is, I tell him about the day I'd sat in the Adirondack chair, imagining him in the other one. He seems a little shy about this, kind of an *Aw, shucks* moment. "Great view," is all he says. But then he kisses me. Just a tiny one, but I'll take it.

We decide to take a tour of the outside before it gets too dark. Max says the clouds look heavy with snow, and when I look up I think he's right. If there's one thing I haven't been paying attention to, it's weather forecasts.

First we stand near Two's grave, facing distant hills that are all gray and black and dark green this time of year. Anyone in the living room can see us, so we don't hold hands or anything, just stand there with our hands in our pockets, and I let my mind revisit that first time I was out here. Two had come out to sit with me. My eyes start stinging now, and I'm sure it's because I'm feeling stressed from a combination of all the crap that's been happening lately, not just about Two. But I don't want to cry. I turn and lead the way toward the back, where I'd thrown the ball for Two that day that feels so long ago now.

"This is a great place for a dog," I say, my back to the house, facing the long open space that's bordered on one side by the view of the hills and on the other by woods.

"You're thinking of Two, aren't you?"

I don't bother to answer. It's kind of obvious that I am, but I still feel happy that Max mentioned him, and that he now gets that the dog was important to me. Kind of automatically my eyes move toward the shed on the edge of the woods, and I head that way. Max follows me inside. There are still some Vote for Etta signs in here, which amazes me; we planted so many.

Max and I turn and face outside, but we don't leave the shed. His arm is around my shoulders, and I lean a little against him. It feels so good, despite all the bad that's happening, to be here like this with him.

Sometimes it's okay when my voice surprises me. "Two saved my life right here."

Max doesn't say anything for about five seconds, and then, "Okay, you're gonna have to explain that one, charmer."

Charmer. God, but I love it when he calls me that. So I tell him how it happened and finish with the hero. "Two just sits there like he's wondering what's for lunch or something. He wasn't even hurt. It was pretty amazing."

I look at Max, who has a really odd expression on his face. Almost as a challenge, I add, "I was part of his pack."

"Ethan, why didn't I know about this?"

"You mean, why didn't I tell you? Or, why wasn't there ever a good time to tell you?"

Max turns to look outside. "I hear you. It's been pretty crazy these last few weeks, huh?"

"Yeah." I'm not sure, but I think that his tone of voice, and the fact that he turned away from me, are saying that he knows it's at least partly because he's limited what we talk about. But I probably have to take some of the blame. I mean, there were those trips to Bangor together. Two's rescue here happened between them, so I could have talked about it on the second trip. I could have talked about a lot of stuff on those trips. But I didn't.

Why not? Was I afraid Max would think I was a loser, spending all that time with an old lady like Etta? Was he giving me the impression that this thing that was eating up the town didn't matter, so anything I said about it would be lame? Was I concentrating so hard on not talking about Kyle's weirdness that I clammed up about lots of other things? Or was I trying to keep Max in a separate compartment of my life, safe from contamination by the rest of it? And am I as scared as he is of being open about what we are to each other?

And what *are* we?

Lots of stuff to think about. Meanwhile, I'm starting to shiver. "Ready to go back?"

Max shrugs. He looks at me again, and suddenly we're kissing. We won't do much in here; it's cramped and cold. But we sure can kiss.

We head back to the house through the first flakes of snow.

Max surprises the hell out of me yet again today when we go inside. Heidi's made hot cocoa, and we're all sitting around the table with Heidi asking Max a few questions about himself, and she tells him a little about her and about Two. Etta's fairly quiet, but that's okay. So am I. And when Heidi tells Max what she does for a living, that's when he surprises me.

"You know about power animals, right? Ethan gave me information about this bird, the junco, that's been following me around. One of them even sacrificed itself, or something. It smashed into the bus window in a snowstorm, right beside me. Does that mean something important?"

If anyone had asked me whether Max had taken in anything that I told him about power animals, or if he'd even really read what I'd printed out for him, I'd have said, "Not very likely." But I'd actually forgotten about that junco that hit the bus window. Max remembered.

Heidi says, "I'm sure it was important to the poor junco! Seriously, though, the messages are not always obvious. How curious are you? Would you be interested in doing a grounding exercise? You might or might not learn something, but it can't hurt."

Max looks at me and lifts one shoulder. I don't say anything, but he says, "Can Ethan and I both do it?"

"You can do it at the same time, if you want. All I would do is talk you into a level of relaxation that keeps the internal mind alert. It's not hypnosis. You don't talk during the exercise, though we can talk about it afterward, if you like."

So we're both going to go into some kind of trance, I guess. Heidi has me get that metal bowl from the living room, the one that had made that beautiful sound the first time I was in this room. She calls it a singing bowl. It's still on the bookshelf in front of the Shakespeare, and I remember one line from when I'd picked it up before: *This above all: to thine own self be true.*

Back in the kitchen Heidi says, "Just sit comfortably." She waits for us to settle. "And now, close your eyes. Listen to the tone, focus on it, and follow it to silence."

That bowl gives the most beautiful tone that lasts and lasts. And it makes perfect sense to follow it to silence. Then she talks me through what sounds like ways to feel, but it gets translated in my head as images. Strong trees, protective nests, buoyant air, deep powerful earth. If Heidi is still talking, I wouldn't know it. I'm in the air looking down on a scene, outdoors someplace. It feels completely natural to be up here, better than being on the ground. I figure I'm flying as Bat.

I'm above an area like the edge of a forest, with lower bushes and then an open field. It's kind of like behind Etta's house. It's not daytime, and it's not night—sometime in between. I've just started to realize that I can't actually *be* Bat, because I can see very clearly, when I hear a sharp whistle, almost a toot, almost like that last part of Dad's whistle. A flash of red appears on the branch of a bush. It's a male cardinal, brilliant even in the dusk. Then it flies away, but another bird is still there—a female, the soft buff tones of her body edged by the rich, deep orange under her wings. She whistles, too, and then there's a flash of red again, and they're side by side once more. I hover and watch as first one of the cardinals takes off and returns, and then the other, and back and forth, whistling. Suddenly the male cardinal lifts off his perch and flies right at me like he wants to strike. I feel my whole body jerk, and I'm terrified. Then I hear Heidi's voice, and I can feel her holding my hand.

"Gently, gently. Relax back into yourself, and leave what you saw just where it is. Take a deep breath and let it out slowly. And again." I hear the bowl sing again. When it's silent, Heidi says to open our eyes.

Heidi keeps hold of my hand. "Ethan, I apologize. You went deeper than I intended. But please know you were never in danger. Take a few moments to come back into yourself." She squeezes and lets my hand go.

Max says he's kind of creeped out. He didn't see anything much, just a kind of gray light, but he says there was someone, or something, watching him. He wants to know what that means.

Heidi says, "It's not unusual that nothing specific appeared to you. But I'm intrigued by the fact that you felt watched. It could be just that you're not quite ready, or not quite open enough, to take advantage of the medicine that power animals offer. I wouldn't let it bother you at all. If you like, we can do this again some time in the future and see if your experience changes. Meantime, it might help for you to contemplate your own life in light of what characteristics you think would help you progress, or support you. Think about what characteristics you'd like to strengthen in yourself."

"Okay." He doesn't sound like he's going to start contemplating right away, in any case. He turns toward me. "Ethan, what did you see?"

Everyone is looking at me, but I don't know what I want to say, or if I want to say anything. I'm still feeling unsettled, even a little freaked out. But I don't see how I can not say something. So I describe what I saw, right up to when the male cardinal flew at me.

Max asks her, "What does Ethan's mean?"

Heidi is still looking at me, kind of intense but still gentle. Finally, to me, she says, "I can tell you only what these animals are said to represent." She shakes her head. "This is what comes of me trying to figure out what someone else's animal is. It's something you need to discover yourself. I might have been off-base with Bat for you, Ethan. If this turns out to be true, I hope it's not upsetting."

"So, what's the cardinal to me, then?" I'm kind of sad; I'm very fond of Bat now, and I don't want him overpowered.

Heidi takes a long breath before she says, "The red of the male cardinal calls to blood in a mystic way. It represents a powerful life force. The female . . . you said they were both coming and going, taking turns?"

"And whistling. They were both whistling."

Heidi nods. "So they both wanted your attention. The presence of both usually represents the integration of male, or perseverance, and female, intuition. When we allow these characteristics to balance within us, that's very powerful. It helps us achieve almost anything. But the red bird flew at you. It's said that he can take you on a spiritual path from which there is no turning back. And someone on this path must take great care not to lose himself in his mission. Again, balance is essential. If you let the power of the red bird take over, you'll lose the intuition of the female."

No one says anything for a minute, but then Heidi smiles and says, "You, young man, are one powerful energy. Below your surface, there are worlds expanding in all directions. People like you often become shamans or priests. Tuck that into the back of your mind for now. How do you feel?"

How to answer? "I feel okay, I think. Kind of tired." My head is spinning, actually, because it's kind of like Heidi's telling me my quest for balance is not just something I want, but it's something I need. Like if I don't find it, I'll get sucked down some path that a stronger personality wants me to go on.

God, no wonder I try so hard not to get involved! I risk a glance at Etta, who had once told me to make sure I wasn't hiding out of cowardice. She's looking at me, her eyes thoughtful rather than intense. We're in synch again, it seems. About time.

I ride with Etta as we drive Max home. She lets us sit in the backseat together, and we hold hands, our fingers playing together as we watch the groups of kids out for Halloween in spite of the inch or so of snow already on the ground. I'd completely forgotten about Halloween. I bet no one will venture down Etta's driveway, and no one's getting anything at my house. I feel so separate from it, but it's more than just being too old to care about wearing costumes and collecting candy. Somehow I've moved to the next level. I feel this; I just don't know what it means.

Just before we get to the Modines', Max gives my hand a hard squeeze and lets go. I want him to stay with me. I want him to stay with me all night, to warm my bed, to be there when I wake up alone in my own house. I have to stop myself from calling to him.

Over dinner, Etta and Heidi talk about the election and what Etta's going to do to get out into the public again, with only one full day left. Voting day is Tuesday. I'm only half listening, wondering how I'm going to figure out who—or what—is trying to drag me out of balance.

Etta and Heidi have stopped talking, but I barely notice until Etta says, "You're looking pensive, Ethan. Thinking about your brother?"

I blink stupidly. Duh. Maybe I should be, but I'm not. "Not at the moment. Mom said she'd call me around eight. I was . . . I was thinking about how some people want to pull you down their religious path."

Etta nods. "I know what you mean. I'm not advocating religion, Ethan. But it seems to me that most people need to believe that someone somewhere understands why things happen, especially when things seem to make no sense. And if they can get others to believe it, too, their belief is validated."

"They want to be lied to?"

Heidi asks, "Who's lying?"

"Well . . . you know, there's really no way to control things, is there? There's no way we can get things to be the way we want. Sure, people pray, but it doesn't usually work, does it? It only seems to, and only once in a while. So, I mean, it's like with this election thing. With ID. They have to lie to believe that evolution can't be true. They have to lie to themselves, and to each other, and they try lying to us. Why don't they admit that science can describe what's going on better than . . . better than fucking Revelations?"

Heidi says, "Language, Ethan."

"Sorry."

Etta says, "Science seems pretty cold to most people, I think. The stories it tells are full of cold facts. And factual stories fascinate only some people. Most people prefer stories about people, about life. Stories they can relate to, that make them feel good, or at least stories that give them hope."

Heidi is nodding. "Not many people change the way they live or the way they think because they heard some facts. They might change small things, but nothing big. People need inspiration to change."

This all makes me feel a kind of hopelessness. It means Sylvia has no chance at convincing anyone that ID isn't science by approaching the issue rationally. And Max can't convince people with science that there's nothing wrong with us just because we're gay. I set my fork down a little too hard, and it clatters loudly and splatters sauce across the table. "But look what religion did to Kyle! And it's making all those ID freaks afraid, and they do terrible things. It uses fear, and threats. That's how it gets people to do things."

Heidi mops up my splatters with a paper napkin. "But it also gives them hope. It calls for fasting, but then you feast. First sacrifice, then joy. Science doesn't offer rewards."

"What was Kyle's reward, then?"

Etta says, "Kyle's problem was not his religion. His disease is what got to him."

"Religion made it worse. And God didn't help!"

Heidi raises one hand as if for calm and sets it down slowly. "I don't think God's role is to solve all the mysteries for us. It's to help us live with them. This is one reason that my own belief system relies so heavily on a broader spiritual world. This way I have alternatives. I have sources of strength that don't rely only on my own understanding, or only on someone else's interpretation, and I don't have only one place to go when I have questions."

This doesn't help me. "So what am I supposed to do? I'm surrounded by some people who want me to believe that there's no way God created everything just like it is, and others who want to convince me that's the only way it could be! And if that's not enough, there are people on both sides who think everyone should be just like them, and no one should be gay!"

Etta is looking at me, drumming her fingers. "Ethan, what part do you think Max plays in your life right now? Does his being in it make things easier or harder?"

Is she suggesting it's one way or the other? I look at Heidi. Does she even know about me and Max? About me? I just gave her a hint. . . .

Heidi smiles. "Ethan, no one has said anything to me, but I have to say it's pretty obvious that Max is special to you. If I've misunderstood, let me know."

I look down at my plate. "I think you understand." I look up at her. "But he doesn't want people to know."

"Do you want them to know about you?"

Time to stop avoiding this question, I guess. "Yes."

"Why?"

"I don't want to hide. I don't want to pretend, or lie, or make it look like I agree with people who think there's something wrong with me."

"What steps have you taken?"

"Well, I have a boyfriend. Sort of. Max."

"Sort of?"

"I mean, he won't really come out at all, so we have to hide. His sister knows about me. He's out to her. And my mom knows. Her lawyer, I think, because he guessed. My friend Jorja, sort of. And Shane. And you guys."

"Shane Jenson? Tattoo Shane?"

This puzzles me, partly because I'd never heard his last name, partly because he knew the name Heidi Wolcott. "He knew who you were, too. I went to talk to him after Two died, when Etta wouldn't . . . you know. Wasn't ready to talk to people."

Heidi asks, "Not Kyle, then? He doesn't know? Or your father?"

"No."

She nods. "Do you wish more people knew?"

"I don't know. I mean, I *want* to be out, you know? But . . ."

"Indeed, 'but.' There are consequences. And not all of them are about you. It's a path you should move down thoughtfully. What about Max? Who knows about him?"

"His sister. Me. You guys."

"As far as Max knows, we don't know anything. If we are to find out, he must tell us."

"Ha. That's not likely."

But Heidi just smiles. "There are a number of things Max is avoiding, aren't there?" I wonder if she means it was Max avoiding his animal, and not the other way around.

There's something I've been avoiding, myself. "Should I tell my dad?"

"Oh, sweetie, no one can tell you that. At any rate, I think he needs to get through at least some of his recovery period before he hears something that might surprise him. He's going through so much right now. Sometimes that's a good time to reveal something to someone. But not always. And I can't advise you."

So. I still have to find my own answers. This sucks. "And what about balance for me? If Cardinal wants to push me down some spiritual path, where do *I* get balance?"

Heidi laughs. "I'm sorry, Ethan. I've been treating you like you understand more than you do yet. I'm getting the sense you aren't ready to let go of the idea of Bat as yours. Is that true?"

"I like Bat. It feels comfortable."

"That's okay; he has plenty to teach anyone, and I still think you need his medicine. The Cardinal pair brings different perspectives. It includes the female, and that's where balance comes from. But you're right not to let the male cardinal come at you too soon. I think you're what I call a sensitive, which means you're very receptive to the difficulties of others—and often to what could help them. If I'm right, you'll need to learn to protect yourself without locking yourself away."

I'm shaking my head. "It's too much stuff to think about at once."

"Then don't think. Just feel, and hold on to Bat as long as you want to. And if Cardinal frightens you, then let me present an alternative. It could be that he's being way too pushy, and if you protect yourself without hiding, you'll soon know whether the cardinal pair is for you. Personally, I'm thinking that someday you'll be ready for Raven."

Now I shake my head, hard. "Raven? Oh, I don't think so! That's all about multidimensional stuff, and mystery. Secrets, magic, the void. Shape-shifting."

Etta laughs.

Heidi doesn't. She says, "That's right."

My iPhone rings, and I jump. It's Mom. "I have to answer

this." I go into the dark living room, where I can see through the picture window that everything outside is obscured by snow.

"Where are you?"

"At Etta's. How is everyone there?"

"Still looking good, thank God. Or whoever. I'm staying here, like I planned. Are you all right being at home alone? Should I ask Etta to have you stay with her?"

"She has just the one bedroom. I'm good. I'll be okay."

"There's a storm coming in. Can you make sure the driveway is shoveled in the morning? I'd like to come get you tomorrow so you can see Kyle and your father. Can you miss school?"

"Sure. Max asked Sylvia to run interference for me. She knows what's going on."

"I'll call the principal's office tomorrow, too, just to be sure. Ethan?"

"Yeah?"

"I want you to know how much I appreciate being able to rely on you. This will be over soon, and things will be better. I promise."

Almost what Dad had said. "I know. It's okay, Mom. Call tomorrow and let me know what time you'll get home, will you?"

"Of course. Good night, sweetie."

She hasn't called me that in . . . forever?

Back in the kitchen, I offer to help with the dishes. I'm not ready to go to my totally empty house. Then we all go into the living room, a place I've never spent more than a few minutes in, and Heidi gives us each a mug full of something that tastes kind of like hot apple cider, but it has a bite to it. I like it a lot. It warms me inside.

Lots of snow is hitting the picture window, and I ask Etta if she knows who will plow her out tomorrow. She smiles and says she does know, but she's not telling. She also says someone will take care of my driveway, or as much of it as they can around my dad's pickup. I try, but I can't get any more than that out of her, so I go back to sipping my drink until my eye falls on the singing bowl, which someone has put back. The Shakespeare books are right there, too.

"Whose books are those?" I ask.

Etta answers, "The ones on the shelves you're pointing to were my father's."

"So is he the one who wrote out the stuff about being true to yourself?"

She smiles. "Yes. If there's one person who could make that claim, it was Dad. We should all be so lucky. But I guess it's not luck. It's up to each of us, isn't it?"

No one answers. No one needs to.

I finish my drink and ask if there's more. Heidi smiles, and says yes, but it won't taste quite the same. She fetches me what really is just hot apple cider now, and I think I can guess that whatever else was in the first mug was alcoholic. The second mug is still good, though.

I'm half finished with this one when Etta says, "I need to get you home before the snow gets too bad. Before you go, though, Heidi and I have something we want you to know. It's a confidence, and if you're not comfortable keeping it, say so and I won't go on."

"You want me to keep something secret?"

"Yes, just as Heidi and I would say nothing about you or Max."

"I can deal with that." My curiosity won't let me turn down this opportunity.

"You might have guessed already, but in case you haven't, Heidi and I are both lesbians. And we're together." I just blink at her. "Just like Heidi said earlier, sometimes a time of turmoil is the best time to reveal something surprising. We think you're strong enough to take this one, which might be a surprise but shouldn't be upsetting. I hope we're not wrong."

Something's coming up from inside me. At first I don't know what it is, but then there's a sputter, and then a giggle, and I have to set my mug down. Then I'm laughing. Of course! How could I not have known? God, even Shane knew! *Friend* was the word he echoed oddly after I said it. Etta and Heidi are both laughing with me now. No wonder she didn't go back to New York.

On the drive home, with snow piling up by the inch and me with no worries about shoveling it tomorrow, I feel supported, somehow, in a way I never felt before. I know I can handle whatever's going to happen next. I'm still in a pack. A secret, wonderful pack.

I do the dishes from this morning, more for something to do than anything else, and make sure the outside lights are on in case my secret snow plower comes for the first time while it's still dark. I should feel really weird being alone in the house like this. I guess I do feel a little strange, but I don't feel alone. And I wish Etta were still here so I could say that having Max in my life is making things better. Come to that, having her in my life is making things better, too.

When I head up to my room I stop at Kyle's door and flip on the light. Mom really cleaned up; you can't tell anything awful happened in here, ever. It's ready for him whenever he gets out of the hospital, though he won't have a door for a while. Maybe we can even bring back the hangers and the lightbulbs.

I sit for a few minutes on the side of my bed, Edgar in my hands. Raven? Heidi thinks I'm destined for Raven? I can't even figure out Up. But I did figure out about my need for balance, and I already knew about my own male–female integration, something the cardinal pair is supposed to mean. So . . . who knows?

I think about the way I'd felt driving home from Etta's: strong, protected, not alone even with all this terrible stuff going on around me. To fortify my network, I picture the different people. And then something jolts me upright.

Jorja.

I grab my phone and dial her house, even though it's nearly ten o'clock. No answer. I've left enough voice messages by this time—two? three?—so I just hang up.

I can't sleep, thinking of Jorja. To put her out of my mind, I think about my folks. Lots of times you watch a TV show or a movie, and there's this family that something terrible happens to like the death of a child, and the family falls apart, the parents split, all that stuff. So what's going on here? Does it take the near death of a child to bring my folks together? Maybe it's just that a catalyst changes the situation from whatever it was to something else? Whatever, it really seems like they're together again. I just wish it was enough happiness to help me get to sleep.

But I do sleep, and I have this dream. It's a stupid dream, and it doesn't feel anything like my trance at Etta's. I don't see any real meaning in it. It's just a jumbled mess created by all the horrible things happening lately, mixed with Jorja's—and maybe Kyle's—fixation on Revelations. On that stupid beast.

Jorja's down in this sort of pit area, and it's all dark like we're in Mordor or someplace, and she's running around trying to hide behind rocks and looking for a way out of the pit, and there's this beast chasing her. I can't see it well enough to describe it, but it's big and ugly and nasty, and there's no doubt its intentions are anything but good. I'm up on the edge of the pit, scrambling around for tree roots or vines or anything I can drop down to help Jorja escape, and of course being a dream it never occurs to me that this is pointless, that the beast could grab on to the vine, too, and maybe pull me in. For some reason I'm not personally afraid of the beast. I am afraid for Jorja, though, and I'm frantic that I can't do anything to help her.

I wake up a few times, but each time I fall asleep again I go back to the edge of that pit, and Jorja's still in there desperately trying to avoid the beast. Finally I get up, maybe around four, and go downstairs. I drink some of Kyle's orange juice and sit in the dark living room, almost but not quite wanting to look in Kyle's Bible to see if the beast can be overcome by garlic or silver bullets or something, not quite having the energy to turn on the computer and do some online research. Town plows have gone by on the road, and there's a berm at the end of my driveway that's maybe two feet high. I'm watching the near white-out conditions outside when I see a smaller truck approaching, slowing, and turning into my driveway. I press my face against the window to see who it is.

It's Mr. Hyde. Nancy Hyde's husband. Nancy Hyde, who had stopped talking to Mom for supporting Etta. I laugh out loud. How do you like that? Etta Greenleaf must have called the Hydes and not only convinced them to plow her out but also to make sure we're okay.

Life's a funny thing.

I turn on the lamp beside me and wave. Mr. Hyde waves back.

Chapter 15

Mom comes to get me around eleven. I've already texted Max to let him know why I won't be in school, and Mom has already called the office. Mr. Hyde has come back at least once more, the sun is now out, and I've shoveled the steps and around the pickup.

Mom comes in, stomping off the unavoidable snow that sticks to everything when it's fresh, and hangs up her coat. She looks tired but happy. "Ethan, you did a marvelous job on that driveway!"

I shrug, thinking she can't have looked too closely; a plowed edge looks very different from when the snow is shoveled. "Thanks, but I can't take all the credit." I'd kind of like to, but the fact that it was Nancy's husband who plowed us out is too good to keep quiet about. "Mr. Hyde came by at least twice."

She freezes. "What? What did you say?"

"Etta must have called him. She told me someone was going to plow her out and would come by here, too. And I saw him."

She kind of gropes for the back of Dad's easy chair and sits down in it, and before I know what's going on she's sobbing and sobbing.

"Mom! What's wrong? Is everything okay?"

She nods, but she can't speak right away, just reaches for the tissue box and goes on crying. I sit on the hassock in front of her, not sure whether to be worried or not.

Finally she manages to say, "It's all right, Ethan. There's just been too much shit going on." She takes a few ragged breaths. "When things have been horrible and someone does something really, truly nice, it can make you lose it. That's all." She blows her nose, cries a little more, and then gets up. "I'm going to take a shower. Then we'll have some lunch, and I'll take you to see Kyle and your dad."

We have some canned tuna and soup in the cupboard, and I throw lunch together so it's ready when she comes downstairs. She hugs me when she sees it.

At the hospital, they've put Dad and Kyle in the same room. Dad looks tired and groggy but cheerful; guess it feels good to be able to save your son's life. Kyle looks exhausted, and he's still hooked up to more stuff than Dad is, but he's alive. He's not terribly chatty, but he lifts his right arm and smiles as well as he can. I smile back, forcing myself not to let it show how grossed out I am, just like Mom had been, by the sight of that bandaged stump.

But it's what Kyle needed. And who am I to say otherwise? Maybe I can't believe the bit about it being possessed, but there's no doubt that Kyle needed that hand gone. It made no sense to us; we just had to believe him. And even though I know it's not the same, because being gay is how I was born and who I've always been, and Kyle wanting his hand gone is only the last few months, it's kind of the same in terms of other people accepting it. Mom and Dad both accepted that taking Kyle's hand off was the best thing, and they made sure it happened. Now I just need to get Dad to accept that letting me be who I am is something he needs to do, too. For me. Because it's best for me. It's truth for me. And I don't want to be untrue to myself or to anyone else.

Mom tells Dad about Mr. Hyde plowing so he won't worry about it. He'll be here a few days before he can go home, and then he'll have to be kind of careful for weeks—no lifting things, and no plowing, that's for sure. Kyle will be here a little longer, and his recovery will keep him out of school for a while. Given how much he's missed already, he might even have to repeat the school year. Which would put him in the same year as me. Which would be really weird. Guess that's one of those bridges we can't cross just yet.

We leave just after three. On the drive home, Mom says she needs to sleep in a bed, and besides she has to vote. I just stare at her; I'd forgotten all about it, and I can't believe she remembers at this point, either.

Mom makes me wait in the car while she goes in to vote. There are people standing around holding signs, and a few of them are repeats from the town hall meeting, but mostly the signs just have candidates' names on them. And there are lots more for Etta than for Carl Phinney. I can't help wondering if somewhere between the fight at school and Two getting shot, sensible people started to see where the violence was coming from.

Fortunately I have my earbuds with me, because the line is kind of long for our little community, despite the overnight storm. There are several things up for a vote today; it's not all Etta and Carl and the one school board seat. But it still feels like that.

It doesn't take very long for them to figure out who wins the seat. Etta's lead is so extreme that by six o'clock, before the polls are even closed, it's official. If the voting had been last week, say on Thursday, there's no way I would have believed this. But so much has happened since the town hall meeting, and having Mr. Hyde plow for us *and* for Etta tells me that the wall—something that's been building up to separate friends from friends, and neighbors from neighbors—is crumbling. I'm no longer worried about what the reaction to Etta's victory will be. Like water after it breaks through a dam, we've found level. We've reached some kind of balance.

* * *

Mom sends me off to school on Wednesday, and I'm bummed when Max doesn't sit beside me. He nods at me, but he keeps going down the aisle. I would have thought he'd gotten over some of his reluctance. I try to tell myself that it's not reasonable for me to expect him to sit with me all the time, and even though this is true, sitting separately today—and the curt little nod he gave me—kind of hurts.

Whatever.

I have another mission today, anyway, so I use it to keep my mind off the fact that Max is distant all day at school. After Biology, I wait for most of the kids to leave so I can talk to Sylvia. She gives me a hug and asks about Kyle. I tell her just enough to get by; it's not Kyle's new kidney that I want to talk to Sylvia about.

"I need to ask someone about this, and I'm not sure who to go to," I open. She moves over to the corner away from the door and sits in a student chair. I sit in the next one over. "I've been trying to reach Jorja. She hasn't been in school in days, and every time I call her house there's no answer. I've left messages . . ." My voice kind of trails off as I see the look on Sylvia's face change from wanting to hear what I need to an expression that shuts me out.

"That's not something I can talk about, Ethan. All I can say is that it's my belief she'll be all right, but her family is going through something rather difficult right now, and—"

"*Her* family? What do you think mine is going through?"

"But your family is pulling together over it, I think, yes?" She waits for my nod. "Tell you what. I'll see what I can do about getting some information to you. I'm not sure what that will mean, but I know you're worried."

That doesn't seem like much to offer me. "You *think* she'll be all right? What's that supposed to mean? She's not all right now?" The look on Sylvia's face tells me she's not saying anything else. "What do I need to do, show up at Mrs. Glasier's Teen Meet to find out what's going on?"

Sylvia shakes her head. "I don't think they'll be able to tell you anything there, either. Just let me see what I can do, Ethan, okay?"

What can I say? Should I tell Sylvia about my beast dream? I decide it wouldn't help.

Max still doesn't sit with me on the bus. This time he barely looks at me. I could be anybody, or nobody. Something's wrong; I'm sure of it. But how the hell am I supposed to find out what? Christ, I don't need anything else to be wrong!

When I get home, Mom's in some kind of nesting frenzy. I can smell household cleaner, there's no clutter in the kitchen, and the rug in the living room looks like it was just vacuumed.

At first she doesn't stop what she's doing, doesn't look up from her bent position as she pulls things out from the front closet floor. Then she stands and pushes hair off her forehead and looks at me. "Let's sit for a minute." And she heads for the kitchen table. I sit across from her and wait.

"Okay, so I don't want you to get your hopes too high, Ethan. Sometimes troubles push people apart, and sometimes it brings them together." She pauses, and I'm thinking, *Yeah, I already figured that much out*, but I don't say anything so she'll keep talking. I think I like where this is going. "So, anyway, I've asked your father to move back in."

She sits back, sighs, and rubs her face a sec. "I'm not exactly perfect, either, so we've talked some things out. And at this point it seems stupid to keep going forward with this divorce just because we started down that road. So I hope you won't be too upset that you aren't likely to be seeing Mr. LeBlanc in the future." She smiles.

I smile back. I'm not sure what to do here. Should I get up and give her a hug? Should I laugh? Cry? Both? I just say, "I guess I can live with that." And, of course, I could just possibly run into Guy again at This Time For Sure someday.

"How are you, Ethan? How are you feeling, aside from the obvious?"

"I'll be okay." I'm wondering if I should tell her about my experience at Etta's last night when it occurs to me I need to talk about something else. "Um, Mom, do you remember what you said when I told you I was gay?"

She nods, doesn't give me anything else to go on.

"I'm not going to change my mind about that. It's real. It's me. So, I guess I need to know if you can live with it."

She takes a deep breath. "What was it I said? When you told me? That I wouldn't be happy about it, I think. And also that you'd still be you. I meant both those things, but I think part of the not being happy was only from not understanding it. The rest is because of how hard it could be for you. Maybe you think you're in love right now, and maybe you are, at least for your age. But if you didn't already know what some of the problems might be, you'd be telling everyone about your boyfriend. You're not doing that. You haven't even told your father, right?"

I shake my head, worried about where she's going with this.

"Now, it seems to me that knowing there will be problems doesn't mean you should try to be something you're not. So, my sweet boy," and she grins at me, "I can live with it. But I'm also worried about you because of it. Does that make sense?"

It doesn't feel much less anticlimactic than it did when I brought it up weeks ago, but it does feel more positive. Lots more positive, actually. "I guess so. I'm just trying to figure out if I should tell Dad."

We lock eyes for a few seconds. "I won't kid you. I'm not sure there's a good time to tell him that. But I think it's safe to say now is a really bad time. Is there some reason you want to tell him now?"

I shake my head. "No. I just don't want to lie to him. And you're right about Max."

"You're still keeping your promise, aren't you?"

"Yes." At least for now.

"Okay. Good. Now, why don't you go get a head start on your homework while I finish up the closet and get dinner started."

But there's more ground I want to cover. Different ground. "Mom? Do you, um, have you heard anything about Jorja?"

Something about the look on her face tells me she has. "Why do you ask?"

"She hasn't been in school for days, no one answers the phone, and Sylvia was very mysterious when I asked her about it today. What's going on?"

I don't like the long pause before she answers. "Can we talk about this maybe tomorrow?"

"Mom, it's freaking me out. Is she all right?"

Mom stands and comes over to me, and I stand for her hug. "She will be, Ethan. She will be." She pats my shoulder, and I want to believe her, but I'm not sure I do.

I push away. "Why won't anyone talk to me about her? Why won't you tell me anything?" I don't mean to shout, but it kind of comes out like that.

Mom sighs. "All right, Ethan. I was just trying to keep the daily drama to a dull roar, but keeping you in the dark is just making it worse." We both sit down again. "She's in Bingham, as a matter of fact."

"Bingham?" My mind is a blank, other than recognizing the town Etta and I drove to on our first outing. "Why?"

Mom pulls her lips into her mouth like she's not sure what to say next, or maybe how to say it. "She's staying with another family there. It might be for a while." She watches my face, which is twisting in confusion. "Ethan, things were really bad for her at home. I don't know how much she told you, and it's her story to tell, not mine. But things were bad. I don't know where her mother is, or why she's not answering the phone, but her father is in jail."

"For what?" My voice squeaks like it hasn't done in a year.

"Let's just say he was making life impossible, and Jorja's mother wasn't helping."

I'm on my feet now. "That's not enough! What was he doing?"

Mom stays in her chair, but her voice is hard. "Ethan, I've told you all I can."

"Well . . . I—Can you at least give me a telephone number where I can reach her?"

Mom thinks for a second. "No, but I will see if it's possible to ask her to call you. I'm not even sure about that, but I'll try. That's the best I can do. Now, homework."

Upstairs I'm tempted to call Max, but I'm afraid I might sound sulky. So I consider texting. And then I decide to wait until he contacts me. I pick up Edgar and hug him. Almost immediately my phone rings. It's Max!

"Hey. D'you wanna go to Marra's for a little while?"

"Marra's?" I'm trying to figure out how to let him know I'm mad at him without actually being mad at him. And I'm trying not to sound too excited that he's called.

"You know. The victory party. I figure it'll be good to put in an appearance. Especially you, since you and your mom helped her so much. I hear Marra's asked Etta to make an appearance herself. What d'you say?"

I want to resist him. I really do. But it's just so I can sulk, and I know that. So instead I say, "I guess. Why not?"

"Great. I'll meet you there. I'll probably get there eight-ish."

I hear my voice say, "K." *I'll meet you there?* Something heavy lands inside my chest. Why would I assume he'd pick me up? And why isn't he picking me up? He knows we're kind of stretched over here just now, and it would be nice not to burden my mom with taxiing me around. Christ! Will I *ever* have my own license? I sit at my desk a minute, breathing deeply and telling myself this is nothing, before I go talk to Mom, who's in her room.

"Marra Whitfield is having a victory party for Etta. Is it okay if I go over for a little while around eight?"

Mom's still on her cleaning binge, closets again. Maybe she's making room for Dad's things to come back? She sits on the bed and wipes hair off her forehead. "On a school night?"

"The election was yesterday. By the weekend it'll be old news."

"I suppose you'll need a ride."

"I could just take the car."

"No, you can't. You can drive over, if you want, but not without me."

* * *

Max isn't there yet when I arrive at around ten after. The party is about like you'd expect. Loud music, and every once in a while someone throws confetti from someplace. What stands out is how many kids are here. And lots of them had been either undecided, in terms of the two warring camps at school, or even on the ID side, at least initially.

Marra has a big banner with one of Etta's slogans hung across a big open doorway. It says, GOT SCIENCE? PROVE IT. She seems really pleased to see me. "Hey, Ethan! I knew you'd come. Is Max with you?"

Ha! I'm not the only one who thinks he should have given me a ride. Interesting, though, that *she'd* ask me this. "He's supposed to be on his way."

"Great! Then the debate team will all be here."

Gregory waves from the kitchen, and I go in to see how he's feeling. Sylvia's in the kitchen, too, and Mr. Coffin. They're chatting in a corner, and for the first time I wonder whether there's anything between them. Behind my ear, the wall phone rings.

"Ethan!" Marra shouts. "Can you get that?"

I have to plug my other ear against the party noise and ask whoever it is to repeat their name.

"Ethan? Is that you? It's Etta. Marra asked if I'd stop by. Could you tell her I'll be there in about twenty minutes?"

Marra's thrilled the woman of the hour will be here soon, and she makes me help her gather some kids together to throw confetti as Etta makes her entrance.

Max is still missing when Etta arrives. But it's not the green Forester that pulls up to the house. It's a cop car. I'm watching out the window as one cop walks her to the door. It seems they're still worried about her safety. She comes in alone and is immediately covered in colored paper bits. The shouting is tremendous, and kids crowd around Etta. I have to say, this really surprises me. I mean, I know we've all been through a kind of war, and she represents our cause, but . . . Maybe everyone's just beyond ready for a party. For something to celebrate. Because, really, if the ID side hadn't caused so much trouble, the Marra Whitfields of the world wouldn't have made such a fuss about Etta. The election would probably have gone relatively unnoticed, and the voting would have been no more heavy than usual.

Etta finds me and wraps an arm around my shoulders, telling her adoring throng that she couldn't have done this without my help. But she doesn't stay very long, and by the time she leaves I'm feeling furious with Max, who's still not here as far as I can tell. I'm standing in a corner of the living room, scoping out the crowd and thinking I'll go check the kitchen in case he got here and I didn't notice, when Jamal Mason appears in front of me.

"So," he says, and takes a gulp from his cup. I'm thinking he'll go on from there, but he doesn't.

I pick up the conversational baton. "Quite a scene, huh?"

"Sure is. Um, listen . . . You and Max. Is that, you know, exclusive?"

Thank God he's keeping his voice low. How the fuck am I supposed to respond to that? All I can think of to say is, "What do you mean?"

"Well—because if it's not, I thought, you know, maybe . . ." And he stops, like I'm supposed to know what he's getting at. I'm just starting to get a little pissed, like he's going to say something nasty about a personal fact of mine he's not even supposed to know, when he says, "Maybe we could go out sometime. See a movie, whatever." He takes another drink, his dark eyes boring into mine, not pleading, not challenging, but somewhere in between.

"I—I didn't know you . . ." Didn't know what? Didn't know he was gay? Didn't know it's that obvious that I am? My voice is almost a whisper. "How did you know?"

He shrugs. "Love the tat. Plus, I've noticed you. And I've noticed you and Max. So what I want to know is whether there's room for me, too." This kid has such a sexy smile. It makes me smile, too.

"Wow. I, uh, you know. I didn't think anyone knew. About me." So the tat is a little more obvious than I'd thought. Or maybe just to other gay people?

"You might be surprised."

I blink at him, wanting but not daring to ask what that means. "Do they know about you?"

He shakes his head. "Don't think so. Mostly they ignore me."

"What? Why?"

"I'm black."

This gives me pause, but just for a second. "Well, I'm not ignoring you now. I just don't know how to answer you. I mean, Max and I..." Christ, how to say anything about this that wouldn't make Max furious if he ever hears it? And how mad am I at him, anyway? "We're pretty focused at the moment, if you know what I mean." This much is true enough, at least for me.

"So right now's not good, but it's not out of the question."

I don't know how to describe this feeling. Someone noticed me. Someone wants me. Someone whose darkness only adds to his sex appeal. "It's not out of the question. It's just not the best timing."

He nods. "K. Maybe I'll check back another time." And while I'm still in shock, he disappears again.

Someone pushes me from the side, and I hear Max's voice in my ear. "What was that about?"

I will *not* react. I will *not* look at him right away. "Discovery mission," I say, hoping that's vague enough to make him wonder.

"Oh?"

But I'm not giving him any more. I still won't look at him. "Been here long?"

"Just before Etta left." Not a word about being late.

We stand there, side by side, sipping from our drinks, surveying the crowd like a couple of tourists mildly entertained at the monkey house at some zoo. Eventually Max says, "Ready to hit the road?"

Now I look at him. "What?"

He shrugs. "Do you want a lift home or not?"

A *lift?* I'm so close to telling him to go fuck himself. Mom is expecting me to call her when I'm ready to go home, so I'm hardly stuck here without Max's stingy offer.

I shrug, too. "Either way." I look back at the monkeys.

"What's with you?"

"What's with *me?*" I can't keep a note of astonishment out of my voice.

He's scowling, but not angry—maybe worried. "Look, Ethan, I . . . Let me give you a ride home, okay? So we can talk?"

My breathing goes all weird. That's the line someone uses when they want to tell the other person *It's not working.* "Fine."

We find Marra, say our good-byes, and as we walk along the road to where Max parked the Sequoia I call Mom to tell her I don't need a ride, that a "friend" is giving me a "lift." I want Max to hear that. Though of course he probably thinks I'm just being discreet.

He doesn't start the car up right away. Staring out the windshield, his voice a little tense, he says, "Was it what it looked like? With Jamal?"

I seem to spend so much of my life torn between those two poles Heidi told me about. I'd really like Max to know he's not my only option; a little jealousy can be a good thing. But I'm afraid of how he'd react if he knew what Jamal had said when I told him I didn't know anyone knew about me, that I'd be surprised. Because if they know about me, they almost certainly know about Max. Jamal did. And it seems like Marra has put us together in her view of things. And if anything will push him farther away from me, it's his fear of discovery. Ha! Discovery mission, indeed.

I stare out the windshield, too. As casually as possible, I say, "What did it look like?" No point in stepping into this with both feet before I'm sure I know where Max's head is.

"Like he was asking you out."

"He was."

"And you said . . ."

Here's the tough part. "He asked if you and I are exclusive. I told him we were pretty focused. He took that for a yes." I hold my breath. Will something explode?

"So you're not going out with him."

I turn to watch his face. "What do you think?"

He doesn't look at me, just pounds the steering wheel once, breathes through his teeth a few times, and then throws his head back against the headrest. "All right. All right." He shifts in his seat to face me more completely. "Look, Ethan, I really like you. I can't get you out of my head, okay? But you... There's something about you, something I can't get. Something that fits in with power animals and spiritual paths and tattoos and bats and Goth, and I don't get it. It doesn't fit on me. It isn't who I am. I always feel like some kind of bourgeois meat-and-potatoes guy next to you. I tried to get there. Sunday? At Etta's? I let that earth mother Heidi lead me into that trance or whatever it was, and all I got was something watching me. It was creepy, okay? Really creepy."

He rubs his face while I try to think of something, anything, to say to that. I don't come up with any words of wisdom before he starts talking again.

"After that, I started to feel really apart from you. Separate. Like we were in two different universes. Dimensions. Whatever. I've gone over and over it in my head, trying to find a place where I can get a foothold in your life. Shaman? Priest? Christ, Ethan! How can I compete with that?"

At last, something I can respond to. "Why do you have to compete with anything? Don't you know how important you are to me? Don't you know you keep me grounded, that without you I'd have gone bonkers weeks ago? My life is crazy right now, okay? But that doesn't mean I'm some kind of out-of-this-world character. And I stopped the Goth look, in case you hadn't noticed."

His voice is small. "I noticed. I wanted to think it was for me."

"It was for you, you idiot! And I'm okay with it. God, I think about you all the time! If you only knew how many nights I've

shot my sheets with you in my head." I have to giggle here.
"Both heads. Max, the only reason we're separate is because
we're both trying so hard to stay out of the other's way. Can we
stop that?"

He looks somewhere between confused and desperate. So I
try to explain. "It always seems to me that you avoid me because
you're terrified someone will know you're gay. I'm not exactly
going to put a banner across the auditorium stage announcing
'Max and Ethan Are an Item,' but I'm also sick and tired of hiding, and lying, and pretending it's okay to think there's something wrong with gay people." I realize I've just said almost this
exact thing to my lesbian friends. It must be true. "And I've been
trying not to make you think that I'm some needy little kid."

We stare at each other for—seconds? Minutes? I can't read
his expression. But he curls a hand behind my neck and pulls
our faces together. We've had hot kisses before. Lots of them.
But this one? This one is on fire. There are flames behind my
closed eyelids. Before it gets out of control he pushes away,
starts the car, and tears out. At first I'm wondering if he's mad
or confused or worried, but he pulls into the trees a little way
ahead, throws the car into park, pulls on the hand brake, and
says, "In the back. Now."

No separation now. No fear of being needy. It's like he has
this searing, desperate need for me, for my body and his together, for celebrating everything about ourselves that's male
and young and in love. He takes me in his mouth and teases
and sucks and pulls, and when I come he keeps going, swallowing everything I give him and wanting more. He's never done
that before, and neither have I, but I do it for him, too. It surprises me that I like it. But I do.

We lie together as long as we dare afterward, and I'm wondering how many more times Max and I will be together like
this before I won't be able to keep that promise I made to my
mother. One of these days, one of us is going to be way inside
the other. And I think I know which way I want it to be. I want
to possess him, and the whole time he's inside me I want to be
the only thing he thinks about. The only thing he cares about.

The only thing he wants. I want Max so deep inside me he gets lost and never finds his way out again.

There's another few semisweet, semihot kisses before I get out of the car at home, and then I watch him drive off, following the red taillights for longer than I can actually see them. Part of it is that I want to have him in view as long as possible, and partly I need a buffer, some time to adjust my mood before I go into that house where Kyle and Dad are conspicuous in their absence. Where, despite the surgical success, worry hovers over everything. I can't bring euphoria in there. It would be cruel.

Chapter 16

Thursday, two tests are on my schedule. One is the makeup test in math from the one I'd missed last Thursday afternoon, but before that there's the test in Biology. Yesterday Sylvia had told the class what it would cover, and she'd made it very clear that it would figure largely into our overall grade. Looking around the room, an intense expression on her face, she'd said that the only excuses for not being present to take it would be hospitalization or death.

Despite the warning, though, Bryan isn't in Biology for the test. A few kids whisper a little as Sylvia starts to hand the test out, but she hushes them and just keeps going.

I do okay, I guess; I'm no genius, but I did all that research when I thought I was gonna have to captain the debate team.

Math I'm not so sure of. But I get through it, and when Max plunks down next to me on the bus ride home, he gives me a grin.

"I have some info for you."

"About what?"

He pulls out a piece of paper with someone's name and address on it. I take it, read it, and start to say, *What's this?* But then I realize it's in Bingham. So instead, I look at Max's beautiful face, still smiling at me, and say, "Is this where she lives now?" Sylvia must have given him this for me. Mom had promised to see if Jorja would call me, but either she's been too preoccupied or she wasn't able to make it happen.

Max nods and says, "I have some more info, too, but not here. Call me when you get home."

This sounds ominous. For some reason, Jorja's with the Cormier family in Bingham, whoever they are. I have only the vaguest notion of what it would mean to have a foster family, or to be one. Did they know what they were getting? Did they know she'd be a heavy-duty-Goth-Christian teenager? Are they nice to her? Do they make her do their housework? Are they trying to make her wear regular clothes and normal jewelry and less makeup?

They might be wonderful people. But the idea of anyone trying to make Jorja give up how she sees herself makes my chest tighten. It's like I can imagine so well how that would feel to me. How it would feel if they tried to force me to be someone I'm not, to stop seeing Max and start dating girls, to have my tattoo removed and give up my bats. Maybe my dad doesn't know about me yet, but he also hasn't said anything really terrible about the kind of person I am. I don't kid myself; my revelation would not be anything he wants to hear. But he doesn't go around muttering about "fucking fags" or anything like that.

It hits me that I don't know whether my mom knows about Etta and Heidi. It's just possible that she does.

I shake off that distraction and make some plans about seeing Jorja. I don't know how, yet, but I know I have to see her. I have to find her and make sure she's okay. I have to ask her why she didn't tell me what was going on. And I don't care whether she's mad at me or not.

As soon as I get home and into my room I close the door and call Max. Once he's on the phone, he's quiet for a few seconds, and all the frustration from when both Sylvia and Mom wouldn't tell me anything comes out. "Max! Out with it!"

"Hey, calm down, will you? It's just that I'm not supposed to know anything. But I heard Sylvia on the phone, talking about it with somebody at the school. It's pretty bad, Ethan. Are you sure you wanna know right now?"

What else can the universe throw at me? "Yes."

"Okay." But he takes another few seconds, anyway. "Her father was abusing her. You know what I mean."

I'm not ready for that, I want to say. *Take it back. Don't tell me.* But it's too late.

I can't speak, even to correct him and say it was her *step*-father. When I don't respond, he goes on. "So they put him in jail, and they sent her to a foster family. Her mother's gone to stay with a sister someplace. So that's why no one was answering the phone when you called."

Suddenly my chest tightens yet again. My best friend was raped by her stepfather, and I didn't even know it. She didn't even tell me. The only thing like this she *did* tell me was that she wanted to avoid sex with boys, and who could blame her with this going on? I can feel my brain cramping. I take a few breaths and then ask, "How long? For how long was he doing that?"

"I don't know any details. I couldn't tell whether it was the first time—if it all hit the fan right away—or if it was going on for a while and it got really bad, or someone else found out. I'm sorry, Ethan. I just don't know."

There's nothing more to say. Nothing more I can say, anyway. "Thanks. I, uh, I gotta hang up. I have to think about this."

"Sure. But, Ethan? Don't go thinking there's anything you could have done."

"Yeah. K." And then, "Max? Thanks."

He's right, of course. But, damn, I wish she'd told me! I'd have made sure someone else knew! I would have made sure it stopped. And suddenly I remember that day when Jorja had called me three times, the day Etta and I stopped at Friendly's. She'd sounded all stuffed up, like she had a cold, or like she'd been crying. Why had she called me three times? She never explained that. So was she . . . you know, did something awful happen to her that day and she was trying to reach me? Maybe even to tell me about it? God!

But I guess it's stopped now, anyway. I sit on the bed, phone in my hand, trying to get up the guts to do what I know I really should do. Finally I find the courage to take the first step: Since Jorja doesn't have a cell, I look up the telephone number for Cormier at the Bingham address Max gave me, and I sit there staring at it for God knows how long. Then I take myself by surprise and just dial it.

"Hello?" It's a woman's voice.

"Is this Mrs. Cormier?"

"Yes. Who's calling?"

"Um, I hope I'm not disturbing you or anything, but... Okay, I'm a friend of Jorja's? Jorja Loomis?" Like this lady won't know which Jorja. "Anyway, is she there? Can I talk to her?"

There's a bit of a pause, and then, "Which friend? May I give her your name?"

"Ethan Poe."

"Just a minute."

Well, it's more like four minutes, but who's counting? But the next voice I hear isn't Jorja's. "I'm sorry, Ethan. She's not feeling up to talking. May I give her a message?"

Not up to talking? I can just imagine the way Jorja might make something like that known, given her circumstances. I feel sorry for Mrs. Cormier. "She hasn't been in school. Doesn't she go to her old school now?"

"Actually, she's not in school at all right now. She's . . . taking a break."

A break? Is she too traumatized to go to school? Is this even worse than I thought? "Can you give her my cell number and ask her to call?" I read it out for her.

"I'll give it to her, Ethan, but please don't be surprised if you don't hear from her. Is there anything in particular you want me to tell her?"

If I say anything at all, it has to be something that will get Jorja's attention. Something with some chance of inspiring her to call me. "Um, well . . . It's kind of hard. . . . Okay, it's just that my brother had a kidney transplant, and they had to cut off his right hand. I just thought she might like to know." I hang up, hurt that Jorja won't talk to me, terrified that Mrs. Cormier will ask me to explain that seemingly irrational sequence of events.

Mom is bringing Dad home Friday afternoon. She makes me go to school, though. For some reason I plunk myself down in a bus seat next to some other kid, and when Max gets on I wink and smile at him. He squeezes my shoulder on his way past, so I know we're okay. We spend the rest of the bus trip texting.

I'm sitting in second period, thinking about what it will be like to have an invalid Dad at home when I get there, wondering whether Max and I will really make it as couple or whether some homophobic idiot will slaughter one or both of us, wondering whether Jorja will ever call and what her foster family thinks of her religious fervor, wondering if she's told them about the beast. But, then, the beast had turned out to be her stepfather.

I remember that dream I'd had, where I watched helplessly from the edge of that pit while a beast chased Jorja around. I hadn't been afraid of the beast, even though at that time I didn't know who the beast was, or that he wouldn't want to chase me, anyway. And now I'm wondering if this is what Heidi meant when she told me I'm sensitive to others. If so, maybe this is why I kept worrying about Jorja when I had no way of knowing there was anything to worry about. She was gone from school only, like, one day before I started worrying.

I'm fishing around in the bottom of my pack for a pen, thinking about when Jorja had told me about the beast, that day we hitched out to Nick's for pizza. In my pack, my fingers encounter something unfamiliar, and I start to pull it out. It's the slave bracelet. And then an idea hits me. I'll hitchhike to Bingham! She'll be home; she's on break from school. I get to Max in the hall before next period and let him know I'm skipping out.

"Cool! Should I come with you?"

"I'm going to see Jorja. I think you'd better not be there."

He shakes his head once. "You're right about that one. Call me later?"

As inconspicuously as possible, I make my way out of school and onto the highway that goes past it. When I'm sure no one can see me, I check an online map on my iPhone for where the Cormiers' house is.

There's quite a bit of traffic, and it's easy getting rides. I'm in Bingham almost before I know it. My last ride drops me off at the end of the Cormiers' road, which doesn't have many houses on it, and it's about half a mile down on the left. There's not much traffic here to get a ride from, but I need the walking time anyway to think what I'm going to say. Provided Jorja's even there. Provided she'll even talk to me.

But by the time I'm approaching the white colonial-style house with the black shutters bolted only onto the front, black mailbox at the road end of the driveway waiting patiently for mail for CORMIER, I haven't come up with anything. I decide the problem is that Jorja is—was?—my friend and I don't approach friends with prepared speeches. I'll just go ring the bell like it's Jorja's house, and I'm here to visit. Which, really, is all true. Sort of.

Mrs. Cormier is short and skinny, reddish brown hair in some style that's never been named floating around her face. But she's nice, and she lets me in.

"I don't know, Ethan. She doesn't talk much. But I'll—"

"Listen, do you mind if I just go knock on her door? I've known her, like, forever, and I really care about her, but I've seen how she can be. Is that okay with you?"

She makes a wry face. "Well, I don't have a problem, but Jorja might. Still, I guess she won't kill you, will she?"

"We'll see." I walk down the short hall toward the door Mrs. Cormier points to, stand there for maybe ten seconds, and then knock. No response; I knock louder.

"What do you want?" Sounds like Jorja: irritated, put-upon, prickly. I turn the handle and walk in. "Get out! Go away! I don't want you here! Mrs. Cormier! Get rid of him!"

I shut the door behind me, knowing Mrs. Cormier might actually be concerned for Jorja's safety. She's probably right outside the door by now, listening, ready to come in if necessary.

I slough off my backpack and coat. Jorja's curled into a ball at the head of a twin bed, as far into the corner as she can get without breaking through the wall. Goth is still with her, and it feels odd that I'm standing here and wearing nothing black at all.

"Hey, it's me," I tell her. "Remember me? The guy who bought you the ear cuff and the slave bracelet? The one who's put up with your guff for nearly a year now?"

She stares at me, her expression . . . malevolent? Terrified? But she doesn't speak. So I do.

"Did Mrs. Cormier give you my message? About Kyle?"

"I don't care about your stupid brother's hand."

"Stupid brother?" Maybe if she hadn't said that, I'd have let her get away with a lot more. But not that. "*Stupid* brother? Kyle's lost his right hand, Jorja! He had to have a kidney transplant! My dad had to give up one of his for him." She doesn't move, doesn't speak. "He stabbed his hand, he cut it, he mutilated it. Then, without anyone knowing, he wrapped something around the wrist so tight it cut off circulation. And then he pounded a chair leg onto it to push in a handful of shit as far as he could so it would get infected!"

She's still staring at me, and I'm still standing there, but I'm practically panting, somewhere between fury and pain. "He got infected, all right. His whole body got infected, Jorja! He was on fluid replacement, antibiotics, and dialysis. Now I know you've had a terrible time. I know that. But you're not the only one." We stare at each other. "Life's not all about you."

That last bit is the trigger, I guess. She practically throws herself off the bed toward me, but I don't flinch. We're almost nose to nose. "You think this is some kind of competition? Whose life is worse? You can't even imagine what my life is like! You can't tell me what anything is about!" Her spit sprinkles my face. She pushes me, and I have to step back so I won't fall. "No one wins! No one!"

And we're back to staring.

"You told me you'd met the beast. I didn't know what you meant. Why didn't you tell me?"

"Tell you? Why should I tell *you* anything? I didn't tell anyone!"

"And look what good that did. It just let things go on."

"Don't you *dare* blame me!"

"Oh, for Christ's sakes, I'm not blaming you for anything except keeping quiet about it. Going on about beasts and demons like *they* were the problem, when it was your own fucking stepfather." Immediately I regret the f-word, given what's happened. "Maybe if you hadn't been so wrapped up in religion you could have helped yourself. You're as bad as Kyle saying the Bible was telling him to cut off his hand. It's a smoke screen for you, too."

"It's not! It's not!" Her face crumples, and she turns away so I won't see.

I feel like a shit, making her cry when so many bad things have happened to her. "Look, I'm not doing this right. I came out here to let you know I'm still your friend, if you want that. Okay, I also came to yell at you for trying to hide, for just disappearing, but that's because we're friends. That's because friends tell each other stuff."

She's recovered enough to wheel back toward me. "Stuff, Ethan? Stuff like your boyfriend?"

I take a shaky breath. "I never said I wouldn't be who I am. You wanted to pray for me, fine. God's answer was no. I'm still gay, Jorja. I'll always be gay. And you've known I was gay, so don't pretend it's some big surprise that I have a boyfriend."

"Don't you know why I was praying for you? Don't you know what will happen to you? And if you care about Max, then I'm warning you it will happen to him, too."

"What? What will happen, Jorja? Will the beast chase us next?"

"Don't you see? It *is* the beast! You being gay. The Antichrist isn't the same for everyone. But it's always a beast, and it's always going to mark you and drag you down into the pit."

I have to shake myself mentally. I have to remind myself that I don't believe any God worthy of worship would make me gay and then say, *Ha, ha! That's your beast, kid. Just try to get away from it.* I didn't choose this. If there's a God, he did, and it's okay. It's not something I'm doing wrong. "What did you do to deserve your beast, Jorja?"

"What?"

"Why did you have to go through all that torment? Why would God do that?"

"We're all tested, Ethan. You know that."

"Did you pass?"

"Yes! But you won't. Not if you keep giving in to temptation."

"What was your temptation? What did you give in to?" I'm trying so hard, here, to make her see that there's no rhyme or reason to her thinking, that this beast thing is just a boogie man that takes the shape of her own imagination. Or her own tormenter.

"Doubt. Doubt, Ethan. Doubt that God would protect me and punish him."

"You mean, jail?"

"Jail?" Her tone is so scornful it makes me take another step back. "Oh, Ethan, you really have no idea, do you? *Jail?* He's going to the eternal fires of everlasting hell! He'll be damned for all time! He'll be in the most desperate agony that will never, ever end!" She stops to take a breath, eyes wide with something that looks like lunacy.

"Why?" It's all I can think to say. "Why would God let all this happen? You think God made your stepfather evil, made him earn eternal torture, just to test your faith?"

"You're blaming me again!"

"I'm not. I just don't understand how you can worship a God who sets things up like that."

"No, I'm sure you don't. You're spoiled rotten, Ethan. You've got the best family, two parents who love you, and a brother who's committed to Christ. If you had gotten him to the kind of people I told you about, maybe he wouldn't have lost his hand."

Stunned. I'm stunned. She's saying it's my fault Kyle's hand is gone?

Jorja's not done with me. "You missed your chance, Ethan. You missed an opportunity God dumped right in your lap."

"That's crazy! You're telling me God made Kyle sick so I could save him and earn—I don't know, brownie points in heaven?"

"I don't pretend to know why God does things. I just know we're supposed to be watchful for chances to prove our faith."

And suddenly it hits me. I can't talk to her anymore. She's entrenched in some circular logic that has an irrational answer for everything, and because it's circular I can't get around it. I was hoping to ask how this whole thing with her stepfather got out, what happened to make someone know about it, what role her mother had played, and whether there was even the remotest chance I could do anything to help. But this? This is madness. Without another word I pick up everything I've dropped on the floor, turn to the door, and open it.

"I hope things get better for you, Jorja."

"I pray that you see the light. I pray that you let God into your heart and see that—" I close the door quietly, her words hitting the other side of it but not sinking into my brain. And I walk down the hall back to the living room, where Mrs. Cormier is standing, looking worried.

"I'm sorry," I tell her. "I hope I haven't made this harder for you. I didn't know she was this far gone. And...I guess I thought I might be able to help. You know, that it might be good for her to see someone she knows. But I must be the wrong someone." What I don't say is that I'm also here to satisfy my own need to know, to understand what happened to my friend.

"Do you have a few minutes to talk?"

This surprises me. I hadn't anticipated a visit with Jorja's foster mother. But—what have I got to lose? "Sure." She gestures toward a chair and then settles on the couch.

She opens. "How much do you know about what happened to her?"

"I know that her stepfather . . . you know. For some time. And she never told anyone."

Mrs. Cormier nods. "And how long have you been friends?"

I lift a shoulder and drop it. "Really friends? Not quite a year, I guess."

"Has she always been religious, all that time?"

"She—yeah, I guess. But it seems like it got crazier the last few months."

More nodding. "Things started to get much worse for her over the summer. I take it you don't go to her church, or follow its teachings?"

"I did go to a Teen Meet, but it was creepy. I left."

She takes a long breath, looks at her hands, looks back at me. "It seems to me—and I'm no psychologist, but maybe this will help you—it seems to me that she needs that black-and-white approach to God so she can believe in the full force of hell. In her mind, she's sent her stepfather there already. The torture that her scripture promised has begun. She needs an extreme religious position to give her this promise. Can you see the sense of that, for her?"

I can feel my face scowling, and I try to soften it. "But—she's condemning everyone else at the same time. She's condemning me."

"I know. And that's very sad. But I think she needs the extremes to keep him as far away from her, psychologically, as possible. What I see is there's a huge chunk of her that's been torn away, and she fills it with religion. And if she allows anyone to dilute the righteousness, make it less extreme, then the promise of Hell is diluted, too. And it could also throw her own salvation into question. And if there's one thing that girl needs right now, it's salvation. I don't think this is a good time to try and talk her out of her religion. I'm sorry it's hurt your friendship, but I have to be on her side, here. Not against you, I don't mean that. But I have to ask you not to make it harder for her. Do you understand?"

"You're telling me not to come back. Not to call her. Is that what you mean?"

"For now. I think that's best. Give her some time to heal. Can you do that?"

I don't need to think hard; why would I want to go on trying to be friends with someone who's condemned me? But ending things like this is too ugly. "Can I write her a note before I leave? You can read it."

She smiles and goes to get a pad and pen, and she leaves me alone. It takes me a few minutes to even know where to start.

> *Jorja — I just want to say I'm sorry all this happened to you. I wish you could have talked with me about it, but maybe even that was too much. Anyway, I'll be around if you want to get in touch.*

I put my cell number at the bottom and sign it with just my first name. Mrs. Cormier is in the kitchen, doing something at the stove. I hand her the note along with the purple and black slave bracelet. "Could you make sure she gets this as well? She loved it, once. Thanks."

"I hope she contacts you, Ethan. She needs friends, she just doesn't know what to do with them right now."

I walk for a long time before I stick my thumb out. I need time to think. But what keeps going around my head are images of the beast. The beast for Jorja isn't the same as the beast for Kyle or, according to Jorja, the beast for me: being gay. A couple of times that idea starts to take hold. But I know—I really *know* it isn't true. Which leaves me with a Jorja who's at least a little insane.

Another whole set of images I get is from that old movie *The Exorcist.* We rented it one Halloween, a few years ago maybe, and I got as much of a kick as most kids out of the grossness and the scary things and the priest flying out the window. But I couldn't sleep afterward, and not because the movie was scary. It was because God was scary. I mean, how could God let something like that happen to this little girl who hadn't done anything wrong? It was like God let Satan take over her, mutilate her, torture her, and then God let Satan kill the old priest so he could get at the young priest and kill him too? WTF?

What was it Mom said when I asked if she believed in God? That everyone defines God their own way? If that's true, then Jorja's defining God in a way that meets her need, that helps her survive what's happened to her. And maybe Mrs. Cormier is right. We just need to let her have that God for now. Maybe forever.

I figure that's about all the closure I'm gonna get, and it's getting really cold, and I'm tired of walking, so I turn and stick out my thumb. Two cars go by, and then a blue sedan goes by, slows down, and pulls over. I trot toward the passenger side and open the door. Before I can ask the guy driving how far he's going, he says, "Hey there. You were in front of me at the town hall, right?"

I look harder at him and nod. "Right." And I climb in, wondering if I should tell him about my role in saving his life.

He pulls onto the road, we exchange a few words about where I'm headed, and he says how great it is that Etta won the election. He chuckles. "Was that your mother who yelled? I can still remember it: 'Professing themselves to be Christians, they commit violence.' Perfect!"

I say something in agreement, and then my voice says, "Um, were you in an accident on this road in October?"

He flashes a glance at me. "Yes. How did you know?"

"Did you know it was Etta who got you breathing again?"

Another quick glance my way. "No. Are you serious? I asked about that, but no one would give me that information. That's—that's unbelievable! Were you there?"

"I was driving her car. She was letting me rack up some driving hours, and we were coming back from Bingham when I saw you miss that deer." I can't think of a good way to play up my great driving skills, but it seems unlikely that's going to have a big impression, anyway.

"Well, I'll be damned. I knew I liked that woman. How d'you like that." He shook his head a few times. "I was lucky on all counts that day. Not only with Etta being there, I mean. I could have been badly hurt, but I wasn't. They're not sure why I stopped breathing. Say, if you're friends with her, do you know what happened to her dog?"

I would have thought I was over feeling sad about Two, but my throat closes a little, and I have to cough. "Someone shot him. They think it was Mr. Galway."

He pounds once on the steering wheel. "I didn't even know she had a dog until word got out about it after the election. It was a pit bull, right?"

"Yes. His name was Two. T-W-O. Etta was One."

He opens his mouth and then laughs and laughs. I'm not sure I get the joke, but I have to laugh a little along with him. It makes me feel better. When the chuckles peter out he says, "That's a woman who should have a dog. Is she getting another one, do you know?"

"I haven't asked her. I think it might be a while."

"Are you a dog owner?"

Good question. And it's one I haven't considered since Two was killed, though I had thought about it before. "No. At least, not yet. I'd like to have one, though."

"Well if you want to consider a Samoyed or a Siberian husky, let me know. I breed both kinds."

I look at him. "Thanks. But I don't know who you are."

He laughs again, and I decide I like this guy. He hasn't even asked me why I'm not in school. I'm glad I helped save his life. "Ed Baker. I live in Holden, but I go back and forth to Bingham. My mom lives there, and she's on her own. Still fit as a fiddle, but I like to check up on her, especially after a storm. And you are—?"

"Ethan Poe."

We ride in silence for a bit, and then he says, "Where is your house, exactly?" I tell him, and he says, "I'm taking you all the way there, Ethan."

"Thanks!" It's just late enough that Mom has probably left for the hospital. I don't need her to know I skipped school, so if I see her car in the driveway I'll have Mr. Baker take me to school instead.

There's no car there, just the pickup, so I thank Mr. Baker again, take the card he offers me, and head inside for something to eat. It's almost one, and I'm starved. I text Max first, though, hoping I'll catch him before lunch hour is over, and I do. I let him know I'm home, that it was kind of a bust but at least I tried. He asks if I'm coming back to school and I say no, I'll wait for Mom, who'll probably be here around three or so. I figure she won't be too pissed that I wanted to be here for Dad's arrival. She doesn't need to know how much school I missed today.

Then something I've been thinking about since Wednesday night hits me, something I need to be alone in the house to do. I won't have another chance once invalid Dad gets home, so before I do anything about lunch I head for what I now, again, consider my folks' room, and I rifle through the drawers on Dad's side of the bed. It takes about half a minute to find what I'm looking for: a stash of condoms. It looks like it's already less than a full box, so I figure he won't miss a few. I grab them, hide them in an envelope in my desk, and head downstairs. Maybe I'll never use them. Maybe I'll be in college before I need them, when I can buy my own easily enough. But—you never know. I don't even know for sure that Max and I would need one, virgins that we are, but I also don't know all the reasons anyone does. Plus it feels kind of like less of a broken promise to my mom if Max and I do it this way. She was worried about me getting sick, is what she said. That's all.

I'm barely done with lunch when I hear a car door slam out front. Thinking it's my folks arriving really early, I head for the front door. But it's not them. It's Max, and I don't recognize the car driving off. Did he hitch, too?

He hugs me before he even takes his coat off. I give him a soda in the kitchen, and he says he thought maybe I could use some company after my disappointing excursion. We sit there for maybe five minutes before we know what we're going to do. But once we know, we're up the stairs in a flash.

As soon as we're up in my room things feel different. In a good way, but different. Softer. Sweeter, somehow. We just stand there, arms around each other, saying nothing for a while. And then I pull back so I can see his face.

Everything disappears from my vision except his eyes, and then he closes them as our faces move together. It's the sweetest kiss we've ever shared. I wouldn't say there's no sex in it, because with us there's always sex, but it isn't *about* sex. It's about us, caring about each other, being right together.

I take one of his hands in mine and lead him toward the bed.

We undress each other, and he kisses every inch of my skin as it appears. Will this be the time? Will I break my promise? I want to. God, I want to! Even once we're naked, hard dicks pointing toward each other, it's still not frantic. I'm thinking that if we're going to do it the way I want, he'll need to be gentle. And he could be gentle today. It was a sign, I'm sure now, that I thought to grab those condoms exactly when I did. Maybe there is a little magic in me someplace.

I reach into the bottom drawer of my desk where I keep my body lotion, and I hand it to Max. I also slide one of the condom packets out.

He takes both, closes his eyes for a second, then looks at me. "For real?" He knows what I want.

I just nod and throw the bed sheets open.

He looks at the place where we'll lie together. "I've never done this with anyone, Ethan. You know that."

"Me either."

"I—I don't really know what I'm doing. I mean, I'm sure I can get this on, it's just—"

I get onto the bed. "We'll figure the rest of it out together."

And we do. We have a few false starts, but we both really want this. It hurts, I can't pretend it doesn't, and Max gets a little worried, but I don't. And eventually he finds a place inside me that makes the pain worth it. I'm hoping it won't hurt so much the next time, but at least now I know how good it can be. At least now I know I can really be gay and be happy with someone. And right now, that someone is Max.

Afterward he's so sweet to me. He keeps dropping kisses all

over my face until I laugh and tell him to cut it out and stop treating me like a girl. "Maybe it'll be my turn next," I tell him as I push him onto his back.

"Was it okay? I mean, you know . . . I didn't hurt you?"

"It was more than okay. Takes some getting used to, but— yeah. I'd do it again." He looks drowsy, but I get up and toss his clothes to him. "If we don't get out of this room before my folks get here, I won't be allowed to *see* you again, let alone . . . you know." I wrap the used condom up in about five tissues and toss it in the wastebasket. I'll do something else with it later.

We're barely back downstairs when I hear Mom's car pulling up.

"I'm gone," Max says. He grabs his stuff and heads for the back door.

"Did you hitch?" I ask his retreating back.

"Yup. Never did it before. It was kind of fun." He winks as he shuts the door behind him; I figure he'll wait until he's sure he won't be seen and then get onto the road to hitch home.

Dad wants to sit in his chair for a bit, and I help Mom get him settled, keeping an eye out for Max. I do see him, but no one else does, and he's out of sight immediately. I have a secret smile the whole time I'm helping Mom make sure Dad has everything he needs.

Chapter 17

Saturday Mom takes me to see Kyle. He has another roommate now, a boy named Charlie who broke several bones and punctured something snowboarding. He has a friend visiting when we get there, and he's full of himself, telling his friend about the magnificent move he was pulling when he went down, about how he knows just what went wrong, and about how it's gonna be perfect the next time he does it. He says he's gonna picture it in his head over and over, visualize it into perfection. Whatever. But then he starts going into how gross his injuries were, how he could see the bone sticking out of his skin.

Kyle's half listening to him while Mom and I think of things to chat about, little news items, stuff at school. At one point when we've run out of subject matter he turns toward Charlie, then back to me, and grins. He jerks his head a little toward his roommate.

"What?" I ask.

"I've got him beat," he says quietly.

Not quietly enough. "What's that supposed to mean?" Charlie says, his voice a little belligerent. "What have you got?"

I'm thinking, *Please, Kyle, don't go into the shit-and-chair scene.*

Kyle grins at him and lifts his right arm up. "Maggots."

Well, I was not expecting that. *"What?"* Has he taken too much pain med or what?

Kyle looks at me. "They used maggots to clean the wound. I had them on for two days."

I turn to Mom for a sanity check.

"Kyle," she says, "please. Let's not talk about that."

"Why not? It's cool!" He lets out a barking laugh. "Science isn't everything. All the antibiotics they have? They couldn't get the infection to stop. They had to use *bugs.*"

"Mom?" I ask. "What's he talking about?"

She sighs. "They put sterile maggots on his wound so they wouldn't have to cut away any more of the arm." Kyle is right. Charlie's bone splinters through the skin is nursery school compared to this.

Evidently Kyle wants the whole story known. "Maggots are fly larvae. They eat only the decayed flesh." He sounds as proud as if they'd hatched from his own eggs. "They leave healthy flesh alone. Anyone who doesn't see the intelligence in that is blind."

And just like that, we're back at ID again. ID. BIID. Whatever. I decide it's not worth pointing out that flies evolved from something at some point.

Maggots. Yuck. I wonder if Kyle would be so over the moon about it if he didn't think using maggots proves his ID point. It shuts Charlie up, and that's good for something. But I'm thinking this image is going to be hard to get out of my head.

Kyle won't be coming home until next week sometime, maybe Tuesday. He's refusing to work with the people who'd like to explore prosthetic options with him. I guess he thinks a demon could inhabit that, too, though for myself, I can't quite picture "stumbling" with a fake hand.

It's weird seeing Dad weak, needing help to get up and taking stairs one at a time to avoid straining his wound. He tries to sleep on the couch at first, but it's not very comfortable, especially after surgery, and he ends up back in his own bed, with Mom. The effect of his slow progress around the house sometimes means he moves really quietly, and he keeps startling Mom, sneaking up on her without meaning to.

It doesn't take him long to get grouchy. Dad's not a man who likes having anyone help him do things he should be doing for himself, and both Mom and I manage to set him off more than once trying to anticipate what he needs and making him feel helpless in the process. Sometimes, even though she's right about what he needed, he pretends he didn't want it at all. I can see that her patient is wearing her patience pretty thin, and mine's not much thicker by Monday morning, when he sneaks up on me.

I'd just finished my shower, my back to the door, still toweling off, when he decides he doesn't want to wait for me to vacate before he comes in to use the toilet. There was no knock, I'm sure of that. And with the overhead fan running to vent steam out, I don't hear the door open, but when I feel the draft of cold air from the hall I wheel around to face the source.

The look on his face—I don't know, scowl? Horror? Fury? Holding on to the door jamb with one hand for support, he points the other at me.

"Turn around!"

"What?"

"I said, turn around!"

Why? What—OMG. He saw the tat. The face, the tone, the posture all tell me he knows exactly what the rainbow colors mean. I stand there, frozen, *not* turning around, towel in my hands dangling down to hide my crotch, but this doesn't make me feel any less vulnerable than if I'd had no cover at all. Turning around? That would be more vulnerable still. I don't do it.

I half expect him to bellow the order at me again, and I'm wondering what will happen if he lunges at me in his condition. We stand there like that, a still photo that begs for a creative caption contest, until I hear Mom's voice.

"What's going on in there? Ethan, don't hog the bathroom." She appears beside Dad, takes in his expression and mine, and maybe she doesn't know what's going on, but she knows it's bad. "Dave?"

He half turns to her, keeping his eyes on me. "Did you know about this?"

She looks at me, puzzled, shakes her head. "About what?"

Now it comes. "TURN AROUND!"

I turn just enough so Mom can see the tat, and I watch her face. Her eyes freeze for a second, but when she speaks it seems like she's trying to downplay things. "No, Dave. I didn't know he had a tattoo with lots of colors in it. But we both knew he had a tattoo." She looks at him like she expects him to explain himself.

"Charlene, those aren't just colors!" He grimaces at me. "Ethan, tell me you didn't know what that meant. Tell me you made a mistake." He's probably hoping I'll ask, *What mistake.*

Okay, this is totally not how I've anticipated telling him, standing here naked and getting colder by the second, dick shrinking into something less than manhood and inked ass there for all to see. Sometimes, though, you just have to play the hand you're dealt.

"No mistake." My chin lifts a little without my telling it to. I wish I had the balls to go back to toweling off, but I don't quite.

Dad grabs a little harder on the door jamb, and Mom decides to take over.

"Dave, this isn't where we should be having this conversation. Ethan, take whatever you need to your room so your father can use the bathroom." She manipulates Dad so that there's just enough room for me to squeak by without actually touching anyone.

Somehow I manage to throw on my clothes, grab my pack, and get downstairs before Dad's done in the bathroom. "Here," Mom says, and hands me a bag with four pieces of bread, some ham slices, and an orange—breakfast for the road. I throw them into my pack while Mom gets my coat, and I'm out the door before I hear the flush upstairs. She calls to me, "I'll try to calm him down, Ethan. Be patient with him."

Patient with him? How can you be patient with someone who wants to tell you that you aren't who you know you are? Christ, but this is *so* not how I wanted to do this!

I'm way too early for the bus, so I just walk along the route it will take and wave it down as it gets close. I throw myself into an empty seat, pull my earbuds out of my pack, and play Queen songs, loud, until Max gets on and sits with me.

He knows right away something's up. "You look like crap."

"Thanks."

"Seriously. What is it?"

I take a shaky breath. "Dad saw the tat."

"Jesus."

We sit there staring straight ahead until I add, "I was getting out of the shower. He didn't knock. Mom intervened and got me out of the house before he could explode completely. But he knows what it means. The rainbow colors."

More silence. Then Max says, "What are you gonna do?"

I shrug. "Mom's gonna try and calm him down. But it'll be ugly."

The day drags, and it goes by much too quickly. I bounce back and forth between feeling terrified to face Dad and looking forward to a chance to stand up for myself, challenge his outmoded opinions, and face him down. At some point that pendulum stops swinging, and I'm both terrified and determined at once. And it occurs to me that taking a stand is something I've never wanted to do. About anything. But now I'm ready. This is me. This is my life.

But I know that even if I stand up for myself, there'll be no facing him down. The only thing I have going for me is that he's too sick to hit me very hard. I can't remember him ever hitting me, actually, other than a few spankings when I was really little. Hitting hasn't been his thing. But all bets are off now. And it wouldn't actually take him hitting me to make things really awful. What if I can't ever see Max outside school again? I keep hoping Mom will call and let me know something, but—no. And I don't dare call her.

Max and I text all the way to his house on the bus after school, even though we're sharing a seat. I can tell he's trying not to let on how much he doesn't want me to mention his name at home, how much he doesn't want to be a part of that discussion. He doesn't even realize that Mom already knows about him. He gives me a heavy look when he gets up. The last thing he texts, after he steps off the bus, is *call me 2nite.*

I take my time getting to the house from the bus stop. I have absolutely no idea what to expect inside. Well, I guess I have some idea. And even though I'm determined to face it, it's still terrifying.

But when I get inside, all is quiet. Mom's cleaning the oven, and Dad's nowhere to be seen, which I take to mean that he's upstairs in bed, resting. No doubt after throwing fits all day.

Mom looks up for a sec when I sit in the kitchen chair nearest her, but she keeps scrubbing. I open with the only thing I can think of to say. "Thanks for this morning."

She scrubs for another thirty seconds, maybe, before she says, "You're welcome." She sits down on the floor and uses the back of a wrist to push hair off her forehead. "Just getting rid of some frustration, here." She looks at me and smiles. It's kind of a sad smile, and I don't know what to make of this.

"What can you tell me?"

"It's probably a lot like you'd expect. He had no idea. We talked until he'd gone round in too many circles and I got dizzy, so I printed out some things for him to read. About the pheromone study, and the animals. He took it upstairs. I can only hope he's read it." She rubs her face. "It might help for you to know something, Ethan. Your father loves both you boys very much. But he's always felt closer to you. Maybe it's Kyle's tendency to be a little stiff, even a little prissy about some things."

"Like the chores list?"

"Things like that, yes. So this has hurt your father."

"Why? I'm still me. You said so yourself."

"I know. It's just . . . It's just that he always felt like he had more of a connection with you. And to find out that something this basic is different—it hurts him, Ethan. You need to understand that so you can understand his reaction. He feels like he's lost a son."

"What, and gained a daughter?" My tone is so sharp it almost makes me wince.

She ignores this. "And also you need to remember that you—and I, actually—have had some time to get used to the idea. It's brand new to him, and now that he knows I've known for a while it's like we were keeping secrets from him."

"We were. We had to. We knew how he'd react."

Dad's voice from the doorway makes me jump. "It's also a question of trust, Ethan."

Up is truth. It's knowing I'm right. I coax my heart out of my throat and stand to face him. "Trust goes both ways." It's like this time, it was someone else's voice. Not mine at all.

"Meaning?"

"Meaning I knew you'd react badly. I knew you'd hate it. So I knew you wouldn't trust me to know who I am."

He shuffles over to the chair across from me, his legs barely moving the front sections of his red plaid bathrobe. "Sit."

Fine. I guess we have to do this. At least Mom's prepared him. She gets up and sits in the chair between us. Dad looks tired. Beaten. Worse than he has since the operation. I guess this is my fault?

"What am I supposed to do now, Ethan?"

"Do?"

"How do I know who you are? How do I talk to you? How do I trust you?"

These questions make no sense to me. I just shake my head, confused. Mom says, "Dave, if you have a question Ethan can answer, then ask it."

Dad doesn't look at her, only at me. "I don't know you. You're like a completely different person to me now." His voice is as tired as he looks.

I don't know where it comes from, but suddenly I feel strong. I feel something powerful supporting me. Powerful but also gentle. "Then let's get to know each other. Where do you want to start?"

He blinks, obviously a little surprised by this response. And maybe by the calm energy underneath it. "How do you know?"

"That I'm gay? That's easy. How do you know you're not?" I want him to think about this for just a second, so I wait about five heartbeats. "Just take those feelings and turn them around a little, and you're there. I *like* girls, Dad. I just don't feel the same way you do about them. I feel like that about boys. It's pretty much the same feeling, I think. Just goes in a different direction."

He looks at me, but I can tell his brain is working harder than his eyes and he's not really seeing me. Finally he says, "I can't get there. I can't understand why you'd want to be with a boy like that."

"And I can't understand why you'd want to be with a girl like that. It feels just as wrong to me as what I want feels to you." Suddenly something Mom had once said about him leaps into my brain: *Your father is an emotional child. He sees everything only as far as it relates to him, which means he can't put himself in someone else's shoes.* Maybe this is partly where my calm is coming from. He's the child. I have to lead. "Dad, I get that you don't get it. I get that you don't like it. But it's real. It's me. It always will be me. So we really need to get through this. You're still my father. We just have to figure out how to go forward."

He leans his elbows on the table and rubs his hairline with his fingers. "I don't see how I can do that."

"I don't see how you can't."

He looks up at me like he can't quite believe I said that. "I don't understand who you are. *What* you are. My mind won't go there. How can I go forward if I don't know my own son?"

Mom says, "Give it time, Dave."

"Time? *Time?* Time's what I'm afraid of! Time will show that he won't grow up into a normal man, that he won't find a girl to settle down with, he won't have kids, he won't have a life!"

This yanks me out of my calm a little. "You still have another son."

"What's that supposed to mean?"

"It's not like you've lost your only chance at grandkids."

"Is that what you—Look, Ethan. I don't know what we did

wrong. I don't even want to know. I just want to know how to fix it. Because right now, something's broken."

Oh, man! "Why? What's wrong with me?" Christ! I want to tell him he knows nothing. He's a dinosaur. He's stuck in the dark ages, a Neanderthal, an ignorant bigot.

"Nothing's wrong with *you!* That's the point. You only *think* there is."

Deep breath. "Dad, there's nothing wrong with me. I'm gay. Both are true."

"That can't be true."

"See, this is what I meant by trust going both ways. You can't see inside my head, Dad. You don't have a TV screen on my heart. You're just gonna have to believe me." I'm thinking I need to get out of here before I do something I'll regret, and this is a good exit line. I start to get up. But Dad yells the word *Sit* at me. He might be the child, but he's still the father. I sit. Hard.

"Young man, I don't know yet what we're going to do about this. But we're going to do something. And in the meantime, you're grounded."

"Dave!" Mom's standing now. "Ethan, please go to your room so your father and I can talk."

That is an exit line. I go all the way up the stairs, stand in the hall, and close my door from the outside just loud enough to be convincing. Then I creep as quietly as I can to the top of the stairs so I can hear what's going on.

"Ethan's done nothing to be grounded *for,* Dave. He's been very helpful with Kyle, he's done everything he could to support me, and he's thrilled that you're home again. All right, he got a tattoo when he shouldn't have, but if he didn't do some things wrong it would be scary."

"Charlene, he—"

She raises her voice. "Listen, will you? Just for a *change?* Listen to what someone else has to say?" I get the sense this is a theme they've gone over before. That this is something that drove them apart in the past. "When Ethan told me he was gay, my feeling at the time was that it might be a phase, or it might be real, but I knew that no amount of my telling him who he is was going to help anything. What will help the most is time."

"I—"

"Listen to me, Goddamn it!" A couple of ticks go by. "*If* he's going through some phase, and if we put up a stink now, he won't want to come to us and say he was wrong. He needs time to figure this out. Time, and a chance to live his life. Because this much I know. If he's really gay, there's nothing in this world anyone can do to change it."

His tone is angry, challenging. "You know this for a fact."

"I do. Did you read anything I gave you earlier?" There's some mumbled sound from him. "Then read it. Read it all, and then read it again. Because otherwise you're telling me that you don't love your son well enough to even try to understand him. And, Dave, I'm not going down that road with you."

It takes me a second to realize what she's telling him: She kicked him out once, and she'd do it again. For me. I have to sit down on the top step to digest this, and to let it sink in that she found all that stuff on the Internet, the stuff I mentioned only because we were helping Etta collect material for her debate. She went searching for it, and she found it, and she gave it to Dad to read. To convince him to accept me.

There's silence, and then Mom's voice again. "Now, Kyle is coming home tomorrow afternoon, if all goes well. And I will not have this household upset by anything that we can avoid. We have to focus on Kyle's—and your—recovery, and that means peace and quiet. Ethan is your son, and you love him. He knows that. But if you keep on like this, you'll convince him that you won't love him unless he's someone he doesn't believe he can be."

Dad sounds almost petulant. "So what am I supposed to do?"

"Do? I—*do?*" I can almost see her pulling her hair out. She heaves a breath so loudly I can hear it from my perch. "Here's what you do, Dave. You treat Ethan just like you were treating him yesterday. No—scratch that. You've been a pain in the ass lately. Treat him like you were treating him when he learned so quickly how to drive Bernie's Camaro. And no, he didn't tell me about that. I have my ways. Treat him like you treated him after he threw himself into the fray to help a classmate and Mrs. Wallace when they were beset by those hoodlums. Treat him like he's the son and you're the father."

Good thing I'm already sitting down, because what hits me then would have made my knees buckle. She's asking him to give me something Shane says only Dog and God can give. She's telling him to give me unconditional love.

Maybe there are some parents who can get there. And maybe I have one of them.

Even so, I'm not happy. Sitting at my desk after dinner, eyes not really focused on the race car fabric Mom used to make my bedspread eons ago, I'm feeling sulky that something small like driving could connect me to my father, and something important—like, who I am—could drive (Ha!) us apart.

Calling Max helps, at least a little. I let him know there were no details covered, no names mentioned. But I do decide to break some news to him.

"Max, I need to let you know something. You know how Sylvia figured out about you and gave you all that material about it?" I wait for his agreement. "Well, my mom didn't exactly figure it out about me. I told her last summer. But she did figure out about you. I mean, about us. You know. She knows I like you."

I wait through the silence, and finally he says, "Okay, so now what?"

Whew. "She stood up for me with Dad. But she did even more. She found a lot of that stuff on the Internet, and she's making him read it."

"So, what are you telling me?"

"I'm thinking we can be a little more open with her. I guess I don't know how that would play out, exactly, but we could keep it in mind." I'm not getting the sense that he's enthusiastic.

We talk a little longer, but things kind of peter out. It's not a good feeling, and I spend a lot of time thinking instead of sleeping. What is Max to me? What am I to him? We've had sex, real sex, and it was great. I love being with him, and he loves being with me. We got over that bump about him seeing me as too weird, or him as too ordinary, or whatever that was. But— now? Is he my boyfriend? Am I his? Are we, like, dating? Friends with benefits? Star-crossed lovers?

I reach for Edgar. *Up, please, Edgar. Take me Up.* I close my eyes. And I swear he says, "No need to fit some mold. Be your own shape."

The word "shape" throws me a little, and I remember that Raven changes shapes and that Heidi thinks I'm headed for Raven. I can't begin to say how nervous that makes me—the idea of changing my own shape. Because the truth is, my shape is gay, and I like Max an awful lot, and together we're whatever shape we are. We don't have to fit some mold. So I guess I'll have to give Max some time, just like Dad and I will have to give each other time, and the real shape of all these things will show.

Time. I guess I've got time. And meanwhile, Bat is still right for me.

Kyle's home when I get there after school Tuesday. As soon as I'm in the door, Mom says, "Oh, good, you're home. I need you to stay here while I go to the store. Kyle's diet is even more fussy than your father's, what with the sepsis he had. Plus I want to get him some immune boosters. He's in his room, but don't disturb him if he's asleep. Just listen in case he calls out; he might need something."

Not that I had anyplace I was planning to go, but I almost ask where Dad is and why he can't babysit Kyle. Then it hits me that Dad's still an invalid, too. I wonder what Mom's days are like lately. I climb the stairs quietly, hoping Dad's asleep and not wanting to wake him up—especially without Mom here to run interference for me. I peek into Kyle's room on the way to mine, and he's awake, a laptop resting on his legs. He looks at me and grins.

I go in and shut the door. Then I realize the door wasn't there when I'd left for school earlier.

"How'd this get here?"

He shrugs. "It was here when I got home. Guess Mom had someone install it this morning."

I point my chin toward his laptop. "Where'd you get that?"

"My church. It's a loaner." Another grin. "I've gotten really good with my left hand."

I have to work hard to avoid saying *Stumbling, too?* Instead I say, "Your church?"

"Yeah. They know what's going on, and the minister's wife brought this over."

They know? Then, where have they been? Jorja had said they should be helping him. "Did they just find out?"

He shakes his head. "No, I called Pastor Moody after I saw that first therapist. So he knew I had this . . . thing. BIID."

I have so many questions I don't know which one to ask first. I start with, "I didn't think you . . . you know, accepted that."

"I didn't. When I told Pastor Moody about it, I thought he'd agree with me. But he didn't. So when he came by to try and see me, and Mom told him to get lost, I didn't fight it. I figured he was as wrong as everyone else."

"Mom wouldn't let him in? I didn't even know he'd been here." And on to the next question. "And now? Do you believe it now?"

He shrugs. "I had a lot of time to think, especially in the hospital. So I guess I'll never really know whether there was a demon in my hand, but I can tell you I feel really great now that it's gone. I was worried that it would move and possess someplace else, but when that didn't happen it occurred to me that a real demon wouldn't be stopped by just cutting off a hand."

I have to sit down. I pull his desk chair out and fall onto it.

He's not done. "So then I thought, maybe it wasn't in the hand at all. Maybe it was in . . . you know." He looks at his crotch, but before I can jump up and scream *No!* at him, he laughs. "But if that were true, it wouldn't feel so great to just be rid of the hand."

This isn't my brother, I'm thinking. *Where did he go? And who is this guy?*

Kyle laughs again. "You look confused." I nod, and he shifts his position carefully. "Maybe you should talk with Pastor Moody. He helped me sort some of this out. And he helped me understand what Dad did for me. What you were willing to do, too. And Mom." I'm just blinking at him. Still speechless. "Could you help me put this thing away? The laptop? I just took some meds that knock me out, so I think I need to sleep for a while."

As I'm finding a place on his desk for the computer, trying like hell not to ask whether laptops—that is, science—are better than maggots, he says, "You know, it might be tough for me to keep up in school. I can't go back yet, and I'm not sure how long it'll be before I can really work on stuff. So we might be in the same classes next year. Wouldn't that be wild?"

Not knowing quite how to respond to that, I grin at him, and before my face relaxes again his eyes are closed, and I swear he's asleep before I close the door from the hall. I turn to head toward my own room and nearly bump into Dad.

He says, "He seems much better."

"Yeah."

We stare at each other a minute, and I get a sense of truce in the air. Then he says, "I'm going down to watch some TV. You doing homework?"

"Yeah. I think I'll do that." I guess he doesn't quite want to sit downstairs alone with me. Plus how would we agree on what to watch? So I go into my room, push in my earbuds, and lie on the bed listening to k.d. lang for a while, on low in case Kyle calls for me.

My phone rings. Max!

"Hey, charmer."

"Hey." I lie on the bed and stare out the window, picturing his face.

"How are things at home today?"

I tell him about my conversation with Kyle, and about how I barely recognize my own brother. "Wow. Guess he really was possessed."

"Interesting point. Maybe I'll have to do what he suggested

and talk to Pastor Moody." This makes both of us laugh. Then he gets kind of serious.

"I, uh, I had this dream, Ethan. Remember at Etta's? How I felt like something was spying on me when we were in that altered state?" He waits for me to say *Sure*. "Well, in the dream? I saw it. It came out from behind this big rock, I guess, and I saw it. It looked right at me."

"And?"

"It was a coyote."

I have to sit up at this. "Are you shittin' me? A coyote was spying on you? Etta says that's a really important power animal."

"It had really piercing dark eyes. Its mouth was open just a little, like it was breathing through it. And it just stared at me."

"Were you afraid?"

"Not of the coyote."

"Of what?" There's a few seconds of silence. "Max?"

"I don't know. It's . . . it's kind of like I was afraid of what it was telling me, but it didn't say anything. It was weird."

"You should look that up. Do a search on power animals. Coyote has something to do with karma." I smile. "You know, kind of like it's great karma that we hooked up." I want him to feel good that he might have a really cool power animal. And that's when I shift my position and see the red plaid bathrobe standing in my open doorway. My eyes flick to Dad's face, which looks nearly as red. "Um, can I call you back?"

"Uh-oh." And we both ring off. I stand to face my father.

"Max?" he says, his tone quiet but cutting. "Sylvia's brother? *He* is your . . ." He can't go on. I can see his fists clenching and unclenching at his sides.

How much did he hear? Will it do any good to pretend Max and I are just friends? Classmates? Not lovers? Ridiculously, my mind goes to my wastebasket. *Christ! Is that used condom still in there? No, trash day was yesterday; it's gone.* By the time all this has flashed through my brain, I know that the expression on my face gives me away.

"Give me that." He holds his hand out.

"What?"

"The cell phone."

Oh, no. This I won't do. "It's mine. Mom bought it for me."

He moves into the room, and I'm trapped on the other side of the bed. "Give it to me!"

I'm shaking my head. There's not much room for me to back up into, but he's wounded and slow. I jump onto the bed, over it, and race downstairs, thinking I have just enough time to grab my coat and get outside, when I see Mom's car pulling into the driveway. Dad's still hobbling down the stairs, so I head outside.

Mom takes one look at me and scowls. "What is it? Is Kyle—"

"Kyle's fine. It's Dad. He knows about Max."

"Christ." She thrusts the bag in her hand at me. "Get the rest." And she heads inside. My protector. My warrior. My Two.

The arguing is under way before I can shut the car doors. I hear Dad first, and I can tell he'd be shouting if Kyle weren't upstairs. "Did you know about *this* before I did, too?"

"Dave, sit, or I'll make them put you back in the hospital. What are you talking about?"

"It isn't enough that he's gay. It isn't enough that he's not a real boy. Now he has a Goddamn boyfriend!"

I want to sneak past them and into the kitchen to unload the bags, but Dad turns toward me like he's going to throttle me.

"Dave! I said, sit down! Now!"

He sits, but his voice gets louder. "Did you hear what I said?"

"All of Canada heard what you said. Stop yelling. Kyle needs to rest. Ethan, put those things away, will you?"

Just what I was planning. I take things out of bags one item at a time, trying not to rustle the bags—though whether I want to be quiet so they'll forget I'm here or so I can hear better I couldn't say.

I can tell Mom's trying to keep things quiet. Calm. Both. Her voice is just below normal volume. "Why shouldn't he have a boyfriend, I'd like to know? If he were straight, he'd have a girl-friend."

"That's not the same at all!"

"Of course it is. Give the kid a break, will you? He's just try-ing to grow up. That's hard for any kid. Look at our other son. We don't need to make it worse for this one."

I can hear Dad breathing, but I can't tell whether it's through his nose or his teeth. Then, his voice pointed and nasty, he says, "Are you sure he's a son?"

That's about all I can take. I leave the rest of the groceries where they are and go in there to face him. They both look at me. My tone just as nasty as his, I say, "Are you sure you're a fa-ther?"

And he's up. Mom steps in front of him but looks at me. "Ethan, go upstairs. Now!"

I catch myself just in time so I don't slam my door. This time I don't want to sit at the top of the stairs. This time I don't want to know what he says about me. But I know for sure that my fa-ther hates me, my mother loves me, and that I've caused an-other rift between them. If Dad weren't an invalid who'd just saved the life of her other son, I think she'd kick him out now.

After this confrontation, life at home is strained, to say the least. Mom may have convinced Dad to leave me alone, essen-tially, but whenever we're all in the same room, there's more tension than oxygen in the air. I'm assuming I'm not grounded, but no one ever really says. I still have my iPhone. And now, in-stead of Dad sleeping on the couch, it's Mom. I offer to let her have my room, but she just shakes her head.

"Thank you, Ethan. But we need to be able to shut some doors between you and your father. I think I'd rather have you in your room."

Armed truce? Is that the right term for this state of affairs where Kyle is the only one in a good mood because he mostly doesn't leave his room and doesn't really know what's going on, and where it's Mom and me in one camp across a no-man's-land from my father? Max is pretty freaked out when I let him know that Dad was listening to our phone conversation and fig-ured out who he is to me. I can tell Max is trying to be calm, and he's not blaming me or anything, but he's not happy.

It goes on like that for the rest of the week. I do my best to help Mom, who's taken as firm a stand for me as I've taken for myself, but with Dad wandering around to keep as active as he can—doctor's orders—she often sends me off to Etta's or even to Max's, driving illegally and alone in her car, to get me out of the house.

Heidi's moved home again, it seems, because she's not always at Etta's, but that's not a bad thing—just their lives returning more or less to normal. Etta is sympathetic, and she lets me rant on and on about Dad. She does her best to help me understand his point of view, but it still always comes back to this: I feel like I'm not his son as long as I can't (or, in his mind, won't) be something I'm not.

At some point I tell Etta the story of what happened to Jorja, and how I'd gone to see her, and what a failure that was. Etta says she'll be surprised if I don't hear from Jorja again at some point. She makes me feel really good about making the effort, even if it came to nothing so far. And she thought it was great that Ed Baker gave me a lift.

On Sunday afternoon Max and I are both at Etta's when Heidi arrives, and Max tells her about his dream. Heidi is impressed, I think, which confirms my understanding of Coyote as an important animal. She talks about Coyote like it's a mirror holding itself up to us, not us holding it up to ourselves, and we're going to see things we might not necessarily want to see. Whether we're cunning or stupid, have good intentions or do mean things, Coyote won't let us get away with not knowing it. So Coyote won't make us stop or start doing anything, but it forces us to see what we're doing. Heidi says this helps us see patterns in ourselves, our lives, and makes us think about how we might change ourselves, or get out of some trap we're in, a trap that could be of our own making. I'm thinking this jives with what Max had told me about his dream in our phone conversation, that there was a scary message from Coyote, who wasn't talking—just holding up that mirror.

"What trap am I in?" Max wants to know.

"Even Coyote won't tell you that directly, Max. He just puts the truth into our faces and won't let us pretend we don't see it."

I have a possible answer to Max's question, but it's not a trap I'm ready to push my own way out of, so I don't say anything. The trap? Lying. Hiding. Not being true to ourselves, so not being true to others. Letting stupidity and narrow-mindedness keep us in the closet. This makes even more sense to me when I remember that Max had said it was only male juncos following him. That would have to be part of the message. I ask, "So it was just Coyote you saw, no juncos?"

Max scowls a little, thinking. "Actually, I haven't seen any juncos at all lately."

On the drive home, though, in the Modine Sequoia, I make a silent pact with myself to take one more step toward escaping from that trap. I decide to tell Kyle. I'm sure this is going to cause a problem, given Kyle's take on this subject, but he's going to find out soon, anyway. He's supposed to come downstairs for dinner tonight, the first time since he's been home after his surgery, and we won't be able to fool him into thinking everything's peachy keen in the family.

I'm deep into contemplation of the possible ways this plan could backfire when Max pulls off the road into the parking lot of a closed-for-the-season tourmaline-and-geode store. He pulls behind the dark building, leaves the engine on, and says, "I think I know what you need."

I'm sure he means sex, and I'm not sure he's right, but we get into the back, anyway.

He just holds me. He holds me and strokes my hair and caresses my shoulder and my fingers. I almost feel like crying. There's a blanket here today, and he's pulled it over us.

At some point he kisses my forehead, and then my nose, and then my mouth. But it's a sweet, sweet kiss. He lies back again, and I don't know about him but the warm feeling around my heart is moving down to my crotch. Then there's another one of those sweet kisses. And then not so sweet. And then he reaches for something else he's hidden back there, which turns out to be a bag with condoms and real lube.

I do need sex. I do. Because I'm sixteen, and because I'm a boy, and because I'm with my lover. It's like we're saying, *We're real. We're true. We're alive and kicking, fucking, kissing, loving, and we aren't going to stop until we're dead.*

Afterward Max parks a little distance away from my house to let me out, saying something about not giving my father any ammunition—and so we can kiss for another few minutes, which we do until we know if we go on any longer it will be a while before I get out and walk the few hundred feet home.

Dad's upstairs when I get into the house, and Mom's in the kitchen working on dinner. I go in there and ask if I can help, maybe trying to put off what I've sworn I'll do. She just says to set the table, that dinner will be another hour or so.

My chore done, I sit down at the table. "Mom? I have to do something, and I don't really want to but I'm thinking I have to."

She turns to look at me. "And that would be—?"

"I have to tell Kyle."

She turns back to the counter. "No, you don't." I'm about to protest when she adds, "I already told him."

"You did? When?"

"About half an hour before you got home."

Okay, this is news. "And?"

"I think you should go talk to him."

"But—is he pissed, or what?" I'm tempted to ask if he and Dad are moving together into some convalescent center to get away from all the immorality at home.

"I think you'll find your brother has benefited in many ways from the loss of his hand." She shakes her head. "I hate to say that, and I know he'll have a hell of a time going through life with only one hand, but without that one at least he has a life." She puts down what she's working on and comes to sit at the table across from me. "You know, I don't like to admit this, but I wasn't completely right about that church of his. You know they brought him a laptop to use?"

"Yeah. I saw it."

"They also didn't agree with his delusion about a demon in

his hand." She rubs her face. "You were right, Ethan. You suggested he should talk to them, and I nixed it."

"Actually it was Jorja's idea. She said they should be helping him to love himself."

Mom gets up, squeezes my shoulder once, and goes back to the counter. "Go talk to him."

Upstairs, Dad's door is shut. I knock lightly on Kyle's door frame, and Kyle, fully dressed and lounging on top of his bedspread, looks up from his church laptop.

"Did Mom send you up?" he asks.

"Yes and no. I was gonna come talk to you, and she said . . . she said—"

"She told me." I can't tell whether the news came as a surprise to him or not.

We stare at each other a minute before I get up the guts to move into the room and pull out his desk chair to sit on. *Up is knowing I'm right. Up is truth.* "Are we okay?"

He half grins. "I'll tell you what I told her. I think it's wrong. I know you believe you don't have a choice, and she showed me all this research that makes her agree with you, but I think there's always a choice with Jesus. And I think it's likely we'll have some . . . uh, interesting conversations about this. Just not right now. Because right now all I want is to be home again, to feel sane again, and get back to some semblance of life. And— well, you're my brother, Ethan. You're part of my life. I don't want to change that." He shrugs. "Maybe at some point I'll actually get you to come to church with me. But I also don't want to add to Mom's troubles right now. I think what you and I should focus on is getting Dad to calm down so we can keep our family together. So I'm not gonna do anything to make that harder. How do you feel about that?"

Wow. How do I feel? How much truth is too much? No amount of conversation will change who I am. No amount of prayer. And, I'm convinced, no amount of prayer *should.*

I say, "You're right about one thing. If we talk about this, the conversations will be interesting. Because I know that I'm gay, and I know that it's not going to change, with or without Jesus.

So I guess he's gonna have to get used to it, because it's how his own father made me. But you're also right that we have a more pressing problem. I want Dad to stay, but I also want him to accept me. And you want Dad to stay, and I'm pretty sure Mom would too if he'd just chill about this. So whatever we can do toward that end, I'm on board."

We're back to staring, but it's not a bad stare. It's more like we're in cahoots, we've got the same goal, and we'll overlook this little rough spot between us for the greater good. At least for now. Because, really, now is what we've got; it's where we are. We should make the most of it.

Chapter 18

At lunch on Monday, I see I have a voice mail from Etta, asking me if it's okay for her to pick me up after school and introduce me to someone really special. I check with Mom, who just wants to know who it is, but I haven't a clue. So we both just have to trust Etta.

She lets me drive the Forester back to her house, and we're about halfway up that long driveway of hers when I hear howling. At first I'm thinking the coyotes are back, but when I glance at Etta she's grinning at me. And something warm and exciting moves up through my body, nearly taking the top of my head off. Etta has a dog again.

"Pull the car over here," she says before we get close to the dog, which isn't a breed I recognize. Is it a mutt? "I'm going to ask you to stay in the car until I call to you. Okay?"

Well, this is ominous. Before I turn off the engine, I lower my window so I can at least hear what's going on. The dog is a large animal with fur that's part light gray and part brownish black, more peppered than spotted. It has kind of a long head, not at all like Two, and its ears are more like a German shepherd. And boy, does this one know how to howl. It's on a lead that's tied to a heavy metal stake I don't remember.

Etta approaches it directly, heading right toward it, not hurrying but totally sure of herself. It stops the noise, looks at her, head down, and bares its teeth. Despite my experience with Two, I don't think I would have had the guts to approach this thing without a weapon.

Etta doesn't stop. When she's close enough, she grabs the dog's collar with both hands and lifts the front end of the animal off the ground as she stares into its eyes. I hear growling, and at first I think it's the dog, but with a start I realize it's Etta. Then she lets go of the collar, makes a kind of "SHHHT" sound, and the dog slowly lies down on the ground, obviously subdued.

Etta unclips the lead from the stake and folds up most of it so the distance between her hand and the dog is pretty short, and she turns toward me, waving me out of the car.

"Ethan, keep your head up. Don't look at her. Approach calmly but not quickly, and pretend she's not even there. Stop a few feet away with your side toward us."

I have to concentrate really hard or I'd be watching that animal for the slightest sign of ferocity. Etta keeps talking, her voice low and calm, encouraging me forward with reminders about not looking, and I'm sure this is for the dog's benefit. White noise, in a way. I stop when I hear her say to.

"Ethan, this is Halfwild. I call her Half. You can look at me now, and at her, but don't stare."

I laugh. I can't help it. Etta's still One, I suppose, and Two will always be Two. But this creature should be called Four, or at least Three, she's so much bigger than Two was, and apparently more ferocious. Etta went from Two to Half but got a bigger dog. When I laugh, Half looks up at me for just a second and smiles, head bobbing a little like any dog relaxing in good company.

"Half, is it?" I ask. "I'm sure you're going to tell me why."

She grins. "She's half wolf, half black Labrador. Our mutual friend and dog breeder, Ed Baker, got in touch with me a few days ago about taking her. I didn't say anything to you before, because I hadn't decided. I didn't know how you'd react, and I

wanted to make my own decision. This morning I decided."
She looks down at Half.

"Will she always be vicious? I mean, I couldn't even get out of
the car, and she was tied."

Etta smiles. "It's easier to manage a dog if aggressive behavior doesn't get a good start. She's still getting used to me, and if
you'd come toward her before I made sure she was calm, her
fear reaction would have sent her into a fury. But we're making
progress."

"She bared her teeth, even at you!"

"Wolves do that when they're unsure about something. It's
not so much a threat as a way of saying, 'I don't understand
what's happening, and until I do I'm on alert.' It doesn't mean
she's going to bite, necessarily." She takes one long breath. "I
have to make sure I stay calm and relaxed with her, at least until
we trust each other. The general consensus about half wolves is
that they're less predictable than wolves or dogs, which means
they're harder to manage."

"You had a lot of practice with a pit bull," I remind her.

"Yes, and without that, I couldn't hope to work with Half. But
Ed told me he was going to have to destroy the animal. Someone who evidently thought it would be a great thing to have a
half wolf got into trouble with this one. They're not good pets,
as you can imagine. And the man just dumped Half at Ed's
property, tied up to a tree near the end of his driveway. Ed saw
the guy and caught him before he could leave, which is how he
knows about the breed and the age; Half is not quite two years
old. Ed has done what he could to manage her, get her to be
more dog than wolf. Spent a few weeks on her, in fact, and
managed to get pretty far along, but he can't spend enough
one-on-one time with her. So he was going to have to put her to
sleep, because he didn't know anyone he thought could handle
this mix." She grins, and I can see pride on her face. "But then
he thought of me."

"Wow." I risk a glance at Half, and she's still just lying there,
relaxed. "Will I ever be able to pet her?"

"Someday. I'll let you know."

"I'll bet those coyotes will keep their distance."

Etta laughs out loud. "Yes, I expect they will. They might not have known what they were getting into with Two until he charged them, but I expect a wolf will keep coyotes at bay."

"And someday will I be able to play ball with her, like I did with Two?"

"I think so, yes. I'm sure she'd love that. The Lab in her will want to fetch." She gives the lead a slight jerk, and Half gets to her feet. I think if she stood on her hind legs, she'd be taller than Etta. I wonder if she'll get much bigger.

We go into the house, where Etta ties her to a huge eye hook that's been drilled into the door frame leading into the living room. She can get to her bed in the kitchen—a new one, not the one Two used—and she could get partway into the living room. But she can't get to the kitchen table or the stove or the sink. Etta has her plan all worked out.

There are cookies, and we sit at the table and talk for a while. Once or twice I forget to be careful, and I raise my voice. Which makes Half bare her teeth and growl. And each time, Etta looks at her immediately, says that "SHHHT" sound, and points to the floor. And each time Half relaxes again.

I can't help thinking this is totally cool. I mean, I saw how Etta handled Two, but he was so well behaved that she didn't have to do much, or do it very often. But the way she works with Half makes me want to try it. So I ask her, and she says she was hoping I'd ask, that she'd appreciate help from anyone who can help Half understand that she's not the alpha. She says it doesn't matter that Half is a she in terms of dominance, and from this animal it can't be tolerated for even a second or there will be trouble.

By the time I need to leave for home, I've learned a lot about handling dogs. And wolves. And while I still have a healthy respect for Half's ability to tear me to shreds, I'm not really afraid of her anymore.

I drive the Forester home with Etta just in time for dinner, so Dad and I don't have to dance around each other for long. But over dinner, I can't help talking about Half. And I can't help letting on how great it was to work with her, to get what it means to think like a dog and to have her obey me. Only as I'm helping with the dishes does it occur to me that talking about Half got me all excited, but working with her had made me totally calm—probably because it was be calm or be eaten. But also because calm worked. Calm helped Half as much as it helped me.

I'm upstairs doing homework when I hear the house phone ring. I ignore it, but maybe half an hour later Mom calls up to me to come down "for a minute." I think she adds that so I won't think this is going to be something dark and awful, but I don't know whether I trust that. I glance into Kyle's room as I pass it, and he's looking at me. I can't read his expression, but I'm pretty sure he's been up here and won't know any more than I do.

Mom pats the couch beside her for me to sit. She's smiling. Dad's in his chair, and he opens. "I just had a call from a man I didn't know. Ed Baker."

I blink at him; why would Ed call here? And why would that make Mom smile?

Dad goes on. "He told me about that incident in October, when you were driving Etta's car. Says you probably saved Etta's life, and maybe the other driver's, too. And then she saved his." He levels a gaze at me. "Is that how you remember it?"

I almost say, *I guess.* But that sounds like when I'd responded to Shane about getting a tattoo. And driving is one thing Dad and I both understand. So I say, "Yes. It is."

"Seems he gave Etta a pretty nasty animal to improve on, from what you've said. And Ed just told me that Etta called him to say you were going to help her with that. So he's pretty impressed with you, what with everything."

I can't think of a good response to this, so I just concentrate on hoping Ed hasn't revealed how we met. That I was hitchhiking.

Dad clears his throat, like he's said more than he intended to, or maybe just nicer things than he would like to have said. I can't tell. And then he says, "Ed asked me if it would be all right with us if he gave you a puppy."

I nearly jump off the couch. A dog! And, like the iPhone, I never even asked for it! I have to clear my throat, too. "What did you say?"

"I told him we'd talk about it. First, you need to understand this is a very generous thing he's doing. He gets a lot of money for these puppies, and this is a gift. Next, there are two things we have to be clear about. The first is that if we get this dog, you're responsible for it as long as you're living here. Your mother is not going to end up being the one to feed it, or walk it, or discipline it, or paper train it, or any of those things. Neither am I. If it misbehaves, it's your job to fix that. Any problem so far?"

I just shake my head; I'm not sure I trust my voice. *Neither am I* implies that he'll be here.

"The other thing is this. Now, I don't mean any disrespect to Etta, or to any woman. God knows your mother is a force to be reckoned with. And from what I know of Etta, I have no doubt she will handle that wolf. But I see this job of putting your dog in his place and keeping him there as something that takes a man, or at least a man's attitude. You have to be firm, and in control, and dominant. And these are qualities I want in both my sons. Whatever else they are."

This last phrase would be a reference to my sexual orientation, no doubt. But I don't react. I just let him talk.

"So I expect you to be a man to this dog, and I also expect you to teach your brother, and me, and your mother what you're learning from Etta. Because I expect that you'll go to college someplace, and you're not likely to be able to take the dog. That means we'll have to keep it, and I will not have you leave us with a willful, disobedient animal." He heaves a quick breath. "Are we in agreement?"

"Yes."

"Because if you don't meet these responsibilities, the dog does not stay. Ed will take it back. Is that clear?"

"Completely."

"Good. And in the spring, we'll convert the shed into a dog-house. Good thing the backyard is already fenced in."

Mom's arm goes around my shoulders, and she gives me a quick hug and kisses my cheek. Even though my mind is racing in all directions at the moment, I know this is her way of telling me that Dad and I will be able to find our way back to some semblance of family. He'll still be here in the spring to help me make a doghouse. This dog will be like a catalyst.

My dog will give us all unconditional love. We'll learn more from him than he learns from us.

I'm gonna have to wait until the weekend to meet my puppy. Ed has a husky picked out for me, a three-month-old male. Names are flying around my brain, but I'm going to wait until I meet him to figure that out. In the meantime, we make a couple of trips—all four of us—to get some supplies. Food, chew toys, a pillow bed, a crate, a collar, a couple of leads, the works. And I spend lots of time at night, after my usual pleasurable homage to Max's sex appeal, imagining taking my dog over to Etta's to play with Half and to the dog park in Bangor.

Tuesday afternoon there's a small package waiting for me when I get home from school. It's from the Cormiers' address. I take it upstairs, a weird feeling in my stomach. Jorja couldn't just send a letter?

There's no letter, really, just a note. I notice the bracelet first, though, because it comes tumbling out onto my bedspread, and I start to get a little pissed off. But when I read the note, it seems like it's not all bad. There's no heading, and no signature.

I'm not ready to talk with you, Ethan. Maybe someday. I'll let you know. And then you can give this back to me again.

At lunch on Wednesday that week, Max and I are sitting across from Marra at a table where a couple of other kids have just left, so the three of us are pretty much alone. Even so, I feel myself duck when Marra says, "You guys got something planned for the weekend?" She raises her eyebrows once or twice like "something" might be salacious.

Max practically pushes his chair back from the table. "Like what? What are you talking about?"

Marra waves a hand like it's nothing. "It's not like I don't *know,* you know." She shrugs. "Anyway, it's my birthday, and I'm giving myself a party Saturday night. Yes, another party! I like parties. So, come together if you want. Or separately. Doesn't matter to me. Okay?" She stands like that's settled, picks up her tray. "See you then!"

I take a deep breath, not sure whether I should look at Max or not. He hasn't moved. We sit there like a couple of idiots for maybe thirty seconds. I can't take it any longer than that. "You okay?"

I hear him breathe. "I'm not sure. She meant what I think she meant, right?"

"I'm gonna say yes." I turn to face him.

He looks at me, and his voice is a hoarse whisper. "What are we going to do?"

A few things occur to me, but in the end I fall back on that perennial teenage gesture. I shrug. "Be ourselves?"

"You're not serious."

"Well—what are our options? I'm not suggesting we go around holding hands or making moony eyes at each other across a crowded classroom."

"So what *are* you suggesting?"

That's not so easy. The idea of responding glibly to Marra's question with something like, *Oh, Max and I are driving to Bangor to get a tattoo and fuck in the back of his parents' Sequoia,* is not any more appealing to me than to Max.

I shrug again. "For starters, I guess stop avoiding being together just to avoid being together. That doesn't mean we're always gonna sit together, but maybe it means we stop being so scared."

"That's—but—what I mean is, if Marra knows, who else does? I mean, there's Jamal, but it seems he's gay, so . . ."

"Guess avoiding being obvious didn't do the trick. They figured it out, anyway."

Max throws himself back in the chair and grabs his hair with both hands. "I can't stand not knowing! When some kid looks at me weird, I'm gonna be thinking, *Does he know?*" He sits forward again. "Okay, like, the day those assholes beat up on me? I knew that had nothing to do with . . . with us. It was because I'm Sylvia's brother." He shakes his head. "Christ, Ethan! If they knew everything, what would they do to me next?"

"Whatever it is, I'll be there. And so will Sylvia, and my mom, and I'd bet Marra, and Etta, and even Mr. Coffin. I don't know what to do, here, Max. I'm clueless. But I really hate pretending that it's okay that some people think I'm some kind of freak." How many times now have I said this in the last few weeks? It's not okay. It will never be okay. And I can't—I *won't*—let them get away with it. "I guess we just take it one step at a time. We don't have to announce when we're getting together just because the straight kids do that. But we already don't go out on 'normal' dates. With girls. We already stand out. That's probably part of how Marra guessed. I mean, look at you. You're gorgeous! What girl wouldn't go out with you? But have you ever even asked a girl out?"

He's trying not to smile. "It's been a while. I guess June."

I laugh so it sounds like a snort. "See? And I don't even know whether hanging with Jorja was enough to give me some camouflage. It just seemed like a good idea at the time."

The bell rings and we have to get to our next class with our own question still hanging in the air. As he stands, almost under his breath, Max says, "One step at a time, charmer."

He's with me. Maybe he's been looking into that mirror Coyote held up for him.

The best part of the week, at least before Saturday, is one of those steps we're taking. Max comes over on Friday for dinner. Mom's the one who says to invite him. She must have broken down Dad's resistance at least a little, convinced him that I really do need a chance to live my life, just like she'd said. Who knows? Maybe she's even had to back Kyle off of some high horse for me. But I'd rather think that it wasn't that difficult. I want to think they're starting—even if it's *just* starting—to see me for who I am, even if it takes longer to accept it. Accept me.

Max coming for dinner tells me he's at least willing to try getting used to being seen as "with me." I still don't know what the right term is for us, so we'll just have to be our own shape.

Still, it's a little weird. We all sit down at the table, with everyone there knowing. You know. I wouldn't say it's a fun event; conversation is a little strained, and Max obviously feels as awkward as I do, but—it's a step. It's a stand. No more duck blinds.

Saturday. Puppy day! I'm up way early, and I make breakfast for everyone. Kyle keeps saying how out of character I'm acting—rising early, being actually useful. I think he's just teasing, and maybe he's even a little jealous. But he shouldn't be; the dog is going to be with the whole family, with all of us, not just me.

Mom lets me drive her car, with Dad sitting next to me. She and Kyle are in the backseat, and the dog crate is in the back of the wagon. It's stupid, but I'm nervous driving with Dad today.

Ed has long rows of covered caged areas along three sides of a huge fenced area behind his house. When we walk into this area with him, the dogs get all excited. I hear some barks and some eerie near-howls from all around us. The Samoyed cages are first, and when I see those gorgeous snow white dogs with their merry black eyes and happy faces, I kind of wish my puppy was one of them. I'm standing there staring at them when something hits my legs from behind. It's two husky puppies tumbling over each other, being chased by two more. They're bigger than I'd expected them to be, and together they almost knock me over. I hear Ed laugh, and when I look up at him he points.

"That's the one, Ethan. That fellow who nearly sent you flying." Ed wades into the fray and grabs one of them by the scruff of his neck. I can't take my eyes off the puppy. He's mostly dark charcoal on his back, feathering into white on his haunches.

His white face is surrounded by black, and he has kind of a reverse widow's peak—white pointing into the black of his forehead. His eyes, circled by black, are blue.

He's perfect. He looks just like me. And his name is Raven.

That afternoon I take him for our first walk together. It's sunny, with that cold blue sky that seems to be very far above you, giving you lots of your own space to exist in. Most of the snow in the fields out behind our house has melted in the sun, but it's been cold enough to keep the ground from being muddy, so we walk out across the open land. Scrabbly, dead-looking blueberry bushes scrape my jeans, and we go along a kind of trail winding around the boulders. I follow Etta's advice: *Lead the dog on the start of the walk. Lead him on the way home. In between, let him explore.* I have a long, heavy stick with me, and a can of pepper spray, in case of coyotes.

When I can't see the house or the road, I let the retractable lead out. I don't let Raven off it; he's still little, but huskies love running. It's what they're born to do. So I'll have to make sure he knows who's boss long before he gets that kind of freedom outside of a fence.

He seems happy enough for now just nosing around rocks, getting tangled in the dead bushes, following some animal scent for a few feet before something else distracts him. So I let my own attention wander a little, let a few distractions in through the cracks of focusing on pack leadership.

It's been a hell of a few months. And I can't point to where it started, exactly. It seemed like things just kept building, piling up on top of each other, sometimes feeding off each other.

The election sure put a lot of dust into the air. Who'd have thought a seat on the school board would have stirred up such a storm?

Really, my own family kind of sums it up. Shows how things can work out. Because what have we got there? There's Dad, mostly Christian I guess though not exactly observant, but still as compassionate as he knows how to be, and I know he's trying really hard to be the father again. There's Mom, whose religion is more *Don't tread on me* than anything else, until someone's in trouble, and then she'll do whatever it takes to help. And Kyle? Maybe he's not so insane anymore, but he's still kind of a fanatic. And he nearly killed himself so he could live. But he's my brother, and he's acting like it. And there's me, the gay kid, the one exploring the world of Raven. And we're a family. We're going to make that work. Thanksgiving is next week. Perfect timing.

I got that tattoo because it represents balance, and I wanted that. Desperate for it. I think now that I was confusing balance with neutrality. Because you don't know what balance is until you've experienced what it feels like to lean away from it.

Now? Now I'm thinking that my tattoo represents a hell of a lot more than balance. Balance isn't enough. Not for me. I want what you get when you know what out-of-balance feels like, and you know what to do about it. And that's more than balance. That's poise.

Now, I want poise.

I pull Raven's leash in close again and give it a light jerk. He looks up at me and smiles, and we turn toward home.

Marra's party is hard for me to go to, because I have to leave the house, which means I have to leave Raven. But it's great to be "out" with Max. He's wearing his ear cuff, and I can't remember that he's worn it since the day I bought it for him. I take this as a good sign.

We don't hold hands or anything, just like I'd said we probably wouldn't, but we're together. I think some of the kids get it, and we don't get anywhere near as many odd looks as I would have expected.

Max wants to leave a little earlier than we'd planned, and at first I'm thinking it's because he's more on edge than I thought. But as soon as we're out the door he puts those fears to rest. We don't make it to the Sequoia before he's wrapped himself around me tight enough that I know he's already got the back of the thing ready for us. We drive for a little while with the heat cranked up, and by the time he parks and we get in back, he's calmer.

"Something I want to show you," he says, sounding a little mysterious. He strips his jeans off, and even in the dark I can tell his eyes are on mine the whole time. Then he reaches into a bag on the side, pulls out a tiny flashlight, and hands it to me. "Point it at my balls."

I laugh. "This isn't what I want to point—"

"Never mind that. Just look." He spreads his thighs apart, and I point the light at a spot—something rectangular—that I don't remember seeing on his thigh. And I know his thighs pretty well by now. I squint, not quite able to see what it is.

As I look closer, I see first colors. Rainbow colors. And then I can see the whole thing. He's had a word tattooed just far enough below his balls so his pubic hair doesn't block it and just high enough that it would be hard for anyone to see. Each letter is a different color.

The word is CHARMER.

My eyes water. I'm not sure whether it's more from knowing how much that must have hurt, on tender skin like that, or from the sweetest emotion I think I've ever felt. But love spends so much time between sweetness and pain that sometimes they feel like the same thing. So I guess it was both.

Author's Note

The inspiration for *The Evolution of Ethan Poe* was a conflict in Dover, Pennsylvania, in which the school board attempted to introduce Intelligent Design into public school science classes.

The types of actions depicted in this book perpetrated by the proponents of Intelligent Design are in some cases similar to, and in some cases identical with, those that occurred in Dover (for example, Dover ID proponents put forth the illogical connection between supporting evolutionary theory and supporting NAMBLA), and the degree to which the town became divided is very much the same.

The Dover conflict went to trial, and in December 2005, the Middle District of Pennsylvania found in favor of the plaintiffs, ruling that teaching Intelligent Design in public school violates the Establishment Clause of the First Amendment of the Constitution of the United States and Article 1, Paragraph 3 of the Constitution of the Commonwealth of Pennsylvania.

The ruling of Judge John E. Jones III[1] declares ID to be "... an imprudent and ultimately unconstitutional policy." Referring to the school board, it further states, "The breathtaking inanity of the board's decision is evident when considered against the factual backdrop which has now been fully revealed through this trial. The students, parents, and teachers of the Dover Area School District deserved better than to be dragged into this legal maelstrom."

Judge Jones went on to say that science does not obviate the idea of a divine creator and that the imperfections that the scientific community acknowledges in current evolutionary theory should not be used as an excuse to disguise untestable, religion-based ideas as science.

---

[1] *Case 4:04-cv-02688-JEJ Document 342. Filed 12/20/2005. Tammy Kitsmiller, et al. v. Dover Area School District, et al.*

The Evolution of Ethan Poe

ROBIN REARDON

ABOUT THIS GUIDE

The suggested questions are included to enhance
your group's reading of Robin Reardon's
THE EVOLUTION OF ETHAN POE.

DISCUSSION QUESTIONS

1. Ethan introduces himself to the reader as "an outlier," by which he means someone who is not in the center of society, someone who is unusual in some way that puts him off to the side. He uses his Goth look and his relationship to Edgar Allan Poe to justify this marginalization outwardly and to make it appear that he's an outlier by choice. Although he takes pride in his ancestor, he lays the real reason for his outlier status at the feet of his sexual orientation. Is he correct, or are there other aspects to Ethan that make him unusual compared to his peers?

2. If Ethan adopts Goth primarily to hide the fact that he's gay and make it look like he's an outlier by choice, what are Jorja's reasons? What is she hiding, or hiding from?

3. Max Modine uses chatter and conspicuously "hip" language to keep from appearing ordinary and uninteresting to Ethan, who fascinates him and even intimidates him a little. It's said that we love someone because of the way they make us feel. What does Ethan see in Max? How does Max make him feel?

4. The day Ethan goes with Jorja to Teen Meet, the group leader, Mrs. Glasier, talks about how the United States is a Christian nation, directly contradicting what Ethan has just heard his history teacher say about the U.S. Constitution. Do you think Mrs. Glasier is representing a valid interpretation of the Constitution? Or do you think her belief system is informing and affecting her understanding of the Constitution?

5. Many religious Christians have stickers on their cars in the shape of the ichthus, the fish. Sometimes the name Jesus is contained within the fish body. On the back of her car, Max's sister, Sylvia—Ethan's biology teacher— has an ichthus with the name Darwin in it. This might represent a conviction that the physical and the spiritual are interconnected, or it could mean that someone worships the physical *instead* of the spiritual. Which do you think is the case with Sylvia?

6. Sylvia is convinced that if the facts are made known to the townspeople, they will understand why evolution is science but Intelligent Design, or ID, is not. And Max believes that if people knew the facts about sexual orientation, they'd stop condemning those who are different from the majority. Do you agree with them? Or do you think presenting people with facts that contradict their beliefs is more likely to cause them to dig more deeply into their positions? If the latter, what does it take to shift people off of beliefs that are unsupported by facts?

7. Hearing that Ethan is getting driving time from Etta Greenleaf in her Forester, and knowing that Ethan's mother is not exactly a calm and collected instructor, Ethan's father borrows a friend's refurbished Camaro and teaches Ethan how to drive a stick shift. What does this say to you about the relationship Dave Poe wants to have with his son? Why do you think he took this risk— borrowing this particular car, a vintage muscle car that his friend probably worked on himself—instead of any number of other standard transmission vehicles? Do you see a male–female difference between manual and automatic transmissions? If so, why?

8. At one point when Ethan and his mother are helping Etta prepare for the town hall debate, Ethan wonders

whether believing the theory of evolution automatically means you don't believe in God. Ethan's mother and Etta both challenge this notion. What are your thoughts? Is there an unavoidable dichotomy between accepting evolution and believing in God, or can the human mind and spirit reconcile the physical and spiritual worlds in a way that preserves the integrity of both?

9. In Ethan's town, as in the town of Dover, Pennsylvania, where a similar battle inspired Ethan's story, some people reacted violently to the idea that ID isn't recognized by everyone as a valid, scientific theory for the origin of species. And the violence in both the real and the fictional communities is instigated by proponents of ID, not by supporters of evolution. Does this surprise you?

10. The history teacher, Mr. Coffin, introduces the black civil rights movement to his class by demonstrating that over time, U.S. society went from violently opposing acceptance of black people to eliminating laws that disenfranchised them, and although complete acceptance is still a future goal, society is moving slowly in that direction. Can you see a parallel for people whose sexual orientation is not heterosexual? Is it possible that as more straight people get to know more people who are not straight, and as they see that the inroads being made are not causing the sky to fall, acceptance of LGBTQ individuals will progress?

11. How do you see the relationship between Ethan and his brother, Kyle, evolving over the course of the story? Where do you think it will go from here?

12. What do you think Shane Jenson's power animal is?